Paris 1934

Victory in Retreat

Paul A. Myers

Paris 1934 ... Fine storytelling and an exciting read

Paris 1934...Fueled by public outrage at massive corruption in the French government, Far Right street fighters topple a French cabinet in early 1934. A new premier moves to present another cabinet to Parliament. All Paris waits. On the chosen night, fired-up demonstrators from a half-dozen Far Right leagues converge on the Place de la Concorde to fight their way across the Seine River bridge and storm the Parliament. Shouting "drive the robbers and assassins out," the rioters battle Paris police on the bridge. The overthrow of the Third Republic seems imminent.

Democratic government in France hangs in the balance. With the memory of the Nazi coup d'etat in Berlin the year before fresh in the public mind, the world waits.

Sorbonne student and part-time reporter Sandrine Durand covers the riots from the foreign ministry at the Quai D'Orsay for an American paper in Paris. She watches spellbound as a column of war veterans attempts to storm police lines and reach the Parliament building. Suddenly, the veterans disperse into the night. Why?

A historical novel with an exciting cast of characters including:

Philippe de Davignon, a polished French diplomat and specialist in German affairs.

Anne de Davignon, the exquisitely beautiful wife of the diplomat and a woman of intensely felt longings.

Jim Potter, a young reporter fresh from a year of covering Roosevelt's New Deal in Washington D.C.

Mac and "Rewrite," the American newspaper editorial team holding forth on the day's events at the local bistro and ready for whatever mischief is in the making.

Sarah, the sharp-witted young American fashion reporter married to would-be novelist and political reporter Bob.

Malka, a politically savvy secretary at the Socialist trade union council and political tutor to Sandrine.

Irene, a young fashion model turned high-fashion dressmaker with the ambition to do what it takes to succeed in the world of Paris couture.

The **Historical Novel Society** describes Paul A. Myers' first historical novel, *Vienna 1934: Betrayal at the Ballplatz,* as "fine storytelling...exciting and romantic."

Cover illustration: The Palais Bourbon was home to the Chamber of Deputies during the Third Republic and sits on the Left Bank across the River Seine from the Place de la Concorde on the Right Bank. The bridge is the Pont de la Concorde. Today, the Palais is the home of the National Assembly, the successor institution to the Chamber of Deputies. (Photo *Palais Bourbon Nuit* by Webster, November 20, 2002, GFDL, Wikicommons.)

AUTHOR

Paul A. Myers lives in Claremont, California with his wife Minche. He is a sole practitioner CPA. He is the author of the historical novel *Vienna 1934: Betrayal at the Ballplatz* and the maritime history *North to California: The Spanish Voyages of Discovery 1533-1603* (viewable in its entirety at Google books). His memoir *Clerk! The Vietnam Memoir of Paul A. Myers* is viewable and downloadable at Scribd.com and describes the author's service as a clerk on the operations staff (G3) of the 101st Airborne Division in Vietnam 1970-71.

Paul A. Myers at Tuileries Gardens, Paris. (Photo by Wahyuni S. Myers.)

More information at: http://sites.google.com/site/myersbooks/

Victory was to be bought so dear as to
be almost indistinguishable from defeat.

—The World Crisis, *Winston Churchill*

SUNDAY

Sunday, February 4, 1934. Sarah sat at the small café table, its marble top circled by a gold-colored metal band, and sipped from her cup of coffee. She looked out the window of the café and across the street to the front of the Romanesque church, the Eglise St.-Germaine-des-Prés, a landmark of Paris's Left Bank. Her eyes took in the upward sweep of the single bell-tower reaching into the gray winter sky. She searched the arched entranceway at the lower left corner of the eight-hundred-year old stone façade for her friend, a young woman. She had not come out from mass yet. There was almost no traffic this Sunday morning.

Turning back to her coffee, Sarah continued reading the smudged carbons of last night's wireless dispatch to Chicago. Her husband Bob, a political reporter for the *Paris Bulletin*, had written the story late last night. It was the weekly wrap-up story, the so-called night lede, to the big Chicago daily that owned the small English-language Paris paper they both worked for, something of a dream job for a young couple just a few years out of college.

Her husband's story described a month's worth of furious street rioting that had toppled the French cabinet the week before. The riots had been triggered by public rage at disclosures of massive public corruption orchestrated by the swindler Alexander Stavisky. When the scandal erupted, Stavisky conveniently committed suicide while the police were beating down his door.

"Or so the police said," thought Sarah, an attractive dark-haired young American who effortlessly glided into the waspishly sarcastic style of the newly sophisticated. She took another sip of her coffee.

She again looked out the window of the café to the entrance to the church. The young woman she was waiting for had not yet appeared.

Sarah turned and looked around the warm, comfortable interior of the café. Small groups of regulars were scattered around tables in the café reading newspapers while smoking and sipping coffee from quite small cups. Some gesticulated wildly with arms flaying and fingers pointing in animated argument about what would happen to France in the coming week. The newspapers spread across the tabletops predicted massive street riots Tuesday afternoon by the Far Right leagues. Rioters would collide with the police forces of the new center-left government of Premier Édouard Daladier. Right-wing rioters would try for the second time in two weeks to topple a French cabinet.

Paris waits, thought Sarah. She, too, pondered the coming week. It was one thing to topple a cabinet, but it was altogether something else to overthrow the Republic.

Sarah finished reading the last page and looked up; she saw a young woman walk out of the entrance of the church and start across the square towards the café. Sandrine was a smooth and swaying study in casual Parisian nonchalance, Sarah thought, the young Sorbonne student moving confidently through her studies towards her professional future. The tumbling mahogany hair framed the white face with dark shining eyes that always said "from somewhere south of Paris," or so Sarah thought.

Sarah was charmed how young French women like Sandrine, at least in Sarah's imagination, could move from the warm bed of a Saturday night *affaire* to the thoughtful meditation of a Sunday morning mass in a centuries old Catholic church in Paris. She, Sarah, had of course been faithfully betrothed and faithfully wed in the Protestant heartland of the American upper Midwest. Her beautiful white wedding dress truly a symbol of her faithfulness, and she smiled to herself, if not quite virginal. It was a faithfulness never regretted, but it was from this experience that Sarah developed a sense of keen curiosity about the path allowed young French women in Paris, if not out in the provinces.

Sarah reached back in her thoughts; she had asked Sandrine about this once. She smiled in recollection at Sandrine's answer: "Oh, the bishops have always taken more money out of the countryside than they should. The people in turn take more love out of life than they should, if that is even possible. I don't know. I don't think so. Life works out." Sarah smiled at the memory.

With Sarah's marriage to Bob came travel to Europe and the urbane sophistication allowed to a young married woman. But as time passed in Paris, a hankering to return nibbled at the edges of contentment, a need to move on in life. Her college friends sent her cards notifying her of baby showers and growing families. Her mother sent her mother's day cards; she wrinkled her nose at the memory.

Sandrine came through the glass door, looked over at a waiter and gave a quick request. Then she walked over to Sarah's table and sat down. She set her coat and handbag on a nearby chair and took off the scarf from around her head. The waiter brought a small café au lait.

Sandrine smiled at Sarah and said, "Oh, it is so nice to see you today, Sarah. It is peaceful today. I am catching up on my studies. The newspaper kept me too busy all last week."

Sarah's shoulders sagged, "I know. Bob worked late every night last week. He's back in our room sleeping now. These riots…I don't know what will become of France."

Sandrine reached out and held Sarah's hand and said reassuringly, "A new government is forming. Daladier presents his cabinet Tuesday night. He is a strong man. He was a frontline soldier in the war. Not an *embusqué* – shirker – like so many of the others."

Sarah looked up, "Yes, he is a good man. But I worry—what will happen if the Far Right leagues get together and try to overthrow the Republic?"

Sandrine's face fell; she had never really thought of that possibility. She said softly, "But the Republic is France. It stood solid through the terrible troubles of the First World War. To be defeated by street riots in Paris? Now?" Her voice trailed off.

Sarah said, "It was a very bitter victory France won in the last war."

Sandrine said softly, "I know. Too much was paid." She sipped her coffee thoughtfully.

Sarah changed her tone as she changed the subject, "I hope you will be able to go with me later in the week and cover the spring openings at the fashion houses. We will have a good time."

Sandrine, her expression coming back to the present, asked, "Do you even think they will have them? This week's riots may be the worst."

In her breezy American manner, Sarah replied self-assuredly, "Too much money is on the line for the houses to cancel the spring openings. Buyers from New York and London are in town."

Sandrine replied softly, "I see."

Turning thoughtful, Sarah added, "If Bob and I ever get back to the States, you could take over the fashion beat. The newspaper is too broke to hire another reporter."

"When do you think you will go back to the States?"

Sarah sighed, "Who knows?"

Sandrine said softly, "I see."

Turning businesslike, Sandrine said, "I'll tell Bob Wednesday if I can make it Thursday for the openings. I'll try."

Sarah said, "Fine."

The two women continued to sip at their coffee and chat as Sunday morning moved towards noon.

Sunday evening, February 4. The station stood empty alongside two sets of rail tracks running between two long concrete passenger platforms. Low-power lights shined down weakly on the polished cement surfaces. The station was a small circle of yellow light against the dark velvety blackness of the cold winter sky.

Across the square from the station, a man in a dark navy topcoat and a squashed-down, broad-brimmed black hat looked at his watch. The train from Paris had departed a half-hour before, he thought. It should arrive momentarily, he calculated. The phone call had said the colonel was on board. The man looked again at the empty station. Just then, as expected, a long black limousine, polished surfaces reflecting the street lamps of the deserted street, pulled up to the curb near the station. The limousine waited.

The man cocked his ear; he heard the sounds of the train approaching, the hiss of escaping steam as the heavy locomotive slowed its approach to the station. A screeching sound of metal wheels reversing against the hard steel surfaces of the rails brought the commuter train to a stop. The man watched the doors to the passenger cars: a door opened, an erect man with the demeanor of a retired officer stepped out of the train and onto the platform. He was wearing a fashionable light brown topcoat and dark fedora hat; an expensive wool muffler was wrapped around his neck and neatly tucked into the front of his topcoat. The man looked over towards the square, saw the limousine, and walked briskly to it. A uniformed chauffeur got out of the driver's side and quickly came around and opened the right rear door. He held it open as the man got in.

Across the square, the man in the dark navy topcoat stepped back into the shadows and watched the limousine move down the street. Several minutes later, the man crossed the square and went into the waiting room next to the passenger platform. He sat down and opened his newspaper. A train going to Paris would arrive in an hour. Most likely the man in the topcoat would return from his errand and be on it. The man would read his newspaper and wait.

The limousine drove down darkened streets and then turned through wrought iron gates and up a gravel drive. Château de Louveciennes. The man in the topcoat looked out the rear window and saw the façade of Ionic columns ahead. *New money likes old châteaux*, thought the man. The limousine stopped in front of the portico, the chauffeur got out and came around and opened the door. The man in the fashionable topcoat got out. The massive front door opened and a butler bade the man to enter. Going through the front door, the butler helped the man with his topcoat and took his hat and muffler.

The man, trimly dressed in a good business suit, walked over to a display case and gazed at the bottles of perfume on display. Several of the bottles were of great style and graced with the symbol of the designer Baccarat. The man knew that packaging innovations had contributed greatly to the worldwide success of the perfumes, making the owner of the chateau one of the wealthiest men in France, at least until the current Depression and a stormy divorce had diminished the great wealth.

The butler ushered the man forward into a large drawing room. A man, dressed in a black business suit and a high starched collar, came across the room and reached out his hand, "So nice to see you again, colonel."

The man replied, "Nice to see you again, Monsieur."

"Please have a seat, colonel."

The colonel took a seat and the businessman, addressed as Monsieur by associates, seated himself in a chair just across from a small coffee table.

The colonel pleasantly started, "It is a beautiful chateau, Monsieur. It was given by Louis XV to his favorite, Madame du Barry, I believe."

"You are well informed, colonel."

"You have maintained it in great taste, Monsieur."

"Thank you, colonel."

The colonel took a sweeping glance around the room and then turned back and looked at Monsieur and began, "The war veterans of the *Croix-de-Feu* thank you, Monsieur, for your generous financial support in the past. Tuesday's demonstrations in Paris may topple the government of Premier Daladier. We would like to know what your views are on whom or what should follow? And do our two organizations have a common interest here?"

Monsieur replied, "We, like you, are Royalists."

The colonel smiled inwardly: Monsieur owned the mass circulation newspaper *L'Ami du peuple*; its working class readership was probably interested in any leader but a king.

The colonel returned to the conversation, "But which pretender should we support?"

Monsieur looked momentarily thoughtful, "It might not be opportune for the return of the Duc of Guise. It might be better that he stay in Brussels," referring to the leading pretender.

The colonel responded, "I would have thought, your origins being in Corsica, that you might prefer Prince Philippe of the House of Bonaparte. He is just over the border in Switzerland."

Monsieur seemed to agree, "Yes, he would be a good choice, but the rise of Nazism under Hitler in Germany and Fascism in Italy under Mussolini suggests that in the immediate term a strong figure from France rather than a prince in exile is needed. It is urgent to eliminate the disorder and corruption of this scandal-ridden parliamentary government. Six governments in less than two years; the Stavisky scandal offers all who are patriotic an opportunity to reorder the state. Social disorder could lead to a Red revolution and a Bolshevik dictatorship in a matter of weeks. Godless Communism would replace decayed democracy."

The colonel watched a wave of real concern wash across Monsieur's face.

Monsieur concluded, "*Solidarité Française* is all for France," naming the Far Right league he financed.

The colonel nodded his head with understanding. He had watched Major Jean Renaud, like himself a veteran of the Great War, command the league's shock regiment of street fighters dressed in their blue shirts, black berets, and jackboots. When street demonstrations had broken out in early January 1934 in response to public rage over the revelations of the Stavisky financial scandal, the Blue Shirts had marched in the Paris streets shouting their slogan "France for the French."

The colonel thought to himself: *of course, a strong man.* Again, he smiled inwardly. With some delicacy, he went onto the next question, "We are, of course, prepared to send the premier and his ministers packing, but we are not sure about driving the President of the Republic from the Élysée Palace. There are five right-wing leagues marching on the Chamber of Deputies Tuesday. Just whose choice would be the new head of state? Who gets to rule, and if Germany is an example, who gets sent to concentration camps?"

Monsieur, somewhat taken aback by the question, had always assumed that he would chose the new leader, a French *führer*, or that he himself might become the French *Duce.* For sure, the times called for a leader of the state, not a weeping president of a republic. Surely, all the leagues were in agreement on that goal.

"Colonel, the task at hand is to sit at the speaker's tribune in the Palais Bourbon. It is time to turn the disgraceful deputies out into the street. We must end parliamentary government. It fails the needs of modern times. The leagues can negotiate the new leadership and form a provisional government once they gain the Palais."

The colonel made an expression of agreement. Then he stood, "I must return to Paris. There is much to do."

Monsieur stood, reached out his hand to the colonel, and said, "Coordinate with Major Renaud. The two of you can achieve great things Tuesday."

The colonel made a small bow, "Thank you, Monsieur." He turned and headed for the foyer.

At the train station, the man in the navy blue topcoat sat reading his paper. He heard the doors of the limousine close shut out in the square. He looked over the top of his newspaper and saw the man in the light-brown topcoat walk along the platform. He stopped and looked down the tracks. Faintly, the sound of an approaching train was heard in the distance. Inside the waiting room, the man continued reading his newspaper. Outside, the train slowly rolled to a stop. The man in the light-brown topcoat entered a passenger car. The man inside the waiting room stood up, folded the newspaper under his arm, and walked outside and got in the next car towards the rear. The whistle sounded; the train slowly pulled away from the station towards Paris.

The train pulled into Invalides station in Paris. The man in the light-brown topcoat got off and briskly walked down the platform towards the exit sign SORTIE and turned and started up the steps towards the street. The man in the dark navy topcoat slowly followed behind and reached the sidewalk in time to see the other man get into the backseat of a black sedan and drive away. Then the man in the dark navy topcoat turned back into the station, descended one level, and went up to a ticket window. He showed the attendant an indentification badge and asked to use a telephone. The attendant opened the door and pointed him to a telephone. He dialed a number and waited for answer.

"Yes."

"*Inspecteur* here. The colonel returned from his meeting. He got in a dark sedan outside Invalides and departed."

"Good. That will be all for tonight. This has been a long Sunday for you, I am afraid. Continue with your work. Police informants say to expect large demonstrations Tuesday night. We will meet Wednesday. Here. After the demonstrations. May be someone will tip their hand. What we're looking for will be hard to find." The line clicked silent.

In an office building near the ministry of the interior, the man at the other end of the telephone line, a *chef de bureau*, hung the telephone earpiece in its cradle and leaned back in his office chair. He looked at the two dossiers on his desk. He knew both by heart. He set the first one in the center of his desk and casually leafed through the pages.

Françoise Coty, perfumer, born in Corsica. Supporter of Far Right leagues. Wealthy, but a divorce and the Depression had taken a toll; he had lost ownership of *Le Figaro*, the leading voice of conservatism among the Paris papers, just four months before. Founded his own right-wing league, *Solidarité Française*, three months ago. Previously he had supported the *Croix-de-Feu*, a large veterans organization, and *Francisme*, a pure fascist street fighting organization modeled on the Nazi Brown Shirts and Mussolini's Black Shirts.

And of course, the *chef* recalled, Coty had started his journey into hate as a supporter of the Royalist *Action Française*. All the Far Right leagues were bastard children of this father organization, an organization born of the anti-Semitic hatreds of the Dreyfus affair thirty years before. The *chef* also knew that the two great writers of the *Action Française* were the incredibly skilful scandalmongers Charles Maurras and Maurice Pujo, masters at fanning inflammatory propaganda across the seething streets of Paris. Already stories were appearing about how black Senghalese troops were being organized by the government into machine gun detachments hidden in the basements of government buildings and waiting to be unleashed Tuesday night on the people of Paris. Monstrous plots entirely from the minds of these two scribblers would be half the reality shaping people's minds Tuesday night, thought the *chef* sadly.

Turning back to the issue at hand, the *chef* moved the other dossier to the center of the desktop. François de La Rocque, retired lieutenant colonel, took over *Croix-de-Feu* in 1931. Good organizer. Successfully cultivates a personal *mystique*. His brother is aide-de-camp to the Comte de Paris, son of the Orléanist pretender, the Duc de Guise. The Duc is the "king" for the Royalist *Action Française*. But, as the dossier showed, the colonel is not much of a Royalist. Interesting, thought the *chef*.

The *chef* leaned back in his chair and blew smoke towards the ceiling, deep in reflection. La Rocque had received secret state funds during the premierships of Laval and Tardieu. The Republic undermines the Republic. Plus money from industrialists wanting a corporative state on the Italian style—destroy the Republic for tame labor unions derisively thought the *chef*. Is this the whole story of Colonel de La Rocque?

So the two leaders met two days before the rumored largest street riots since the Commune of 1871, the last insurrection to tear Paris apart. The smoke drifted up to the ceiling in a twisting ribbon as the *chef* pondered his singular thought. Why?

TUESDAY

Tuesday, February 6, 1934. Upstairs on the second-floor, in a shabby, paper-strewn newsroom, a rotund man in suspenders with a cigar sticking out of the side of his mouth stood in the slot of a large horseshoe-shaped city desk. He spoke to a dozen people, some seated, some lounging against the walls, in the small room, "Listen up, kiddos. Time to go over tonight's assignments. Last night the *Croix-de-Feu* tried to storm the interior ministry…"

Bob Tompkins, a reporter leaning against one of the walls, interrupted, "I was there, chief, they were just going through the motions, looked more like a rehearsal."

The voice behind the cigar replied, "I agree, Bob. Monday wasn't the big night. But all the French papers predict massive street demonstrations tonight." The editor paused, then added, "For once the French papers might know what they're talking about."

The reporters all laughed.

The editor took the cigar out of his mouth and stabbed it straight out as he said, "Here are the angles tonight. First, will the street fighters get into the Palais Bourbon and overthrow the Chamber of Deputies? If so, will they overthrow the Republic and set up a provisional government?"

The editor looked around the room, then said, "One other thing. If you have to mention the Stavisky scandal in the story, remember it is simply 'a two-hundred-million-franc fraud.' Don't confuse the readers with a lot of facts."

Again, the reporters all laughed.

Bob Tompkins threw in another comment, "This morning, the Communist paper *L'Humanité* called for party members to join tonight's demonstrations against the Republic. Communist veterans are to take the lead. Looks like a hot time in the ol' town tonight."

A puff of smoke came sidewise out of the editor's mouth. He spoke around his cigar, disdainfully, "They seem to have forgotten what happened in Berlin last year."

Another puff from the cigar blew out from the editor's mouth like some sort of smoke signal. He turned and nodded to another man leaning against the other wall, "By the way, you all know Bill Wilshire? He's back with us. Just finished a year writing in Spain, right Bill? Got that novel done?"

"Naw, looking for a meal ticket, though."

Everyone laughed. The Depression had run like a scythe through the livelihoods of expatriate American journalists over the past year. France was sinking.

The editor poked his cigar at Wilshire, "Bill, you cover the Place de la Concorde. You can phone in from the Hotel Crillon."

The editor turned back towards the first reporter, "Bob, you cover the ministries over on the Left Bank. You can base at the Quai D'Orsay. Take Sandrine with you. She knows all the press aides over there," and he smiled at the young French woman standing over by the doorway, "Don't you honey?"

She smiled, "*Bien sûr*, Monsieur Mac." Of course. She nodded at Bob.

The editor turned to another reporter, "Take the Élysée Palace, Phil."

The editor continued working around the room handing out assignments. Then he looked at the men, and one young woman, standing around the horseshoe desk and said, "Rewrite will be here ready to go," and he pointed his cigar over to a narrow-faced man with slicked down black hair, a pencil neck, and a turnip-shaped torso. Hearing his name, the man's head popped up like a chipmunk and he grinned while giving the crowd a cross-eyed look. The journalists laughed at the Laurel and Hardy pantomime. Mac continued, "Just feed Rewrite the facts. Leave the prose to all those novels that you're going to write."

Everyone laughed. The group broke up. Sandrine walked over to the man named Bob.

"Nice to work with you again, Monsieur Bob."

"Pleeze. Bob."

"Bob," she said slowly making it sound like "Boob." Then she made a small laugh, "Is that your novel he's talking about?"

"Mine and about a hundred other guys'."

Sandrine smiled, "Oh, you Americans. Tell me, Bob, what did Monsieur Mac mean about the Communists forgetting about Berlin last year? I didn't know there were any Communists in Berlin; I thought they were all in Moscow."

Bob laughed, "You've got that exactly right, Sandrine. Now."

Then Bob turned thoughtful and said, "Last year in Berlin, the Communist unions helped bring the Nazis to power by bringing down the Weimar Republic. The Nazis promptly arrested them—nothing unusual about arresting Communists in Europe; they sort of expect it in fact—and then shipped them in cattle cars to concentration camps. In the camps, the Nazis killed them. All of them. Completely. Something very new. So yes, there are no Communists in Berlin. But there used to be. Now they are mostly in Moscow."

Sandrine seemed startled, "I didn't know this. All of them?"

Bob nodded his head sadly, "Yes, all of them."

Sandrine looked troubled. Then she changed the subject, "How's Sarah? Every lunch with her is a delight. I might even be an American someday." Then she added wistfully, "If I could be like her."

Bob smiled. His wife Sarah was like a big sister to Sandrine. Sometimes he would watch the two of them at lunch: smiling, elegant young women chattering away at the end of the table about fashion and shopping while he and his newspaper buddies swapped stories about the endless crises in French politics. Or talked about the exciting new developments in Roosevelt's New Deal far across the ocean.

"Sandrine, let's go across the river and get something to eat before the festivities begin. Do you know a place near the Quai D'Orsay?

"*Bien sûr.* Rue St.-Dominique."

Arriving at Café Dominique, a small restaurant on a corner two blocks behind the Quai D'Orsay, Bob pulled out a chair for Sandrine at a small table near the window in the falling light of a winter afternoon. A waiter came over, recognized Sandrine, and spoke to her, "Good afternoon, Mademoiselle, business at the ministry today? We're closing soon. Trouble is expected."

Sandrine smiled, "My friend Bob. He's a reporter with the American paper next door to *Le Petit Journal.* Sometimes I work for the Americans, too. We're on our way to the ministry."

The waiter nodded hello to Bob, "Can I get you two something?"

Bob said, "Sure. What would you like, Sandrine?"

"Café au lait."

"Café noir. Grand," Bob added, and then said to the waiter, " We probably have a big night ahead of us. We're here to cover the expected trouble."

The waiter nodded his head and strode back to the zinc bar to fill the order.

Bob turned to Sandrine, "Tonight, let's make our base at the foreign ministry." Bob thought for a minute, trying to imagine how the evening's events might unfold, and then continued, "The *Croix-de-Feu* will have to march right past the front of the ministry to get to the Palais Bourbon," referring to the seat of the Chamber of Deputies in the building next door to the foreign ministry on the river front.

Bob summed up the plan, "You cover the demonstrations at the Quai D'Orsay. I'll be next door at the Chamber of Deputies watching Daladier present his ministers."

Sandrine nodded agreement, then hesitated and asked, "Do you think Daladier can form a government? Your wife is unsure."

Bob shrugged, "I honestly don't know."

The waiter returned and set two cups of coffee down on the circular table.

Sandrine stirred her coffee and then said, as if confiding a family secret, "My father was a lieutenant in the war. So was Daladier. He rose from private to company commander. In the infantry. They were both *poilu*. My father said that one of Daladier's men, when asked if Daladier had been a good officer, had said, 'Better than that. He was a good soldier.' In our house, you can't say more than that."

Sandrine stirred her coffee, and then looked up at Bob, "You don't know what it was like to grow up *poilu*, the pride felt side-by-side with the gnawing sense that the victory had not earned France a peace worthy of the sacrifice."

Bob nodded his understanding—yes, *poilu*, "the hairy ones," the classic definition of the French infantry in the Great War. And here was the daughter of one of them, a beautiful emissary from a painfully remembered reality. Bob looked sympathetically at Sandrine, "What does your father do now?"

She replied, "Oh," and then she straightened up proudly, "he is the head of a *lycée* in Toulouse. The students are everything. They are like the spirits of his dead soldiers to my father."

Bob nodded his head in understanding, "What happens this week is just one chapter in a bad political play. If Daladier does not succeed, most likely politics will muddle along with some sort of coalition government. There will be new elections in France in two years."

Sandrine looked thoughtful and said, "I'm sure you're right. You know politics so well."

Bob smiled and then got out his notebook and a pencil and started to write an outline down the left side of the page.

Sandrine asked, "What are you doing?"

"Let me show you. Do you have a pad to take notes? You can use this with your work for the French papers, too."

"Yes," and she pulled a note pad out of her handbag. "Usually I just take the press handouts and communiqués. Sometimes I write down what the press aides say, or rather tell me to say."

"Well, let me show you some tricks of the trade. Should work for you, too. On these kinds of assignments, you just call in the facts. The rewrite guys on the copy desk write up the story. We just shovel in the facts."

"You don't express your opinion? All the French papers seem to be all opinion, few facts."

Bob smiled and flippantly said, "Well, may be you can change that."

Bob sipped his coffee and then he showed Sandrine his pad. "It's simple. American journalism uses what we call 'the five W's and How.' Six elements. So we just write down on the left hand side of the pad the "who, what, when, where, why and how." Then we fill in the blanks. The one you really want to get right is the "who." Editors hate people calling up about misspelled names."

He pushed his pad over to Sandrine. "Write these down in French on your pad, you know—*qui, que, quand, où, quoi, et comment*. Then I like to put down a simple subject-verb sentence. Tonight, we might write, 'demonstrators storm Chamber of Deputies.' Tells the whole story. A good rewrite man can write a whole news story out this information. So you just call in your story, give the rewrite guy the five W's and how, plus the simple direct sentence that summarizes what happened. He takes it from there. *Voila.*"

Sandrine wrote on her pad and then showed it to Bob. "Like this?"

"You got it. You could write it in English or French, depending on which paper you are calling the story to. Or return to the office and just tear off the page and give it to the rewrite man."

"Bob, tonight, a lot might happen."

15

"Just keep adding short subject-verb sentences for additional paragraphs. Add any additional facts just below each sentence as you go. Just read it to the rewrite guy."

Sandrine finished her coffee and said to Bob, "We better go over to the ministry."

They stood up and Bob left some coins on the table. They walked over to the coat rack and put on their overcoats and mufflers, then took their hats off the rack. Bob held open the door, Sandrine walked out into the cold air of the street. The afternoon shadows were giving way to deep winter twilight. Bob followed.

They came up to the ministry of foreign affairs and stopped at a sentry box outside a small courtyard. A uniformed guard, crisply resplendent in dark blue uniform, red sash, dark kepi trimmed lightly with gold, and a highly effective looking rifle, waved them to the window of the sentry station. Sandrine explained to an older man sitting inside the box, *un ancien combattant*—a war veteran, that they were reporters. She and Bob presented their police press cards. She said they were to see Madame Bardoux. The older man looked up and smiled warmly on hearing the name. Then he held a clipboard down on a small table with a shortened left arm that ended with a metal hook where his hand had once been. With his good right hand, he paged through the sheets of paper until he found the two journalists' names. Bob watched intently, a small ritual repeated daily across France: the disabled war veteran, what the French called so directly *les mutilés*, performing some minor public task. And of course everywhere there were the widows and mothers dressed in black, the black crepe of *deuil*, mournful reminders of the tragic cost of the late war.

The old veteran in the sentry box found the names, smiled his approval at Sandrine, noted the time next to their names, and picked up a telephone and made a call to someone inside the building. Shortly, a receptionist hurriedly came towards them, smiled, and said, "This way."

The uniformed sentry snapped to attention and the receptionist and two journalists crossed the courtyard to the tall wooden doors leading into the ministry. The three walked together up a wide marble stairway to the second floor. They walked through the corridors to the front of the building.

The receptionist extended her arm towards a well-dressed woman of about thirty, "Madame Bardoux." Sandrine admiringly observed that Madame

Bardoux was dressed in a very well tailored black skirt and a black jacket discreetly trimmed with black silk borders embroidered with scrolls and leaves. The outfit was beautifully set off with a high-necked cream-colored silk blouse. *Yes, that is what I want*, thought Sandrine.

Smiling, Sandrine extended her hand and said, "So nice to see you again, Madame Bardoux. Let me introduce you to my colleague, Bob Tompkins, he is a reporter for the *Paris Bulletin* and husband of my good friend Sarah, the fashion reporter that I have told you about."

Madame Bardoux stepped forward, "Suzanne Bardoux," and held out her hand to Bob.

Bob shook the outstretched hand and looked at the warmly smiling woman, struck by the lustrously dark brown hair swept back in an elegant chignon.

Sandrine said to Bob, "Madame Bardoux was the first woman to pass the *concours*— the entrance exam—of the foreign ministry and become a *redactrice*, the entry position to the senior civil service."

Bob said to Madame Bardoux, "I am impressed."

Sandrine turned back to Madame Bardoux, and somewhat in the manner of a schoolgirl, explained, "I have completed my *baccalauréat* at the *lycée* in Toulouse and am now studying for my *licence* in law at the Sorbonne. I hope to become a *redactrice*, too," and then laughingly added, "in one of the social housekeeping ministries."

Madame Bardoux replied, "You would be wise to do so, my dear. But I might add that skill in press affairs is much valued today in all the ministries. You are gaining valuable experience."

Madame Bardoux turned to Bob, "I enjoy your paper. It's great fun for keeping up on American cultural news in Paris. But I am afraid Paris is not so fun anymore. Even for the Americans."

Bob replied, "The Depression has hit America hard, too, I'm afraid."

Madame Bardoux turned thoughtful, "But you still have the dollar. France has struggled. France won the war, but lost the value of its beloved *franc*. It is bleak for so very many."

Bob nodded in understanding.

Then Madame Bardoux gave a small nod of her head and turned to business, "You can see the entire Quai from these windows. There are telephones in the next room to call your paper."

Madame Bardoux smiled politely and asked, "Can I offer you some tea or coffee while we wait?"

Bob replied, "Not for me right now." He turned to Sandrine, "I'm going to go over to the Chamber of Deputies. I'll meet you back here after they adjourn if not before. Will that be OK, Madame Bardoux?"

"Why of course."

"I'll see you later, Bob," replied Sandrine. She turned to Madame Bardoux, "Some tea would be delightful."

Madame Bardoux spoke softly to a secretary standing behind her, who went off to fetch some tea. Then she turned to Sandrine, "Let's go to the front of the building and look out the windows."

Bob turned and headed down the stairway and out the rear of the building. He crossed the courtyard towards one of the rear entrances to the Palais Bourbon.

Quai D'Orsay, home of the French foreign ministry, faces the River Seine on the boulevard Quai D'Orsay. Just to the east is the Palais Bourbon, home in the 1930s to the Chamber of Deputies. Just to the west is the broad grassy Esplanade des Invalides.

Sandrine and Madame Bardoux walked across the room over to tall windows overlooking the wide avenue of the Quai D'Orsay. Across the avenue were elm trees evenly spaced along a wide sidewalk bordered by a small waist-high wall.

Beyond the wall and down twenty feet, the River Seine slowly flowed in its stonewalled channel.

Sandrine pointed her hand and said, "There is the police line backed up by squads of Mobile Guards."

She looked farther up the avenue, "There are the demonstrators. They are nicely formed up in a column. They seem to be waiting."

Madame Bardoux observed, "Yes, they are a column of the *Croix-de-Feu*. A second column is rumored to be forming up out beyond Rue de Bourgogne. They will march on the Chamber of Deputies from the back streets. We think this column outside our window will then try to advance from the north along the river—a two-pronged assault on the Palais Bourbon."

Sandrine wrote this down in her notepad.

Madame Bardoux quickly added, "No direct quotes."

Sandrine replied, "Yes, I understand. I'm learning."

"Yes, you are, my dear," replied the older woman.

With the sun setting in the west, the police colonel strode down Boulevard St.-Germain with five hundred marching gendarmerie troops strung out behind him. On his left was the Palais Bourbon, seat of the Chamber of Deputies. Up ahead the all-important bridge. Earlier in the afternoon, the call had come from the Paris prefecture of police, the nervous voice asking, "Could you scare up some reinforcements from the suburbs and get them to the bridge by nightfall?"

"Yes."

He had been an officer in the war, a *poilu*. He remembered: the desperate calls in the night, the hurried rush forward with troops, turning back the onslaught. He remembered the calls. There was always only one answer, "*Oui, Monsieur.*"

One of the assistant police chiefs came over, and with a sigh of relief said, "You made it."

The police colonel nodded and thought silently to himself: *Yes. Of course I made it.*

The assistant police chief said, "I'll take over now and deploy your men."

The police colonel nodded his assent and made a sweeping gesture with his arm back towards his men, the gesture indicating his release of the command and as a sign to the men that the command had changed.

Over on the bridge, nervously chain-smoking, was a man in civilian clothes, somewhat reluctantly in charge. The police colonel assumed he was the new Paris prefect of police, Georges Bonnefoy-Sibour, who had replaced the long-time and highly popular Jean Chiappe three days before. Chiappe, luxuriously corrupt for a police prefect, had never held the police colonel's respect. The police colonel walked over to the new prefect, stood to an easy form of attention, and saluted, "Colonel Simon, commander of the First Legion of the Gendarmerie."

Bonnefoy-Sibour nodded and gave a weak smile, "Thank you for your prompt assistance. It will be remembered and spoken of." Then he turned away and looked back absently over the bridge to the Place de la Concorde on the other side. The police colonel thought: *sort of dismissed*. He shrugged. *Elan?*

The police colonel turned away and walked across the street and took up a position near the bridge and in front of the Palais Bourbon. He leaned against the balustrade and watched the bustling activity around him. He decided to wait and see how his men did under the pressure of the coming street demonstrations.

As the police colonel watched, an assistant police chief came over to Bonnefoy-Sibour and conferred. The police prefect pointed to the last barricade on the Pont de la Concorde—the bridge—before the Palais Bourbon and said, "To be held at all costs."

A man in a slouch hat, pulled down low over his eyes, a scruffy wool muffler wrapped around his ears and neck, wearing a dull overcoat, turned onto the sidewalk of elegant Boulevard de La Tour Maubourg. He hurriedly walked twenty meters up to an apartment-house entrance, rapped three times in succession on the door, and as the door opened, slipped into the building. The man opening the door whispered to the visitor, "Fifth floor, second door on the right."

Minutes later, on the fifth floor, the man in the slouch hat opened the door to an apartment and walked in. A man standing over by a window turned and walked over, "Ah, Colonel de La Rocque," and the man threw a casual salute, "we are ready."

The colonel took off the slouch hat, unwound the muffler, took off his overcoat and draped it over the back of a chair, and said by way of starting, "Good."

The colonel walked over to the window and looked out into the fading twilight. Night would soon be upon them. He looked through the bare branches of the elm trees lining the boulevard and across the broad expanse of the Esplanade des Invalides towards the river. On the far side of the grassy park and fronting the river stood the beautiful buildings of the Quai D'Orsay, seat of the foreign ministry and the offices of the premier and council of state.

The colonel then swept his gaze westward to the façade of the Hotel des Invalides with its golden dome set in the center of the palace-like building. Below the dome rested the tomb of Napoleon. The colonel idly recollected that Napoleon was the last man to harness the revolutionary fervor of the French masses into a driving authoritarian state. Then he sighed. Today, the Republic must be seen as anointing the leader; the days of an emperor placing the crown on his own head are past.

In the back streets behind the massive Hotel des Invalides, the largest building on the Left Bank, members of the *Croix-de-Feu*—Cross of Fire—gathered in groups, smoking, gossiping, and speculating about the evening's demonstration. Night set in. The men, mostly war veterans, easily formed into ranks as orders were shouted down the streets until two long marching columns, each two-thousand-men strong, assembled in the narrow streets. In the van of each column were younger men, the *Dispos*, trained for street assault.

The first column stepped off leaving the second column behind—later, it would deploy along the river. The first column of marching men wound its way through the nighttime streets behind Les Invalides, turned, and headed down Rue de Bourgogne. Ahead, the men could see the narrow street opening up into the square of the Place du Palais Bourbon. Behind the square the men could see the large multi-columned building of the Palais Bourbon, the home of the Chamber of Deputies. Ranks of closely formed police blocked the way. Behind the police was a phalanx of helmeted Mobile Guards. The column marched forward.

The young men, many with wooden axe handles and staves, pushed into the police line, the surging mass of men behind them driving them forward, the young men yelling and swinging at the police. The police were pushed back into the Mobile Guards, tougher men who started to strike back with batons and bloody the front rank of attackers. But the surging mass of men simply pushed the entire police line back. As attackers fell, others were pushed into their place. The police line fell back, a wobbly line of swinging fists and batons. Police commanders screamed to their men to hold in place.

If the police line were pushed back into the square, the commanders knew, then the attackers would just surge around the ends of the line and into the Palais Bourbon. The rioters would quickly penetrate the hall of the Chamber of Deputies and drive the deputies, sitting in session, from their benches. The rioters would control the seat of the Republic's power and legitimacy. Then, possibly a proclamation of provisional government would be read out from the speaker's tribune. Then, civil war.

Suddenly, shouted orders to halt came through the massed ranks of the *Croix-de-Feu*. The men stopped, fell back, and stood easy. Up front, older men pulled the young men back from the police line, those who protested were slammed against the walls of buildings and the older men shouted in their faces, "To the Invalides. Orders."

Slowly the column reformed, the young men angrily turning their backs on the police line. The reformed column marched back up Rue de Bourgogne, turned right, and then headed towards the large expanse of the Esplanade des Invalides. Reaching the Esplanade, the column turned right again and headed down to the broad boulevard of the Quai D'Orsay along the river. The men could see the other *Croix-de-Feu* column stretched out in a long line west of the buildings of the foreign ministry. In front of the buildings was another police line blocking the boulevard fronting the river. A block past the foreign ministry was the façade of the Palais Bourbon, also facing the river.

As the second column took position alongside the first column, leaders hurriedly conferred. A new assault line was formed. Leaders eyed the police line up ahead, stared at the helmeted Mobile Guards behind the police, disdain welling up inside them. The colonel had concentrated great force on the Quai. Wisely. With certainty bred of hard experience in the war, the front-rank leaders murmured to one another, "We will carry the police line. One push, and we will be on the Palais. We'll drive the robbers away from their corruption." All heads, dark eyes burning with determination, nodded in agreement.

Late in the afternoon, Bill Wilshire walked along the sidewalk bordering the south side of Place de la Madeleine, behind him the Parthenon-like façade of the great nineteenth-century cathedral rose above the Parisian streets of the normally bustling Right Bank, the merchant district of Paris. Wilshire turned down Rue Royale towards the Place de la Concorde, the high buildings on both sides of the street—the ministry of marine on the left, the Hotel Crillon on the right—framing the tall Obelisk jutting skywards from the center of the square. The Obelisk, more than thirty centuries old, stood like a rifle sight framed in the twin-pillars of a rear sight. The Obelisk was a gift from the viceroy of Egypt the century before during the age of the First Empire. The ceremony placing the Obelisk on the square marked a new era of grandeur for the fabled Place, the site where thousands, including Marie Antoinette, had previously been guillotined during the Terror while the jeering crowds of Revolutionary Paris looked on.

Place de la Concorde today. The two fountains are separated by the Obelisk. The Hotel Crillon is on the left, the Rue Royale in the middle with the Madeline neoclassical church at its far end, the ministry of marine on the right. (Photo by the author.)

Straight beyond the Obelisk was a bridge over the River Seine, the Pont de la Concorde. At the far end of the bridge, in the silvery gray light of the winter sunset, Wilshire could see the massive, many-columned façade of the

Palais Bourbon, seat of the Chamber of Deputies. Reaching the end of Rue Royale, Wilshire walked out onto the broad surface of the Place. Across the Place, he could see a few hundred shock troops of the Far Right leagues pushing at a police line strung across the square. Wilshire thought that the scene was not shaping up to be much of a news story. Nevertheless, he took out a notepad from his overcoat pocket and started to take notes; he saw some members of the *Camelots du Roi*, young shock troops of the Royalist *Action Française*, fewer than he would have thought since *Action Française* was the largest of the Far Right leagues. Looking more closely, he saw some of the fifty-man mobile squads of the *Jeunesses Patriotes*—the Young Patriots—dressed in their blue raincoats and berets. By far the largest contingent was from *Solidarité Française*, well financed by the wealthy perfume industrialist François Coty. The young shock troops were militarily well turned out in black berets, blue shirts, and jackboots.

Wilshire took a final look at the desultory pushing and shoving along the police line. This looked like a routine street demonstration, well within the police's ability to control. Interestingly, he saw a lot of Communists among the crowd. Their newspaper had called for direct action this morning. He snapped shut his notepad and turned north and headed for the entrance to the Hotel Crillon. May be he could grab a bite to eat. Beyond the hotel was the American Embassy; possibly some embassy staffers, or other journalists, would be inside the hotel. Someone would have the inside dope. On the bridge, a day was ending, a night beginning.

Back across the river at the Palais Bourbon, Bob Tompkins, having just left Sandrine at the Quai D'Orsay, presented his police press pass to the *huissier*—military sentry— and walked up the stairs to the press gallery. The tumultuous shouts of the deputies followed him down the hallway. Inside the gallery, Bob looked out over the cavernous Chamber with its circular benches forming a three-quarter circle before the raised tribune of the speaker. From the direction of the speaker's tribune, the Communist deputies, seated on the left-side benches, were giving a rousing rendition of the *L'Internationale*. Over on the right-side benches, the Far Right parties were singing *La Marseillaise*, breaking off periodically with shouts at the ministerial bench, "Resign."

Unable to read his ministerial declaration to establish his government, Premier Edouard Daladier asked the speaker for a fifteen-minute suspension. Daladier was the leader of the centrist but somewhat misnamed Radical Socialist party, the party that commanded the parliamentary majority. The speaker, attired in top hat and formal dress suit, mustered his dignity and ordered the suspension. A Far Right deputy strode across the well to the ministerial bench and tried to pull the astonished Daladier off his bench. Daladier, nicknamed the Bull of Vaucluse for his stocky build, was all *poilu*; a veteran of the tough trench fighting of the Western Front in the Great War. He sent the right-winger sprawling.

Bob exclaimed to the reporter next to him, "I'll be damned."

"No, France will be if the Chamber allows the streets to overthrow a constitutional government," replied a British journalist. "I say not the way we do it in London. The king wouldn't approve."

Bob looked at his colleague with open-mouthed astonishment.

When the fifteen-minute suspension ended, Daladier again tried to read his ministerial declaration. But he was drowned out by shouting and pandemonium. Exasperated, he called for a vote of confidence.

The Far Right deputies erupted into a shouting mass and threatened to charge the well of the Chamber and start a free-for-all with Daladier's supporters. Daladier called for another fifteen-minute suspension.

Just then, one deputy, a veteran blinded in the war, heard sharp sounds coming from the bridge over the roar of the crowds trying to storm the Pont de la Concorde. He shouted, "They're firing! You're a government of assassins!"

Fearing the mob, many deputies left the hall. They found the corridors crowded with injured police and Mobile Guards being attended to by the Chamber's own doctors. The wife of the speaker, Madame Bouisson, moved between the wounded handing out bottles of rum.

Earlier in the evening, Tuesday, February 6. On the cold granite stones of the Place de l'Hôtel-de-Ville, young men began to assemble in the late twilight wearing their distinctive blue raincoats and berets. Many were university students from across the river. Older men moved among the milling throng, leaders forming up the younger men into a long column.

Overlooking the broad square was the magnificent edifice of the Hôtel de Ville, the majestic seat of the city government of Paris. Above its multi-storied stonewalls, steeply pitched roofs soared to the sky. At the ground level, hundreds of police stood in a line in front of an arched façade, pushing and shoving to keep rowdy demonstrators from forcing their way into the building. More young men poured into the square. Soon four thousand members of the *Jeunesses Patriotes*—the Young Patriots League—crowded into the square. The older men, like sheep dogs, moved about and cajoled the younger men into the ranks of the long column.

Then, from the arched entrance to the municipal building, sallied forth thirteen municipal councilors, mayors of the *arrondissements,* who strode out onto the broad square. These well-fed middle-aged dignitaries, distinguished by beautiful tricolor sashes draped across their expansive white shirts, took up positions at the head of the column. They were outraged that the national government had sacked the popular Far Right Paris police prefect, Jean Chiappe, a move that undoubtedly disrupted many lucrative arrangements. A state of war between the Hôtel-de-Ville and the national government was virtually declared.

From the head of the now-formed column came a muffled order. The front ranks stepped out and the column made a smooth turn, arms swinging, onto Rue de Rivoli. The column marched northwest singing the stirring national anthem from the Revolution, *La Marseillaise.* As the column marched along the Rue de Rivoli, the marchers, spying onlookers who appeared to be foreigners on the broad sidewalks, screamed out, "France for the French!" Onlookers scurried into the tourist agencies lining the street to seek refuge from the street-marching militants. The column continued striding alongside the Louvre Museum, tramped past the Tuileries Garden, and then out onto the broad expanse of the Place de la Concorde. The column halted well back from the police line guarding the approaches to the Pont de la Concorde. The councilors walked forward and approached the police line; a chief waved them through the line and allowed them to cross the bridge to the Palais Bourbon, home of the Chamber of Deputies.

The *Jeunesses Patriotes,* sullen and defiant, watched the councilors cross the bridge. Then, swaying in their ranks as if building up a reservoir of momentum, they surged forward towards the police line hoping to break through to the bridge. The police, manning three powerful fire hoses as if they were artillery pieces, broke the charge and drove the crowd back. Helmeted members of the Mobile Guard, swinging batons, waded in and roughly pushed the demonstrators farther back. Behind the Mobile Guard came mounted members of the Republican Guard, spurring their horses forward into the crowd while slashing with the flat sides of their sabers. The demonstrators fell back to the middle of the square around the tall Obelisk.

Tuesday evening, 6:30 p.m. Having finished a quick meal, Bill Wilshire came out of the entrance of the Hotel Crillon, astounded to see the surging thousands of new demonstrators pushing the police line back towards the bridge. Wilshire worked his way along the columned portico of the hotel and then across the front of the ministry of marine; he crossed the Rue de Rivoli, and then climbed a short flight of steps into the Tuileries Gardens. He worked his way along a balustraded walkway about a dozen feet above the Place de la Concorde. The entire square was visible from this vantage point. From the walkway, crowds were hurling paving stones and iron grilles ripped from the base of trees at the police. Wilshire noticed the presence of Communists mingling with their fascists' enemies in the insurrection against government order. Below him crowds were surging at the police lines, then the rioters were driven back by charges from the mounted Republican Guards, slashing away with sabers at the crowd. Demonstrators with long sticks edged with razor blades slashed away at the horses and the legs of the mounted police; a number of horses went down, the riders mauled by the vicious assaults of the rioters. Wilshire watched as both sides started to carry their wounded away. An intense, hateful mood of combat spread.

Wilshire backtracked and worked his way back across the square to the Hotel Crillon. Going up to the third floor, he joined twenty French and foreign journalists on an outside balcony overlooking the square.

Tuesday evening, 7:30 p.m. Near the Madeleine, the grand Parthenon-like church two long blocks to the east of the Place de la Concorde, the hard-right fascist street fighters of *Le Francisme* hurled themselves at the police cordon. From side streets poured hundreds of other rowdies. The police lines were swamped and they fell back down Rue Royale with the surging crowd growing stronger every step of the way. The crowds flowed onto the Place de la Concorde adding their weight to massed rioters of the *Jeunesses Patriotes* and the *Solidarité Française.* The massed rioters pushed the police lines off the square and onto the bridge.

Tuesday evening, 8 p.m. On the Place de la Concorde, the crowd surged forward behind a large Tricolor flag waving back and forth as a rallying point. Thousands were singing *La Marseillaise.* In the van, *Jeunesses Patriotes* pushed back the police line farther onto the bridge. Police charges broke the center of the line, but the mobs surged around the ends. Again, the police played their firemen's hoses onto the rushing rioters. The rioters, pushed forward by those surging behind them, drove ahead to the hose fighting line, captured two of the fire hoses, and turned them back on the police. The police retreated to the middle of the bridge and formed a triple cordon shoulder-to-shoulder. Outnumbered ten to one by the rioters, the police buglers sounded the last mournful call, the traditional fanfare that the police were about to fire if the forces of rebellion mounted their assault. Riot had become rebellion.

Suddenly, a mob of *Solidarité Française* broke through the line at the north end shouting, *"Á la Chambre!"* They pushed across the bridge heading for an all-out assault on the final police lines guarding the Chamber of Deputies. Startled and panicky, individual policemen and Mobile Guards saw the black berets storming at them, heard the thunder of jackboots on the pavement. They opened fire with automatic pistols. Six rioters in the front rank went down. Other police fired over the rioters' heads. The charge was broken. Mounted police with swords drawn spurred their horses forward into the teaming ranks of the rioters. Women in the crowd started screaming, "Assassins! Assassins!"

Across the Place de la Concorde on the third-floor balcony, the journalists listened as gunfire sounded from both sides of the bridge. Suddenly, a cleaning woman standing in their midst buckled at the knees and dissolved onto the floor. Bill Wilshire rushed to her side; blood spurted from a hole in the middle of her forehead. She had died before hitting the floor. Indeed, someone had fired high.

Tuesday evening, 8:30 p.m. At the Quai D'Orsay, Sandrine heard the gunfire on the bridge. She turned away from watching the *Croix-de-Feu* who were strung out in a column north of the foreign ministry. On the Pont de la Concorde, Sandrine saw the demonstrators retreating back across the bridge towards the square on the other side of the river. She stood transfixed as she watched the riotous melee on the Place de la Concorde. Then, hearing shouted orders, she turned and saw the column of *Croix-de-Feu* coming to attention, getting ready to march. In the front ranks of the column were war veterans with medals pinned to the fronts of fading uniforms from the Great War. The column moved forward, arms swinging in cadence, the men lustily singing *La Marseilles*. The column hit the police line and pushed it back, a breakthrough to the Chamber of Deputies seemed imminent. Sandrine furously wrote notes in her notepad.

Coming up the avenue from the other direction were reinforcements of helmeted Mobile Guards, brandishing white batons and ready to crack heads. The veterans' column broke under the police assault. Falling back, the veterans carried off their wounded, taking them back to the Invalides station north of the Esplanade. Just beyond the foreign ministry, the veterans reformed again on a broader front, putting the *dispos* in the front ranks, young toughs trained in street fighting. The column waited to move forward.

Sandrine watched apprehensively as she wrote notes in her pad and thought to herself, "They're sure to break the line on the next go."

Tuesday evening, 8:30 p.m. Next door at the Palais Bourbon, Bob Tompkins watched Socialist leader Léon Blum confer with Daladier and then rise to speak, "We have not forgotten what the fascists did to the parties of the left, and to government of the law, in Germany and Italy when they overthrew those democratic regimes with street violence."

Nodding at Daladier, Blum shouted out his argument, "Our vote for the government is not a vote of confidence. It is a vote of combat!"

The vote of confidence in Daladier's government carried almost three-to-two for the third time on this historically troubled day.

With the roar of the crowds in their ears, the remaining deputies left and headed for the rear gates. The speaker rang down the adjournment.

Tuesday evening, 9 p.m. On the other side of the Esplanade des Invalides from the Quai D'Orsay, Colonel de La Rocque looked out the window and watched as his men formed into a new column along the river. His men were ready to make a second assault at the police line in front of the foreign ministry. The telephone rang, an aide answered.

The aide turned to the colonel, "For you."

The colonel came over, picked up the receiver and put it to his ear, and spoke into the mouthpiece, "Colonel de La Rocque here."

He nodded his head, "Yes, that is good news."

"Tomorrow?"

"Does Daladier know?"

"Not yet, you say."

"Doumergue, are you sure? He has turned the President of the Republic down on this before."

"Pétain? Minister of defense. Good."

"What of Laval?"

"Minister of the colonies. Good."

The colonel clicked the phone off and handed it back to the aide. He walked back over to the window, caught up in his thoughts. He considered his options, then looked across the Esplanade as his men continued to form up along the river. He turned to the men in the room and said, "We have prevailed at the Élysée Palace."

Turning to his deputy, the colonel said, "Quickly get over to the column. Pull them back. Then send them home for the night. Tell them our mission for today has been accomplished; the deputies have abandoned their benches. Important announcements will issue tomorrow. From the President of the Republic."

The man came to attention, "Yes, colonel," and departed.

Inside the foreign ministry, Sandrine watched out the window as men ran to the front of the *Croix-de-Feu* column and grabbed at shirtsleeves, pulling men around and then out of the ranks. Shouts went up, some men in the ranks protesting, "No, no, not now."

Other men shouted back, "Yes, orders from the colonel. We have won our objectives for the day. Follow your orders. Tomorrow will be a truly new day for France."

Slowly the column broke up, men walked back up the avenue along the river towards the Invalides station. Others walked across the grassy Esplanade towards the neighborhoods they had come from.

Sandrine wondered what had happened.

She turned away from the window and walked over towards the secretary and asked after Madame Bardoux. The secretary pointed her down the hallway towards an open office door.

Sandrine walked down the hall and looked into the office and saw Madame Bardoux speaking with a well-dressed man sitting behind the desk, obviously a senior official. Sandrine lightly tapped on the thick wooden door and Madame Bardoux turned and said, "Come in, my dear."

The man smiled and his eyes lit up as Sandrine entered the spacious office.

Madame Bardoux said, "This is the young woman of whom I spoke. Let me introduce Mademoiselle Sandrine Durand," and she turned to Sandrine.

Sandrine held out her hand.

Madame Bardoux said to Sandrine by way of introduction, "Monsieur Philippe de Davignon, a senior member of the office of Central European affairs. He specializes in Germany."

Davignon stood up and came around his desk. He wore a well-pressed white shirt with the pointed collars of the modern style and a medium-width dark maroon silk tie. He wore an almost-black charcoal gray suit with deep gray pinstripes tailored to a trim Parisian look. Not London at all. He would of course appear sleekly French at the international conferences. Davignon took Sandrine's hand in his own, brought it up halfway to his bowed head, gave it an air kiss, and then let the hand down. He stood up in a business-like manner and gave her hand a nice diplomatic handshake and said, "*Enchanté.*"

Sandrine was charmed by his effortless gallantry. She smiled and said, "Thank you." Then thinking about the business at hand, Sandrine looked at Madame Bardoux and said, "The *Croix-de-Feu* has turned away. What happened?"

Madame Bardoux replied, "Let me say, unofficially of course, that the police outside have told us that Colonel de La Rocque gave the order to fall back and disperse. His lieutenants are saying that the *Croix-de-Feu* has gained its goals. He says that the government has heard the voices of the street. His followers have been told that important announcements will be made tomorrow."

Madame Bardoux then became thoughtful, "Interestingly, Colonel de La Rocque said that announcements will come from the Élysée Palace, from the President of the Republic. That sounds like a shake-up in the government. It sounds like Colonel de La Rocque knows something we do not."

Davignon nodded his head in absent-minded agreement while smiling lightly as he watched Sandrine intently.

Madame Bardoux changed the subject, "Monsieur de Davignon has been increasingly interested in the press coverage in both the French and English-language Parisian papers. He feels that the English-language press more accurately reports the ministry's position. Since you work with both French-language and English-language papers, we thought your experience might give you some insight into this question."

Sandrine said, "As you know, I pick up your communiqués and press hand-outs, or make notes of what your press spokesman says, then I give them to *Le Petit Journal.* Then I go up to the second floor and drop off copies to the Americans at the *Paris Bulletin.* The French editors rewrite to their point of view. Sometimes they reprint the communiqué, but of course it all sounds very official."

Davignon listened attentively. Sandrine could see that she really had his attention.

Sandrine continued, "The Americans are different. They take a simple who, what, when, where approach to their news stories. They like facts arranged in a descending order of importance, like a waterfall. They like to summarize the main point in one opening sentence. I just give them as many facts on a sheet of paper plus the press handouts as I can."

Davignon nodded in agreement, "The political level wants to do a better job of getting the government position out to the public in an understandable way. The American papers in Paris do a good job, but the public of course reads the French papers."

Sandrine smiled, "Yes, I know. Many of the French papers have fanned the flames of tonight's disturbances."

Davignon sadly nodded his head in agreement.

Just then Bob Tompkins came walking up the hall and, looking into the office, saw Sandrine, "Oh there you are. The receptionist said there is going to be a briefing for reporters in the reception area."

Madame Bardoux smiled at Bob and said, "Quite correct. I am going to give the briefing. But first come in and let me introduce you to Monsieur de Davignon."

Davignon stood up and turned on a charming smile, "Pleased to meet you. Sandrine was telling us about how Americans write their news stories. Very interesting." Turning to Madame Bardoux, he said, "You better attend to your press briefing," and he smiled at Bob.

Madame Bardoux said, "We better not keep the others waiting," and she extended her arm to usher Bob back into the hallway. She followed him out.

Sandrine stayed behind momentarily and turned to Davignon, smiled brightly, and, displaying her finest charm, said, "I hope I have the opportunity to discuss press relations further with you, Monsieur de Davignon."

Davignon smiled, "Yes, we can keep in touch after the disturbances. Through Madame Bardoux, of course."

Sandrine replied, keeping the cadence of the conversation in perfect time, "Of course." She smiled charmingly. Then she turned and followed the other two down the hall, leaving a small harmony behind.

A small knot of reporters was standing in a circle talking about the evening's events. Madame Bardoux took her place in front of them. She said, "Okay, we can begin."

Madame Bardoux spoke crisply, "The *Croix-de-Feu*, apparently on Colonel de La Rocque's orders, has withdrawn and the men have gone back to their homes for the night. On this side of the river, the demonstrations are over."

"Premier Daladier has gone across the river to meet with President Lebrun. Later he is expected to meet with some members of his cabinet."

"We have been told that he will return, probably early in the morning hours, to Quai D'Orsay. As most of you know, he has his offices and residence here pending completion of new quarters at the Hotel Matignon. We expect that he will issue a statement to the press when he returns."

The reporters turned to one another with a ruffle of conversation and murmurings. *Another long night.*

Madame Bardoux concluded, "There are telephones for you in the next room. And some coffee and baguettes. I and my staff will be down the hall."

Bob turned to Sandrine, "Let's phone in our stories. Then you better go back to your flat and get some sleep. Sarah would never forgive me if you stayed out working into the morning hours. Give me the phone number of your French paper and I will phone in the communiqué for you."

Sandrine wrote out the number on a sheet of paper and handed it to Bob, "Thanks, Monsieur Bob. I'll call in my story and tell them to expect the communiqué from you. It will be too late for the morning edition anyway."

Fifteen minutes later, Sandrine came up to Bob, "My paper will be expecting your call. I'm taking off now. Please say hello to Sarah for me. May be I'll see you at the Oasis tomorrow?"

Bob said, "I'll tell her. We'll all be there."

"Goodnight, Bob." Sandrine walked over to the far side of the room and descended the stairs to the courtyard.

Tuesday evening, a little after 9 p.m., Place de la Concorde. From the Hotel Crillon, Bill Wilshire watched the roar of the crowd as the rioters, driven off the bridge by police gunfire, turned in a frenzy on fire crews trying to douse flames in the ministry of marine, the grand edifice next door to the hotel. Naval guards were holding the surging throng back at pistol point. Suddenly, the roar of the crowd died away. To the north side of the square a long column of thousands of war veterans, members of the mainstream *Union nationale des combattants*, the UNC, came marching in from the Champs Élysées with flags and banners held high, medals pinned across their chests, singing *La Marseillaise.* Many of the veterans carried hand-painted signs: WE WANT FRANCE TO LIVE IN ORDER AND HONESTY. The rioters made way for the marching column; the police saluted the flags. The column crossed the square and proceeded up Rue Royale and then turned left towards the presidential palace, the Élysée Palace.

Tuesday

Wilshire hurried outside and fell in with the leading marchers. The veterans marched up Rue Saint-Honoré to the Élysée Palace intending to petition the President of the Republic, Albert Lebrun. The marching column was stopped by a police barricade, which refused to give way. The veterans grew surly and belligerent with the front ranks pushing into the police line, fists swinging and arms flailing at the police batons. The veterans pushed the police back and over to the side of the street. The veterans surged forward, the angry tide sweeping through a second barrier. In front of the palace, the veterans met closed ranks of mounted Republican Guards, sabers drawn. The Republican Guards spurred their horses into the massed men, sabers flashing, and drove the veterans back, leaving fifty-three seriously wounded lying on the cobblestoned street.

Wilshire scribbled notes in his pad; he had never seen the Republican Guard break up a rioting mass quite so harshly. The veterans retreated back to the Place de la Concorde, adding their angry numbers to rioters milling in front of the police lines guarding the bridge. More angry rioters, many of them Communists, poured into the square from surrounding streets. Wilshire followed, mesmerized by the crazed, unfocused hatred of a crowd looking for a fight.

Wilshire looked at his watch, 10:30 p.m., almost the hour of emotional midnight for a Paris street riot. The crowd in the square now formed up in close ranks almost as one body and surged toward the bridge. Firemen at the front of the police line played three hoses on the on-rushing rioters while Mobile and Republican Guards broke the charge. The rioters, sullen and angry, regrouped and surged forward. Repulsed, the rioters armed their front ranks with stones and large men with strong arms to hurl them. They surged forward again. Twenty assaults were mounted. Each time the rioters charged, some of the defenders on the police line went down. As assault followed assault, over a thousand police and guards were evacuated back across the bridge to overwhelmed aid stations inside the Palais Bourbon. Holding the bridge had become a war of attrition. Wilshire saw, that on the police lines, assistant chiefs and other front-line leaders had fallen disproportionately. The police leadership was being decimated.

At 11:30 p.m., the rioters reformed yet again with tougher, angrier men coming into the front rank. Shouts went up, the rioters surged forward, red-hot intensity fueling deadly hatred, the police line buckled and some of the police started to flee back over the bridge, fearing for their lives.

At the last police line, the police and guards aimed their machine pistols at the screaming, stone-throwing rioters charging onto the bridge. They fired. Some rioters fell, the others fell back onto the square. The rioters started to reform again before the dazed eyes of the police and guards manning the police lines. Many of these rioters were men who had "gone over the top" in the Great War. They were without fear. *They are going to come again.*

Left Bank, Pont de la Concorde, 11:30 p.m. Colonel Simon, the gendarmerie commander who had turned over his men to the Paris police that afternoon, watched. He heard the gunfire. He watched the wounded police and guards stream back across the bridge. The police lines must be weakening, dangerously so, he thought. He looked across the bridge, eyes smoldering with contempt at that almost useless spectator, the prefect of police, Bonnefoy-Sibour. The prefect stood there nervously chain-smoking but not issuing any orders, giving no instructions, seemingly wondering what had happened to all the assistant police chiefs. No police leader was in sight.

Colonel Simon cinched the belt of his greatcoat as he had so many times before. He looked across the bridge, saw what had to be done, and started to walk forward in a determined and forceful manner. He was heartened by the smiles of the wounded limping back across the bridge, weary police and guardsmen who now recognized that authority was moving forward in the determined stride of one forceful leader. Surely the forces of order would prevail, they thought.

Colonel Simon came up to the mounted Republican Guards, "Who is in charge here?" The sabers pointed towards a rider in the center and a little out front. Colonel Simon walked over, "I'm Colonel Simon of the First Legion of the Gendarmerie. I'm taking command. I want you and your men to lead the charge. You are to clear the square and stay. We are going to hold the square. I will follow with the Mobile Guards, gendarmes, and police. We are going to hold the entire square. Understood?"

"*Oui, Monsieur.*" The saber came straight up and was held out in front of the commander's face towards the colonel. All the other mounted Republican Guards immediately knew the order. Horses formed up, the mounted line straightened, hooves clattered on the stones.

The weary Mobile Guards, gendarmes, and police saw the mounted Republican Guards come into a precise and straight line, the riders' backs straighten, the commander centered and in front of his men. They too understood.

Colonel Simon came in among the weary men, "The Republican Guard will lead the way. They will drive the rioters from the square. We will follow and drive the rest out. We are staying on the Place de la Concorde. Do you understand? The Place de la Concorde is going to belong to the forces of order. Tonight. All night." Turning his head and nodding towards the square, "They have had their day."

The men smiled, stood a little straighter, took a grip on their batons, and formed into two or three ranks. Men stepped forward and took the place of missing leaders. Hands waved at Colonel Simon. He nodded at the commander of the Republican Guards, took a couple steps towards him, and uttered those never-to-be-forgotten words from the Great War, "*Avancez.*"

The Guards spurred their horses forward, holding a tight line, and moved into the square. The rioters buckled, fell back, and then broke and ran for the streets leading away from the square. The police and Mobile Guards followed on foot driving the rest before them. The square was cleared as fast as the horses and walking police lines could cross it.

Bill Wilshire, watching from the Hotel Crillon, looked at his watch. It was almost midnight. He had never seen anything like it. He watched the lone man in his greatcoat follow behind his men, then wave and nod approval at the commander of the mounted guard. As Wilshire watched, the man turned over command of the police on the square to one of the remaining assistant police chiefs. Then the man turned and walked slowly back over the bridge. So this was how the Great War had been won, Wilshire thought. Men like that. He looked up at the stars shining in the dark night.

Tuesday night, 11:45 p.m., Élysée Palace. In the spacious lobby of the presidential palace, Phil Roberts turned to a blank page in his notebook. He had already telephoned in two stories to the *Paris Bulletin*, the last one just an hour before about the Republican Guards breaking the war veterans' surging assault on the streets outside the gates of the palace.

A press aide came over to the waiting reporters and said that Premier Daladier was coming to report to the President of the Republic. Just then, a dark-haired, thickset man, escorted by an aide and several policemen, came through the entrance and walked purposively towards the presidential office. The door of the office opened and President Albert Lebrun, tears streaking down his distraught face, came out with both arms outstretched plaintively asking, "What are we to do?"

The premier took the President's hands in his own and replied calmly, "The government is determined to maintain the security of the population and the independence of the republican regime. There is evidence of an attempt by armed force against the security of the state."

The two men went inside the office and a guard closed the door.

Several minutes later the door opened and Premier Daladier came out, nodded at the reporters, while one of his aides came over and explained that the premier was on his way to the ministry of the interior to confer with members of the cabinet. A statement would be forthcoming after the meeting.

Phil Roberts and several reporters followed the official party out through the gates of the presidential palace and across Place Beauvau to the ministry of the interior. The fortress-like building was ringed with police and Mobile Guards; the reporters went to the sentry box and showed their police press passes under the supervision of the premier's press aide. The reporters trudged inside and flopped down on sofas and chairs in the lobby. The official party ascended in elevators to the suite of offices maintained for the interior minister.

Wednesday morning, 2 a.m., ministry of the interior. The premier's press aide stepped out of the elevator and walked into the lobby, gently nudging reporters' legs and shoulders as he went, good naturedly saying, "Wake up. Final news call." The reporters woke up, rubbed their eyes, got out their pads and pencils, and looked at the press aide.

"Let me read you a communiqué," he said and looked down at his handwritten statement.

"Bands armed with knives and revolvers attacked the police. They opened fire on the defenders of order and many police were wounded. There was a real armed attack on the security of the state."

"These assaults were broken and the objectives of the rioters were not reached. Necessary measures are being immediately taken to prevent any new attempt."

"The country desires order and peace. The government is determined by all means given it by law to insure the security of the people and the independence of the republican regime."

The press aide looked up from his statement, "Let me speak, unofficially of course. The premier, as minister of defense, has ordered some army units to the outskirts of Paris as a precautionary measure."

One of the reporters broke in, "What measures has Interior Minister Frot planned for tomorrow to prevent new riots?"

The reporter was referring to the dashing young minister, Eugène Frot, one of the cabinet's Young Turks, fiery and intense, ambitious to make a name for himself in the new government. The minister was rumored to be the authority behind the use of armed force to break the back of the riots.

The press aide sighed and said, "Minister Frot is preparing to implement strict preventive measures against those plotting against the security of the state while strongly backing the premier's movement of military forces to the outskirts of Paris."

A reporter called out, "Does that include preventive arrests?"

The press aide quickly and crisply replied, "Only legal actions will be undertaken."

The press aide looked around, "That will be all."

Wednesday morning, 3 a.m., Quai D'Orsay. In the reception area of the foreign ministry, a press aide moved about waking up the soundly sleeping reporters, "The premier is returning from the other side of the river. You can speak to him outside his residence. It has been a long night for him. Here are copies of the communiqué just given to your colleagues over at the ministry of the interior."

Bob Tompkins stood up, stretched, and reached out for one of the communiqués being handed around. He read it and then said to the reporter next to him, "What does all this mean? What happens tomorrow?"

The reporter grumpily answered, "I don't know."

Led by the press aide, the reporters moved out the door and into the courtyard towards the entrance to the premier's residence. A large black touring car drove up. Several policemen got out and surveyed the reporters and then turned and said something to the people in the car. Premier Daladier and an aide got out and started towards the residence.

One of the reporters shouted, "What are you going to do?"

Premier Daladier stopped, turned around, and with a wan smile said, "Save the Republic." He waved wearily.

WEDNESDAY

Wednesday, February 7, 1934. Early in the morning, in a spacious, high-ceilinged office in the ministry of the interior, black-bearded, saturnine-faced Eugene Frot reviewed the previous night's cabinet meeting with an aide. The often dashing, always debonair minister was businesslike. "I told the premier that the national police forces were greatly weakened by last night's riots. Two thousand have been injured. I told him we might have great difficulty controlling another day's riots. The premier understood."

Then the minister put the dilemma to the aide, "But he does not want to further inflame the situation. I understood. So he has brought military units only to Saint-Cloud just outside the city."

Frot paused and collected his thoughts, then he turned to his aide, "The premier has been minister of war in the last four governments. He feuds with General Weygand," referring to the army commander-in-chief, "and he does not trust the general. The general has well known Royalist sympathies. Possibly he has contacts with," and the minister paused to consider his words, "shall we say, those agitating against the Republic."

The aide nodded his head in understanding.

Frot continued, "On my own authority, I have ordered the prefect of police to arrest as many of the leaders of the riots as he can find." With scorn he added, "Turns out that is not many. The attorney general of course objects." Frot made a frown of disgust at the pusillanimity masquerading behind a mask of mere legal formalities. Not much dash there.

Just then, the dark wooden door to the office opened and another aide ushered in a somewhat rumpled man, an official from the police intelligence bureau of the Sûreté Générale, the national police agency.

Frot turned to the man, "Ah, good morning, Monsieur. What have you for me this morning?"

The man came across the broad carpeted floor and took out some papers from a file and spread them on the desk before the minister. "Not good news,

I am afraid," said the man. He continued, "The reports from the police informants are bad."

Frot scanned the reports, periodically pointing out a typewritten paragraph to his aide. The Far Right leagues were planning even larger demonstrations for today. There had been runs on all the Paris gun shops. Thousands of weapons had been bought. The demonstrators were going to bring guns and grenades to this new round of demonstrations.

Then there was another series of reports, more disturbing. Several of the groups had held tribunals. Yes, the minister of interior had been condemned to death for ordering the police to fire. The sentence would be carried out before dark. Not much in the way of formalities here, Frot bitterly thought. The young minister's shoulders sagged; he raised his hand to his mouth. *Yes, stripped of dignity, then fed to the mob.*

Frot turned to the police official, "Would you excuse us. Please wait outside."

The minister looked at his aide, then turned and picked up the telephone, "Get me the President of the Republic."

"Monsieur le President. This is Minister Frot. Disturbing reports. The government must resign as soon as possible."

The President of the Republic, distressed and weeping, said plaintively, "Thank you for your call, minister. You have done your duty. I will call Premier Daladier." He rang off.

Frot looked at the now silent earpiece. He nodded at his aide, tapped the phone cradle several times, and heard the operator come on the line. "Please put me through to Premier Daladier."

"Hello, Daladier here."

"Monsieur le Premier, I have just spoken with President Lebrun."

A harsh and insistent voice came over the line, "You have!"

"Yes, Monsieur le Premier, I have read the police intelligence reports. The leagues plan unspeakable violence for tonight. The government must resign."

"Ah yes, and you of course have told this to the President of the Republic?"

"Yes, Monsieur le Premier."

"Your commitment to cabinet government has gone absent without leave. I will get back with you later, minister." The line went dead.

Wednesday morning, Quai D'Orsay, 11 a.m. Premier Daladier put down the telephone. Frot had lost his nerve. If he ever had any, thought the premier. The telephone rang again. The premier picked it up, "Daladier here." The premier listened with growing disgust, then he replied.

"Léon," the premier said into the mouthpiece, referring to Léon Blum, chief of the Socialist Party, "you are the only one urging me to stay and fight. I understand—the Republic is threatened. The threat should be met. But I don't think the Chamber and Senate will support a state of siege. The leaders of the Chamber and Senate are on their way to see me. Nevertheless, I greatly appreciate your support. Events may prove you right, I am afraid." The premier put the earpiece back on its wishbone and thought—*yes, it was a bad precedent. Foreign capitals will notice. Berlin especially.*

The premier's thoughts were broken when an aide opened the door and announced, "The presidents of the Senate and the Chamber, and the party leaders, are here to see you, Monsieur le Premier."

"Thank you. Show them in."

The delegation entered the wide office and took up the chairs arranged in a semi-circle in front of the premier's desk.

The president of the Senate began, "If you stay, Edouard, you will have to fight. The police forces are greatly weakened. The army, we think, would do its duty. But to shoot at the war veterans might be too much to ask of it."

Daladier listened thoughtfully; he gathered his thoughts, "I took office two weeks ago to reestablish orderly government after public indignation overthrew the previous government. I did not accept this high office to deploy the soldiers against the citizens."

Just then the telephone rang. Daladier picked it up, "Daladier here."

He spoke into the mouthpiece, "Yes, Monsieur le President."

He listened, and then repeated, "To avert civil war. Yes, the cabinet understands. I will be at your office at 1 p.m." He placed the receiver back on its wishbone.

Daladier turned to the men sitting before him, "I am going across the river. I will turn in the resignation of the cabinet to the President of the Republic."

The men stood up. Then Daladier stood. He shook hands all around.

Wednesday, noon, Left Bank. Sandrine found a telephone and called the *Paris Bulletin*. Rewrite answered. Sandrine spoke, "This is Sandrine. I have finished my classes, such as they are. Do you want me to pick up any releases this afternoon?"

Rewrite drawled, "Let me check."

A few moments later, Rewrite came back on the line. "Monsieur Mac says go to the Palais de Justice. Something's cooking over there."

"Cooking?"

"You know. Happening. Just go over and nose around."

Sandrine answered, "I will," and she hung up the receiver.

The main entrance to the Palais de Justice 1933.

She started walking down Boulevard St.-Michel towards the river. Then she walked across Pont St.-Michel and stopped halfway across. She looked over towards the twin rectangular bell towers of the massive cathedral of Notre Dame and once again thought of all the events, the revolutions, and outbursts of discontent that had occurred within view of its bell towers. She had been told that from the days of the First Republic the Palais de Justice had been built across the square from the great cathedral to establish the equality of secular law with the power of the Church. She turned and continued across the bridge and walked up the Boulevard du Palais. She turned into the entranceway of the massive stone edifice, walked through one of the wrought-iron gates, and into the spacious courtyard of the Cour de Mai. At the far end of the courtyard, just in front of a great flight of steps leading up to the colonnaded façade of the Galerie Marchande, jostled a crowd of angry lawyers in their distinctive black robes and white collars. Some were shouting towards the building, "Assassin."

Sandrine looked across the crowd of men and then she saw a woman, also dressed in the robe and collar of *une avocate*, a lawyer. Sandrine walked over to her and asked, "Who is the 'assassin?'"

The woman turned, guessing that Sandrine was a reporter, and smiled, "Minister of Interior Frot gave the order to fire on the demonstrators last night. He is also a lawyer. He has betrayed the ideals of the profession."

A distinguished older man appeared at an open window.

Sandrine asked the *avocate*, "Who is he?"

"He is the president of the Bar Association."

The older man shouted out, "Please send a delegation to the offices of the Bar Association."

A delegation quickly assembled and went inside the building.

The *avocate* looked at Sandrine, glanced at her notepad, and said, "The lawyers feel disciplinary action is called for."

Sandrine wrote this down.

A lawyer from the delegation appeared at the door and beckoned the crowd inside.

The *avocate* said to Sandrine, "Come with me."

Sandrine joined the throng and went inside the building and stood with the others on the massive marbled floor of the main corridor of the building.

Solemnly, two lawyers put a cap and robe over a small wastebasket in the middle of the corridor. The president of the Bar Association stood in the background, as if presiding.

One of lawyers spread some fluid on the cap and robe. He took out a match and lit it. Then the robe and cap ignited in a blaze and the assembled lawyers clapped and a few cheered.

The *avocate* turned to Sandrine and said, "They have just burned Monsieur Frot's cap and robe."

One of the leaders of the delegation then called down the corridor, "Tomorrow, the Order of the Attorneys will meet to discuss striking Monsieur Frot's name from the membership roll of the Paris bar."

Sandrine wrote this down in her notepad. She turned to the *avocate* and said, "Thank you. I must be off to my newspaper. Before I go, could I get your name in case I have a future need for *une avocate?*"

The *avocate* smiled like a familiar aunt and said, "Of course," and handed Sandrine a small white business card beautifully scripted in black.

Sandrine smiled, put the card in her handbag, and smiled at the graciously mannered woman: *yes, I want to be like that.*

The woman read Sandrine's thoughts, smiled thoughtfully, and gave a small bob of her head.

Sandrine turned and headed down the marbled corridor towards where bright light was coming through the open doorway. She walked across the courtyard and out of the Palais, down to the river, and walked along the sidewalk looking at the fashionable apartments lining the Left Bank quay. Presently, she made a turn and entered the tree-shrouded, triangular Place Dauphine and found an empty bench.

She took out her notepad, opened to a blank page, and headed it "English." She left a blank space in the top lines, then below this space she wrote down who, what, when and where for the story. She arranged other facts in descending order of importance. She looked at what she had written and tried composing a lead sentence in her mind. Then she started to write, erased some of it, and wrote some more. Finally she looked at her handiwork and smiled. This should do. Just like Bob Tompkins taught me, she thought.

Then she opened another page and headed it "*Français.*" She wrote all the information down in French. Then she closed her notepad and put it back in her purse. She walked across the small park and onto a street leading out to Place de Pont Neuf, the small square between the two spans of the ancient stone bridge. She turned and strolled east across Pont Neuf towards the Right Bank and the newspaper offices up on the hill.

Phil Roberts sat in the lobby of the Élysée Palace with other reporters waiting for some official to say what was happening. So typical, he thought, events swirling all around Paris, and here at the center of the Republic the reporters were told nothing. Just then the massive front door opened and the dark, heavy-set figure of Pierre Laval came striding into the lobby with some conservative deputies trailing behind. The door to the presidential office opened and President Lebrun, tears streaking down his florid face and hugely upset, said to the approaching figure of Laval, "Doumergue has refused me. Says he's too old and too tired."

Laval, purposeful and decisive, said, "Monsieur le President, let me speak with President Doumergue," and he walked around the President and into his office.

Roberts quickly interposed himself between President Lebrun in the lobby and the door of his office. Roberts watched Laval pick up the telephone and speak into the mouthpiece, "Get me President Doumergue." Doumergue had been President of the Republic in the 1920s.

"President Doumergue?"

"Yes, Pierre Laval here. The Republic calls you. Seven former premiers ask that you head an all-party government. We are meeting in the Quai D'Orsay this afternoon. We will be at the train station to welcome you in the morning."

Laval listened, and then he said, "Yes, our recommendation is that you appoint Marshal Pétain as minister of war."

Laval listened and replied, "Good. We will see you in the morning, Monsieur le President."

Laval turned to President Lebrun as he came back into his office. The massive door swung closed leaving Roberts standing outside with the lasting image of a smiling Laval speaking with the President.

Roberts had his story. He spoke with the other reporters and then he said, "Seven premiers are going to meet at the Quai D'Orsay this afternoon to form an all-party government." The reporters headed for the telephones to call in their stories.

Bob Tompkins listened to the press aide at the Socialist Party head-quarters, "The executive committee of the General Confederation of

Labor has sent out ninety telegrams to the departmental labor unions to hold themselves in readiness for all eventualities. This is not going to be Germany."

The telephone rang and the press aide picked it up. "Yes, I understand." The press aide turned to Bob and said, "Daladier has resigned. The confederation has called for a twenty-four hour general strike Monday," the press aide paused and looked at his notes, "against the threat of fascism and for the defense of public liberties."

A secretary came up and gave the press aide a mimeographed handout. The press aide scanned it and gave a copy to Bob, who started to read it aloud, "All the reactionary elements of capitalism have been mobilized...for an assault which aims at the republican regime...if the reactionary rising is victorious our liberties will be killed. More than our salaries...we stand by our liberties, for liberty itself."

The press aide said, "As you can see, the workers of Paris see last night's riots as a reactionary uprising."

Bob moved forward, "Who is going to follow Daladier?"

"We have been told former President Doumergue has agreed to head an all-party government. We on the Left believe that it is essential at this time that a non-party man like President Doumergue should head the government, a man firmly in the republican tradition. If any Right politician tries to take the premiership, then the Left will have to take to the streets. There cannot be another Berlin where the Right seizes the government."

Bob said, "Okay, but what is the Socialist Party going to do?

"President of the Chamber Fernand Bouisson is a Socialist and he has agreed to join the new government."

Bob was quick to spot the hole in the statement, "But what is Léon Blum going to do?"

The press aide gave a weary smile, "The Party leadership is going to stay outside the government. We will be a minority, but we are a minority with real force behind us. We put many of the Radical Socialist deputies into the Chamber on the second ballot in the last election. The Left commands broad public support. The Right can turn out a crowd in Paris; we can turn out the whole country."

Up on the hill and just down Rue Lamartine from the newspaper offices, lights shined brightly from inside the Oasis bistro, casting a warm yellow glow onto the sidewalk in the early evening darkness. Bob Tompkins approached the door. Walking inside, he saw a big round table surrounded by American newspapermen. Along the zinc bar were half a dozen French workers having a *pastis* before heading home. A large woman, Madame Royer, stood at the end of the bar dressed in black and wearing a white apron; she was talking with two of the Frenchmen. She kept an eye on the table full of boisterous Americans for what she knew were the inevitable calls for the refills. The dayshift guys were knocking back drinks and swapping stories with the nightshift crew, who were getting ready to go up to the newsroom and put out the next morning's edition.

Bob pulled up a chair and waved at Madame Royer, always simply Madame to the Americans, who nodded her head. Then Bob turned to the group, "I'm bushed. What a day. The Communists turned down a call from the Socialists for a peaceful anti-fascist demonstration tomorrow. Instead, they have called for a massive Communist rally on the Place de la République for Friday. I spent the afternoon with the Socialists and the labor unions. They at least know what they are doing. They're calling for a twenty-four hour general strike next Monday. But no street demonstrations. Tell me what happened around the rest of the city?"

Bill Wilshire chimed in, "Daladier came back from the Élysée Palace mid-afternoon and put out a short statement saying that the government did not want to employ soldiers against demonstrators. That's why the cabinet turned in its resignation." Wilshire shook his head in disgust.

Phil Roberts broke in, "What should he have done, Bill?"

Wilshire started to speak, earnestly, "Phil, Daladier won a big vote of confidence in the Chamber of Deputies last night. Either the parliament is sovereign or the streets are. If a bunch of fascist street rowdies will use bloodshed to overthrow the regime, then I think it was the duty of the republican government to defend the Republic by force if necessary. I saw the mobs last night. Angry yes. But leadership, no! It was absent. Daladier should have put some infantry and cavalry around the Palais Bourbon and the demonstrators would have been cowed and gone home."

Roberts calmly interjected, "Bill, what I heard was that Frot caved in this morning. The police informants were telling the Sûreté Générale that Far Right leagues were planning armed fighting tonight. Secret tribunals had condemned the minister of interior to death. The sentence was going to be carried out before sundown. Frot lost his nerve. He immediately telephoned President Lebrun."

Wilshire sarcastically cut in, "And President Lebrun started weeping—again—and so the government had to change—again."

Roberts smilingly nodded and then continued, "There's more. The Paris councilors and most of the deputies and senators representing Paris put out a public appeal this afternoon calling on President Lebrun to demand Daladier's resignation. The municipality is at war with the national government."

Wilshire responded, "So the Right takes power without an election. Seems to me I've seen that somewhere before. Rome, Berlin."

Rewrite, sitting next to Mac, popped in, "New Orleans?"

Everybody laughed thinking about Huey Long of Louisiana.

Bob Tompkins looked at Wilshire, "It's not quite the same as Berlin. The leadership of the Far Right leagues was missing in action Tuesday night. In particular, the *Action Française* leaders. Maurras was home writing poetry to his friend's wife and Pujo has been hiding for two days. These guys are writers, not street revolutionaries."

Rewrite jumped in, pounding his wine glass on the table, "Hear, hear for the scribblers."

Roberts smiled and said, "The Right's not taking power. Instead, it is similar to what occurred in Great Britain, an all-party national government. Mush. President Lebrun approved a meeting that was held this afternoon at the Quai D'Orsay. Seven former premiers plus the leaders of both houses met to seek common ground. A measure of agreement was reached to support an all-party government under former President Doumergue."

Wilshire seemed dubious, "Agreement between French politicians is rare and hardly long lasting," and he held his wine glass up in front of his face and fixed it with a cross-eyed stare.

Roberts laughed and continued, "Bill, Daladier came in two weeks ago to improve the government. That became impossible. Let some other politicians try to square the political circle. French politicians love to form new governments."

Wilshire brought his wine glass down, took a big sip, and said contemptuously, "Doumergue is just an old wheelhorse politician."

"May be that's all that is required. Just an old horse pulling the party wagon," replied Roberts. Wilshire nodded.

Sandrine came in, removed her overcoat and hung it on the coat rack, and came over and pulled up a chair from another table. Bob made a space at the table for her and said, "Sarah wanted me to give you this letter. She hopes you can make it tomorrow."

Sandrine took the letter and said, "Thank you." She opened the letter and read the enclosed message. She smiled and turned to Bob, "Tell her I will be there."

Mac, the city editor, spoke across the table to Sandrine, "Thanks Sandrine for picking up the story about Frot at the Palais de Justice. It will run in tomorrow's paper."

Sandrine replied, "Oh, thank you, Monsieur Mac."

Bob turned and asked Sandrine, "By the way, where you've been? We've been here for almost an hour."

"Oh, I was downstairs at *Le Petit Journal* for the Frot story. I did just as you said. I wrote down the who, what, why, where, and when. I put other facts into paragraph order, and then I sat in Place Dauphine and wrote a nice lead sentence. I did it in French, too. I was downstairs with the editor and I wrote out the story for him." Sandrine's eyes brightened and she said, "He said he would give me my first byline." She sat up straight, folded her hands primly on the table, and smiled triumphantly at the men seated across the table. She looked at Mac and said slowly, "My first."

Mac put on his Hollywood bad guy look and scowled at her, "He's just trying to get in your pants, Sandrine."

Sandrine quickly put her hand up to her mouth in horror, "Oh, no. But I am a good girl," and she thoughtfully paused. She placed each arm across her chest just beneath her bosom and hugged herself warmly, rocking back and forth, "I will tell him that he will have to start inside my blouse first." She beamed at Monsieur Mac, "In France, certain preliminaries must be followed with a good girl." She gave Mac a long, provocative smile and slowly said, "A very good girl."

Rewrite brought his hand banging down on the table, "Shot you down again, chief. How many times does that make? Six? Twelve?" He turned towards the bar and called out, "Madame, a glass of champagne for the showgirl," and pointed at Sandrine.

Mac tore out a sheet of paper from a notepad and took his pen and scribbled a message on it. Then he turned to Rewrite and barked, "Okay, errand boy. Take this message up to the numb nuts that pretends to be the night editor. Tell him no if's, and's, or but's."

Rewrite stood up and snatched the message out of Mac's hands and held it to his breast, "I'm going to entitle that novel that I'm never going to write, *The Editor Who Couldn't Get to First Base!*" He smiled good-naturedly at Sandrine, winked, and walked out the door.

Sensing an opening, Roberts broke in, "Sandrine, what happened at the Palais de Justice?"

Sandrine replied, "Oh, all the lawyers were in the courtyard demonstrating against Monsieur Frot, the minister of the interior. They believe he ordered the shooting of the demonstrators last night. There were cries of 'Assassin' and even worse."

Roberts interjected, "So what happened?"

Sandrine explained, "Monsieur Frot's cap and robes were burned in the main corridor of the Palais."

Wilshire broke in, "So much for dash and flash. Long live the minister."

Roberts added with a confidential air, "My sources tell me he was really unnerved this morning. He finally understood the power of the streets."

An American reporter came through the door and said, "Rioting down by the Gare St.-Lazare. The mob's heading for the Madeleine."

Mac took a long pull from his wine glass and set it down on the table, "Okay kiddos, you know the drill. Let's go."

Bob turned to Sandrine, "You better go home. I'll tell Sarah when I get back tonight that you will meet her tomorrow."

"Thanks, Monsieur Bob." Sandrine smiled at him as she took her leave.

THURSDAY

Thursday, February 8, 1934. Early in the morning, the *inspecteur* walked across Place Beauvau eyeing the sandbags stacked in front of the large wrought iron gate guarding the entrance to the ministry of the interior. He watched the sharp glances thrown at him by the gendarmerie guarding the building. He walked up Rue de Miromesnil for several minutes, stopped, then knocked on the door to a large apartment building. The door opened and he stepped inside. He waited for the door to close behind him; he showed his identification to the man standing behind a small podium-like desk. The man nodded and pointed down the hall to an elevator, an *ascenseur*, situated in a wire-mesh rectangular column in the central space of the building.

The *inspecteur* rode the elevator to the fifth floor, got off, walked down the hallway and knocked on an unmarked door. The door opened and the *chef* waved him in, "Come into my office and we can talk." The two men walked through the vacant secretarial area.

The *inspecteur* sat down and the *chef* walked around his large desk where several dossiers were spread out across the desktop. The *chef* sat down in his chair. He asked, "What have you found?"

The *inspecteur* brought out a small notepad and paged through it, "The Far Right press, lead by Monsieur's newspaper *L'Ami du Peuple*, is calling Colonel de La Rocque's *Croix-de-Feu* by the nickname *Froides Queues*. The cold rear ends. Everyone on the street believes the *Croix-de-Feu* could have stormed the Palais Bourbon."

The *chef* smiled and said, "We can conclude that the 'coordination' between the colonel and Monsieur last Sunday night at Chateau Louveciennes was not all that Monsieur hoped."

The *inspecteur* smiled and nodded his head, "The question on the streets is—why?"

The *chef* said, "May be I can help. We have the transcript of a wiretap made by general intelligence to a flat near Invalides where Colonel de La Rocque had his secret command post. The other party was someone close to former Premier Laval. See for yourself."

The *inspecteur* scanned the typewritten transcript, murmuring as he went, "They knew Tuesday night the government was going to change on Wednesday…here, Pétain was mentioned for minister of defense…the colonel knew he had already won, so he called off his shock troops…so, he just wants to rearrange the furniture inside the Republic. He doesn't want to put a *führer* into the Élysée Palace."

The *chef* leaned back and looked up at the ceiling and asked rhetorically, "Does Berlin?"

The *inspecteur* replied, "No informant even whispers about any involvement by the Nazis. The trail of course from Marcel Bucard and his *Francists* to Rome is a well-lit road."

The *chef*, staring at the ceiling, added distantly, "Almost is if someone wanted us to follow that road."

The *chef* sat up and turned directly to the *inspecteur*, "What of the German embassy? They're right down the quay. They could watch everything Tuesday night from the upper story windows."

The *inspecteur* answered, "I have not been able to find any link from the embassy to any of the Far Right groups."

The *chef* leaned back, "Ah, Caesar's wife remains pure."

The *inspecteur* said, "Monsieur once had some dealings with Germans. But the trail went stone cold before the Nazis even came to power."

The *chef* responded, "Yes. But I think the Nazis are there. I feel a presence, some one sitting behind a desk in Berlin and thinking about Paris. I think the Nazis are playing us very deep."

The *inspecteur* said, "I will keep watching."

The *chef* summed up, "Yes, but keep a careful distance. We should not be too close."

The *inspecteur* asked, "What are we looking for?"

The *chef* said, "Somewhere in the future, the Nazis will do something. We will be watching. We will see that someone in Berlin seems to be unusually well informed about policy at the highest levels in Paris. Then we can find the source."

"What will we do then?"

"Why, we will keep watching," and the *chef* smiled and repeated softly, "Always watching."

Late Thursday morning. Sandrine walked up the sidewalk of Avenue des Champs Élysées. The massive grandeur of the Arc de Triomphe was straight ahead, framed between the trees lining the extravagantly wide sidewalk. She came up to a sidewalk café, stopped and scanned the tables. She saw Sarah and walked over, "Good morning, Sarah." She sat down.

"Oh, I am so pleased you could come. I covered the morning shows already. Let me fill you in. Would you like a coffee?"

"Yes, thank you."

Sarah waved at a waiter, "Monsieur, café au lait for my friend."

"*Oui, Madame,*" and the waiter turned and went inside.

Sarah pulled out her notepad, "This morning was fabrics. Chanel created a sensation with its new high-relief prints that give the illusion of being covered with festoons of fringe, ribbons, and feather trimmings. And Chanel's gingham-checked taffetas went into a really smart line of afternoon frocks. The announcer said the hemline was the highest level seen so far this season; twelve inches off the floor." Sarah made big eyes, "Let me tell you, feminine virtue is being put to great risk."

Sandrine laughed, "Oh well, the Puritans' dresses are at least taking on some color."

The waiter set down a coffee on the small metal table in front of Sandrine.

Sarah continued, "At another salon, slim models walked down the runway in beautiful evening gowns. Get this. The announcer said the gowns were adaptable 'to all figures.' In English, that means the gowns can be sold in New York to wealthy American matrons with big behinds!"

Sandrine laughed, "Sarah, you're so much fun."

Sarah, eyes flashing, replied, "The other big development is capes, hip-length Spahi capes for afternoon and evening wear. Just in case Madame wants to pick up a matching police baton in white and join the local police line."

"Fourrures André Brunswick: le grand couturier de la fourrure"
by Louis Gaudin, c. 1930. ("The grand couturier of furs").

Sandrine rather wistfully asked, "Doesn't it seem strange that these shows are going on even as Paris is overrun with civil riot."

Sarah responded, "I'll let you in on a secret. We're talking the big money here. Behind those big behinds in New York are even bigger purses. One of the American papers wrote that if today there were more people in the United States buying the new Paris summer line, then there would be fewer barricades in the Place de la Concorde. *Vive le couture.*"

Sandrine softly said, "I'm sorry I missed the morning shows."

Sarah airily responded, "Oh don't worry. We'll catch the last of the big Summer Openings this afternoon."

Sandrine smiled and finished her coffee. She looked at Sarah.

Sarah stood up, "The next opening is right up the street. Then we'll go back to the paper and write our stories. I'll show you how."

The two women walked up the wide sidewalk chatting and laughing as they went. Sarah thought to herself, oh so deliciously—*to be young, size four, and in Paris!*

Late Thursday afternoon. Sarah and Sandrine walked up Rue Royale in the lengthening afternoon shadows towards the Madeleine, the massive Corinthian pillars of the church standing in front of the deeply shadowed façade. The two women looked with keen interest at the evidence of riotous vandalism all along the street that led from the Place de la Concorde to the Madeleine. Businesslike, they were headed for the newspaper offices a half-mile or so up the hill beyond the Madeleine.

Sandrine said, "This was from last night's riots; it wasn't here Wednesday morning."

Sarah looked, "I didn't imagine."

At the Place de la Madeleine, Sandrine and Sarah turned onto the Boulevard de la Madeleine; they were greeted with a vision of warlike devastation along the entire boulevard to the Opera. All the street lamps had been overturned. Every news kiosk was a smoking ruin. All the billboards had been destroyed. Many of the shops had been ransacked.

Sandrine spoke, "This is the work of hooligans and street toughs. Looting is not about politics."

Sarah said, "Look in the middle of the street. There's a huge hole. A gas main must have exploded. And the water mains must have burst," as she looked at the puddles of soot-blackened water among the debris. Sniffing the burnt-charcoal odor in the air, she added sourly, "The entire street smells like a giant brazier. Civilization was put to the crisp." She gave a short, bitter laugh.

Sandrine said, "Let's turn here. I know a quick way to the newspaper offices."

Sarah turned and took a final look at the street and its terrible desolation, "Yes, I simply didn't know."

Thursday evening. Sarah and Sandrine descended the stairs from the newspaper office onto the sidewalk and turned down Rue Lamartine. Sarah spoke, "They'll be at the Oasis. Well on their way, I'm afraid."

Sandrine cheerfully replied, "Oh, they'll be all right. They're fun."

Sarah responded somewhat seriously, "They've been up two or three nights in a row covering the riots. It takes a toll."

The two women entered the little bistro, took off their hats and coats and hung them from a row of pegs already bulging with hats and overcoats.

Mac joyously shouted across the room, "Ladies night at the Oasis. Come right over. Civilization has made it through another day."

One of the men dragged two chairs up to the table and Sarah and Sandrine sat down. Sarah leaned over and kissed her husband Bob on the cheek, "Have a good day, dear?"

"We filed a big roundup story on the riots last night," and he swept his hand by Phil Roberts and Bill Wilshire. "Then stories about the old government and the new government."

Mac interjected across the table, "And what have the lady journalists been occupying themselves with? A tea at the embassy perhaps?"

Sarah leaned back and airily pronounced, "Oh nothing as serious as that, Mac. Sandrine and I have been up on the Champs Élysées covering the Summer Openings at the fashion houses."

Mac, eyes glistening, yelled back towards the zinc bar, "Madame Royer, please, two glasses of champagne for the winners of tonight's Marie Antoinette award. Intrepid journalists covering fashion shows while the Republic burns. Hear, hear."

Sarah broke in, "I will skip telling you about the Mainbocher show which featured gowns for what the announcer said were 'stylish stouts.' You're not married yet."

Rewrite, sitting next to Mac, chimed, "Mac, she thinks you're going back to America to get married."

Mac harrumphed, "Never. A down-on-the heels countess from Hungary maybe."

Sarah continued, "Lucien Lelong exhibited his new line of evening gowns. The décolletage is high in the back," she made a long pause, "and in the front the décolletage is low and made with a deep V." Sarah turned and swept her glance around the table, "Should make this year more interesting for you guys, just in case any of you wind up somewhere where evening gowns are present."

Mac replied, "The peasants scream for bread and the capitalist class offers them fashion shows. Champagne for the lady journalists! We will go to the revolution with low-cut evening gowns!"

Sarah reached into her purse and took out her notepad. "I wrote a little news dispatch just for you, Mac, and all the rest of you dormitory boys in short pants. Let me read it."

Sarah began, "France, with deepening unemployment, anxiously viewed the display of major new product lines by its leading export industry, a sector employing hundreds of thousands of workers, with the expectation that new products will conquer new markets in New York and London during the summer selling season."

Mac held up his hand palm out, "Stop." He leaned way back in his chair and put his head even further back until he was looking at Madame from quite upside down. He called to her, "Madame, one round of humble pie for *les petits pantaloons.*" The small pants.

The men around the table brought fists down on the table and chanted, "Hear, hear."

Mac leaned back yet again and called back to Madame, "Serve mine red and in a glass."

Rewrite echoed, "*Moi, aussi.*" Me also.

The others, banging glasses on the table, yelled like cannons firing off a salute, "*Moi, aussi,*"

"*Moi, aussi.*"

"*Moi, aussi.*"

Madame, smiling broadly, came over with a tray of glasses, set them around, and then poured deep-satin-like red wine from a big bottle. She smiled at the two women, "*Bon nuit, Mesdames,* the francs run free tonight! As always when you two are here."

Mac pulled out a copy of the *Le Petit Journal*, opened it to page two, and carefully spread it across the table. "Sandrine, here is your story. It came out this afternoon on page 2. Your byline is here."

Sandrine anxiously looked at the paper and said, "Let me see." She pulled the paper over to her side of the table and, beaming, showed it to Sarah and Bob. "See?"

Bob looked at Sandrine and said softly, "I think Mac has more."

Mac turned grave, "But Sandrine, that dumpy little French rag is not your first."

Sandrine looked at him quizzically.

Mac pulled out a copy of the *Paris Bulletin*. He spread page one across the table and smoothed it out. Then he said triumphantly, "Here, page one, look above the fold, here's your story with your byline on it. See, the story under the big headline. What's more, this paper was on the streets this morning. Hours before that French rag. Your first byline was American—and of course it was bigger and better, sweetheart. That's the American way."

Sandrine smiled, "Oh, my dreams are fulfilled. I always wanted to be first with an American."

Sandrine put Mac in the middle of her stare and then slowly and ever more vigorously shook her shoulders, her loose breasts shimmying beneath her soft wool sweater. She turned on a wide seductive smile. She batted eyelashes above dark flashing eyes.

Pandemonium broke out across the table. Rewrite, his smile came on like a light, shouted to Madame, "A bottle of champagne for the showgirl!"

The other men banged their fists on the table, "Show, show. More, more."

Mac turned and beamed at them, "Didn't I tell ya!"

Sarah looked at Sandrine and shouted over the din, "Sandrine! How could you? The minks are on the runway," and swept her hand past the reveling men on the other side of the table, "we'll never get them back in their cages now!" She looked at Bob with bemused wonderment and took a long sip from her glass. She said to her husband, "We're a long way from Iowa!"

Bob smiled and nodded, "Yes, a long way from Iowa."

The door to the bistro swung open and a young man in a leather jacket and broad-brimmed floppy hat, something of the student about him, and a young woman, also in a leather jacket and wearing an oversized working man's cap, walked in. They looked around, saw Sandrine, smiled, and gaily waved. They took a step over to a row of coat hooks and took off their overcoats and hung them up. Above the row of coat hooks was a long shelf for hats. They punched their hats into a semblance of shape and placed them on the shelf. Thick wool mufflers were hung over the tops of their overcoats. The young woman ran her fingers through her short brown hair, brushing it back, reestablishing the part along one side of her head, giving it a sort of workingman's look above a cute feminine face.

Sandrine called out, "Oh, Malka, you and Pascal are here!"

The couple turned and smiled at Sandrine, then looked at the other people at the table and smiled at them. They walked over to the table, the young man deftly grabbing two chairs along the way. He pushed one chair in next to Sandrine and the young woman called Malka sat down. The young man pushed a chair in beside her and sat down.

Sandrine turned back to the table, smiling, and announced, "These are my friends, Malka and Pascal."

Bob waved at Madame and said, "Two glasses." Madame moved to bring two glasses over to the table.

Sandrine said to the group, "Malka's a secretary at the *Confédération Générale du Travail*, the CGT. She's a real Marxist." Then Sandrine added, "But not a Communist."

Malka smiled, "No, not a Communist. They have their own trade unions. Like our leader Leon Blum, I have kept to the 'old house,'" she said referring to

Leon Blum who famously kept the French Socialist party out of the Moscow orbit and its dictatorship of the proletariat with a famous speech in the 1920s saying he was going to stay with the 'old house.'

Then Sandrine looked over at the young man and said, "Pascal's a student at L'Ecole Polytechnique. Some day he is going to build a great bridge. Aren't you, Pascal?"

Pascal diffidently answered, "Well, I hope to help build something."

Mac leaned across the table squinting at Pascal's breast pocket and asked, "What's dat?"

Malka laughed and said, "Oh that's his prize possession. Show it to him, Pascal."

Pascal reached into his pocket and pulled out a small, eight-inch long slide rule with a small chrome clip attachment that held the device to his pocket. Pascal beamed, "It's a slide rule, small, but very accurate."

Mac peered at the little slide rule, "Does it add and subtract?"

Pascal laughed, "No, you have to do that yourself, but it multiplies and divides easily. And miraculously it can raise a number to a power."

Mac straightened up and looked around the table and said, "I would rather try to raise the dead than raise a number to a power."

Everyone laughed.

Sandrine smiled and smugly told the group, "Malka tells me—we tell secrets—that late at night, snuggled up under the blankets, Pascal whispers his dreams to her. He is going to build a great bridge."

Mac's eyes went wide, his head reared back, "Pascal unlocks the secret. What French women really want! Whisper to them sweetly about bridges. Who would have thought? Which side of the slide rule gives you that answer?"

Sandrine gave a small laugh and continued, "Pascal is the only Socialist at L'Ecole Polytechnique."

Pascal interposed, "That's not quite true. There are others. Most of us are followers of Jean Coutrot, a brilliant graduate of our school. He just founded Le Centre Polytechnicien d'Etudes Economiques. The center brings together graduates who have risen high in the elite branches of the civil service and industry with economists and leaders of the trade unions."

Mac, eyes burning with amusement, "So, you are all going to design a better society? With the slide rule?"

Pascal, turning earnest, replied, "Oh, no, we feel that capitalism can only be made to work if the technicians who really run the industries, banks, and trade unions can be brought to a guiding position. The technocrats are the only people who really understand the complexities of twentieth-century industrialized society. The politicians and intellectuals simply lack the knowledge of what makes the modern world go round."

Rewrite banged his glass down, "Hear, hear. The elite will tell us the world goes round when we all know it is simply flat and flies through the universe like a saucer!"

Mac laughed, and then turned thoughtful, "The Communists are marching tomorrow. They have a scientific theory, too. Are you marching with them?"

Pascal replied, "No. We are not enamored with the 'totalitarian mystique.'"

Mac playfully ducked his head down, peered over the top of his wine glass, and meekly asked, "No exchange programs with Berlin?"

Pascal laughed, "No. But we do observe that a powerful state can put people back to work."

Mac said, "A weak state can too. Our publisher loves putting people to work, preferably at the lowest possible wage. We're testimony to that. Calls it the virtue of a free market."

The newspapermen around the table pounded the table with their glasses, "Hear, hear."

Malka said, "You need a trade union. Solidarity with the working man."

Mac laughed and swept his hand around the table at the newspapermen and said to Malka, "We're too disorganized to be anything but Democrats. That's a political party in the States."

Malka smiled, "But you do have Roosevelt."

Mac lifted up his glass towards Malka, "*Salut.* By the way, I like your haircut."

Malka laughed, "Sandrine calls it 'Socialist Realism.'"

Mac sternly replied, "Well, I'm glad you're Socialist. We wouldn't want Sandrine palling around with a bunch of Bolshies. The publisher wouldn't understand," and looking at Pascal, "You don't know how reassuring that slide rule is."

Malka and Pascal smiled and lifted their glasses in turn.

Sandrine broke in, "We have to leave. We have classes tomorrow, and Malka her work." Malka, Pascal, and Sandrine stood up and went over and got their overcoats, hats, and mufflers and put them on. Then they walked out, turning back to wave at the friends around the table.

Rewrite said brightly to Mac, "I know. I will title the novel that I am never going to write: *How the Engineer Designed the Path to First Base.*

Mac laughed and said to the group, "Looks to me like he got to home plate with Malka. Imagine that, and him being an engineer, too," and gently nodded his head at the wonder of it all.

Everyone laughed.

Then Mac looked thoughtful and said, "Sandrine is something, isn't she?"

Heads nodded around the table.

Then Mac turned and said to the people at the table, "Bill hasn't been with us for a while. Time for a bedtime story. Let's write the novel again." He looked over at Bill Wilshire, "What was the name of that guy from Michigan who wrote the big novel, used to be a correspondent in Paris?"

Wilshire looked down at the table and mumbled, "Hemingway."

Mac sort of grumbled, "Yeah, Hemingway. Something about the sun rising in Spain. Yeah." Then he turned and smiled at everyone else at the table with eyes laughing. He said to Rewrite, "Let's write our own version. How did he describe the English broad, you know, Lady what's-her-name? Sort of like Sandrine."

Rewrite straightened up like a chipmunk and said with well-rehearsed practice, "She had curves like a racing sloop, and you missed none of it with that wool sweater."

Mac, thinking back about Sandrine shimmying in her sweater, said, "Yeah, you see a lot of that here in Paris." Then he looked over at Sarah.

Sarah looked into her wine glass, then she looked over at her husband, and softly intoned, smiling at Bob, "We had such a damned good time together in Paris."

Mac smiled like a schoolmaster and turned and looked at Phil Roberts, "Phil?"

Phil Roberts, taking his queue, looked up at the ceiling, remembered the final line from the novel, and then created his own line of remembrance about all their days in Paris, "Yes. Paris. Wasn't it pretty to think so."

Mac turned his head down the table, made a sidewise glance at Bill Wilshire, then slowly looked back at Bob Tompkins and put him in the center of his gaze. He solemnly intoned, "See, that's the problem Bob. The great American novel about Europe has been written. The guy from Michigan did it. I hear that Stein woman said to him, 'Why don't you go to Pamplona and see the bulls?' Imagine that. Now he's sitting in Key West knocking back drinks on his royalties. The streets of Paris are empty for guys like you."

Sarah looked at her husband, smiled wanly, and nodded wistfully in agreement.

At the other end of the table, Bill Wilshire slowly nodded his head up and down. The novel he wrote while in Spain was a clump of paper in his trunk back at the room he shared with his wife.

GENERAL STRIKE

Friday afternoon, February 9, 1934. Sandrine walked up to the sentry box outside the Quai D'Orsay and showed her police press pass, signed the register, and walked across the courtyard and into the foreign ministry. The receptionist smiled and said, "Madame Bardoux would like to see you. Upstairs on your left."

Sandrine climbed the sweeping staircase and then turned down the wide marble-floored corridor to Madame Bardoux's office. She entered the outer office and a secretary smiled and waved her to take one of the chairs. Presently, Madame Bardoux came out and invited Sandrine into her inner office. Sandrine went in and sat down.

Madame Bardoux spoke, "I have a press release on the appointment of Jean Louis Barthou as minister of foreign affairs. It is a distinguished appointment. His recent experience as president of the War Reparations Commission gives him direct experience with German affairs, the issue of the hour."

Sandrine jotted this down in her notepad and then said, "I'm young. Could you tell me a little about his background?"

Madame Bardoux smiled, "He has decades of front-rank ministerial experience and brings a reputation for probity from his term as minister of justice in the Poincaré government. The appointment rises above politics. All in the ministry are pleased to serve again this distinguished minister."

Sandrine wrote this down in her pad, put the mimeographed press release in her handbag, and looked up at Madame Bardoux, sensing more to come.

Madame Bardoux cleared her throat, and then said, "Monsieur de Davignon would like to speak with you. He has been reading the English-language papers." She stood up. Sandrine followed suit, and the two of them went into the corridor and walked down the hall.

At the entrance to Davignon's office, Madame Bardoux gently knocked on the open door, smiled, and said, "Monsieur de Davignon, here is Sandrine Durand." She extended her arm to wave Sandrine into the spacious, high-ceilinged office, gave Sandrine a weak smile, and then turned and returned to her office.

Davignon said pleasantly to Sandrine, "Please be seated." He watched with interest as she took a seat across from his desk.

Davignon held up a copy of Thursday's *Paris Bulletin* and said, "I read with interest your story about the burning of Minister Frot's robes at the Palais de Justice yesterday. The Americans must be very pleased with your work," giving a sly smile that suggested the Americans were at least pleased with something.

Sandrine, never one to miss even the slightest hint of masculine interest, saw the second side of Davignon's compliment and pleasantly responded, "Oh, the Americans heard the editor of *Le Petit Journal* was going to give me my first byline. Mac, the editor, said they wanted to be first," and she paused and smiled, "with the biggest."

Davignon leaned back in his chair and smiled and thought *yes*. Eyes twinkling, he said, "I see." He set the paper down and then said, "We here at the ministry, of course, want to encourage your career with both newspapers, particularly the Americans. They put out a more objective account, and of course many of their stories are later published in the American papers. For example, your friend Bob Tompkins," and Davignon flashed a smile, fishing for some hint at the depth of this friendship, "has his stories published page one on the front page of the Sunday Chicago *Daily Bulletin*, a very important American paper."

Sandrine, expecting the one sally and a little surprised at the second, took them in order, "Oh, I am a close friend of Sarah Tompkins, Bob's wife. She is like a big sister to me." Sandrine watched the ease come over Davignon's expression and decided to place a slightly more encouraging opening before what she saw was now an obviously interested man, "She is my closest contact among the Americans, my only confidante."

Then Sandrine shifted in her chair and said, "I know Bob is respected by the other Americans, but I didn't know he was so widely read in America."

Davignon pleasantly added more sugar to the brew, "Our ambassador in Washington comments upon his stories frequently. Read at the highest levels in Washington, I believe."

Sandrine, caught off guard, stammered, "Oh, I didn't know."

Davignon looked at her and said, "You seem surprised."

Sandrine, regaining her composure, replied, "Oh, I am just putting together in my mind the seriousness of what you have just said with the table-thumping good time the Americans have at the bistro next to their office, the Oasis. Great fun."

Davignon smiled, "Yes, the newspapermen live a lively existence. Their dollars go a long way in Paris."

Sandrine turned thoughtful and decided to share some information, "Bob has been trying to write a novel, like all the other young Americans. His wife Sarah strongly," and Sandrine paused and searched for words, "and lovingly, wants him to concentrate on his journalism career. She feels he has great talent for it." Sandrine looked warmly at Davignon and said, "I look forward to sharing with her what you have just told me. It will mean a lot to her."

Davignon gave a little bow of his head. He continued, "And I have something for you. Possibly another story," and he smiled and looked inquiringly at her.

Sandrine looked at him with interest, "Yes, I would like that." *Yes, a friendship of mutual interest*, she thought. *Yes*.

Davignon watched: *did he see what he just thought he saw?*

He paused, and then said, "If you hurry, you can go out to Le Bourget airport. I am told that Minister Frot is about to take an airplane to Morocco. Undoubtedly there will be an aide from the ministry of the interior there who can confirm this to you. You will have another story. No need to tell anyone about my involvement."

Sandrine wrote this down in her pad and said, head down, "Of course." She looked up and smiled, "I better get going," and stood up.

Davignon stood up, came around his desk, and gently put his arm around her waist to escort her out the door. In the corridor he said softy to her, "May be we can meet?"

She smiled and looked into his eyes, "I would like that very much," and turned and walked down the hallway.

Friday afternoon, February 9. Sandrine got out of the cab, paid the driver, and walked up to the small wooden building that served as the terminal for Le Bourget airfield. Inside she walked across the polished concrete floor of the waiting lounge while looking out the large windows at the two-engine airplane sitting on the tarmac outside. A policeman in a gold-trimmed, dark blue kepi and wearing an even darker navy blue cape, its interior liner a resplendently bright red, walked over to her smiling, "Mademoiselle?"

Sandrine fumbled in her handbag and pulled out her police press pass and said, "I was told that Minister Frot is departing this afternoon from Le Bourget."

Smiling, the policeman said, "Where did you hear that?"

Sandrine, returning the smile, "Oh, some one in a ministry in Paris."

Eyes twinkling, the policeman said, "Ah, a ministry in Paris. Yes." He turned and looked at a young man in a black suit standing over at the far side of the terminal and waved him over. The young man started walking over.

The policeman turned to Sandrine, "Here, we have another man from a ministry in Paris. May be he knows your someone in a ministry in Paris." The policeman smiled and gave Sandrine a long up-and-down look of thoroughly masculine appraisal. Coming to a delighted look of approval, the policeman said, "Possibly this someone in the ministry in Paris is a man?"

Sandrine dipped her head in agreement and smiled slyly, "*Bien sûr.*" Of course.

The sharply dressed young policeman smiled in acknowledgement and took a step back as the young man in the black suit came up, "Mademoiselle. What can I do for you?"

Sandrine showed her police press pass and said, "I have been told that former Minister Frot is leaving by airplane from here for Morocco this afternoon."

The young man looked at her and said, "You are possibly well informed. Possibly not. However, if you sit over there and look out the window at the airplane you may find out whether or not you are well informed. Or not."

Sandrine smiled, "Thank you."

The young man bowed, "At your service." Then he walked back to the small knot of men standing at the far side of the room.

Sandrine walked over and took a seat on a wide comfortable chair in front of the large window. Soon a large black car pulled up on the tarmac between the building and the airplane. Three men got out. Sandrine stood up and walked over to the window.

Yes, he was what she had been told to look for—a youngish man, with a spade beard, and a devilish look. Well dressed, some might even call debonair, a gay blade in a Bal Musette sort of way, thought Sandrine, thinking about the cheap Paris music halls for picking up women. She laughed to herself. Yes, obviously, a man of self-important charm. But she had a hard time finding him—she searched for the right word—*intriguing*. What little elegance Sandrine could see seemed to be at sixes and sevens with itself. She had been told he was something of a ladies man. To each her own, she thought.

Out on the tarmac, the man with the beard shook hands with the other two men and then strode over to the airplane and ascended the small steps of a boarding ladder into the main body of the plane. The steps were folded up into the cabin and the door closed. The propellers revved up and the plane taxied along the apron to the end of the runway, swung around, stopped, revved its engines to a high pitch, and then let its brakes go and swiftly gained speed down the runway. The plane easily lifted off and climbed rapidly into the gray winter sky.

Sandrine walked over to the end of the room towards the young man in the black suit. She asked, "Morocco?"

The young man nodded affirmatively.

Sandrine smiled and walked over to the other end of the room to a desk with a receptionist and asked to use the telephone. She called the newsroom of the *Paris Bulletin*. She spoke into the mouthpiece, "I have the story on Minister Frot." Then she recited the hastily written-down facts from her notepad into the mouthpiece.

Friday evening, 8 p.m., February 9. Bob Tompkins walked down the darkened boulevard towards the Place de la République, the large square within easy walking distance of the newspaper office on Rue Lamartine. Coming into a circle of dull yellow light from one of the remaining street lamps, he stopped and looked at the posters plastered on the wall. In the center was a pasted-up bulletin from the new government emblazoned—*La patrie est endanger*. The country is in danger. Under the headline, a message from the new premier, Gaston Doumergue: "Citizens…a government of truce and justice…I invite you in turn to your duty to renounce agitation and demonstration and place the interests of France and the Republic above all else." Next to the government poster was a flaming red poster proclaiming that the Communists would return to the attack against the fascists. The poster announced a mass demonstration to be held Friday on the Place de la République. Next to the Communist poster was a Socialist placard urging the citizens not to submit to the loss of democratic rights. The Socialists called for a general strike on Monday—to be peaceful and without street demonstrations.

Place de la République with "Statue to the République" by Léopold and Charles Morice erected in 1883.

Having finished reading the posters, Tompkins continued down the sidewalk toward the Place de la République. Approaching, he saw that the large square was screened off from the boulevard by a double-ranked police line. Tompkins walked up, showed his press pass, and asked for the command post. A space opened in the line and a black-coated arm pointed towards a group of men standing around the central monument of the square, a large classically robed statue of a woman personifying the Republic on top of a tall pedestal.

Tompkins, spotting a familiar face, went up to an assistant chief and asked, "What's happening?"

The police chief replied, "The Communists are organizing. They have called for a demonstration on the Place de la République to protest the rise of fascism. Police Prefect Bonnefoy-Sibour has declared no street gatherings are allowed in keeping with the new premier's appeal for calm. We are on the square. The Communists are not. We are here to see they obey the law."

Tompkins inquired, "The Socialists?"

The chief gravely replied, "They're not here. Their leaders have said to stay home and prepare for the general strike Monday. The Communists are spoiling for a fight; the Socialists want to show the world a peaceful face. We will see."

Tompkins followed up, "Do you expect trouble?"

The chief looked at Tompkins with slight disbelief, "Yes. The hooligans want to loot the shops." Then the chief added contemptuously, "Wreck the working class district in a show of solidarity with the working class."

Just then there was the sound of a motorcycle. The police line opened, and the motorcyclist entered and came up to the command post. The motorcycle policeman reported, "The rioters have formed up in front of the Gare de l'Est," the large train station several blocks to the north of the square.

The police chiefs whispered amongst themselves, heads nodded, and one of them strode out across the square. He pointed his arm up the boulevard, shouted instructions, and a large detachment of baton-wielding police formed up. Behind the police ranks was a phalanx of Mobile Guards on foot. Several dozen mounted Republican Guards brought their horses up in two ranks behind the Mobile Guards. Several police scout cars pulled up alongside the flanks of the leading police ranks. The police perimeter opened and the battalion-size force marched up the wide boulevard towards the square in front of the train station.

Tompkins hurried across the square and attached himself to a police chief following behind the horse-mounted Republican Guards. As the lead elements approached the train station, Tompkins ran around the edge of the police formation, across a street, and past the parish church of St.-Laurent. He found a wall overlooking the square in front of the train station. He hoisted himself up onto the wall, found his footing, and looked out across the large iron-fenced square where thousands of demonstrators had assembled. As the police ranks approached, front-line police commanders ordered the crowd to disperse. In response, the crowds shouted, "Fascists!" Then the multitudes let loose with screamed insults at the police ranks adding extra ugliness to an already mean situation.

The leading police ranks waded into the crowd, white batons swinging, while Mobile Guards worked their way along the fences pushing the edges of the crowd back into the station. The police grabbed hundreds of rioters and moved them back swiftly into waiting police trucks and vans. Standing on the wall, Tompkins wrote in his notepad that many of those apprehended were dazed and bleeding profusely from head wounds suffered from the swinging police batons.

One group of rioters, returning to the fray from inside the station, attacked the police with lumps of coal, knocking one policeman out of his scout car. The rioters quickly surrounded the downed policeman and, as Tompkins watched, he was badly beaten by the mob. Suddenly, Mobile Guards crashed in viciously swinging their batons and rescued their comrade. Some assailants were grabbed by the Mobile Guards and clubbed with batons again and again as they were dragged to the waiting police vans.

As the police broke up the crowd in front of the train station, a shout went across the square to the police chief. Arms and fingers pointed down the nearby side streets. Shouting crowds of tough looking characters started looting the shops. Smaller detachments of police started down the side streets to assault the looters. Then suddenly Tompkins heard the sharp crack of pistol fire coming from the upper stories of the apartments on the narrow street just across from his perch. As Tompkins watched, the police advanced down the street; he saw one policeman go down from gunfire. Almost instantly he heard the answering report of gunfire from the police machine pistols, gunfire that had been mistakenly described as machine gun fire during the Tuesday night riots. Tompkins watched the police advance down the street. As the police came upon barricades blocking the street, they formed up, often drawing pistol fire from unseen shooters, and then charged the barricade, often under short fusillades of fire from their own supporting machine pistols. Shattered glass fell from upstairs windows where police suspected snipers; wooden shutters splintered. The barricades fell; the rioters fell back. The street came under control.

As the police moved into the side streets, Tompkins descended from his perch, walked across the now vacant square, and then down the boulevard to the Place de la République. He walked over to the police commanders, smoking and talking in hushed tones near the statue in the middle of the square. Bob went up to his acquaintance, who saw him approach and stepped outside the circle of police commanders to answer his questions. Starting off, Tompkins asked, "How many wounded?"

The police chief succinctly responded, "A dozen police were shot and seriously wounded this evening. Another twenty-five in the hospital from injuries in the street fighting."

Tompkins wrote the numbers down and followed up, "The rioters?"

A terse reply, "At the train station—eight hundred arrested. Communists."

Then the police chief looked at Tompkins and spat out, "On the side streets, hooligans." He turned away from Tompkins and stepped back into the circle of the command group.

Gunfire and the tumult of riot could be heard in almost every direction from the square except to the north where the newspaper office was located. Police detachments were being reformed and dispatched to the surrounding neighborhoods. Tompkins turned to another police official standing nearby and pointed at the detachments forming up. The police official, quietly conscientious, said with calm assurance, "The neighborhoods are coming under control. All will be settled before dawn."

Tompkins wrote down a summation, then turned and walked towards the perimeter. The line opened and he walked out to the boulevard and started the journey back to the newspaper office a half dozen blocks away. He composed his news story in his head as he walked along the now deserted streets in the cold wintry night.

Saturday afternoon, February 10. The long black limousine glided through the open gates and into the courtyard of the military barracks outside Paris. Inside was the recently appointed minister of defense, a general who sixteen years before had been the hero of Verdun. A military aide got out of the front passenger side of the car and took two steps back and opened the rear door to the saloon of the limousine. The aide came to crisp attention. An elderly man, short gray hair under a kepi military cap elaborately embossed with gold oak leaves, wearing the uniform of a marshal of France, got out of the car. An honor guard stepped forward, the commander took an additional two steps forward, snapped his boots together at the heels, and brought his right hand up in salute, and said, "Marshal Pétain, the Republican Guard."

The marshal brought his baton up to the level of his shoulder and replied, "Colonel."

The two officers strode over to the far side of a long column of double-ranked Republican Guards standing at attention, white batons held diagonally across chests emblazoned with decorations. The marshal walked slowly along the line of guardsmen intently looking at the well-disciplined troops; the colonel followed two steps behind. Reaching the end of the column, the two officers turned and headed across the courtyard.

On the far side of the courtyard a detachment of twenty mounted cavalry guardsmen were drawn up in a long line, the chestnut-colored coats of the horses gleaming in the afternoon sunlight, saddles polished to a high sheen, plumed feathers coming out of the top of the ceremonial dress helmets of the mounted guardsmen, sabers held downward alongside right legs with tips towards the ground.

In the center of the courtyard, the adjutant shouted, "Present arms."

The guardsmen promptly brought the sabers up and pointed the tips forward over the tops of the heads of the horses. The marshal strode along the column of cavalry. Reaching the end, he turned and walked out into the middle of the courtyard and took position in front of the color guard. The colonel followed and took position two steps back.

Another officer escorted two guardsmen, each carrying a bugle, from the side of the courtyard out to a position three steps in front of the marshal. The officer stopped and saluted. The marshal raised his baton, then lowered it. The two guardsmen stepped forward, spoke with the marshal, and showed him their bugles. The marshal looked at the bugles. He watched as one of the men showed him the dents in his bugle made by stones thrown in Tuesday night's riot on the

Pont de la Concorde. Then the two buglers and the escorting officer stepped back, the officer saluted, and the three men walked back across the courtyard.

The marshal looked back at the adjutant, who promptly ordered, "At ease."

The guardsmen stood easy. The marshal spoke, his voice reaching across the courtyard, "The buglers have told me that Tuesday night on the Pont de la Concorde that they advanced under a hail of stones and sounded three trumpet calls on the bugle. The forces of disorder were warned, in the traditional way, that the forces of order were going to the final resort, gunfire. Loyalty to order, and to the Republic which maintains that order, is the duty of all. You, guardsmen, have done your duty."

The marshal looked back at the adjutant, who shouted, "Attention." The guardsmen came to attention, horses were brought to close order.

The marshal walked across the courtyard, his aide opened the door to the limousine, and the marshal got into the rear seat. The aide closed the door and took his position in the front seat. The limousine slowly turned and drove out the gates of the barracks.

Underneath the colonnade at the end of the courtyard, Phil Roberts scribbled into his notepad. Earlier that day he had watched Premier Doumergue take the oath of office. Afterwards, the premier had gone with President Lebrun as they visited wounded members of the police, Mobile Guards, and Republican Guards in hospitals across Paris. Marshal Pétain's visit to the barracks of the Republican Guard was a final public statement in support of the Republic and disavowal of the Far Right leagues' attempt to overthrow the Republic. In particular, Marshal Pétain had put the lie to the Far Right's propaganda that the police had fired without first giving the customary bugle call.

As Roberts walked out the gates to look for a cab back to Paris, he collected his thoughts for a wrap-up story to wire to Chicago. He concluded that the French Republic was much stronger than many had thought Tuesday night. The threat had passed.

Monday afternoon, February 12. Sandrine sat with Malka and Pascal drinking coffee in the warmth of a café along the broad boulevard of the Cours de Vincennes in the eastern working-class section of Paris. Sandrine cheerfully bantered, "This is a wonderful day. I have never seen Paris so quiet, so well-ordered, and so good-tempered on what is supposed to be a day of revolution."

Malka smiled and replied, "That is because the workers have heeded the call of the CGT's general secretary not to confront the police in the streets. The workers have respected the need to keep important public services functioning while stopping the rest of the capitalist working machinery across the nation. The workers want partnership with the industrialists, not revolution. So the workers are not tearing up the cobblestones of Paris like the fascist bandits."

Sandrine laughed, "You have a great future as a street organizer, Malka."

Pascal pointed out to the immensely wide avenue, "Look. The crowds are starting to form into ranks."

Sandrine looked out and saw many marchers carrying red flags and displaying placards announcing that they were Young Communists from this and that district. Almost like going to a football game she thought.

Pascal excitedly pointed, "Here come some police." Then he gave a small satisfied laugh, "Look at that."

Sandrine smiled as she watched the policemen good-humoredly pass their hands over the students' pockets to see whether they had any weapons. All passed safely onto the avenue. No hooligans today.

Malka pointed to the far side of the avenue and shouted, "There are our Socialists. Look. Leon Blum is marching at their head with several deputies," referring to the charismatic Socialist party leader.

Pascal added, "There, the Communists are starting forward with Marcel Cachin at their head," referring to the Communist party leader.

Sandrine stood up and said, "Let's go. We'll march with the Socialists."

The three left the café and crossed over to the far side of the avenue and fell in with the Socialists ranks. The order to move rippled across the crowd, and the column tramped forward behind large flowing red flags. Then over the sound of marching feet came the stirring sound as all the marchers—Communists and Socialists—broke into rousing choruses of the *L'Internationale*, the great marching song of the parties of the left.

The columns swung into the wide circular Place de la Nation and started to march around its huge circular space. Several marchers darted out and climbed the giant bronze statue, *The Triumph of the Republic*, with its majestic woman symbolizing the Republic standing on top of a globe. The woman is bravely striding forward while looking up Rue du Faubourg St.- Antoine towards the Place de la Bastille, the traditional corridor of support for the Republic. One of the youths hoisted a red flag to the top of the statue as the crowds lustily cheered.

*Place de la Nation and the statue "The Triumph of the Republic"
by Aimé-Jules Dalou and erected i3n 1899. Dalou was greatly
influenced by iconic painting "Liberty Leading the People"
by Eugène Delacroix.*

As the column marched around the circular square, Sandrine looked down each side street leading away from the great square. Mounted Republican Guards backed by Mobile Guards and police on foot cordoned off each avenue leading from the square towards central Paris. Passing in front of Boulevard Voltaire, she saw double lines of forty horsemen blocking the avenue.

The column continued marching. Just as Sandrine came in line with Boulevard Diderot, the marching column stopped. The marchers looked down the boulevard. As they watched, an order was heard coming up the boulevard from a Republican Guard officer. The horses picked up their forelegs, almost prancing in place, and gave off a staccato burst of shod hooves coming down on the cobblestoned street like muffled gunfire. The mounted line moved forward a couple of yards. The crowd good-naturedly waved, took up their song, and continued marching around the square.

Sandrine shouted to Malka, "Obviously a good day for a peaceful demonstration."

Malka smiled and passed over a small flask of brandy, "This is a great victory for the rights and privileges of the people against fascist totalitarianism." She nodded at the majestic statue in the center of the square, "The Republic again triumphs against the forces of reaction."

Late Monday afternoon, February 12. A courtly, well-dressed middle-aged gentleman briskly walked down a street in Faubourg St.-Germain near Boulevard St.-Germain. Along the way he would tip his stick and greet the well-to-do ladies of the *haute bourgeoisie* neighborhood as he met them on the sidewalk with, "*Bonjour, Mesdames.*" Presently, he came to the door of an elegant apartment building, entered the door, spoke to the concierge, and walked up the curving staircase to the third floor. He knocked on one of the doors, it opened, and he walked inside. A man stepped forward from the group of people gathered in the front room and said, "*Bonjour, mon colonel.*"

Colonel de La Rocque crisply asked, "Reports?"

The man replied, "The general strike has brought all private business to a halt. Public services have only been interrupted symbolically; public workers are on the job. All is calm across Paris. The Communists and Socialists are having a big rally at the Place de la Nation. It is peaceful. There is some small fighting in a few of the provincial capitals."

The colonel took stock, "Good."

The man looked quizzically at the colonel, "Good?"

The colonel turned and spoke to the wider group, "Yes. We must learn from the Left. They are peaceful and orderly. The Far Right was way too violent last Tuesday night. We in the *Croix-de-Feu* must organize ourselves as the voice of a new spirit across France in the service of order and authority. We need to transform ourselves into a more broadly based political movement. We have a singular opportunity to add millions to our membership rolls across the entire country while the Far Right leagues tear up paving stones in Paris."

Heads nodded in agreement. From the dining room, a woman called pleasantly, "Colonel, lunch?"

He turned, bowed his head slightly, and gallantly said, "*Mais oui.*" The colonel added in a voice of exquisite politeness, "Some Bordeaux, perhaps?"

The woman replied, "*Mais oui, mon colonel.*"

The group filed into the dining room. The colonel sat down, the others followed.

One man asked, "Colonel, you were an aide to Marshal Foch in the World War," referring to the legendary marshal who led the Allies to victory in 1918.

"Yes, that was my duty and my pleasure."

The man continued, "At the Versailles peace conference in 1919, the marshal demanded the French border be pushed east to the Rhine River. He told the Big Four there was no international guarantee that could prevent the complete defeat of France from another invasion across the Rhine."

Another man put his wine glass down, "The Americans and British never understood. Even Clemenceau could not prevail against the Anglo Saxons."

The colonel sipped his wine and nodded his head in agreement.

Another voice added sorrowfully, "Thirty times invaders have crossed the Rhine to invade France, five times within the past century. How could they not understand?"

Another voice said contemptuously, "The Americans and British wanted the German market back, profits before peace."

The first man nodded in agreement and said, "After the Treaty was signed, Marshal Foch said, 'This is not peace, but a truce for twenty years. The next time the Germans will make no mistake."

Someone else said, with a touch of dazed amazement, "In that case, we have five years left."

Another man looked up to the head of the table and said, "Now I understand, colonel, we must strengthen the French state for the coming struggle."

The colonel set his wine glass on the tablecloth and looked down the table and said simply, "Yes."

As darkness approached on a small street in a pleasant *bourgeois* neighborhood in one of the outer *arrondissements*, a policeman walked along the sidewalk holding the hand of a young boy. Finding the house number he was looking for, he turned into the little walkway and knocked on the door of the comfortable ground floor flat. A woman answered the door. With a look of surprise she saw her son; then she looked beseechingly at the police officer.

The policeman bowed his head and gravely said, "The school has asked me to escort your son home and explain to you that your son tried to get the other students to join the general strike. It is not allowed, Madame. The Republic leaves him to your motherly instruction." He tipped his hand to his cap in salute, turned, and walked back to the sidewalk.

The mother shushed her son quickly into the house, "*Vite, vite.*" Quick, quick.

RENDEZVOUS

A Wednesday afternoon, April 1934. Late in the afternoon, Sandrine walked along the Rue de Rivoli, the sidewalk deeply shaded by the Museé de Louvre. Crossing the square bordered on the opposite side by the Comédie Française, she walked a short block to Rue St.-Honoré. Yes, just as she remembered: *there was the café.* It was five o'clock in the afternoon. She was wearing a girlish navy blue pleated skirt, a white blouse, and a gray sweater—only slightly dressed up from the normal wear of a university student coming from her classes. Almost businesslike, she thought. She smiled to herself. From the tables on the *terrasse* one could see the Opéra House farther up the broad avenue, the green of its copper roof contrasting with the golden gilt of its bordering façade.

Walking inside Sandrine passed a small musical trio; a violin, cello, and piano were playing a pleasant tune of popular melody, a pleasing background for the intimate conversations of couples scattered across the tables of the inner café. She surveyed the clientele: well-dressed older men in earnest conversation with buoyant young women, demure in demeanor, and, quite as obviously, interested in outlook.

Philippe de Davignon caught her eye with a small wave and a broad smile. He was sitting at a small table over by the far wall. Sandrine walked over. Philippe stood up and held out his hand to her, "So nice you could come, Sandrine." A waiter hovered behind her holding the chair. She sat down, folded her hands on the table in front of her, and warmly said, "Thank you for inviting me. I have so looked forward to this."

The waiter came up with a bottle of wine wrapped in a white napkin. Philippe said, "I took the liberty of ordering a nice light Bordeaux."

"Fine."

The waiter poured two glasses of crystal clear wine into the glasses.

Sandrine looked around the dining room with an appraising glance at the murmured conversations between the couples and good humouredly said, "Ah, you look almost too young, and possibly, can it be, I am too old?"

Philippe laughed, "You have a marvelous sense of humor, Sandrine."

Then he said, "These young women, like you, are all students. Paris abounds in young women working their way through university, or so they say."

Sandrine laughed and then said with a touch of seriousness, "*Au contraire*. But I am different."

Philippe interrupted, "Of course you are." He leaned forward and put her in the center of his gaze.

Sandrine continued, "I have just come from my classes. In two years I will have my *license* from the Sorbonne," mentioning the French equivalent of a bachelor's degree.

Philippe smiled his warm approval and asked, "Do you plan to follow in the steps of Madame Bardoux, or do you think you might have a career with the Americans?"

Sandrine leaned back, glanced upwards at the chandelier beyond Philippe's head, and posed a rhetorical question, as much to herself as to him, "Ah yes, *les américains?*"

"You could be a journalist."

"Yes, but I have said to myself, 'No Americans.' I am French. I learned English to work with them, not to become one."

"Sandrine, I understand. I am from northeast France, near Germany, and I have had to work very much to stay French, and to keep the French thinking that I am French. On the other hand, I have a deep commitment towards working to develop friendships between these two difficult peoples. That has been my life's work in the foreign ministry."

Sandrine tentatively slid a question across the table, "And where is your wife from?"

Philippe nonchalantly replied, "She is also from the northeast. We have known each other since childhood. When we were eight years old, we were a delightful couple. We were best friends before we were lovers."

"Does she share in your work?"

"Very much so. She has a wide circle of acquaintances in the German community here in Paris. We try to stay in close touch with the more humanist elements in that community, both inside and outside the embassy. There are some humanists, even now, you know. Possibly some day, now starting to look distant, we will be able to build a better future together with them. We spent several diplomatic tours in the French embassy in Berlin. It was a vibrant and exciting city in the 1920s. So much seemed possible."

Philippe shifted the conversation, "If not a journalist, then what?"

"I thought a career in one of the ministries."

Philippe replied, "If the economics stay grim, that might be difficult."

She turned philosophical, "I think, for a woman, lasting happiness in Paris must be from independence, which is always earned, not given."

She took a sip of wine and turned reflective, "On a story for the Americans, I met a woman at the courts, *une avocate*. A lawyer. Another year or two of school, which is possible for me, then I would master my own professional destiny."

"That is important to you?"

"Above all else."

"Possibly I could help."

He reached over and took the wine bottle from its stand and adroitly poured some of the lightly golden liquid into her glass.

"Thank you."

"We should, may be, discuss a more intimate arrangement between us."

She smiled and ever so slightly nodded her head, "I am listening."

"I have a very nice flat in the outer reaches of the Sixth. You could have it. I could meet you there, now and again."

"I have a small flat near St.-Germain-de-Prés. My mother and my aunts provide for me. I think I shall keep it."

Philippe's brow furrowed; an unexpected turn in the conversation, a conversation he had so confidently imagined in his walk over to the café.

Sandrine smiled, the suaveness of Philippe's manner had been everything she had imagined while she also walked across the bridge to the Right Bank. Her eyes were light with merriment at his unconcealed perplexity. Yes, she would do well in this relationship.

Ah, a negotiation, thought Philippe. He asked, "Just what do you want in this intimate arrangement between us."

"An intimate relationship."

Breathtakingly direct, he thought. "That is what I am offering."

"I hope that is what you want, you desire."

Changes the transaction—exceedingly well, he thought.

"Yes," he said slowly and looked at her with smoldering dark eyes.

She saw the desire burn through the savoir-faire, the more primitive longing take hold. *Yes, this is something I want to do,* she thought, *with him.*

He saw her acquiescence, so unspoken, but so direct.

"Yes, truly you are not so young as the others," and his eyes toured the room in a glance taking in the mademoiselles seated at the other tables. *Yes, she is unlike anyone else.*

Sandrine made a small laugh.

"Monsieur, I am not looking for a husband."

Philippe's eyes lit up and he recaptured his wit, "Good, my wife would not approve."

"She approves of other things?"

"We have certain understandings."

Sandrine looked at him inquiringly, her eyes asking for more.

Philippe thought for a moment, "Total loyalty to each other. It, like your independence, allows other things to be possible."

Sandrine nodded her head, the insight sinking in, "Yes, I like that." She looked directly at him and said approvingly, "I am sure she would not want to lose you."

He said sincerely, "There is no fear of that."

He watched the relief in Sandrine's eyes. He wasn't sure whether it was because Sandrine would not want to disturb a marriage vow from some deeply held belief from her Catholic girlhood, or whether it was a desire to maintain her independence.

Sandrine looked playfully at him, "As you can see, I only need a very little, shall we say, keeping."

Philippe laughed and his demeanor relaxed, "Delightful."

She looked at him and softly said, "Yes, we have an arrangement." An unspoken question hung in the air. She looked across the top of her wine glass at him, "Soon?"

"Would Thursday afternoon around five be convenient? At the flat?"

A wonderful meeting of minds she thought. "Yes, perfect."

He reached into the side pocket of his jacket, pulled his closed hand out and slid it across the table and into her hand, "Here is the key. The address and some directions are on the slip of paper. There are silk kimonos in the closet."

Sandrine bantered, "Do you do this a lot?"

"The kimonos? No, they belong to my wife and me. Sometimes we stay at the flat when we are in town over the weekend."

Sandrine said, "You are charmingly discreet," and slipped the key and paper into her handbag.

"Let me walk you outside. May be we can walk along the river *ensemble* for a while. Together. It is beautiful at sunset this time of year."

"I would like that very much."

He got up and came around and held her chair as she stood up. They walked through the restaurant in close and easy familiarity. *Not quite a Madame de Davignon,* Sandrine thought. *Just the right distance, though.* She smiled.

Thursday afternoon, April. The sun was setting to the northwest, a golden glow coming down the cobbled street out where the Sixth *arrondissement* meets the Fifteenth. Sandrine walked up the street with a sense of warm expectation that was as golden as the sunset. She turned down a small street, walked along an ivy-covered wall, and came to a gate. She peered in, saw the small gardened yard, the bright red flowers of the bougainvillea in romantic profusion, and walked up to the porch. She tried the door. Locked. She got out the key. The door opened. She went in. She walked around. Two rooms, one with a small kitchen and a dining table with four chairs. A water closet with sink, a modern toilet, and a bidet. Yes, of course, a bidet. Towels on a rack.

In the sitting room, there was a large four-poster bed with a dark red bedspread interlaced with silky blues and greens. She sat on the bed and bounced a little, testing it. Very luxurious. She looked at the large, darkly wooded armoire against the wall. She stood up, walked over to the windows, and let the drapes close.

She walked across the room to the armoire and opened it. Yes, there were the kimonos. A large black one with white and gold images of large birds. Next to it hung a slightly smaller Imperial red kimono with golden flowers stitched in patterns. There was a third, jade green with cream white songbirds. She took the red kimono out and carried it into the bathroom and hung it from a hook. She removed her clothes, folded them and placed them on the chair.

She filled the sink with warm water; she turned the water on in the bidet to a soft burble. She felt the cool water on her thighs, then she stood up and stepped in front of the sink. She used a wash towel to complete her toilet, and then rubbed herself happily with a big fluffy towel. She dabbed some perfume here and there. She reached out and took the kimono off its hook and put it on, the slightly rough silk exciting on her bare skin. She thought for a moment and decided to leave her clothes folded on the chair. She went back into the bedroom and sat down on the bed. She lay back putting her head into the plumpish pillow and stared at the ceiling, waiting.

She heard him come through the gate and onto the porch. She swung her legs off the bed and stood up. The door opened and Philippe came in. He was wearing a dark business suit after a day at the ministry. He smiled warmly at her and walked up to her. He held a small grocery bag in front of him, the neck of a bottle of wine sticking out of the top. He craned his neck forward while holding the bag between them and gave Sandrine a kiss on the cheek. Then he stood back and gave Sandrine a playfully appraising up-and-down look. With a warm smile, he pronounced her, "Magnificent."

Then he thrust the grocery bag at her and said, "Here, why don't you put these in the kitchen while I change clothes."

Sandrine smiled warmly and with a hint of submissiveness said, *"Bien sûr."* Of course.

She took the bag and walked into the other room. She put some cheese and a baguette on the table and then went over to a cupboard and took out some small plates, a cutting board off the counter, and a bread knife and some other utensils from a drawer. She held the wine bottle up to the light, a vintage Bordeaux from an estate near Toulouse. She smiled. She found a corkscrew and pulled the cork out of the wine bottle. Then she re-corked the bottle and set it on the table. In the next room she could hear Philippe putting clothes on a chair, heard the armoire open, the rustle of a garment being removed. Then he went into the bathroom. She heard water run. He came out and she heard him softly call, "Sandrine?"

She turned away from the table and walked into the other room, a tingle of expectation on her flesh. She stood in front of him. He was wearing the black kimono. The scent of eau de Cologne came to her. He smiled at her, then held his arms out and cupped her shoulders while he made a relaxed look up and down her sheathed body, his smile widening, his pleasure in her appearance growing. Then he stepped forward and enveloped her in his arms and bent his head down towards her upturned face and gave her a kiss. He pulled his face back a couple of inches, looked into her eyes, and then pushed his lips onto hers in a crush and passionately reached into her yearning mouth with his tongue, feeling the insistent playfulness of her tongue in return. She pushed her hips into his and twisted. Their passion ignited.

Sandrine opened her eyes to the soft gray light of early dawn. Recollections of sensual pleasure seemed to caress her body, bringing a smile to her lips. She lay back in the pillow and listened to the breathing of Philippe beside her. She lingered in the memory of the previous night, a memory that was like a warm and tender embrace, an evening of small intimate harmonies. *As it should be.* Then, thinking of the day ahead, and comforted with the assurance that last night would be followed by many more, she slipped out of bed, picked the kimono off the floor, and walked quietly in bare feet to the bathroom.

She put on her clothes, completed a small toilet, and then stepped back into the bedroom and walked around to Philippe's side of the bed. She sat down on the edge, leaned over, and kissed him on the cheek, waking him up. "I have to go, *mon cheri.* Let me know *la prochaine fois*—the next time." He smiled at her, his eyes bright with happiness. She was doubly reassured. *You see the eyes. You know.*

Early on Sunday morning, Sandrine walked down Boulevard St.-Michel towards the river, the five-story apartment buildings towering above her and shading the street. Ahead, the morning sunlight glistened off the moist marble in the spray of the fountain in the middle of Place St.-Michel. On a corner of the square was the Brasserie Dalmatienne, a place of strong coffee and spicy Yugoslavian sausages, a favorite of Malka's, whose parents had come from Serbia before the Great War; some would have said "escaped" from that angry Balkan republic.

Small tables dotted the *terrasse.* Sandrine saw Malka sitting at a table at the end of the *terrasse,* stirring a cup of coffee. Sandrine walked over, sat down, and asked, "Have you seen Irène?"

"No, but she will be here," Malka said.

Soon a flaxen-haired young woman, tall and slender, well turned out in a light summer dress, approached and sat down, "Good morning."

89

Sandrine and Malka replied, "Good morning."

A waitress came up and Sandrine said, "Coffee and a baguette, *s'il vous plait.*"

Malka added, "Try the sausage. Really tasty. A touch of the old country."

Irène said, "I thought we were in the old country?"

Malka laughed, "The Dark Ages start a thousand miles east of here."

Sandrine added, "I'm told the new Dark Ages are just east of the Rhine River."

Malka replied, "Ah, the girl from the Quai D'Orsay speaks."

Irène interjected, "Try the melon. It is coming into season."

Malka laughed, "And so are we…affaires…marriage…babies."

The other two young women laughed and Irène said, "Malka, your affair with Pascal must be going well. Now it is talk of marriage and babies."

Malka laughed, "I work as a secretary for the trade unions. A *bourgeois* life in an outer suburb is our idea of heaven. Pascal will do well. He is so committed. He truly loves me."

Irène smiled, "I just hope for one good affair—at a time."

All of them laughed.

Sandrine asked, "But doesn't one man mean a loss of independence? You become the kept, not the keeper."

Irène said wistfully, "Independence? In 1934? In this Depression?"

Irène added softly, "Since coming to Paris, I have been an artists' model and then a runway model, for some of the very best fashion houses on the Champs Élysées. *Tres chic.*"

Malka brightened, "Oh good, more stories from the *haute monde* of Paris fashion. I can share the tales with the secretaries at the Confederation."

Irène made a mock scowl and continued, "Wherever I worked, I always wound up on my back looking at the ceiling—over some man's shoulder."

Malka pouted, "But isn't that glamorous?"

Irène replied, "Sometimes with some men you really get into, shall we say, the galloping enthusiasm of the moment."

Malka said, "Yes, the girls will like to hear about the galloping enthusiasm of the moment."

Irène said with an air of worldly resignation, "Other times you just have to get past the smell of garlic."

Malka turned up her nose.

Sandrine said, "But you have a good job."

Irène replied, "Shop girl for the Bon Marché department store. Barely enough to pay rent. But I work on the side for a small dress shop on Rue du Cherche-Midi. Madame says she will bring me in as a partner. My dream."

Then Irène turned to Sandrine, "You said you had a request for me?"

Sandrine answered, "Yes, I have been invited to a cocktail party out in Neuilly. Philippe is a senior official at the foreign ministry. His wife will of course be the hostess. I want to make a good impression."

Malka asked, "On the husband or the wife?"

Sandrine answered dryly, "Both."

Irène said, with shrewd calculation, "Interesting. So it is Philippe, is it?"

Malka now heard the clue that she had missed, the intimate significance of the first name reference, "This is getting interesting. Our little girl is first names with a senior official at the Quai D'Orsay. I thought you were just picking up press handouts for the Americans?"

Sandrine responded, "I got to cover the February riots from the Quai D'Orsay with Sarah's husband Bob. I met Philippe that night."

Irène leaned back and airily pontificated, "And you are a good girl, so you couldn't have an affair with your friend Sarah's husband. How American! So you picked up a potted palm at the foreign ministry? How English!"

Sandrine said, "Oh no, he's not a potted palm. He is a senior official dealing with Germany. He had postings to Berlin, and before that in the Rhineland when the French army occupied it."

Irène insinuated knowingly, "And he has a nice little flat back in the Fifteenth."

Sandrine straightened up a little bit, put on a touch of ruffled dignity, "Yes, it is very lovely flat, just inside the Sixth." Then she smiled and added, "No garlic. Beautiful shoulders."

Malka laughed, "Our little country girl comes to the big city."

Irène adds, "So our little country girl needs to dress up as the *femme fatale*."

Malka gleefully piled in, "How about Sandrine as a vamp? Like the Hollywood movies."

Sandrine rolled her eyes, "Please. I want to dress like a smart young professional bustling down the hallways of the ministry."

Irène relaxed and put her hands on top of Sandrine's hand, "Sandrine, that will be easy to do. Our dress shop does just that. We do a lot of wives of ministry officials, wives of the well to do, stylish but understated. And the American women."

Malka, slightly perplexed, looked at Irène and asked, "The American women?"

Irène said, "Yes, the ones down near the river. The ones who like women."

Malka replied, "Oh, those."

Irène said, "Yes, those."

Irène turned to Sandrine, "How old is this couple? In their forties?"

Sandrine said, "No, I think their mid-thirties. Why do you ask?"

Irène looked furtively at Malka, considered the wisdom of revealing real secrets, then decided to speak, "Malka, this is for your coffee breaks. At the Bon Marché, I made extra money consulting with women on their dresses, their wardrobe. I started going to their apartments, surveying their wardrobes, custom fittings, and such. Then there was the brush of your hands on their bodies. Intimations begin. Then you are invited to meet the husband. You develop a rapport. Soon, you find yourself between them."

Malka smiled broadly with relish, "Ah, the decadent aristocrats."

Irène smiled, "Bored aristocrats I would call them. You add some fire to fading embers."

Sandrine listened intently.

Irène continued, "The houses would be out in Neuilly or Right Bank. Then I would be invited to the country houses for weekends. No garlic. Beautiful perfume."

Malka broke in, "Oh yes, all those little impermissible things out at the chateau, out beyond the sight of *bourgeois* morality."

Irène said, "Yes, impermissible things with the husband and the wife. Together. Interesting experiences. You are the excitement."

Sandrine asked, "For both of them?"

Irène said, "Yes. It is easy work, mostly touching, the brush of lips, and a pinch here and there. For the couple, you bring them to a great intensity—*ensemble*, together."

Irène looked at Malka, "There is more to sexual life than babymaking in the suburbs."

Malka said softly, "So I see."

Sandrine said, "One couple or are there others?"

Irène replied, "There is a very discreet circle. Other women approach you, diffidently, discreet inquiries are made. Fashion consulting appointments arranged, an invitation to stay for cocktails. It just happens. Shall I say the fees from the fashion consulting are very good. The dress shop sells more dresses; Madame is very pleased. She understands. The word gets around in the right circles; more weekends are arranged."

Malka, returning to high good humor, said, "Oh, I can't wait for the next coffee break. Are there any princesses, or marquises, or, let me see, comtesses in this fairy tale of ravishing adult love and forbidden longings?"

Irène laughed and said, "Oh, your friends are never going to believe this. They will think you made this all up."

Malka made a pert smile and replied evenly, "About goings on in the great apartments, in the chateau, with the ministers' wives, the wealthy society women—the trade union secretaries will believe every word I say—with total conviction."

Sandrine laughed and looked at Irène, "She's right. The Americans also."

Malka asked, with interest and concern, "Irène, you have so much—your style, your beauty, why?"

Irène looked at her evenly, "Why? I am going to have a beautiful shop on Rue du Cherche-Midi. A grand apartment. A nice house with a walled garden out in the country. Then, Mademoiselle, I shall pick my lovers."

Malka chided, "From which sex?"

Irène airily replied, "I like the galloping enthusiasm." Then she smiled conspiratorially, "For now."

Sandrine shifted the conversation and said softly, "Independence?"

Irène said, "Above all else."

Irène looked directly at Sandrine, "Remember, when beauty fades, a woman's best friend is property." She turned and looked at Malka, "For you, a good husband I think."

She turned back to Sandrine, "For our aspiring civil servant, the beautiful young woman who desires to be a *fonctionnaire*, I wish for you a big, handsome desk."

Sandrine and Malka laughed.

Irène sipped her coffee and concluded, "Paris teaches lessons. Women always pay a price for the lessons. Be sure to get what you want at the end of the lessons."

Irène looked inquisitively at Sandrine, "Just what are you looking for in a married man?"

Sandrine answered, "It's attraction." She brightened, "An adventure."

Malka interjected, "No dreams about him leaving the wife for you?"

Sandrine said, "*Au contraire*, he goes back to the wife. He is utterly devoted to her, anyway, so he is quite safe. Besides, I picked him. He is very sophisticated; he effortlessly understood that it was I who was opening the door. I was impressed."

Irène smiled, "So we see. You have it all figured out."

Sandrine looked at Irène with her own insight about Paris, "Paris gives experience. Why else come here?"

Irène put down her coffee cup and concluded, "I agree. That's why I left Lille. Let's go over to the shop. I have a key. We will make you a fashion plate for your cocktail party. One other thing Sandrine..."

"Yes."

"You are not quite right about the cocktail party; it is not just about impressing this couple. You want to impress every man at the party. Of course, that will then impress the women. Paris is about building a circle of acquaintances. That is right behind property," she concluded. "Care to come with us, Malka?"

Malka, "I wouldn't miss it for the world—except for my own *bourgeois* wedding of course."

The other two chimed, "*Bien sûr, Madame.*"

An afternoon in May. Sandrine saw him first—a young man standing in the doorway gawking into the disarray of the newsroom. She nodded at Mac, seated in the slot of the big horseshoe-shaped news desk. He turned and looked at the young man, "Come in. What can I do for your?"

"Hi, I'm Jim Potter. I'm looking for the publisher."

Mac's eyes brightened and he rolled his cigar between his lips, "Yeah, heard about you, kid. Been expecting you."

Mac stood up and walked around the news desk and stuck out his right hand at the young man, who awkwardly put a foot forward and pushed out his right arm like he was grabbing for a life ring in a lonely sea.

Mac said, "Pleased to meet you."

The young man broke into a warm smile and said, "Boy, am I glad to be here."

Sandrine watched the young man and saw the relief spreading across his face from the warmth of the welcome. He was tall, had strawberry blond hair, with a rangy and angular frame in a loose fitting suit, sort of like a young family man in one of those refrigerator advertisements in the *Saturday Evening Post* magazine that she found so fascinating. The loud yellow of his tie was in clashing contrast to his brown suit; may be that was the style in America now. She would ask Sarah.

Mac said, "Let me take you down the hall to the publisher. He's expecting you."

The two stepped out into the hall and turned down the hall towards the publisher's office.

A few moments later Mac came back and took his seat in the center of the horseshoe, smiling, and said, "New kid from the States. Guess he has an 'in' with Chicago or something. Been working in the Washington D.C. bureau."

Rewrite popped his head straight up and said, "Why would he leave D.C. for here?"

Mac guffawed and said, "Hear he wants to be a foreign correspondent. You know, the excitement, the exotic assignments."

Rewrite tilted his head, made wide his eyes, "Here? On the *Paris Bulletin?*"

Sandrine thought about it to herself: *yes, since the February riots, Paris has settled down. The cabinet plods along.*

In a few moments the publisher, beaming a big smile, stepped through the doorway with the young man on his arm and ushered him in like giving away a bride, "Here he is, Mac."

The publisher turned to the young man, "Mac will fix you all up." Then he turned and went back down the hallway to his office.

Mac pointed to a chair next to Rewrite and said, "Sit down. How's your French?"

"Well, urhh, I had some in college."

"I know. If it were any better, they would have assigned you to Rome. Doesn't matter. You'll learn. We all did."

Jim looked around the room, saw Sandrine, and smiled a shy boyish kind of smile at her.

Mac said, "This afternoon you can work here with Rewrite. You know how to use a mill?" and he tapped the top of one of the upright typewriters on the desk.

Jim brightened, "You bet."

Mac nodded and continued, "Tomorrow morning you can continue with Rewrite. In the afternoon, you can go with Sandrine," and he stopped and nodded towards Sandrine, "and she can take you round to some of the ministries. Introduce you. Pick up some handouts."

"Gee, I'd really like that."

"Do you know anything about the Saar?"

"I hear they have a plebiscite coming up on going back to Germany."

"Hey, you know more than I thought."

Mac smiled at Sandrine and then said to Jim, "Sandrine can take you to the Quai D'Orsay tomorrow afternoon and you can talk to some of the bigwigs about the Saar. It's an on-going story for us. Remember when you write, always keep the 'Nazi menace' angle in mind when writing about the Saar."

Jim exclaimed, "The Quai D'Orsay? The French foreign ministry."

"The one and only."

"Wow."

"Oh, Sandrine is our French copy girl. She's a student at the Sorbonne. So, college boy, meet college girl," and he extended his open palm towards Sandrine.

Jim stood up and went over and extended his hand to Sandrine, and with a sudden and surprising upsurge in assurance, or so it seemed to Sandrine, said, "Jim Potter. Glad to meet you."

Sandrine smiled and pleasantly shook his hand, "I will meet you across the river after lunch tomorrow. I have classes in the morning. Let me write down directions." She handed him a slip of paper.

Mac broke in and said, "Rewrite will take you to the Hotel de Lisbonne later this afternoon. Fix you up with a room. Most of the staff lives there. Rent's cheap, nice neighborhood. Near the Luxembourg Gardens."

Mac then looked around and said, "Everyone else is out on assignment. Or getting drunk. Tell you what, tomorrow after work you can meet us across the street at the Oasis, our own little bistro, and I'll introduce you to the whole gang."

Mac turned to Sandrine, "Can you manage that, honey? Get Cub Reporter here to the Oasis tomorrow afternoon."

Sandrine made a small curtsey, "Delighted, Monsieur Mac. But what does 'cub' mean."

Mac laughed, "It means a baby bear. Slang for a new reporter."

Sandrine looked at him quizzically. *These Americans.*

Jim sat at a small table under the awning of a little café on Rue St.-Dominique a couple of blocks away from the grassy Esplanade des Invalides. He had been able to find the Esplanade easy enough. Then the street and the café were just where Sandrine had said they would be. *Piece of cake.* He drank his coffee and took a bite from his ham and cheese sandwich. Looking up, he saw Sandrine walking up the sidewalk towards him. She smiled and came over and sat down.

"Let me get you a coffee?"

"No, thank you. Finish yours and then we'll get over to the foreign ministry. There will be plenty enough to drink at the Oasis later."

"Yeah, I really heard about that," Jim smirked. "The Americans' own little bistro." Then he asked, "Why do they call it the Quai D'Orsay?"

"That's the name of the riverbank and street in front of the ministry. Sort of like your White House."

"I see. You know people there?"

"Yes, I know a few officials. I met them while working with Bob Tompkins during the February riots."

"You work with Bob a lot?"

"Some. I work with his wife more. You will like Sarah."

Jim took a final sip of coffee, set the cup down, and stood up. Sandrine stood up before he could come around and hold her chair. Independent. Jim left some coins on the table and the two of them started walking up the sidewalk.

They checked in at the guard kiosk and then entered the building, nodding at the doorman. They ascended the grand staircase to the second floor and Sandrine went up to a secretary and murmured some words. The secretary waved them towards an open office door. Sandrine stood by the open door and ushered Jim into the office with a wave of her arm. Then she followed him into the office. A pretty woman of professional demeanor stood up. Sandrine said, "Jim, this is Madame Bardoux."

The woman extended her right hand, palm down, towards Jim and said, "*Enchanté.*"

Sandrine added, "This is Jim Potter. He's the new American reporter. He has just come from the Washington bureau."

Madame Bardoux's interest was suddenly peaked, "That must have been an exciting assignment what with Roosevelt and the new American administration."

Jim looked down for a quick moment and then looked back up with a bashful look on his face, "Yes, ma'am, but it was my first job and so I was pretty junior. I always wanted to be a foreign correspondent and then this came up."

Madame Bardoux said, "I see. Sandrine tells me you are interested in the Saar."

"Well, sort of, yes actually, I don't even know where the Saar is. But the editor says I am interested in it. The Nazi menace and all. So here I am."

Madame Bardoux gave a small laugh at his fresh-faced honesty and smiled, "We have arranged for you to meet with Monsieur de Davignon, one of the ministry's experts on Franco-German relations."

Madame Bardoux looked at Sandrine and then back to Jim and said with a thin smile, "Sandrine knows Monsieur de Davignon well."

Sandrine stepped forward, slightly assertively, and said with a touch of finality, "Yes, quite well." She smiled to put an end to the little exchange.

Oblivious to the feminine exchange, Jim glanced around the well-appointed office and thought to himself: not government issue. More style than a senator's office.

Sandrine ushered Jim out into the hallway and said, "Monsieur de Davignon's office is just this way."

They came up to an open door. Sandrine rapped lightly on it and called in, "Monsieur de Davignon?"

A pleasant voice answered, "Oh, Sandrine. Come in. Your American friend?"

He stood up as Jim came in and held out his hand, "Philippe de Davignon at your service. Sandrine speaks highly of you. Please sit down."

Jim sat down, a touch of wonder in his expression as he looked at Davignon, the combed-back black hair, the bright white shirt, the well-tailored pinstripe suit: the complete French diplomat. This is the real thing, Jim thought.

Sitting down, Davignon leaned back and steppled his hands on the desk, "Do you have any questions?"

"Yes, I looked over the clipping file this morning. Why is the Saar a separate territory administered by the League of Nations? Seems like it is part of Germany."

"Yes it is. During the Great War, the Germans devastated the factories and coalmines in northeast France. It was a deliberate policy executed by the German army at the behest of German industrialists. They wanted to destroy France as a competitor. Very brutal. The coal mines in the Saar were given to France as compensation."

"You don't like the Germans."

"To the contrary, I am from the northeast. My family has been there for centuries. I know Germany and Germans well. Speak the language; love what is good in German culture. My hope is to build cooperation between two peoples who should be neighbors, not enemies. In particular, the Rhineland is one of the beautiful places of Europe."

Jim shifted in his seat, "If the Saar goes back to the Germans, what happens to the coal mines?"

"That is one of the questions at issue. Most likely the Germans would have to buy them back."

"What are some of the other issues?"

"Well, if the Germans get the Saar back, the steel industry in the Saar still needs access to French iron mines in Lorraine. Everything is interlocked."

"I see." Jim looked down at his notebook, "Why did French troops march alongside the Saar border last week?"

Monsieur de Davignon sat back, "They were routine maneuvers. France wants to maintain stability before the League of Nations takes up the Saar question next week in Geneva."

"I see. Is France playing for time?"

"Oh, sounds like an American gangster movie. But yes. Time. Since the beginning of the year, the French government has believed that the Hitler regime is not as solid as it seemed."

Jim looked startled, "They look pretty tough."

Davignon took on a slightly superior tone, "In 1917 at the height of the Great War, Germany was united, but then she broke. She is not as united now as she was in 1917. Today, Germany is not solidly nationalist but is riven through and through on questions of conscience. Protestants, Catholics and Jews are together in undercover revolt. The resurrected militarist spirit can be broken again."

"Why do you think that?"

"Hitler has had many setbacks. Then there is a new development: Russia will also be at Geneva and may well come into the League of Nations. Confidential conversations are underway. We feel the only way Hitler can save his regime is by compromise. He, too, is going back to the League of Nations in Geneva."

Davignon looked at Jim to see if his argument was connecting. He then said with a touch of Gallic grandeur, "He is being pushed that way by the rigor of facts."

Jim wrote in his notebook and then looked up and asked, "What do you expect to happen at Geneva next week?"

Davignon eased and smiled, "On background, from a high official, France expects a date to be set for the Saar plebiscite early next January."

Jim saw the scoop and exclaimed, "Great," and wrote this down.

Davignon looked at Jim and then thought for a moment. He reached over and pulled a sheet of paper from the side of his desk, "Let me give you on background some excerpts from Foreign Minister Barthou's remarks that he is delivering to the Chamber of Deputies tonight."

Davignon then began to read from the paper as Jim copied the words down in his notebook, "Will there be war? I do not think so. France does not want it and the government will do everything possible to avoid it."

Davignon looked up and said, "France's only insistence is that the Saar plebiscite should be free, sincere, and complete."

Then Davignon turned back and read from the minister's speech, "A solemn promise of Germany is not enough for me."

Jim finished writing and looked up, "Great. The editor will be pleased."

Davignon looked over at Jim and smiled. He stood up signaling the end of the interview. He looked warmly over at Sandrine and agreeably nodded his head.

After crossing the river and going up the hill, Sandrine turned to Jim, on the sidewalk outside the newspaper office, and said, "I'm going to file a story with my French editor. I'll see you upstairs a little later."

Jim replied, "Okey dokey." He turned and went up the stairs two and three at a time to Sandrine's amusement.

Entering the newsroom, Jim called to Mac sitting in the slot, "Think I got something. The guy at the foreign ministry gave us some quotes from Foreign Minister Barthou's speech to the Chamber of Deputies tonight."

"You mean Davignon?"

"Yeah, that's him."

Mac smiled, "He gives Sandrine lots of little tidbits. Let's see how you use that mill, kid."

"I'm on it."

Mac pointed over to the wall at a vacant typewriter and said, "Make a carbon. May be we'll send it to Chicago."

"Wow, really?"

Mac looked back at him and put on a dumb dog expression, "Yeah, really!"

Jim turned and went over to the long table and sat down at the old upright, laid out his notes, and started to type.

Mac looked at Rewrite and said approvingly, "Both hands, too. All the fingers. What will these college kids do next?"

About a half hour later, Sandrine came up, said hello to Mac and Rewrite, and looked over at Bob Tompkins finishing a story and asked, "Is Sarah going to be at the Oasis, too?"

Tompkins looked up, "You bet. Chance to meet someone from Iowa. Wouldn't miss it."

Hearing the word "Iowa," Jim snapped around and smiled at Sandrine and said, "Just a second, I'm almost done." He typed another paragraph, looked at it, and then pulled the sheets of paper out of the typewriter in a whirl of meshing gears. He sorted the story into the carbon and the original and looked over the copy one more time.

"There," he pronounced and stood up. He took the two copies over and handed them to Mac.

Mac handed the carbons to Rewrite and said, "Give it the works."

Then he turned and read the originals. He looked up at Jim and said, "Hey, pretty good."

He turned to Rewrite and said, "Put this on the wire to Chicago."

Bob Tompkins looked over with some interest and thought, "Hey, the kid knows some stuff."

Bill Wilshire turned and looked up. He remembered his first day as a journalist in Paris nine years before—right at this desk. It had been such a promising start, he thought wistfully. He stood up and said, "See you at the Oasis."

Mac turned to Sandrine and said, "Thanks for helping out, Sandrine. You get a story in downstairs?"

"*Oui*, Monsieur Mac," and she gave a nice curtsey.

Mac turned to Jim, "Keep it up. You can work with Sandrine going around to the ministries when she's available. Right, honey?"

"*Bien sûr*, Monsieur Mac."

Mac turned to Jim and said, "Why don't you and Sandrine go over to the Oasis. The other staff is already there. Meet the guys," and he looked at Tompkins, "and the girls?"

Tompkins said, "Sarah is probably already there."

"Good. She makes the party."

Sandrine grabbed Jim by the hand and led him over to the stairwell. The two clomped down the stairway to the street in a staccato of shoe soles rapping away on the old wooden stair steps.

Sandrine and Jim walked down the street half a block and came up to the *terrasse* of the bistro. At the far end of the *terrasse*, a couple of the small tables had been pulled together in a row. Bill Wilshire was sitting at one and speaking with Sarah Tompkins. Jim thought she was terribly attractive.

Sandrine went over and sat down next to Sarah. Sandrine turned and held her hand up in front of Jim, who was standing by her shoulder, and said, "Sarah, this is Jim. He's new. He's from Iowa, wherever that is."

Sarah, amused, said, "You've got that right, honey. Wherever that is!"

Jim pushed a chair in and sat down next to Sandrine. In a good-natured challenge, he said to Sarah, "Aw, come on. Just who do you think is running the New Deal? Why, men from Iowa, that's who."

Sarah looked at him with mock disdain and said under an upwards-tilted nose, "Pray tell."

Just then Mac and Rewrite came up and took two chairs right across from Jim and Sandrine. Bob Tompkins sat down between his wife and Bill Wilshire.

Wilshire, eyes tinkling, said, "Jim, here, is just about to tell us how Iowa is running the New Deal."

Mac said pleasantly, "He should know. He just spent a year in the Washington bureau covering the New Deal," and turning to Jim, "Didn't you, sonny?"

Sarah turned and looked keenly at Jim, a dozen questions dancing behind her expression, "You left Washington to come here?" She looked over at her husband, wish and longing across her face.

Jim said, "Well, yes, but it is sort of long story."

Wilshire broke in and said, "First, let's hear who's running the New Deal?"

Mac caught Madame Royer's eye and said, "Wine, wine." Then he looked at Jim and back at Madame, "And a beer for the boy."

Jim said, quite honestly, "Thanks." Then he looked at Wilshire, straightened up, and put on his storytelling smile, "Why, over at Agriculture we have Hank Wallace."

Jim turned to Sandrine and said, "That's the Department of Agriculture. It has half the total employees of the federal government. It's the big cheese in Washington. Almost half the American economy is farms, and they're hurting."

Wilshire asked, "So what did Wallace do?"

Jim leaned back, a sense of pride spreading across his face, and replied, "Why not much. He just refinanced almost the entire farm economy of the United States. He does more finance in a week than the Treasury and Federal Reserve do in a month."

Wilshire punched back, "Okay, hayseed, hometown boy makes good. Who else?"

Jim didn't miss a beat, "Why there's Harry Hopkins. He's a graduate of Grinnell College."

Jim turned to Sandrine and said, "I went to Grinnell. I was the editor of the paper there."

Then Jim looked over at Mac and said, "Hopkins is sort of why I got the job in Washington."

Sarah broke in, dark eyes flashing intently, "Tell us how you got the job in Washington." The intensity behind her query made it sound like she was asking for the key to the universe.

Jim looked at Mac, and Mac said, "Go on. We're dying to know."

Jim took a sip of beer and said, "Well, I graduated in June 1933. Went up to Chicago looking for a job. Went into the *Chicago Bulletin*. A nice receptionist looked at my letter from the president of the college and then showed me into an editor's office. He asked me where I was from. Well, I said, 'I'm from Grinnell College. Out in Iowa. You know Harry Hopkins went there.'"

Mac leaned back and smiled, "This is getting good."

Jim looked at him, "The editor told me to sit right there and he'd be back in a minute. He came back and said, 'The Colonel says since you know Hopkins why you can start in the Washington bureau next Monday morning. Hopkins is not his kind of guy, but he's news.'"

Jim looked at Mac, "I started to explain that I didn't exactly know Hopkins personally, and the editor broke in and said, 'Let's not confuse the Colonel.' You get on a train to Washington and be in the bureau office next Monday. You got the job. Take it."

Jim straightened up and repeated his answer, "Well I said, 'Yes siree.' The editor called his receptionist over and said, 'Fix him up for Washington.' Then her turned to me and said, 'Good luck.'"

Wilshire shot a question in, "What happened when they found out?"

Bob Tompkins listened intently as Jim spoke, now and again looking at Sarah, reading her mind.

Jim said, "Now comes the fun part. I hopped a sleeper to Washington. Found a room and then asked around for the location of FERA, the agency that Hopkins was heading up. I got there just three weeks after Hopkins started."

Jim turned to Sandrine, "Hopkins only got to the New Deal on the seventy-seventh day of the famous Hundred Days. I read a story about that my first day. Hopkins got there and his desk was still sitting in the hallway. He sat down and started writing telegrams and wired five million dollars out to put people to work before the workmen could even get his desk into his office."

Jim looked across at Wilshire, "The following Monday morning I went to his office, a ramshackle old office building, introduced myself to a receptionist, and she pointed down the hallway and gave me the name of man. I went up and introduced myself. He looked me over and said, 'Wait here.' He stood up and went into the office behind his desk. Next thing I know Harry Hopkins comes out, reaches out his hand and says, "From Grinnell College? Pleased to meet you, my name is Harry Hopkins."

Jim opened his eyes wide for emphasis, "I said, 'Yes sir, Mr. Hopkins. I just got a job starting as office boy and cub reporter at the Chicago *Bulletin* office.'"

"Then Mr. Hopkins smiles at his assistant and says to me, 'The Colonel's politics are a little to the Right of us. But, hey, the reporters down at the bureau are okay.'"

"Then I said, 'The people in Chicago got a little confused...'"

"Mr. Hopkins broke in, 'A little confused!'" He turned to the other guy, 'That's rich.'"

"Yes, sir. I said I was from Grinnell and that that was where you were from also. They thought I meant that I knew you."

"Then Mr. Hopkins said, 'Well now you do.' He turned to assistant, 'Call the Washington bureau.' The assistant had them on the line in a jiffy and Mr. Hopkins takes the phone and says, "Hi, Robert. Yes, Harry Hopkins here. Yes, young man here from Grinnell College. Yes, name's...' and he looks at me and I say 'Jim Potter,' and Mr. Hopkins says, 'Jim Potter. Good man.' Hopkins listens for a while and then says, 'My regards to your wife,' and hands the phone back to the assistant."

"Then Mr. Hopkins turns to me and says, 'There you are,' and sticks his hand out in a handshake and with his other arm turns me around and has me heading for the door, sweet as could be." Jim smiled at the recollection.

Bob Tompkins broke in and asked, "Did you get to cover Hopkins while you were in Washington?"

Jim replied, "Some. Quite a bit actually. The big stories went to the older reporters, but Hopkins' assistant would sometimes call me with small scoops."

Mac asked, "What was your next big Hopkins story?"

Jim took a pull from his beer, put the storytelling look back on his face, and said, "In November. Hopkins came back from a Midwest tour. The economy just wasn't turning around. A lot of people were out of jobs. Winter was coming. And then the way I hear it, Hopkins had lunch with Roosevelt and, like in a football game, just busted the play wide open."

Sandrine watched Sarah and saw that she looked at Jim with utter fascination. Sandrine wondered why Washington held her in such awe.

Jim looked at Sarah and said seriously, "Hopkins knew the winter was going to be desperate."

Sarah nodded her head in sorrowful acknowledgement.

Jim continued, "Roosevelt asked Hopkins how many jobs would have to be created."

Jim then solemnly gave Hopkins' answer, "Four million."

Jim turned to Sandrine and explained, "That's a really big number."

Jim turned back to the group and continued, "Roosevelt coolly calculated that four million jobs would mean four hundred million dollars."

He turned to Sandrine and added, "That's a lot of money. More than all the corn in Iowa a couple times over," and he smiled down the table at Sarah, who gave a faint smile back.

Jim then looked at Tompkins, "Roosevelt told Hopkins to get the money from Harold Ickes' Public Works Administration. Roosevelt told Hopkins to simply 'straighten it out' with Harold," and Jim laughed.

Jim again turned to Sandrine by way of explanation, "Ickes does big long-lasting jobs like dams and irrigation projects. Costs lots of money but they don't really create many jobs."

Tompkins asked about Ickes, "Didn't the Old Curmudgeon put up a fight?"

Jim replied, "Yeah, sort of. Right about then some one came up to Hopkins with a project that would take a lot of time and assured Hopkins that 'it would work out in the long run.'"

Jim laughed and said, "Hopkins, exasperated, said, 'People don't eat in the long run—they like to eat every day.'"

Glasses came down on the table and everyone laughed. Mac looked intently at Jim with rising interest. Tompkins put his chin in the palm of his hand and pondered thoughtfully the excitement of the Roosevelt New Deal. Sarah stared at Jim utterly transfixed.

Rewrite perked up, like a child, and asked, "Tell us the end of the story. Did he get the four million jobs?"

Jim said, "You bet. Hopkins put four million people to work in thirty days. All the Nay Sayers—and that was most of Washington—were left almost speechless."

Jim turned serious, "I went down to Baltimore Christmas week and interviewed dozens of men standing in payroll lines for the first time in eighteen months. Let me tell you, you write that story and you really believe."

Sarah, tears at the corners of her eyes, nodded her head in understanding and looked at Sandrine with warm approval in her eyes.

Jim brightened and said, "Not that the Republicans didn't get in their licks; they said of all the men out in the parks and public lands with shovels, or even a rakes, why they called them, 'Leaf rakers.'"

Sandrine broke in, "How noble that these Republicans support leaf raking. That is exactly what we need here in France. The people without jobs could go out into the parks and gardens and forests and clean them up. You Americans are so inventive."

Sarah laughed and said, "Why, Sandrine you are so right. But the Republicans are against giving the unemployed anything. They say it will weaken the unemployed workers' 'rugged individualism.'"

Sandrine looked quizzically at Sarah, "How can that be? Working outside in the open air will make them healthier. Factories are not such good places."

Tompkins gently interjected, "You're quite right. But actually, any kind of work helps. What Hopkins understands is that it is people's dignity that has to be encouraged."

Sandrine answered, "Of course. I thought everyone would understand."

Mac, looking sidewise at Rewrite, said to Sandrine, "You would have loved Coolidge."

Turning to Rewrite, Mac asked, "What did that guy that went back to New York, the funny guy, say about Coolidge?"

Rewrite primly recited like a schoolboy in church about Coolidge, "A man who doesn't pray isn't a praying man."

Sarah laughed and then jumped in, "What did Dorothy say when she was told that Coolidge had died?"

Rewrite primly folded his hands and closed his eyes, "How could they tell?"

Sandrine laughed and elbowed Jim in the side good naturedly, "You Americans!"

Mac looked at Sandrine and said, "Then there was Hoover."

Rewrite folded his hands neatly on the table before him and recited like a choirboy, "Everything seemed to die in his hands. I believe a rose put in his hands would wilt."

Sandrine watched fascinated as these long ago *bon mots* from almost forgotten bistro sessions rolled off Rewrite's tongue.

Mac looked at Sandrine and summed up, "Noble is not a word that goes in the same sentence with Republican. Not leastwise with people who work."

Sarah looked at Sandrine and nodded her agreement with a warm smile.

Mac then turned to Jim and asked, "Then what happened?"

Jim took a sip of beer and leaned back and drawled, "Well, in January, and let me tell you it was cold, six degrees below zero in Washington D.C., why even the Congressmen felt the chill, that four-hundred million from Ickes was running out. But twenty million Americans were now dependent upon some form of federal aid."

Jim let the words sink in. Then he continued, "Roosevelt sent Hopkins up to Congress and he asked for nine hundred and fifty million more. The Republicans yelled that the Congress were a bunch of 'dumb driven cattle.'"

Jim turned to Sandrine and said, "At least that's what they said in polite company."

Mac laughed.

Jim continued, "Well, the Congress really hated it," and Jim paused, "privately," and then he followed, "but the country was overwhelming in its support. The Congress heard. They looked at their calendars, and low and behold, it was an election year. They voted the money."

Tompkins said, "That's quite a story."

Jim replied, "Hopkins went on the cover of *Time* magazine."

Sarah, collecting her thoughts, asked quietly of Jim, "You left all of that to come over here?"

Jim sort of straightened up and said, "Yeah, sort of. See the Colonel came to town. The chief assigned me to drive him around. He asked me what I wanted to do and I said, 'My dream is to be a foreign correspondent.' Well, two weeks later came a telegram telling the bureau chief to send me to Paris. Here I am."

Sarah looked at her husband and turned back to Jim, "You make it sound so simple. But Bob and I have been trying to figure out how to get back to the States. He's not going to be a novelist in Paris, but his journalism could be a real career—for us."

Jim broke in, "You bet. His stories are page one in the Chicago paper, page three at the worst. People in Washington are really following Bob's stuff." Then Jim turned and looked at Bill Wilshire sitting quietly over on the other side of Mac, "You, too, Bill. Your stuff really gets read. On the other hand, everyone says the Colonel's journalists are sitting in Paris drinking wine while the stories are in Berlin and Washington."

Wilshire groused, "I know. The French national unity government is sliding sidewise while the madmen in Berlin are throwing thunderbolts. But how do I get there?"

Jim said to Wilshire, a bit thoughtfully, "Let me see what I can do. Get the tom-toms beating."

Sandrine asked, "Tom-toms?"

Jim looked at her, "You know, drums," and he beat out a tattoo on the tabletop. Sandrine smiled and nodded. *He's so colorful.*

Then Jim looked at Sarah, "Getting back to the States? Let me nose around. The Washington bureau chief is a great guy. With the Colonel, you slide the question in the right way, and you never know."

Sandrine watched Sarah, the longing in her eyes, the furtive glances at Bob, and the great seriousness in her face as she said to Jim, "We would really appreciate that, Jim."

Sandrine pushed her chair back and said, "I have to get back across the river. I have classes tomorrow morning."

Sarah straightened up and said, "Yes, you're so right. Bob let's walk back with Sandrine?"

Bob nodded.

Sarah turned to Jim, "Would you like to walk back with us?"

Jim pushed his chair back and stood up, "Walk through Paris with the two most beautiful women in Paris. Who wouldn't?"

Bob and Jim started walking down the sidewalk. Sarah and Sandrine followed, Sarah softly explaining to Sandrine the new hopes and vistas, things almost too good to hope for, that seemed to be unfolding with the arrival of Jim in Paris.

Mac watched them go and then turned to Rewrite, "May be there's more to this guy than a corn cob sticking out of a shirt collar."

An afternoon in May, Neuilly-sur-Seine, just north of Paris. The afternoon sun streamed through the elm trees lining Boulevard de la Saussaye, dappling the broad sidewalk with flashes of light against the moving mosaic of shadows cast by the leaf-laden limbs of trees heavy with spring growth. Sandrine walked along the sidewalk admiring the splendid homes of the fashionable suburb. The *grandes maisons* were set back behind high walls lining the sidewalk, the lawns and façades visible through wrought-iron gates hinged to massive stone pillars, the pillars seemingly symbolizing the immovability and wealth of France's ruling class. She glanced at the street numbers emblazoned on dark bronze plaques as she passed.

Coming to a small side street, she turned right and then followed a turn to the left. An open gate, a glance at the street number, and Sandrine turned inside and walked up the carriageway past numerous cars parked along the smoothly stoned surface, here and there a driver lounging by a front fender smoking a cigarette or speaking softly with another driver. The drivers turned and watched her walk up the curved drive and turn into the walkway. Their eyes followed her as she delicately went up the steps, hips ever so slightly swaying, to the large portico. She crossed and went through the open space—two large front doors were swung wide open—onto the black-and-white tiled floor of a two-story tall circular vestibule reaching towards the roof if not the heavens. Sandrine glanced at two classical statuettes situated in small alcoves on either side of the foyer. To her left, her eyes followed a grand staircase sweeping up to the second floor, beautifully accentuated by a black wrought-iron balustrade; classical frescoes adorned the wall in a smooth upwards arc following the stairwell's ascent.

The cool air of the foyer reinforced the sense of good taste intersecting refined perfectionism.

Sandrine handed her handbag and summer evening coat, along with a small beret-like hat, to a maid crisply dressed in a traditional black dress with a white cloth barrette holding her smooth black hair in place, a small white apron coming down from her waist. The maid made a small curtsey, "Mademoiselle."

Sandrine smiled and walked over to a full-length mirror on the side of the foyer and straightened the front of her dress as she surveyed her image: a long elegant light wool blue dress coming down to mid-calf, high-waisted with a medium-wide black belt cinched with a simple square bronze buckle, going up to a sleeveless top and curving neckline trimmed in white. The navy blue was "just a touch light" according to Irène, soft to the eye for a spring afternoon. Nice white shoes went with the afternoon party. *Irène was a treasure*, thought Sandrine.

Sandrine walked over to a butler and handed him a small handwritten card; he escorted her over to the entrance of a large drawing room and announced her. Looking through the tall windows on the far side of the room, Sandrine could see guests mingling on the verandah outside. Beyond the stone verandah was a large garden interspersed with small paths. On the edge of the verandah, the lyrical tones of chamber music were coming from a string quartet. The butler pointed down to the far end of the drawing room to two women standing in front of a large stone fireplace and pointed towards one and intoned, "Madame."

Sandrine thanked the butler and started to walk across the large Persian rug towards the two women. The woman identified as Madame turned, brought herself into a posture of well-poised composure, and smiled at Sandrine. She watched admiringly as Sandrine approached: the lustrous raven-dark hair, the slender body well proportioned, the easy assurance of an elegant carriage well complemented by the long blue dress. She thought: *yes, Philippe was quite right*.

As Sandrine approached, Madame held out her hand and said pleasantly, "Mademoiselle Durand, I believe, *enchanté*. Anne de Davignon." She gave a warm and welcoming smile and turned to the other woman and by way of introduction said, "Here is the young woman Philippe speaks so highly of. She works with the American newspaper people." She looked questioningly into Sandrine's face, "You are a student also?"

Sandrine pleasantly responded, "Yes, Madame."

The other woman gave an appraising glance; so many young women were "students" nowadays, all seeking shelter from poverty's storms from some "teacher." A man who could pay the second rent on a Paris flat could make a selection of his own choosing, she thought somewhat bitterly.

Madame de Davignon moved the introductions along, "Please call me Anne, my dear."

Sandrine made a small curtsey and said, "Anne."

Madame de Davignon beamed.

The other woman stepped forward, offered her hand, and said, "*Enchanté.* My name is Charlotte. And yours?"

Sandrine quickly replied, "Oh, yes, my name is Sandrine."

Sandrine looked around the large drawing room, the couches covered with damask, end tables from the Louis Fifteen epoch on their elegantly curved legs, but mostly she gazed at the large tapestries. She turned from one to the other, making almost a half circle while the two other women watched.

Sandrine turned to Madame de Davignon and said, "They are beautiful. How long have they been in your family?"

Madame de Davignon, momentarily caught by the perspicacity of Sandrine's question, very knowingly and warmly replied, "Centuries."

Charlotte looked startled. She had been here dozens of times. That the tapestries were family heirlooms of centuries standing had not occurred to her. Yes, now she could see, of course, that they were.

Madame de Davignon smiled at Sandrine and said, "Let me take you out to Philippe. When you are through speaking with the men, please come back and I will show you the house. I look forward so much to showing it to you and getting to know you better."

Madame de Davignon lightly put her hand on Sandrine's arm and guided her out through the open French doors onto the verandah. The two walked over to a group of men and women gathered around Philippe.

Philippe turned and smiled and said by way of hearty welcome, "Here she comes. The girl of the Americans." He waved to a waiter, who moved to bring over a glass of champagne.

Madame de Davignon let Sandrine's arm go and left her standing next to her husband, who proceeded to introduce Sandrine to the men and women standing in a small circle.

Philippe said, "Sandrine is now working with a young American reporter covering the Quai D'Orsay. The two work closely with Madame Bardoux and are writing stories on the Saar issue, aren't you, Sandrine?"

Sandrine spoke to the group, "Yes, we go around to the ministries, collect handouts from the press attaches, and write up routine business. But the longest stories are about the international politics of Europe. The Americans are quite interested."

Philippe interjected, "Sandrine, Bertrand here," and Philippe pointed towards one of the men, "just spent a year touring across American and writing about it for French newspapers."

Sandrine said, "Oh, Jim tells me a lot about America. He is from Iowa. And he just spent almost a year in Washington D.C. working as what he calls a little bear reporter."

Bertrand laughed, "What the Americans call a 'cub reporter.'"

"Yes, that's it. A cub. Why, I don't know. He's really sort of a puppy."

The others laughed.

Bertrand asked inquiringly, "He gave up a job in Washington D.C.? A lot is happening there right now."

"Yes, he says he always wanted to be a foreign correspondent. He seems to know someone called 'the Colonel' in Chicago."

Bertrand let his breath out, "Whew, that's high up." He said to the group, "The Colonel owns many newspapers."

Sandrine listened to this comment with keen interest.

Bertrand then smiled and explained to the group, "All the young men in the middle of American want to go to a big city, and those who can want to come to Paris. They hear about the girls in Paris," and he smiled at Sandrine. "There is always talk in America about small-town virtues, but that of course just gets the young men wondering what the lack of virtue in the big cities might be like."

Sandrine said, "You are quite right. I think Puritanism is something they look forward to after marriage."

The group laughed again, American provincialism, of course, being a great source of mirth.

Sandrine said, "They have lots of little white churches made out of wood with one small steeple. I asked him about the cathedrals in Iowa and he said there weren't any."

She looked at the group and commented, "Strange. I asked him how could people in Iowa appreciate the majesty of God's grace if they could not see the soaring spirit in the high ceilings of a cathedral."

She answered her own question, "He says they don't think about grace, rarely about forgiveness, and mostly about Hell and Damnation."

Heads nodded in understanding. She continued, "He said that the sermons in the little white churches about Hellfire and Damnation always led to grave warnings about the evil of liquor."

Sandrine said to the group, "I can see one should not live in a land without cathedrals. But I was amazed to find out that the Americans had outlawed all alcohol in the whole country up until just last year. This prohibition law was even included in their constitution. Seemed to me to be a subtraction from the rights of man."

Heads nodded in further understanding. She continued, "I asked him, 'What about the vineyards in Iowa? What did they do?'"

She looked teasingly at the group, "He looked at me with blank astonishment, uncomprehending—vineyards in Iowa? Apparently there is only corn."

Bertrand laughed, "There are only a few vineyards out in California. Americans don't know wine."

Another member of the group, perplexed, said, "Really? Are they backwards or just primitive?"

Sandrine continued, "I asked about these people who don't drink wine and go to the little white churches."

"He said they are all very devout," and then she said, with a look of genuine puzzlement, "He called them Bible Thumpers. I asked about the Bible."

"He said the Bible they read was the greatest book ever written. Even he believes this. He said it was the King James Version of the Bible."

She now spoke quite seriously to the group in an emphatic tone, "I told him it was absurd to imagine God speaking through the voice of an English king." She shrugged her shoulders and said, "And in a language so lacking in melody and song."

The group laughed and Bertrand said, "She is quite right. They slavishly follow their Bibles. But Sandrine," and he nodded at her, "Bible Thumper is sort of a slang."

She straightened up, mildly affronted, "Oh, no, he is quite insistent on this. He says they gather in their churches," and she smashed the heel of her hand into the open palm of her other hand for emphasis, "and they thump their Bibles. He is very clear on this."

Bertrand smiled and nodded his head, winked at Philippe, and said, "I am sure you are right, Sandrine."

Then Bertrand spoke knowingly to Sandrine, "Iowa and the other corn states are the progressive states in America. The people are hardworking, quite earnest, and the towns and cities are clean and usually prosperous. Undoubtedly your young American is proud to be from Iowa."

Sandrine said, "Yes, he is. But he also seems to be glad to be out of Iowa."

Laughter rippled out from the group across the verandah.

Bertrand said, "You need to see what the Americans call the Midwest and its corn economy against the American South and what is called the cotton economy. I traveled across the southern states, the red dirt country, the shacks, ramshackle towns, and everywhere black people—the Negroes—almost in rags. They are in debt slavery."

Philippe interjected, "Weren't the black people freed in the American Civil War?"

Bertrand said, "No, they just traded one set of chains for another. You go across what the Americans call the Deep South and you see this awful hatred the white people have for blacks, the hatred hanging like the long strands of moss that hang from the limbs of the great shade trees on the plantations. It is to go back into the Middle Ages. Very feudal."

Philippe decided to turn the conversation to a happier track, "See Sandrine. Your young friend comes from nice people in a good land."

Sandrine said to Bertrand, "Thank you. There is so much I don't know about America."

Madame de Davignon came up to the group and stood next to Sandrine. She politely interjected, "I thought I would show Sandrine the house."

Philippe graciously nodded agreement, and Sandrine and Madame de Davignon turned and walked back into the drawing room.

Madame de Davignon said, "Let me show you the library. It is just beyond the drawing room." Madame de Davignon held out her left arm to point the way through the far door.

Inside the library, Sandrine saw wooden bookshelves lining the walls and reaching halfway to the ceiling. Above the bookshelves were large oil paintings of men and women stiffly and elegantly posed; the paintings marched around the three walls of the room and ended on either side of the large fireplace. She took the regiment of portraits to be ancestors of the two distinguished families. Looking over her shoulder at the wall behind her, she beheld another large tapestry with a soft grayish beige field sharply set off by brown and green trees and hunters mounted on rearing horses with hounds baying after the chase. Very aristocratic, thought Sandrine.

Turning back to the gallery of portraits, Madame de Davignon said, "Some of these are Philippe's forebears, some are mine. He is of course a younger son; his older brothers manage the estates and industries of the family in the northeast."

Sandrine nodded in understanding; she had heard vaguely that Philippe de Davignon came from a wealthy family of industrialists. Other murmurings had said that Anne de Davignon was from a branch of one of the Two Hundred Families, families that had owned much of France's wealth since the time of Napoleon. Many of the families were original shareholders in the Banque de France, founded by Napoleon. Malka and her friends were quite bitter about these people. They felt the families were enemies of the Republic, not supporters of the country. Sandrine, from a family of small landowners in the south, was at once distrustful of both the industrial wealth centered in Paris and Marxist workers in the industries, who by definition were landless, and therefore to Sandrine's family hardly French at all. Sandrine's father rented out her grandparents' farm to a neighboring farmer, but the land was kept. Not to be sold.

Madame de Davignon guided Sandrine around the room making pleasant small talk about this and that ancestor. Then she pointed her arm down a hallway to the other end of the house. They walked by a spacious book-lined study and Madame de Davignon said, "Philippe's study." They continued past another open door, a small bedroom seemingly decorated as the bedroom for a small girl. At the end of the hall, a large door opened into a spacious bedroom with tall French doors that opened to a small patio. Small blooming flowers danced around the edges of the patio. Behind the flowers were dark green shrubs in front of a brick wall separating this small sanctuary from the larger garden beyond. Trees just outside the walls shaded the patio.

In the center of the room was a large canopied bed with a massive mahogany headboard. Along the wall opposite the bed was a long hardwood dresser with a gilt mirror above. At each end of the dresser was a large armoire for hanging clothes. Sandrine walked along the dresser admiring the small pieces of pottery and sculpture decorating the space. She came up to a small framed portrait of a young girl, possibly nine years of age or so, with smooth blond hair and questioning childlike eyes. Sandrine gazed at the picture and said, "Such a beautiful child," and looked at Madame de Davignon expectantly.

Madame de Davignon, somewhat startled, said, "Yes, that is Philippe's niece. She is a favorite; she lives in the northeast," then awkwardly she added, "Yes, she is a favorite of both of ours." Madame de Davignon looked wistfully at the picture.

Sandrine felt she was intruding into some special area. She turned and continued over to the windows and looked out on the patio. Madame de Davignon came up alongside her and put her hand on Sandrine's shoulder and murmured, "This is my own little Eden. I stare outside early in the morning before I get up. I listen to the birds chirp and watch the leaves rustle."

Sandrine said softly, "It is so peaceful. Secure." She walked towards the center of the room and then turned with her back to the bed and said, "Thank you very much for showing me your house. It is lovely."

Madame de Davignon said, "My pleasure. We better be getting back."

The two women turned and walked out into the hall and towards the drawing room. Entering the drawing room, Charlotte saw them and broke off from a knot of other women and came over to them, "There you are," and then to Sandrine, "Did you enjoy your tour?"

"Yes, very much so."

"And where do you live?"

Sandrine said pleasantly, "I live on Rue du Dragon near Place St.-Germain-de-Prés. I have a small flat."

"Oh, you live in one of those little dormers?" referring to the cramped servant rooms in the attic space of Paris apartment buildings.

"No, that is one more floor up. They are quite vacant. I am on *le troisième étage*. I have a two-room flat. It was re-done after the war. It has its own water closet and a small kitchen. I have four maiden aunts..."

Charlotte took a breath, *yes, the maiden aunts, part of the cost of the war.* She nodded her head in understanding.

Sandrine continued, "They are prosperous and see to my good keeping in Paris," a light smile crossed Sandrine's face as she said *to my good keeping.*

Madame de Davignon caught the touch of irony: *she was just as Philippe said.* She appreciated the subtle dig at Charlotte, the mild one-upmanship, the younger woman one dance step ahead of the older.

Charlotte said, "I see." The kitten knew how to play.

Just then, Philippe came up to the women and said, "I promised Sandrine that we would have her home for her studies." He turned to Sandrine, "Let me show you out to our car and driver. He will take you home."

Sandrine turned and held out her hand to Charlotte, "So nice to have met you."

Then she turned to Madame de Davignon and held out her hand, "I really enjoyed meeting you. Thank you for showing me your house."

Madame de Davignon took her hand in both of hers and said, "Yes. I so enjoyed meeting you. Could we have lunch together? I would so enjoy it."

Sandrine, momentarily startled, smiled and said with smooth assurance, "Of course. I would like that very much. Some Friday at noon…maybe at the café on Place St.-Germain-de-Prés?"

"Yes, I know it well. That will be fine."

Philippe smiled at this warm interchange, put his hand gently on Sandrine's elbow, and guided her towards the front door. As they walked across the room, Philippe bent over and whispered, "*Jeudi soir?*" Thursday evening?

Sandrine looked up at him, "*Bien sûr.*" Of course.

He could see the desire in her lustrous dark eyes. A sense of longing rose deep inside him.

As Sandrine and Philippe walked across the room, Madame de Davignon watched with a single-minded focus as Sandrine's hips softly swayed under her summer dress. Madame de Davignon was seemingly enchanted, thought Charlotte.

Charlotte rustled her dress and said huffily, "Anne, your husband is parading his mistress in front of you. And you graciously give her a tour of your house. And now you want to have lunch with her?"

Madame de Davignon turned and faced Charlotte directly. With a blank gaze, eyes utterly far away, Madame de Davignon softly said, "Sometimes we share."

Then she turned her head back and watched Sandrine walk towards the front door, her gaze continuing on Sandrine's hips moving under her dress. Madame de Davignon was seemingly transfixed.

Charlotte went white with astonishment: *well, yes, there had been the rumors... that last diplomatic posting in Germany...the night life in Berlin...with the avant garde...the decadence...some rumors about girls.*

She watched Madame de Davignon's eyes intently follow Sandrine out the front door, and then she reached back even further into her memory: *before that... there was something in the Rhineland...way back in the twenties...a girl...something else?*

NEW BEGINNINGS

Monday, June 25, 1934. Bob Tompkins clomped up the wooden stairs to the newsroom in the heat of early afternoon and walked into the newsroom.

Mac looked up, "I've been waiting for you, Bob. Better sit down. I've got news from the publisher," and Mac nodded his head down the hall towards the publisher's office. "It's from Chicago. You've been transferred," Mac paused ominously, "or fired." He made a half-hearted frown and then smiled.

A look of puzzlement spread across Bob's face. Times were tough. What would he and Sarah do?

Mac brightened, "But it might be a big break. The Hayseed from Iowa seems to have done you a favor."

Bob looked skeptically at Mac.

Mac waved a telegram in his hand and said, "You're being transferred to the Washington D.C. bureau. On the Colonel's orders. At full pay. As a political reporter."

Mac looked at the telegram and read, "No more first-rate American talent covering second-rate Frog politicians from the wine shops of Paris. Want Tompkins D.C. September latest."

Mac looked over at Tompkins and smiled, "Sarah gets a stringer job. They want someone to cover the Missus. Seems Eleanor has a big agenda."

Bob scratched his chin and said thoughtfully, "Where the action is." Then he added happily, "Sarah will be thrilled."

Mac said, "You'll have to leave right after Bastille Day."

Bob said, "I know."

Mac turned thoughtful, "Bob, the novel didn't turn out, but you now know how to write a helluva news story. You'll be a prizewinner in D.C."

Bob smiled, eyes warm with friendship, "Thanks."

"Remember us wretches in the wine shops covering the Frog politicians."

Bob stood up and said, "I'll be buying tonight at the Oasis."

Saturday, June 30. The big taxi swayed from side-to-side, the headlight beams searching for a break in the jammed automobiles pushing down the broad Alleé de Longchamp towards the racecourse at Longchamp. Tall trees framed the bullet-straight boulevard as if it were a tunnel; the glow of the long line of headlights projected dark shadows deep into the surrounding forest of the Bois de Boulogne, the large forested park to the northwest of Paris. In frustration, the taxi driver bumped the steering wheel with the open palm of his hand; it was important to show the passengers that he was trying. They didn't care.

Sarah exclaimed, "What great fun! Midnight horse racing at Longchamp. What a way to start the *Grande Semaine* – the Big Week."

Sarah pushed her champagne glass over towards her husband Bob for a refill, "We're going back to America in style, honey!" She pulled back, "Watch the dress!" She quickly swept the loose folds of her black velveteen dress under her thigh. "Don't want to splash the goods."

Sarah brought the now bubbly glass back to her lips and sipped, "Haven't had so much fun since Ann Arbor."

Jim exclaimed, "You went to Ann Arbor?"

Sarah said, "Got me out of Iowa, kiddo."

Jim said in a leering sort of way, "Oh, I heard about the girls at Ann Arbor."

Sarah straightened up, "Okay, Hayseed, what did you hear?"

Jim drawled, "Oh, those raccoon coats. Hip flasks under the girls' dresses. Then in those rumble seats, why the boys start looking for the flasks."

Sarah excitedly coaxed him on, "And then what? Come on, buster, what?"

Jim stammered, "Well, you know what…one thing leads to another…"

Sarah all but yelled, "Then what?"

Jim, really flustered, "Well…"

Sarah then said triumphantly, "Well, yes, I do know. I'm a married lady," and she beamed at Sandrine and Irène.

Jim said meekly, "Better give me a glass of champagne."

Sarah loudly said to her husband, "One glass of champagne for the Hayseed."

Then with her other hand she leaned across and gave Jim's knee a good wobble, "You'll like the champagne. But of course its not quite so much fun as necking in those rumble seats! But hey, this is pretty swanky, right?"

Jim replied, "Aw shucks, Sarah. I've never seen anything like this." Then, neck craning and eyes looking out of the rear of the big cab at the boisterous, honking traffic, he asked in a voice full of wonder, "All of these people going to the race track?"

Sarah popped, "Paris has been talking of nothing else for weeks. I've got us tickets to see the races from the grandstands and then supper and dancing in the paddock after the races. All the jazz bands in Paris will be playing. Thousands of the best known figures in Parisian society will be here."

Bob added, "Word is that spending will reach several million francs tonight."

Jim added thoughtfully, "You sure don't see that money on the streets of Paris. Most people are really scraping."

Sarah cut him off, "Let's let it go for one night! We've got two weeks of evening fetes and smart afternoon garden parties all capped off with Bastille Day in two weeks."

Then Sarah looked over at Sandrine and said with mock seriousness, "International commerce demands a never-ending stream of news stories on the newest fashion trends: who was at whose garden party, the glittering dresses of the costume balls, and most importantly, the newest Paris fashions on parade." Then in self-satisfied triumph Sarah smugly said, "Sandrine and I are going to do our duty. Aren't we, honey?"

Sandrine stretched her head back and laughed, "*Bien sûr, Madame.*" Of course.

Sarah looked down at her champagne glass and said quite happily, "Then back to the States and home."

She looked across at her husband and said, "Someday I will tell my daughter about the wonderful Paris parties." She smiled warmly at her husband.

He gazed back at his wife, eyes alight with merriment, and smiled. Babies had been crisscrossing his wife's mind ever since the reassignment to D.C. came through.

Sandrine held out her glass, "I'm so happy for you, Sarah. Thank you for getting Irène tickets, too. We'll have a lovely time."

Irène, sitting next to Sandrine, said, "Thank you, Madame."

Sarah replied, "Sarah, pleeze. And Irène, before I leave I'm stopping off at your dress shop so you can get my measurements. That way I can get one authentic Paris fashion outfit a year back in the States. What your dress shop does for Sandrine is a show stopper."

"I'd love to, Madame."

The taxi pulled alongside the rear of the grandstands; a huge awning was spread over a thousand tables arranged for dinner. The taxi stopped and the driver came around and opened the double rear doors and the five revelers got out.

Looking over at the restaurant, Sarah said, "The dinner was sold out before I could work my magic." She held her nose up in the air and sniffed, "We'll have to settle for supper and dancing after the race."

Sandrine said, "That's fine. Right now the Paris Opéra should be putting on a performance in front of the box belonging to the President of the Republic. We can see it from the grandstands."

Jim said, "I hear American jazz."

Irène said, "There's lots of jazz bands here tonight. Do you dance, Jim?"

"You bet. You girls are in for a treat."

Sarah looked startled and then looked at Jim archly, "You? Dance? With girls? A treat?"

Sandrine smiled and gaily said, "I can't wait. Do you know the new American dances, Jim?"

Jim stretched tall with a boyish look of kindergarten pride and said, "You bet. I can Lindy Hop with the black people. Lots of hot times in D.C. and out in the roadhouses of Virginia. Before that on the riverboats in Iowa."

Sarah looked at him sharply, "All with good girls, I bet."

Jim smiled, "You bet. Girls from my college and from my hometown."

Sarah said dismissively to Jim while winking at Sandrine, "Good girls. Their femininity stops at their neckline."

Irène laughed, "If that were true, Sarah, there would be no fashion in America."

Sarah harrumphed, "There almost isn't."

Jim turned to Irène and said, "Sarah went east of the Mississippi River to college and ever since she thinks she's a sophisticate, too worldly for the small-town virtues."

Sarah interjected, "Since when has closed-mindedness been described as a virtue?"

Jim wrinkled his nose at her.

Sarah leaned over towards Jim and whispered loudly, "Remember, buckoo, the real excitement starts below the neckline."

Jim's face reddened and he got mildly flustered. Sandrine leaned into him, grabbed his arm in hers, looked up at him with laughing eyes and an adoring manner and said, "We'll have fun dancing tonight, won't we?"

Jim smiled and said with a touch of self-mockery, "Yessiree, Bob. We'll have a hot time in the ol' town tonight." He reached out with his free arm and pulled Irène over to him in a hug. The three lurched forward together.

Sarah leaned against her husband's shoulder and wrapped herself around his arm while they walked towards the grandstand. Happiness radiated across her face.

Sitting in the grandstand in the center of the little group, Sarah spoke to Sandrine and Irène, "Tonight exceeds all expectation. All the smartest women in Paris are here," and she lifted her champagne glass, "why, even us!"

Sandrine and Irène laughed. Sandrine said, "All these women in full evening toilet, complete with jewels. The high evening coiffures. It is like being in a palace with Marie Antoinette."

Sarah put on a serious air and asked Irène, "What do you think? You're the professional."

Irène looked out across the fashionable crowd with an even gaze, "The brilliant headdresses—all those paradise feathers—are new, a colorful addition to the evening stylescape."

Irène took a sip of champagne, then took a second look out across the crowd, and continued, "Tomorrow, the French papers will talk a lot about the capes. The hip length is an innovation from the winter capes that reach well below the knee. Obviously, you can only do colorful capes with paradise and ostrich feathers when there is no threat of rain. The colors—the glistening white capes and the others in all those pastel shades—put real gaiety into summer couture. The capes are all pure decoration, no pretense of function."

Sarah said, "Great observation. I'll add for the American papers that Peter Pan hats were seen in great abundance. The rakish single feather will give a sharp look to the fall dress suits for women in town. The hats will do well in America this fall."

Sandrine chimed in, "I'll write about the Empress Eugénie hats trimmed with feathers. They're a playful addition to a regular suit outfit, which can come across as too severe."

Sarah smiled, looked appraisingly at Sandrine, "Severe? Depends upon whose hips are swaying underneath the dress."

Irène laughed and replied to Sarah, "Sandrine really knows how to, shall we say, present what is below the neckline to admiring public view."

Sarah smiled, "You can say that again."

Sandrine playfully batted her eyelashes at Sarah.

Jim looked onto this little feminine theater of conversation with fascinated revelation: *the women, they all know.*

Suddenly, a display of fireworks went off, rockets arcing up into the dark sky and erupting into beautiful starshells of color.

Jim exclaimed, "Wow, just like Fourth of July back in Iowa."

Bob said, "That was the last race. Time to go across to the paddock for supper and dancing."

The five of them stood up. A score of jazz bands and dance orchestras started playing; sound came from all directions. They walked across a carpeted walkway leading from the grandstand to the paddock. Sarah gave tickets to the concierge, who led them over to a white-draped table. The women sat down as Bob, Jim and the concierge gently pushed chairs under the resplendent dresses, the folds of the dresses making a soft rustle as the women settled in. A waiter came up and poured white wine into tall glasses.

Jim took a sip of wine and looked up and surveyed the crowd. Suddenly, he said, "My gosh, there's Monsieur de Davignon from the foreign ministry."

Sandrine momentarily looked startled. Sarah glanced at her—searchingly. Then Irène smiled knowingly at Sandrine. Sarah caught Irène's smile, too. *Girls with secrets.* She knew Sandrine visited the ministries, but this. She wondered.

Jim stood up as Davignon approached. The effortlessly aristocratic diplomat was dressed in dark evening clothes, bright white shirt and black tie, clothes that magnificently set off his dinner companion's head-to-foot white ensemble. With his right arm, Davignon guided forward his beautiful and exquisitely dressed wife. Sarah of course presumed the lady to be his wife. The well coiffed lady looked intently at the ground before her as she put one slippered foot in front of the other while holding the hem of her dress off the grass with white-gloved hands. Like a queen walking across a garden, Jim thought.

Bob stood up, and then Sarah, Sandrine, and Irène in order. The group moved away from the table and formed a small circle with Davignon and his wife, like hundreds of other chattering circles of friends spread across the tabled social setting.

By way of introduction, Davignon said, "I thought I saw you." Looking at Bob and Sarah, and then Jim and Irène, he said, "I don't believe you have met my wife, Anne. Sandrine, of course, already has."

Sarah was in rapt fascination at his little disclosure. *Sandrine knew the wife, too?*

Anne de Davignon stepped gently forward, lowered her hem, and shook hands in turn, "*Enchanté*," she murmured.

Madame de Davignon looked at Sandrine and smiled in warm recognition, "You look beautiful tonight, Sandrine." With a slightly appraising look, she added, "Once again, you are beautifully dressed for the occasion. Your dress is quite charming."

Sandrine dipped in a slight curtsey and said, "The dress comes from my dear friend Irène's dress shop." Sandrine held her arm out towards Irène by way of introduction.

Madame de Davignon graciously addressed Irène, "Why, of course. There is a pleasing similarity between your dress and Sandrine's." Then Madame de Davignon swung her gaze at Sarah, "And of course, I believe we have seen the slim lines of your ensemble before, haven't we? Paris couture. A Lucien Lelong, perhaps?"

Sarah laughed, "Of course, you have a fine eye. I write fashion articles for our paper back in Chicago. I am easily bought off by the leading houses."

Madame de Davignon arched her head back and laughed, the thin diamond necklace at her throat sparkling in the light, "Well you should. You wear their clothes exceedingly well."

"Thank you."

Turning back towards Irène, Madame de Davignon inquired, "Ah, *ma couturière*, where is your shop? I must visit."

Irène looked brightly, "Rue du Cherche-Midi. Just down the street from the Bon Marché."

Madame de Davignon engagingly replied, "I know the area well. I look forward to it. My friends and I are always on the lookout for the rising talent."

Irène, copying Sandrine, made a small curtsey and said, "Thank you."

Madame de Davignon turned back to Sandrine, "We must have that lunch we spoke about, Sandrine. After Bastille Day?"

Sandrine replied, "I would love to. How about the following Friday at Place St.-Germain-de-Prés. Across from the church."

Madame de Davignon said, "I know it well. I look forward to it." Then she made a sweeping glance across all three women, smiled, made a small curtsey, and said, "Thank you for the pleasure of your acquaintance."

Monsieur de Davignon turned to Bob Tompkins and Jim Potter and said, "Let us not dampen the spirits of this beautiful evening with any talk about the dross of politics." He smiled warmly to end the little social interchange.

Bob Tompkins, after taking a glance at Jim, replied, "Our sentiments exactly."

Monsieur de Davignon nodded his head at the two Americans, looked at his wife, and with his glance pointed her back towards their table across the paddock. The French couple turned and worked their way through the tables and chattering groups of socialites.

As a bustling corps of waiters was clearing plates away, an American Negro jazz band set up behind a large dance floor laid down for the occasion. The sounds of instruments being tooted and rhythms being tapped out wafted out across the tables. A tall American Negro trumpet player came up to the microphone and in thickly accented French said the band had just come over from Chicago and New York. Then he expansively announced that they would start with some foxtrots and then jump into *le jazz hot*. The audience gave a chorus of approval and clapped hands happily.

Jim said, "Now we can get going. Sandrine, let's dance." He stood up and walked around and held her chair as she arose. The couple walked out to the dance floor with dozens of other young French and American couples.

The bandleader faced the band, then turned and spoke over his shoulder into the microphone, "The latest from the Duke. Took the Cotton Club by storm. 'Stormy Weather'," he intoned and waved his right hand in a horizontal flash and the band took off with the moody dance piece. Couples started slowly gliding around the dance floor in a luxurious foxtrot, the men guiding the women in slowly circling arcs, the women moving in easy swaying motions to the subdued rhythms.

Jim expertly guided Sandrine around; she quickly got into following his movements, marveling at his ability to so effortlessly guide them across the dance floor. Other couples looked over, some almost enviously, at the young couple's display of grace and movement.

With another slash of his arm, the bandleader brought the number to a close; the couples stopped and politely clapped.

Sandrine said, "Please ask Irène to dance. She will love it."

"Love to."

Jim guided Sandrine off the floor and back towards the table. Sandrine slid into her chair while Jim eased behind Irène and leaned over her shoulder and whispered with polite charm, "Mademoiselle?"

"*Bien sûr.*" Of course. Irène stood up as Jim held her chair.

The music for the next dance started while Jim escorted Irène towards the dance floor. At its edge, Jim took Irène's left hand and held it high while launching her in a graceful swirl out onto the dance floor. He pulled her forward and caught her waist with his right hand, brought her in to a dance embrace, then moved their interlocked hands to shoulder height as he pushed off into a now faster foxtrot. The couple glided between other swirling couples moving in time to the music across the dance floor.

Irène's flaxen hair glistened in the arc lights and bounced softly on her covered shoulders, the white evening dress resplendent on her slim figure.

She looked at Jim and said, "Sandrine is so lucky to have you Americans as friends."

Jim laughed, "You think so. But she always says, 'Never an American.'"

Irène said, momentarily thoughtful, "She is very French. Committed."

Jim smiled, "So I have seen."

Irène's smile brightened, "But I know her like a sister. She just hasn't met the right American yet."

Irène gave a warm smile, an invitingly nice smile, possibly on behalf of her "sister," Jim thought.

The song ended, the couples stood together and politely clapped. The band-leader looked out across the dance floor and caught Jim's eye. He said, "May be we'll heat it up with the next number. Some of you look like you can cut the rug. May be a Lindy Hop." He smiled and nodded at Jim.

Jim turned to Irène and said, "Let me get Sandrine for the next number?"

Irène said, "Yes, please do." She smiled with a sense of accomplishment.

Jim guided Irène back to the table, held her chair, and smiled at Sandrine and said, "Next?"

Sandrine stood up, on her face a smile of eager expectation that Jim had never seen before. Excitement. He guided her out to the dance floor. As Jim and Sandrine stepped onto the dance floor, the bandleader said, "We're going uptown and up tempo. Something hot from the Savoy ballroom in New York." The bandleader turned and faced the band, made a quick upswing with his hand, and then slashed to the right as the band took off with one of the latest American swing tunes. The bandleader kept time by moving his trumpet with the beat.

Jim guided Sandrine out onto the floor, took her left hand up in his and swept his right arm around her waist bringing her comfortably up against his hip. With an upward lift of his left hand, he led Sandrine in a backwards arc out across the floor, moving her along in a fast-moving foxtrot. She looked at him and smiled almost to the point of laughter. *How gay this was.*

Then Jim lifted his left hand high and swung her out in another circling arc; she twirled and he brought her back into a dance embrace. Then he repeated the maneuver with his right hand and deftly guided her in a circle in the other direction. She smiled at him with a look of enchantment. He swung her out with his left again, then brought her back, stepped out of the way and sent her off in the other direction, raised their interlocked hands high, and twirled her around again. He brought her back to a dance embrace. She beamed at him.

He said triumphantly, "Now we're ready to go."

Sandrine broke into a wide smile of expectation.

The bandleader looked out at Jim and Sandrine with a nod of approval, looked back at his band, brought his trumpet up to his lips, and broke out with a high-register, sizzling hot solo.

Jim sent Sandrine on a swing out, twirled her, brought her back, swapped hands behind his back, periodically let her hands go and brought his together in a big clap, lowered his hips and waist, swung his shoulders, and kicked his feet in a rapid fire chattering step while snapping the fingers on his outstretched hands. Sandrine kept a two-step going while watching Jim do a virtual solo dance number. Then she started swinging her arms bank and forth, leaned towards Jim, and got a really hot Charleston going, hands and knees crisscrossing in flashes of motion. The other dancers, now standing back and watching, roared approval and clapped hands.

Finishing his improvised solo swing dance, Jim reached out towards Sandrine, grabbed her outstretched arms, brought her in towards him, and then stepped back out of the way like a bullfighter as he led her by him with his upraised left hand. He twirled her around on an inside turn and then brought her flying back towards him and into a dance embrace. On they went: he would bring her around in turn, send her flying with one of his long arms, lift a wrist and bring her hurtling back in, then lift her up off the floor like a ballerina while sending her out in the other direction to the end of their joint reach. Outside turns followed by inside turns, over the heads, around the waists, and reverse swing outs followed in a dazzling array of flashing legs and stomping feet. The other couples stood clapping time, the men moving their feet in time, the women ever more boisterously swaying their hips and clapping their hands as they watched Jim and Sandrine fly this way and that on the dance floor. The hot trumpet blared its notes across the dance floor, its plaintive sounds reaching into the far recesses of the audience's emotional souls, touching chords of feeling never before plucked.

Finally, the bandleader blazed out the final shrill notes of his solo and brought his trumpet down in a sweeping motion. Sweat beading his cheeks, he turned and faced the band and with his hand set the band onto the bars of one last chorus. Then abruptly, he brought his hand down in one sharp movement and the band stopped on its final beat.

Jim stopped, dropped his hands, faced Sandrine, and bowed his head towards her with a look of exhausted happiness. The other couples clapped enthusiastically. Sandrine, face flushed, smiled warmly with a glow of approval at Jim. She said, "I never imagined."

Jim stepped over, took her arm in his, and guided her back to the table. Sarah stood up clapping exuberantly as they approached. Bob and Irène stood and clapped warmly.

Sarah looked across the expanse of tables and nodded at Sandrine, "You have admirers over there."

Sandrine turned and saw Philippe and Anne de Davignon warmly smiling, standing at a distance while intently clapping. Madame de Davignon, her face radiating approval, looked at Sandrine with keen interest while whispering something to her husband. Sandrine smiled and waved. The Davignons waved back. After a minute, the Davignons turned and spoke to their friends and the party moved through the crowd towards the parking area.

Sarah watched the Davignons walk away with curious interest.

Bob nodded over towards the eastern horizon. Sarah exclaimed, "My goodness. Dawn is starting to break."

Bob calmly said, "We have a rendezvous with the cab in ten minutes. We better get going."

Irène looked at Sandrine and said, "You were simply wonderful, Sandrine."

Sandrine hugged herself with her arms like a little girl. She looked at Jim while replying to Irène, "Oh, he is simply marvelous. These Americans." Then she directly addressed Jim, "Even the ones from Iowa."

He smiled and thought, with a small sense of deliverance: *Yes, I'm a long way from Iowa.*

Sunday, July 8. Sandrine led Jim by the hand along the sidewalk towards the Porte de Vincennes just north of the Bois de Vincennes, the large and beautiful park along the southeast edge of Paris's working class neighborhoods. She said, "I never thought I could tire of garden parties and evening soirees. But Sarah just keeps me going. The paper must get someone else to do this when classes begin."

She looked up at Jim, "You can help me, maybe. I want to get back to working the rounds with the ministries. That is where I hope my future lies."

Jim smiled and said brightly, "A girl who likes politics more than fashion?"

Sandrine replied, "Law comes out of the political process."

Jim asked, "Is that what you are studying?"

Sandrine replied, "Yes, the first level degree here in France, like your college degree, is called a *license.* That gets you into the professional civil service. Another year on top of that qualifies you to be, for a woman, *une avocate*—a lawyer in English."

Suddenly, Jim broke off the conversation as he looked goggle-eyed up the broad boulevard leading towards central Paris. In the middle of the boulevard he saw the massed phalanx of helmeted mobile guards, backed by horse-mounted Republican Guards. "Wow!" he said.

The forces of order were blocking the way towards downtown Paris where thousands of *Croix-de-Feu* veterans were going to light the flame at the Arc de Triomphe later in the day. Jim continued, "Boy, they sure don't want to let the Leftists get near the Rightists."

Sandrine laughed and said, "We will meet my friends and you can see first hand the dangerous Leftists and may be even share a glass of wine with them. Or beer."

Jim, turning away from gazing up the boulevard, laughed, and said, "Today, a bucket of ice water will do. It's over ninety degrees today. Just like Iowa on the Fourth of July."

Now, looking down the boulevard, Jim exclaimed, "Look at that," and he pointed towards a group of demonstrators stoning a police car. Then he pointed farther along the boulevard at another group, "They're replacing the French flag with red flags on the buses."

Sandrine said, "That means they're Communists. The Socialists would never remove the Tricolor."

Jim looked at her questioningly, "Why's that? I thought red was the color for the Socialists, too?"

Sandrine answered, "It is, but the Socialists are loyal to France. The Communists are loyal to the International in Moscow. They believe in world revolution."

Jim asked, "And you. What do you believe?"

Sandrine smiled and replied, "The workers need a better future in France, not another revolution. We had one; it led to tragedy."

Sandrine then said, "Over there," and she guided Jim towards a large group of demonstrators in ebullient good humor massing on Boulevard Poniatowski.

Jim looked at the crowd forming up in loose marching formation and said with abashed wonder, "There must be thousands of people here today."

Sandrine said, "I've been told tens of thousands will be here today."

Jim exclaimed, "Wow."

Sandrine pointed over to some people standing under the shade of a tree, "There's Malka and Pascal."

Jim and Sandrine walked over. Jim held out his hand to Pascal, "Nice to see you again." He smiled at Malka.

Sandrine hugged Malka and kissed her on both cheeks. Holding her arm towards Malka, Sandrine looked at Jim and said, "Malka works in the big office building belonging to the Confederation of Trade Unions. A Socialist bastion, right Malka?"

Malka laughed, "Yes, this is an exciting day for the parties of the Left."

Jim asked, "Let me step into my newspaperman role. Why?"

Malka laughed again, "Normally, the Communists call the Socialists dupes of the capitalist class and traitors to the working class. But now, the two parties have joined together into what everyone is calling the Common Front." She winked at Jim and said, "Solidarity is the great virtue appreciated by all the parties on the Left."

Jim looked at groups of young men patrolling the around the edges of the gathering crowd in blue berets, blue shirts, and red neckties, "Who are those guys?"

Pascal said, "The Red Falcons. Those are the defense troops of the Socialist party, the Left's answer to the *Croix-de-Feu* and the other right-wing leagues. They keep the right-wing leaguers from disrupting our demonstrations."

Sandrine laughed, "See Jim. There's some 'red' on the Socialists. So it is not just the color of the Communists."

Malka turned to Sandrine, "I have a surprise for Jim," and she looked over at Jim. "I have a real Communist waiting for us at the café."

Jim opened his eyes wide at Malka and said, "A real Communist?"

Malka looked back at Jim and made eyes, "Yes, a real Communist. I told him a capitalist would buy him a beer today."

Jim said, "We're going to meet a capitalist, too?"

Malka laughed, "You're the capitalist."

Jim jerked his head back in feigned astonishment, "Why, I'm not a capitalist."

Malka said, "You're an American. Same thing."

Jim pulled himself up and put on his best busybody air, "Why, I'm a New Dealer."

Malka replied, "Good. Roosevelt fascinates my Communist friend. The 'traitor-to-his-class' label fascinates him. I think that is because he doubts that if he had a grand estate on a big river that he would be a traitor to his class," and she laughed.

Malka said, "Look, the crowd is starting to march. We better join them." The two couples walked over and took up station in the slowly walking formation as it moved west along Boulevard Poniatowski.

Jim walked with Sandrine and exclaimed, "Look at all the red banners. And me right in the middle. They won't believe it back in Iowa."

Then he turned to Sandrine, "What do those banners say?"

Sandrine looked at the banners and replied, "Those with the words '*Front Commun*' are celebrating the establishment of the Common Front between the Socialist and the Communist parties. Other banners say 'Workers Unite,' while others say 'Down with Fascism.' Fascism is the real enemy here today."

Near Porte Dorée on the western edge of the park the massed marchers slowly made a semicircular throng around the raised speaking platforms used for large open-air meetings.

Sandrine turned to Jim, "You can improve your French. Both the Communist and the Socialist speakers are going to grandly proclaim the solidarity of the workers on the one hand, and much more seriously, condemn the imprisonment of Social Democrats and Communists in the Nazi Reich."

Jim replied, "I'll try."

After almost an hour of speeches, Pascal came over and nudged Sandrine, "It's incredibly hot. The café is down near Lac de Gravelle. Right on the River Marne. It will be cooler there."

Sandrine said, "Let's go." She turned to Malka, "I might have a special treat today, too. Philippe de Davignon and his wife Anne might joint us. Representatives from the *haute bourgeoisie*, if not the aristocracy, for your Communist friend."

Malka laughed, "Irène told me about meeting them at the midnight horse races. She is quite excited by Madame de Davignon's interest in her couture."

Malka then widened her audience to take in Pascal and Jim, "Irène of course has no interest in whether a man is of the Right or Left, just whether he plans to stay vertical or wants to go horizontal!"

Jim's eyes widened, "Irène?"

Malka smirked at him.

The two couples pushed their way to the edge of the crowd and then started walking along a gravel walkway towards the southern edge of the park. Coming to the large outdoor café, Malka said, "Look. Over there. He saved a table and some chairs for us." The two couples pushed their way through the throng of people to the table.

A young man stood up and nodded at Pascal. He looked towards Jim. Malka held out her arm towards the young man and turned to Jim, "This is my friend Sergio. He's very Marxist."

Sergio held out his hand. Jim reached out and shook it and said, "Glad to meet you."

Sandrine stepped forward and kissed Sergio on both cheeks, "Nice to see you again, Sergio."

Sergio smiled warmly. The five of them sat down.

A waiter walked over and Pascal pointed around the table indicating beer for the men and white wine for the women.

Jim asked a question of Sergio, "What makes for a Common Front now?"

Sergio replied with well-rehearsed doctrinal correctness, "The Left is taking a common stand against the fascism of the French Doumergue government."

Malka laughed and broke in, "That was yesterday, Sergio. This afternoon both the Communist and Socialist speakers out there," and she pointed back into the center of the park, "are protesting the German government's treatment of Communists and Socialists." She turned and said to Jim, "Tens of thousands are being sent to concentration camps. Many have been murdered."

Jim softly said, "A common enemy."

Malka, dropping her gaiety, replied, "A common enemy to all, I think. Not just the Left."

Jim nodded, "I agree."

Sergio added, "But today's demonstration signals that in the next election, the parties of the Left will be the Communists and the Socialists. The Radicals will have to come to our agenda, not the other way around."

Malka nodded her head in agreement. Then she picked up the thread, "The rumor is that the Socialists' National Council is considering a proposal from the Communists for united action in what they call 'the struggle against fascism and in defense of laboring and democratic liberties.'"

Jim said, "Well, who could be against that?"

Malka smiled, "No one. But there is another dimension. Our leader," and she looked warmly over at Pascal, "our leader Leon Blum and the others are determined to maintain the independence of the Socialist International. There is going to be no taking direction from Moscow."

Sergio mildly scowled, "Moscow is the home of the true revolutionary vanguard."

Malka took on the look of a kindly schoolteacher and looked at Sergio as if he were a schoolchild, "But each countries' own socialist party is best positioned to advance the revolutionary goals of socialism in that country."

Sergio smirked in silent non-acceptance of such doctrinal deviancy.

Pascal looked at Jim and spoke up, "But Blum and the others acknowledge that the progress of fascism in Germany and Italy has become too serious to refuse cooperation with other parties of the Left, including the Communists. Both have compromised here."

Sergio nodded his head in agreement and then continued, "If a compact can be worked out, then in the next election, when the voting gets to the second round, the Socialists will support the Communist candidates in the final vote."

Malka laughed and said, "When the voting gets to the second round, the Communists will support the Socialists in the final vote."

Jim laughed and said, "I see. It depends where you sit."

Pascal smiled and said, "Actually, the Leftist candidates with the most votes in the first round get the votes of the others in the second round."

Sandrine chimed in, "In the last election, the Socialist candidates got a lot more votes than the Communist candidates. They will most likely be the Leftist party to form a new government. Not the old and tired Radical Socialists. That's the difference this time."

She looked over at Malka and shivered her shoulders in childlike anticipation, her breasts bouncing underneath her blouse, "It's so exciting. Something really new."

Jim looked at her with a new appreciation, the sheer vivacity of her optimism was enchanting to him.

Sergio shrugged his shoulders and said, "Who's the capitalist that's going to buy me a beer?"

The phrase broke Jim's reverie about Sandrine, somewhat to his annoyance, he noted. He turned to Sergio, smiled, and said, "No capitalists today. Just a New Dealer from Iowa."

Sergio looked perplexed, "Iowa? What's that?"

Sandrine laughed and said, "A place on the other side of the world from Moscow."

Jim looked at Sandrine with great affection. Malka and Pascal looked at Jim. Then they turned and smiled at each other.

Sandrine looked up, "Here they come!"

All heads turned and they saw an elegant couple approach, dressed casually in studied elegance. Pascal jumped up and grabbed two nearby chairs and brought them up to the table. He held the chair for Anne de Davignon, who graciously slipped into it while looking over her shoulder with a disarming smile at Pascal, "Thank you." He was smitten. Malka smiled.

Philippe nodded at Sandrine and then said hello to Jim. Then eyeing Sergio's Communist party badge, he engagingly asked, "Well, whom do we have here?"

Malka answered, "My friend Sergio."

Philippe replied, "Sergio, well, I'm pleased to meet you. Philippe de Davignon," and held his hand out across the table.

Sergio looked mildly perplexed, smiled, and shook Philippe's hand.

Philippe asked, "What do you do?"

Sergio came alive and responded proudly, "I work for the state railways."

Philippe leaned back, "Well, we both work for the same employer. I work for the foreign ministry. We are both servants of the Republic."

Sergio gulped and looked beseechingly at Malka.

Malka laughed, "Sergio thinks the State should be the servant of the workers."

She took a sip of her wine and added, "Sergio has never looked at members of the foreign ministry, shall we say, as comrades. He doubts the common struggle."

Davignon laughed and then easily slid into his answer, "Well, the workers should be a major voice in the operation of the State. Europe's best future is with social democracy. But who should lead the way? The Communists or the Socialists?" He looked around the table.

Davignon fixed his gaze on Malka, "You must be the Socialist?"

Malka smiled charmingly, "Right you are. I work for the Confederation of Trade Unionists."

Davignon looked at her, made a glance at Sergio to bring him into the sweep of his conversation, "What is happening today here in this park is very important. The world must protest the hideous treatment of the Communists and Social Democrats in Germany by the Nazis. The savagery of the oppression darkens the future for the entire world."

Malka turned sad, "Yes, but to be honest, there is much discouragement about the fate of the German Social Democrats here in Paris."

Davignon softly said, "We must take heart and work for a solution. Foreign Minister Barthou works tirelessly for this goal."

Looking at Sergio, Davignon added, "Having the Communists make a common front with the other parties of the Left is important to all our futures. World peace might turn on the effort."

Jim watched as Davignon held the others in rapt attention, almost trance-like, to his self-assured charm. Born to the pinstripes, thought Jim.

Davignon turned to Pascal, "And you, what do you do besides escort this beautiful young woman to the park?"

Pascal replied, "My name is Pascal. I'm a student at L'Ecole Polytechnique."

Davignon exclaimed, "An engineer."

Pascal added, "A civil engineer. Building bridges. But I'm afraid right now we spend too much time in officer training practicing blowing up bridges."

Davignon picked up, "But that sad fate cannot last forever. Somewhere in the future, we will need to build bridges into Germany. There is only one political challenge for my generation, and yours, and that is a union of all European countries."

Pascal looked keenly at Davignon and asked, "What must occur for a union to come into reality?"

Davignon replied, "First, economic integration. You integrate coal and steel. Get coal moving east over those new bridges you are going to build, get steel coming west across other bridges. You need lots of bridges. You integrate the western provinces of Germany into the eastern provinces of France. Once that prosperity is established, Germany and France become virtually unbreakable partners, not historical enemies." Davignon looked off into the distance, the arguments further away from the present than he dared to admit.

Sandrine watched the fleeting sadness pass across Philippe's face. There could be so much more "there" than just an adventure, she thought wistfully. The seriousness. She was very relieved that he had brought along his wife.

Sergio interjected, "And the lords of coal and the barons of steel unite to break the power of the workers on their iron anvil."

Davignon looked quickly at Sergio, "Right you are."

Sergio jerked his head up in amazement, surprised at Davignon's sudden agreement.

Davignon quickly turned his gaze at Malka, "That is why economic integration must be led politically by the Social Democrats."

Turning back to Sergio, he explained, "Only the Social Democrats have the political heft to move to this future democratically."

Sergio countered, "Only the workers have the revolutionary determination to defeat the capitalists in class struggle."

Davignon replied, "Violent revolution is a terrible road to go down. We don't want to repeat the Great War."

The others gathered around the table drew back at the mention of the Great War, the dark presence increasingly on so many people's minds in France.

Sergio held his ground, "Only the Communist International has the fighting power and revolutionary will to defeat the fascists. The Nazis are not going to be defeated at the ballot box. That time is past. Only workers organized for violent struggle will be able to carry the day."

Davignon sighed, "If you are right, it will be a very violent future awaiting all of us."

Anne de Davignon took on a slightly pained expression and softly said to Malka, "We know from firsthand the ugliness of the Nazi regime."

Sandrine looked at her questioningly and asked herself if Madame de Davignon's sense of despair had something to do with her niece, the little blond girl in the picture on the bedroom dresser. She knew the Davignons were from the northeast, like Irène. Both the Davignons and Irène were fluent in German. May be the Davignons had relatives on the other side of the border. She wondered. Both Davignons seemed unusually attached to the little girl.

Late in the afternoon of this blazingly hot Sunday with the summer sun still high in the west, Phil Roberts walked up the Champs Élysées towards the Arc de Triomphe, situated magnificently in the center of the Place de l'Étoile. Thousands of police supervised crowds numbering in the thousands, while steel-helmeted Mobile Guards blocked all the approaching avenues. Behind the Mobile Guards, hundreds of mounted Republican Guards backed up the cordons. The government was taking no chances on the rumored "bloody Sunday" clash between the forces of the Right and the Left.

In a decision made months before, this evening was the turn for the *Croix-de-Feu* to revive the flame of remembrance over the Tomb of the Unknown Soldier.

Approaching the Arc, Roberts saw some French reporters and sauntered over and stood next to them. Several nodded a greeting at him. Just after six o'clock, a compact contingent of war veterans, in superb close order drill, marched up the avenue following behind a *Croix-de-Feu* color guard displaying a magnificent array of colorful campaign flags and a flowing Tricolor. Behind the flags and in front of the color guard, in a dark blue army uniform, chest ablaze with decorations, strode Colonel de La Rocque, somber and determined.

The crowds uncovered as the flags passed, here and there polite applause: respect was pervasive. One of the French reporters leaned over and whispered at Roberts in good natured jest, "Not like your Legionnaires, eh?" Roberts remembered his last sight of the now middle-aged and rotund, overfed, and over-intoxicated Legionnaires as they struggled to maintain a semblance of order while following the beautiful American colors down the Champs Élysées. He smiled and nodded.

The procession halted. The color guard moved underneath the vast Arc and formed a square around the Tomb of the Unknown Soldier. A bugle sounded a melancholy call. Colonel de La Rocque advanced and performed the ceremony of reviving the flame of remembrance, a small ritual performed each evening at six. A muffled order was given. The veterans formed up and then marched through the Arc de Triomphe to the Avenue Foch on the other side.

As the veterans dispersed, the French reporters approached Colonel de La Rocque. Roberts tagged along.

One of the reporters shouted at de La Rocque, "Colonel, what do you think of the Front Commun's threat to disrupt your ceremony today. Was that a provocation?"

Colonel de La Rocque turned and addressed the reporters, "The *Croix-de-Feu* wanted nothing more to do this Sunday than to honor the great sacrifices in the World War. Our paramount concern, as always, is to support the dignity of France." The colonel tipped his open palm to the brim of his gold-leaved kepi in salute, pivoted on his foot, and walked away in the company of his aides.

Roberts wrote down the colonel's brief statement. It was beautifully said, thought Roberts. Millions of middle-class French across the entire country would read it in tomorrow's papers: the *Croix-de-Feu*—maintainer of order, keeper of the country's dignity.

Thursday, July 12. In the fading twilight of evening, the American newspapermen crowded around the small sidewalk tables jammed haphazardly together on the *terrasse* of the Oasis, circular columns of smoke rising in the air, glasses of red wine sitting on the little tables interspersed with half-drunk glasses of beer. Hands gesticulating in the air, fingers stabbing across tables as if to impale the other person with the point of the argument, the men jousted about the tumultuous events cascading through the early summer days of Paris.

Mac looked at Bob Tompkins and asked, "What did the foreign minister have to say in London, Bob?"

Bob looked at the others around the table and replied by way of explanation, "I just got back from London with Foreign Minister Barthou. He claims the British and French governments are in agreement on the need for additional regional security pacts in Europe."

Bill Wilshire pushed in, "Hah, no such thing is going to happen. The British government is avoiding continental security pacts like the plague."

Bob politely turned to Wilshire, "There's a new angle. Germany signs the regional pact and then returns to the League of Nations in Geneva. The British government gets a revival of the disarmament conference, its real interest in European politics."

Wilshire skeptically replied, "Okay, but that's a lot of 'if's' you got lined up."

Mac pushed his cigar out into the middle of the table, "What about Italy?"

Bob crisply answered, "Barthou wants a southern pact covering Italy, Yugoslavia, Greece and Turkey."

Mac smiled, "A plague of pacts, huh?"

Bob laughed, "Pactomania is the word of choice."

Wilshire interjected, "Here I'm on firmer ground. There's no evidence Mussolini is going to do a pact just to please France."

Mac summed up, "Il Duce says a plague on France's pact."

Wilshire replied, "Exactly."

Bob looked solemnly at the two of them, "It's not a board game. Barthou may be the last statesman in Europe truly looking for a road away from war. He fails...and...*après moi, le déluge.*"

Mac turned thoughtful, "You're probably right, Bob. But what do the men in Berlin really want?"

Phil Roberts leaned across the table to answer Mac's question, "Tomorrow we find out. Chancellor Hitler is making a speech to the Reichstag, supposedly to answer the French proposal. A guy in the foreign ministry says that perhaps the whole future of Europe depends on Hitler's answer. All Europe waits. Or so he says."

Mac replied, "May be. May be not."

Mac looked up the sidewalk and saw Sarah and Sandrine leisurely walking towards them chatting about the fashion shows they had seen that day at various garden parties. Arriving, each woman grabbed a chair and dragged it into the circle of men, Sarah pulled up next to her husband Bob, while Sandrine pushed in beside her.

Mac beamed and welcomed the two women, "Ah, the fashion ladies are here. Let me see what they've been up to?" He pulled out some clippings from his coat pocket. He started to read, "The Princess Facigny Lucinge wore purple velvet with a pinky mauve dress."

He looked over the top of the clipping and spoke across the table, "I really like that description—'pinky.'"

He turned back to the clipping again, "The Marquise de Polignac was in white chiffon with a long pale-green chiffon sash…green satin sandals completed the nymphlike picture."

He put down the clipping, "I had never thought of the ol' hag, excuse me, the marquise, as 'nymphlike.'"

Sarah broke in, "You're thinking of Princesse de Polignac. The marquise is quite pretty."

Mac replied, "My goodness, gracious sakes, you're right. It was the princesse. How could I forget? And me, a boy off the streets of Brooklyn. Why my Irish grandmother used to tell me, 'When you're with the quality, don't confuse a marquise with a princesse.'"

The newspapermen all laughed.

Sarah leaned back in her chair, a look of severe appraisal across her face. "Of course, how could you? Millions in Singer Sewing Machine Company money makes the princesse an American goddess."

Mac smiled a wicked smile and rubbed his hands together, "Princesse or goddess, the story was a French gentleman stood outside the princesse's townhouse, outraged that the princess had seduced his wife, and shouted up to the princesse to come down."

Mac blew a cloud of cigar smoke out across the table and looked at the listening newspapermen and then gave a "here-it-comes" glance at Sarah and Sandrine. All was set.

Mac hit the punch line, "The French gentleman shouted up to the closed windows, 'If you're the man I think you are, you will come down and fight me.'"

Glasses banged down on the table, bursts of laughter rippled across the *terrasse*.

Hugely self-satisfied, Mac turned to Madame Royer and said, "White wine for the lady journalists."

Mac looked up the street and saw Jim approaching, "Well, well, boy reporter is going to join us." He looked at Madame Royer, "Sasparilla for the boy reporter."

Madame Royer looked at him like he was crazy. Rewrite chirped, "Get the young man a beer." Madame Royer smiled and turned to the bar.

Sandrine looked at Jim and caught his eye, "Sit over here by me, Jim. There's room." Bill Wilshire scooted his chair to one side.

Jim brightened, grabbed a chair, and pushed in next to Sandrine, "Thanks. I missed you at the foreign ministry today."

"Oh, I was with Sarah at the fashion shows. Besides, you know all the ministry people now."

Mac looked across at Jim, "Was that a book I saw sticking out of your pocket, Jim?"

"Why, yes." Jim smiled. "Mark Twain's *Innocents Abroad.*"

Mac's eyes widened, "You don't say. You are reading *Innocents Abroad?*"

Jim earnestly answered, "Oh yes, what with Bastille Day coming up. I wanted to read about Paris." Then giving a leering in-the-know adolescent smile, Jim puffed up and said, "I read about the can-can. Don't want to miss that."

Mac's eyes widened further, "The can-can, you say? Here hand me the book."

Jim reached into his pocket and pulled the book out and handed it across the table to Mac. Sarah looked on with keen interest, skeptical of Mac's brotherly interest in Jim's book.

Mac riffled through the book and found the page he was looking for. "Let me read," he said, "The music struck up, and then—I placed my hands before my face for very shame…"

Mac placed one hand over his eyes and continued, "But I looked through my fingers." Mac spread his fingers so he could peek across the table like a small boy.

Then he continued reading, "They were dancing the renowned 'can-can.' A handsome girl in the set before me tripped forward lightly to meet the opposite gentleman, tripped back again, grabbed her dresses vigorously on both sides with her hands, raised them pretty high, danced an extraordinary jig that had more activity and exposure about it than any jig I ever saw before, and then, drawing her clothes still higher, she advanced gaily to the center and launched a vicious kick full at her vis-à-vis that must infallibly have removed his nose if he had been seven feet high."

Jim exclaimed, "Yessiree, Bob, that's it. You know all the good parts of the book, too?"

Mac nodded sagely, "Well, of course I do. I was young once, too."

Mac lifted his wine glass, took a sip, winked at Rewrite, and said, "So Jim, you want to see the can-can?"

Jim said, "Oh yes, at the Moulin Rouge."

Mac replied, "Well, how about Saturday night? It's Bastille Day. The joint will be jumping."

Jim responded, "Would you? You guys are sure swell."

Mac solemnly said, "Why, of course. The boys and I will be happy to oblige. We'll go after the reception at Madame Weldwhite's mansion. She invites all the American journalists every Bastille Day. From her apartment, why we'll take you to see the can-can at the Moulin Rouge."

Sarah looked disbelievingly at Mac, sensing some mischief afoot, and rolled her eyes, "Oh, no."

Sandrine laughed and looked at Sarah and said, "Oh, they'll have fun. That's what Bastille Day is for."

Sandrine turned to Jim and said, "I have to go back across the river. I have lectures tomorrow. Do you want to walk back with me?"

Jim said, "Of course I do, Sandrine. Let's go." He stood up and held Sandrine's chair as she grabbed her handbag and stood up.

Sandrine turned to Sarah, "I'll see you for coffee, tomorrow?"

Sarah looked up with a smile, "About noon?"

Sandrine said, "Fine." She turned and grabbed Jim by the arm and started down the sidewalk.

Mac watched the two of them walk down the sidewalk and then turn the corner and start down the hill. He sat his glass down, "Where were we?"

Rewrite perked up, "Oh, we're going to see the can-can Saturday night."

Mac replied absentmindedly, "Yes, let the Hayseed see the girls' underwear."

Bill Wilshire gave a snort, "I remember that first summer in Paris. Living over near the Sorbonne. That first time a French girl came up to my room with me. Got past the underwear pretty fast."

Sarah smirked, "Lot's of firsts that first time, right Bill?"

Bill replied sheepishly, "Yes. Parts of my education were left incomplete in Iowa."

Sarah replied, "Well, weren't we all. Then be careful who you call Hayseed."

Mac slapped his wine glass down. "Right. It's our duty. After the can-can, why we'll walk home by Rue de la Huchette. There's that little place over there...with the smoked windows."

Rewrite's eyes brightened, "Yes, *une maison de joie. Le Panier Fleuri*—a basket of blossoms. A 'little moment" for our hayseed. *Une demiheure* or *une heure?*"

Sarah looked aghast, "You wouldn't?"

Mac smiled like a Cheshire cat.

Sarah's voice fell, "You would."

Mac solemnly declaimed, "Time to take the Protestant out of the Hay-seed."

Bill Wilshire stared into the distance and said dreamily, "I remember the last time I was in Paris. Rue de la Huchette. Sometimes we would stop by in the afternoon and have a glass of champagne with Madame Mariette and her girls."

Sarah dismissively rejoined, "Just window shopping, Bill?"

Wilshire airily replied, "Improving our speaking of the French language. The champagne was expensive enough as it was without, as we shall say, the other entertainments."

Sarah gaped at him with open mouth disbelief.

Rewrite jumped in, "Oh, another title for the novel I am never going to write — 'Lies, Damn Lies, and Bill Wilshire taking champagne with the ladies at *Le Panier Fleuri.*'"

Bill Wilshire dropped his eyes into his wine glass and sighed, "Oh, well."

Sarah looked at him, "Bill, you're virtue is safe with me. I won't whisper a word to your missus."

Wilshire looked up, smiled, and then went back to his wine.

Rewrite turned to Mac and pronounced a new plan, "I spoke to Elliott Paul and he said the last time he was in Paris that the best was to have a 'double date' with your favorite and the small *chic* brunette Mado. He promises simply undreamed-of delights."

Mac brought his palm down on the table and expounded, "By God, a double date. That'll take the Puritan out of the Protestant!"

Bob Tompkins looked at his wife, smiled, and shrugged.

Sarah rolled her eyes and said, "Frat boys."

Rewrite looked at her and made himself up into a little prissy face, "Please, 'fraternity' to you, little Miss Sorority."

Sarah leaned way back and looked at the ceiling, remembering back to Ann Arbor: *Yes, the Spring Formal. Afterwards, the rumble seat. The groping hands.* She dropped her glance and looked lovingly at her husband. She smiled warmly in remembrance.

Friday noon, July 13. Sarah walked across the Place Eglise St.-Germain-de-Prés searching the crowded tables of the café across the street. Spotting Sandrine sitting at the edge of the *terrasse,* she walked over and sat down. A waiter approached and Sarah crisply requested, "*Un café, s'il vous plait.*"

Sandrine set her book down and looked up, "Catching up on my reading today. You Americans keep me busy."

Sarah sighed, "I want to speak with you. Mac and the other boys, and they are boys," she spit out the words with disgust, "anyway, they are going to take Jim to some cathouse after they take him to see the can-can dancers tomorrow night."

"Cat house?"

"You know, a bordello. With *filles des joie.*"

Sandrine smiled, "Oh, men and Bastille Day."

"It's not just that. They think he's never been with a girl. They came up with a whole new meaning to the American word "hayseed" for him, as being some sort of virgin."

Sandrine laughed, "Oh, Sarah, French men do that all the time back in the villages. Take the sons to *une maison.* Uncles are the worst."

Then she looked at Sarah with a touch of wonder, "But usually the boys are much younger. Babies almost." She struck a poise of maternal concern.

Sarah rolled her eyes, "Iowa is different."

Sandrine said thoughtfully, "Yes, so you all keep telling me."

Sandrine looked momentarily thoughtful, "Here in Paris, it is better than the villages, I think. Here the girls grab the boy and sneak him off into some corner. It's a dull boy who doesn't get grabbed."

Sarah sighed, "Well, that would at least be an improvement."

Sandrine took a different tack and said, "Well, what Mac and the boys are planning is very American," and she turned and said with added emphasis, "after all." With a sense of detached amusement, she continued, "That is the only reason the Legionnaires ever come back to Paris, I believe. The houses."

Sarah laughed and said, "Yes, come back and relive that first conquest over a French girl, and then what the Hell, lift a glass to the Armistice." She thought of the boozy American Legionnaires staggering down the Champs Élysées behind their flags, the victory of their youth increasingly a boozy montage seen through a middle-aged alcoholic haze. Sarah made a wan smile.

Sandrine smiled comfortingly, "See, there you feel better."

Sarah sighed and said, "Nevertheless, Sandrine, not to be the Old Maid, you could grab Jim at Madame Weldwhite's reception and take him for a long walk along the Seine and then drop him off back at the hotel."

Sandrine pouted and said impishly to Sarah, "But Mac and the boys might think less of me?"

Sarah moved her head in a half-circle of disbelief, "Think less of you? Come on. But Jim is your friend, too. Take him home. Leave him to some future romantic fate at least of his own making. Or some French girl's grab."

Sandrine smiled evenly, "We'll see."

QUATORZE JUILLET

Saturday, Quai D'Orsay, July 14, 1934. The American reporter followed the receptionist up the sweeping marble stairway to the second floor of the foreign ministry, utterly quiet this Saturday morning of Bastille Day, the year's biggest national holiday. He followed her down a hallway. She stopped outside a tall open doorway, turned, and held out her arm directing him into a spacious office. The well-dressed figure of Philippe de Davignon rose from behind a large mahogany desk and held his hand out, "Welcome, another American I see. I so enjoy your other colleagues on the *Bulletin*."

"Bill Wilshire," the reporter said by way of introduction.

"Yes, please sit down," and Davignon held out his hand towards the empty chair.

Wilshire sat down.

"What brings you to the ministry this morning?"

Wilshire shifted in his seat, "We are interested in the French government's reaction to Chancellor Hitler's speech to the Reichstag last night in Berlin. You are one of the ministry's senior experts on Germany."

Davignon took a breath, "My remarks this morning must be unofficial of course."

Wilshire opened his pad, "Of course." As an afterthought Wilshire added, "I was a correspondent in Vienna for the past several years and have been to Berlin often."

Davignon quickly said something in German.

Wilshire smiled and said, "*Ja.*"

Davignon smiled and said, "Of course."

Wilshire pulled out a teletype.

Davignon asked, "What's that?"

"Frederick Birchall's dispatch last night from Berlin for the *New York Times*."

Davignon said, "Excellent. May I see?"

Wilshire pushed the long teletype across the desk.

Davignon started to read out loud, "Before the German Reichstag assembled in the Kroll Opera House tonight…he spoke for an hour and a half evidently under strong emotion…as again and again with clenched fist…he denounced the treachery of rebellious Storm Troop leaders and enunciated his determination ruthlessly to exterminate such perfidy as theirs and keep faith with the German people who put him in power."

Davignon took a deep breath and looked up at Wilshire, "This word 'exterminate' comes up again and again in Hitler's speeches. It's in his book *Mein Kampf*."

"I know," replied Wilshire. "It's troubling."

Davignon nodded his head sorrowfully. He continued reading, "Yet it was an accounting without vouchers except the Leader's word; an assertion without proofs…a report supported solely by the intensity of the emotion with which it was rendered."

Davignon looked at Wilshire, "The reporter uses the phrase about the intensity of emotion as if the speech were art, which it is, I guess, a new phenomenon—the political mass communication of evil."

Wilshire nodded his head in agreement.

Davignon turned back to the teletype and said, "Here's Hitler's own words: 'One puts down mutinies by eternal law. If I am confronted with reproaches as to why I did not invoke the judicature of the ordinary courts then I can only reply: In that hour I was responsible for the fate of the German nation and thereby I was the German people's supreme judge.'"

Davignon looked at Wilshire again, explaining, "The authoritarian leader always assumes the role of sole judge of the nation's security, the authority from which there can be no appeal. They stress the singularity."

Wilshire nodded his head in understanding.

Davignon glanced down at the teletype and said, "Of course, one of the kaiser's sons, Prince Auwi, is in the Reichstag resplendent in his brown Storm Trooper uniform." Davignon shook his head and sarcastically added, "The old aristocracy supports the guttersnipe corporal for a few fancy uniforms."

Davignon kept reading and then spoke, "Here is Hitler's accounting: seventy-seven dead. Storm Troop Leader Ernst Roehm of course leads the list." Davignon continued reading and then slapped the desk with his palm,

"Incredible. Hitler says three men were shot for mistreating prisoners. As if he had never heard of Dachau."

Then Davignon looked at Wilshire, "This is completely unofficial but our intelligence reports the number of dead as being in the hundreds, possibly more. It is called the Night of the Long Knives in Germany."

Davignon continued scanning the teletype, "Here is the political elimination of what is left of the last German government. Hitler said: 'General von Bredow worked only according to the activity of those reactionary circles...' Bredow is shot. Now former premier General Kurt von Schleicher is described as being in conspiracy with Roehm. Von Schleicher is shot."

Davignon set the teletype down and calmly began speaking to Wilshire, "Schleicher's assassination is very significant. He has long been called the 'Field Grey Eminence' since he was the army's political ambassador in Berlin. He was also the Hohenzollerns' chief stalking horse in Berlin for a return of the monarchy," referring to the name of the last kaiser's family dynasty.

Davignon leaned back in his chair, looked up at the ceiling and continued, "We had thought that the army and the old aristocracy would eventually assert a moderating influence on the Nazis. Von Schleicher's murder ends that hope. The army will be completely intimidated by a failed corporal." Davignon turned his eyes back to Wilshire with a look of complete disgust. "The royals have been bought off with some black SS uniforms and daggers." Davignon gave Wilshire a bleak look.

Then Davignon's face hardened, "Our reports—eyewitness accounts—say that six men in civilian clothes came into von Schleicher's driveway and summoned the General and his wife. Then they riddled them with bullets gangster style. The henchmen sped away with tires squealing like in an American movie. Cold blood."

Davignon leaned back in his chair and became reflective, "The blood purge of the Brown Shirts signals another great change. The name of the Nazis is, of course, the National Socialists. The purge ends what little "Socialist" was in the party. The Brown Shirts were the working class and lower middle class wing of the party; many of their leaders like Gregor Strasser had called for a 'second revolution' against the 'debt slavery' of the workers. Strasser was murdered just like von Schleicher. Now, the working classes' aspirations have been utterly crushed. It is now an all-nationalist party built on the hate of others."

Wilshire looked questioningly at Davignon, "Why did the Nazis destroy the social appeal of their party to millions of loyal followers?"

Davignon collected his thoughts and replied, with an air of resignation, "One theory, which I had not really accepted, says that the Ruhr steel magnate Fritz Thyssen, a big bankroller of Hitler, demanded the destruction of all working class opposition to the steel trust."

Wilshire asked, "What is Thyssen's goal?"

Davignon answered, "German steel is shut out of France, Britain, and the United States. He needs markets to the east. That is the real motivation behind the more 'living room' argument that Hitler makes. Thyssen dreams of a rebirth of the old Berlin-to-Baghdad axis that Germany pursued in the First World War with its alliance with Turkey. The dream demands the absorption of Austria, Hungary, the Balkans, the Ukraine—the entire Danube basin."

Wilshire said, "Russia would never stand for such a German expansion."

Davignon agreed, "That is part of Foreign Minister Barthou's hopes for a Russian agreement—contain Germany on the eastern front. It has nothing to do with being friendly with communism; it's all about power politics."

Wilshire looked at Davignon and asked, "You have a reputation for wanting to build trade agreements with Germany around steel and coal along the Rhine river valley?"

Davignon wearily said, "Yes, and that goal will be with me to my last breath. For Germany and France to someday live in peace requires integration of the steel and coal communities between the two countries. It is fundamental."

Davignon grew intent and then he began to recite the lecture that was in the center of his lifetime thinking, "First you get economic cooperation underway. The wealthy can see the immediate profits. Building on those benefits—you buy the elites in both countries, they then buy the politicians—you slowly get some political cooperation. The Versailles Treaty of 1919 instead imposed huge economic costs on everyone, which has destroyed almost all hope for political accommodation. The English economist John Maynard Keynes pointed this all out in 1919 in his famous little book *The Economic Consequences of the Peace*."

Wilshire responded, "Yes, I read the book. Now I see how it plays out in European politics. Thyssen is not interested in cooperation."

Davignon said, as if acknowledging a new reality, "No, some experts say the Nazi party is Thyssen's personal possession. His Ruhr coal needs iron ore from

France's province of Lorraine. As long as Thyssen's demands are Germany's, then war with France is the means to those ends. Iron to feed the new eastern markets."

Wilshire replied, "But you don't believe that?"

Davignon answered, "Oh, I believe Thyssen's influence. But my guess is that Hitler will own Thyssen, not vice versa. Hitler is the king scorpion of conspirators. He strikes lightning quick. As we have just seen."

Wilshire wrote some notes, "I see."

Then Wilshire looked closely into Davignon's face. Yes, Wilshire could see the disgust in his eyes, but he could also see that there were other troubling thoughts sending the diplomat's eyes scuttling this way and that, a nervous flicker of worry and concern. Something darkly troubling had clouded Davignon's outlook, something personal, thought Wilshire. But what was it?

Taken aback by this startling interlude, Wilshire looked down at his notebook. He broached a new topic, "Hitler didn't answer the French proposal about a new security pact for Central Europe that Foreign Minister Barthou offered in London last week. Where does European security stand?"

Davignon returned to the conversation, "You are, of course, quite right. New security agreements...disarmament...Germany going back to the League of Nations?"

Then Davignon composed himself and sat up, "Today, Foreign Minister Barthou is speaking in Bayonne and will say that a new era might open which will permit the effect of the disarmament pacts to be discussed. Barthou's statement will include his heart-felt belief that there is no more noble search than the search for peace and that his goal is to bring back results."

Davignon looked at Wilshire, "The foreign minister is very persistent, very dogged. He is an old man; he offers his life to this noble goal."

Wilshire nodded and then looked at a story in a French newspaper he had brought with him. He summarized, "The newspapers say the pact scheme won't work, especially with Britain hanging back, and that the treaty's chances of ever seeing a gathering of signatories seem as remote as that of seeing, in this generation at least, Aristide Briand's European federation take substance."

To underscore his point, Wilshire spread a London *Times* out on the desk and began to read, "Yesterday, the House of Commons cheered Sir John Simon's statement that the French understand that the British are not undertaking any new obligation beyond the original Locarno agreement of a decade ago. The British government is not going to guarantee any continental boundaries from aggression." Wilshire commented, "The House of Commons is almost as isolationist as the U.S. Congress."

Davignon replied, "Of course, the British are on their island, the Americans across the sea. The British believe that the creation of opposing blocs of countries creates tensions that will inevitably lead the opposing alliances into war as happened in 1914. They see themselves as pragmatists, not isolationists."

Then Davignon looked at Wilshire evenly and explained, "Barthou will continue. A new era is still possible. Eventually, and this is what I continually work towards, a European federation will come into being. That is the grand dream. Someday Briand's grand vision will be realized. My belief, which I just shared with you and which I have discussed with your colleague Jim Potter, is that economic integration, such as German and French coal feeding German and French steel mills, will be a future basis for peace. Sadly, Europe today is not like the United States."

Wilshire smiled, "If it makes you feel better, you have convinced the entire staff of the *Daily Bulletin*."

Davignon brightened, "Yes, but by my arguments or Sandrine's incandescent presence?"

Wilshire laughed, "Some of both."

Sandrine pointed across the crowds of people thronging the garden in front of the columned façade of the Hôtel des Invalides and said to Jim, "There. We can stand up on one of the cannons out by the moat. We will be able to see the square." The two of them elbowed their way through the crowd to one of the cannons overlooking the Place des Invalides and the grassy Esplanade beyond. Jim helped Sandrine to stand on one of the cannons; he stood beside her as a balancing post.

They looked beyond the crowd to the semicircular square of the Place des Invalides. Along the edges of the square, uniformed infantry companies stood at rigid attention in the surprisingly cool summer weather. In the center of the square a long line of soldiers, airmen, and sailors stood. President Lebrun, followed by a group of officers, was working his way down the line. He would stop, face one of the uniformed men, an adjutant would read out an order, the President would step forward and pin a decoration on the man's chest, the man would salute, then the President would step back. The President would then turn, take several steps to the next man, and repeat the little ceremony. The President slowly worked his way down the line giving thanks from the Republic for brave service.

Sandrine said, "Look. He's almost done."

Jim watched as the President pinned the last decoration on the last sailor in the line. The President then walked into the center of the square; he stood and faced the line of this year's heroes. The adjutant barked out orders, the men in the infantry companies snapped rifles in front of their chests to present arms, the Tricolor and other flags of the color guard dipped and then came proudly back up, and the band struck up *La Marseillaise*, the national anthem of France. A deep upwelling of sound came from the crowd as all joined in singing the stirring anthem and its collective call on the memories of the crowd of the great sacrifices made in the World War, a memory which continued to haunt the life of France.

As the last notes drifted across the Esplanade, Sandrine jumped down from the cannon and said to Jim, "Let's hurry. We can walk down the Esplanade and across the bridge to the Grand Palais. I know where we can get a good view of the reviewing stand for the parade."

Jim said, "You're driving today."

She turned and smiled at him, dark eyes sparkling.

They walked across the grass of the Esplanade towards the river. Sandrine pointed and said, "See. Over there is the Quai D'Orsay. It was there last February where I watched the *Croix-de-Feu* form their columns down along the river for their assault on the Chamber of Deputies. Then, on the cusp of success, they dispersed. I will never forget. I still don't know in my own mind what happened. Calculated opportunism or respect for the Republic."

Jim asked, "That is the night you made your first contact with Madame Bardoux and Monsieur de Davignon?"

Sandrine answered absently, "Yes." Then she added, "Both Bob Tompkins and I were there that night. I was just a helper."

Hôtel des Invalides, the Place des Invalides, the Esplanade, Pont Alexandre III, Avenue Alexandre III (today Avenue Winston Churchill), Grand Palais on the left, Petit Palais on the right, the Avenue des Champs Élysées. Place Clemenceau is at the intersection of Avenue Alexandre III and Avenue des Champs Élysées.

With thousands of other people, Sandrine and Jim joined the bustle and walked across the Pont Alexandre III to the Right Bank, through the parkway of the Cours la Reine, and up Avenue Alexandre III. Tricolor bunting hung from wooden staffs angled out from the lampposts. Sandrine and Jim walked with the jostling crowds toward the Grand Palais and the Petit Palais, which face each other across the broad avenue.

Reaching the Grand Palais, Sandrine pointed and said, "Up there. Above the steps and out on the wing by the statue. We will be able to see the reviewing stand across the street on the steps of the Petit Palais."

They walked over and edged their way up the steps to the distinctive twin-columned portico of the Grand Palais. Soon the dignitaries started to assemble on the reviewing stand across the avenue, then a wave of applause spread across the crowd as President Lebrun took his place at the front of the reviewing stand draped in the ubiquitous red, white, and blue tricolor bunting.

Sandrine pointed at the reviewing stand and said, "The man in the turban behind the President is the Sultan of Morocco. The other man with the green tricolor sash is the premier of Rumania, a Little Entente country. Behind them is the French cabinet."

Jim looked and saw Premier Doumergue and the cabinet, all standing proudly with tricolor sashes across their bright white shirts. Some wore decorations from the Great War.

Sandrine looked down the avenue towards the direction of the bridge and said, "I can hear them."

Jim's eyes followed Sandrine's gaze down the avenue. He could see the lead infantry regiment come across the bridge. Just then Sandrine pointed into the sky, "Look. See the airplanes."

Jim looked up and saw formations of aircraft approach. He said to Sandrine, "Those are pursuit planes in the front. Behind them are the bombers."

Sandrine watched the planes fly overhead, "There must be over a hundred of them." Then she looked down the avenue, "Here come the soldiers."

As the infantry regiment came up the avenue and passed in front of the reviewing stand, an officer shouted an order and the soldiers' heads and eyes snapped right towards President Lebrun. The President saluted the colors.

The infantry regiment was followed by a detachment of soldiers riding in the latest-model motorized vehicles. The officer in the lead vehicle stood and saluted the reviewing stand as his vehicle passed. President Lebrun solemnly returned the salute.

As the motorized troops passed, Jim turned and looked up the avenue towards Place Clemenceau on the Avenue des Champs Élysées. He watched the color guard, holding high the Tricolor and attendant battle flags, enter the square. Behind it was the army marching band. Next came the infantry regiment. As he watched, the color guard turned left onto Avenue des Champs Élysées. At that instant the army band swung into a thundering rendition of *La Marseille* with the drums rolling and the brass blaring. Moments later Jim watched as the lead rifle company of the infantry regiment swung left in a beautiful wheeled turn and started marching up the grandest avenue in Paris. The thunderous cheers of tens of thousands of onlookers thronging the broad sidewalks reverberated across Paris.

Jim turned to Sandrine, "Imagine what it was like in 1919 when the allied armies marched through the Arc De Triomphe and down the Champs Élysées." He let his mind savor the imaginary memory and the magnificence of the great allied victory over Germany in the Great War.

Sandrine said, "My father marched in that parade. He told me he thought of all the men who weren't there, the widows in black along the sidewalks, the legless men in their little pushcarts. Yes, a great day, but the cost was almost unbearable."

Jim nodded solemnly and turned back to watch the troops marching past the reviewing stand. The last of the motorized troops went past. Next came caterpillar artillery units with tractors towing wheeled artillery pieces. On the tractors soldiers rode and periodically waved to children along the side of the avenue or blew kisses at the many young women twirling the hems of their light summer dresses at the soldiers. The tractors gracefully served from one side of the avenue to the other displaying the easy maneuverability and surprising speed of this new and advanced military technology.

Following the artillery, a unit of officers wearing field khaki and marching behind a large flowing flag of Belgium stepped along, many waving to the crowds.

Sandrine turned to Jim, "There is always a large detachment from one of France's many allies. These are Belgian reserve officers." She laughed, "Regulars would never wave. You should see it when the British come with their bearskin caps and bagpipes."

Behind the Belgians came a contingent of quite young French naval cadets in beautiful dark blue uniforms and marching as the lead element of a series of officer training detachments from the *grandes écoles.*

Sandrine pointed to one of the student detachments and said, "If we look, may be we will see Pascal marching for the École Polytechnique."

Jim said, "He seems more like an anarchist or artist than some swaggering drill officer."

Sandrine laughed and said, "Pascal and Malka feel strongly that all French political groups should be represented in the officer corps, not just impoverished aristocrats braying for the return of the king."

As the parade continued, Sandrine looked this way and that, pointing and smiling, obviously proud of what she saw. Like a child at a county fair, thought Jim. Soon enough, the last elements of the parade—some Paris fire trucks— hove into view.

Jim said, "Let's get up to the Oasis. The gang will be there. There's supposed to be a street party nearby and later a wealthy American lady is hosting a party for American journalists at her Right Bank mansion."

"Anything else?"

"Ah, Sarah told you. Come on. The boys are just going to take me out and see the can-can dancers. My gosh, it's in Mark Twain."

Sarah put her arm through his, leaned up and kissed him on the cheek, and said, "I think tonight you are mine. After the party, I'll take you over to the Left Bank—where we belong."

"You and me?"

"*Toutes les deux.*" Both. "But don't tell anyone. Promise?"

"I promise," he replied. Now, for the second time that day, he saw her dark sparkling eyes flash. Her words resonated deep inside him: *you are mine. . .belong. . . tous les deux.* Both.

Walking down the deeply shadowed Rue Lamartine in the summer twilight, Sandrine and Jim approached the *terrasse* of the Oasis and saw the boisterous *Paris Bulletin* crowd whooping it up around pushed-together tables covered with red-splotched white table clothes. Sandrine grabbed a chair and pushed in next to Sarah; Jim crowded in alongside Bob Tompkins.

Sarah said to Sandrine, "You're just in time. There's a big street ball with dancing over on Rue Fontaine. We're about to leave." Then Sarah dipped her voice and spoke conspiratorially, "Keep your boyfriend with you tonight. These boys are looking to go out of control."

Sandrine, eyes bright, smiled, "Don't worry. I'm going to hold him tight." She winked.

Mac called out over the table, "Let's roll the show over to the street party. Afterwards let's meet down at the Rond-Point on the Champs Élysées. There are some horse cabs that can take us up to Madame Whiteweld's apartment. We'll never get through the crowds otherwise. The mansion of *la grande madame* is near the Étoile at Rue Presbourg and Avenue D'Iena," describing a fashionable neighborhood near the Arc de Triomphe.

Five minutes later the Americans were swaying up the sidewalk of Rue Fontaine in good-natured camaraderie. An entire block had been roped off and couples were dancing in the street to a big band playing a rollicking American jazz tune. The *terrasses* of the cafés were overflowing with celebrating revelers. Beautiful multi-colored Japanese paper lanterns were hanging from trees and lampposts creating an exotic aura.

On the bandstand, a woman in a sequined sheath dress, low cut across an up-thrusting bosom, crossed the stage to shouts and applause and stood up next to the big microphone. She gave a wave to the band to start the music and then started belting out a nightclub *chanson.* Young people got up from the tables and flowed out into the street and started dancing.

Mac shouted to the other Americans, "They're broadcasting the street party back to the States. May be we should sing the Star Spangled Banner?"

Bob Tompkins shouted at Mac, "Better not. The French might think we're the American Legion and run us off the street."

Mac laughed, "You're right."

A group of French men and women, hearing that the music was being broadcast to America, surrounded the bandstand in front of the microphone. The *chanteuse* belted out her last chorus, bowed her head, and the crowd exploded in applause and cheers. Then a young woman in the front shouted, *"Pour les américains,"* and started singing the *La Marseillaise.* The crowd quickly picked up the stirring melody, and at the choruses the men heaved chests and bellowed like big deep-throated fire trucks, "*Marchon, marchon...*" Wine bottles passed around. The fever built.

With the last chorus of *La Marseillaise* dying away, the band picked up with a fast-step American swing piece, the crowd on the street clapped in delight, and couples broke out into dancing. Young couples took to the center and started in with some red-hot swing dancing, girls flying and twirling, men reeling them in with outstretched arms.

Jim, eyes wide open, said, "Wow. They're good. As good as the black people on the riverboats back home."

The swing piece died away and the *chanteuse* came back out and started singing a sultry torch song. The dancers stood in the street and slowly kept time to the swaying beat with soft handclaps. One of the young women started slowly doing a twisting dance, hips swaying, luxurious rolls of her shoulders and breasts undulating under a soft cashmere sweater, hands clapping above her head. The crowd made a circle around her and she slowly twisted in the center before the ever more intense gaze of her audience.

Languorously she reached down and grabbed the bottom of her sweater and slowly started to pull it over her head.

Transfixed, Jim said, "Look at that. Why I never..."

Sandrine, intensely watching the young woman, said, "She is an *artiste*."

Bob laughed and said, "She's probably a model just having fun doing for free what she does for money during the week."

The young woman pulled the sweater off revealing a black brassiere against pale white skin. She waved the sweater like a flag over her head and then threw it into the crowd. She moved to remove her brassiere.

Jim exclaimed, "She wouldn't!"

Sarah laughed and said, "She would and she will."

The young woman unclasped her bra and pulled it off as the crowd cheered and she gaily waved it back and forth over head while continuing a now erotic dance of swaying hips and swinging breasts.

The young woman, the center of all attention, continued her swaying, twisting dance ever more suggestively moving her hips. Then the song ended and the band brought its piece to a crescendo-like close. The crowd clapped, the young woman deeply bowed from the waist, and one of the women in the crowd handed her sweater back to her, another her brassiere. She pulled the sweater over her head and chest and tossed the brassiere to her boyfriend. The crowd clapped and hooted.

Sarah said pleasantly to Jim, "She obviously has a sense of decorum. She kept her skirt on."

Jim looked at her, "You're kidding. *Everything*. In the street?"

Sarah started to walk away and said gaily over her shoulder, "The night is still young, Hayseed."

Jim looked at Sandrine, "I never imagined."

Sandrine stood up on tiptoe and kissed him on the cheek and mimicked, "The night is still young." She stood back and looked at him with dancing eyes and a smile he had never seen before.

"I'm a long way from Iowa."

Mac called out to the others, "See you down at the Rond-Point, or Madame Whiteweld's for sure," and he gave Rewrite a shove down the street, "Let's go, bucko."

"Bucko yourself, when do we get to see the can-can girls?"

Mac put his finger to his lips, "Shush. Later."

Sandrine caught the can-can girl remark and thought: *yes, Sarah was right.* She smiled to herself and turned to Jim, "Let's follow. We'll just follow along. I know the way."

Jim said, "As I said, you're driving today."

Sandrine turned to him, "Yes I am. And you're staying with me. Don't want you winding up, shall we say, dancing with the wrong girl."

Jim looked at her, "Honest. I would never think of it."

Sandrine replied, "No, but some others might," and she laughed.

At the Rond-Point, Mac looked around the turning circle situated in a park-like wood and then pointed, "Over there. Down the avenue. There's some horse cabs."

The group of boisterous journalists walked over shouting, "*À la maison Weldwhite*. Who's got the wine?"

Sandrine grabbed Jim by the elbow and headed towards the rear of the file of horse cabs. She saw Sarah and Bob start to walk over, but Sandrine shouted to Sarah, "We'll see you up there."

Sarah's face brightened in sudden recognition and she smiled, "See you up there," and gaily waved and turned her husband towards one of the other cabs. The couple piled in behind Mac, Rewrite, and others busily hoisting wine bottles to the sky and screaming, "*Vive la France.*"

Sandrine stepped up into the rear of the horse cab, its top shoved all the way back behind the luxurious rear seat of the carriage so that the passenger seats were open to the sky. She turned back and offered a hand to Jim. He stepped up and she pushed him gently back into the rear seat. Sandrine turned and stood up on tiptoe and spoke to the top-hatted driver, who was sitting up high on the driver's seat. The seat was well forward and majestically above the carriage's front seat affording the passengers well-paid-for privacy. He put his hand to his hat brim and said, "*Oui, Mademoiselle.*"

Sandrine turned and sat down in the rear seat and sank back languidly in the soft cushions and snuggled up next to Jim, holding his arm. She said sweetly to him, "We'll go up the Champs Élysées. The crowds will make way for the horse. So romantic. With my true love," and she leaned over and nuzzled his cheek with her own.

Soon they heard the driver jingle the reins, heard the hoofs of the horse take its first steps, and the carriage slowly glided forward. The procession of carriages moved through the crowd-thronged avenue. Sandrine turned sidewise along Jim's long body and draped her leg over his and pushed her thigh into his; she reached across and caressed his chest and nestled her head onto his shoulder and stared out at the crowds dancing in the street.

Jim receded into a pleasant languor; may be a little too much wine, he thought. He stared out at the festive crowds, the street dancing. As he watched here and there he could see tambourines keeping time, girls on the sidewalk dancing. Yes, Sarah had been right. They were not wearing their skirts, or anything else for that matter, like something out of medieval street fair, a burst of wantonness before Lent.

Jim whispered to Sandrine, "They're not wearing their clothes."

Sandrine whispered back, "May be they're happy."

After a while Jim stirred and asked, "The other cabs are turning."

Sandrine said, "I told the driver to go up around the Arc de Triomphe. It's beautiful at night all lit up. I want you to see it."

Jim nuzzled against Sandrine and said, "Fine. You're driving."

The cab came up to the Étoile and slowly started to work its way through the crowds surrounding the magnificent arch, floodlit against the black sky, draped in tricolor bunting. Slowly the cab worked around the great circular square and started back down the Champs Élysées.

Sandrine slowly opened the buttons of Jim's shirt and caressed his chest. Then she briefly sat up and unbuttoned her blouse and took it off.

"Sandrine, what are you doing?"

"I want to feel your skin with mine."

"But the driver."

She leaned over and kissed him, "We'll give him a big tip."

She dropped her slip and removed her brassiere and then put her blouse back on but did not button it, "Modest enough for Bastille Day," she said.

She leaned over, kissed him, and let her breasts play across his chest. Then she pushed her lips against his and searched deep inside his mouth with her tongue and pushed her breasts into his chest.

She raised her head back a little, kissed him quickly with pursed lips, and said, "Most of you has melted away," and looked at him mischievously, "but not quite all." She pushed her hips into his pelvis. "There," she sighed.

She rolled away from him a little bit and reached down and pulled her dress up a little and reached under it and started to pull her underdrawers down.

"What are you doing?"

"I won't be needing them." She pulled the cotton drawers over her ankles and put them in her handbag.

"*Amour, mon amour,*" she whispered into his ear. She undid his belt buckle and pants and slid her hand down, caressed and squeezed.

Jim gave out a low moan, "Here?" And incredulously, "Now?"

"Here, now," she murmured. She pulled her skirt up and draped it over Jim's waist, finished wiggling his pants down, and then slid over on top of him and spread her skirt like a tent over his midsection. She moved herself slowly over his masculinity while grabbing his pectoral muscles in her hands and digging her fingers in. She leaned down looking into his face, eyes flashing, then dipped her lips and kissed him.

She slid slightly up, positioned herself, and then slid back down over him, arching her back, and letting out a long, sighing moan, "*Mon amour.*" She slowly started to rock, working on building her pleasure, looking down at him with ever-deeper rapture, kneading his chest muscles with her fingers.

Jim looked up at Sandrine, her breasts swaying tantalizingly above him inside her open blouse, *he never imagined...like this...here...with her.*

He looked out the side of the carriage, here and there people pointing at them, laughing, sometimes clapping. Beyond Sandrine's shoulders he could see the tophat of the driver, eyes resolutely forward, the slow clomp of the horse pulling the carriage down the avenue, and the ever more exquisite feeling of Sandrine on top of him.

She felt his hands tighten on her waist, then pull her down, she felt his paroxysm begin inside her, and then she let her mind go and felt the beginning of her own wonderful sympathetic response, the waves of pleasure inside her. She arched her back, clasped his chest, dug her nails into his flesh, and slowed to a convulsive easy rocking of her hips over his.

She sighed, "*Voila, mon chéri,*" and collapsed on his chest, burying her face behind his ear, kissing his neck, wrapping her arms tight around his chest, making small undulating movements with her hips, slowly climbing down from the mountain of her pleasure.

After a while, she lifted off, slid over and helped him pull up his pants. Then she lay her head down on his chest and made little curlicues on his stomach with her fingers. The carriage continued down the festive Champs Élysées, the young lovers caught up in their own solitude amidst the shouts of the multitudes. Eventually, the carriage pulled over to the curb and came to a stop. The driver said, "Place de la Concorde, Mademoiselle. It is as you wished it?"

"Yes, as I wished it. Thank you." She turned and whispered in Jim's ear, "Ever so much as I wished it."

She got out onto the street and as Jim stood up in the carriage behind the driver, she said, "Please pay the driver," and added with a smile, "and give him a big tip."

Jim paid the driver. He stepped down out of the carriage and the driver turned to them, "*Bon soir, Monsieur et Madame.*"

Sandrine turned to Jim, "I love the sound of that. *Monsieur et Madame.*"

Jim put his forehead against her forehead and looked at her. "So do I. But we missed the party. Where are we going?"

"I want you to see the Place de la Concorde tonight on this very special night. It is wonderfully lit up. Then we'll go to your hotel. It will be the quietest place in Paris tonight," and she smiled at him. "We'll make love."

"What was all that?" He nodded up the avenue.

"A celebration, *mon chéri*, a celebration. You are my man. A wonderful big man." And she thought to herself with great satisfaction, *yes, a wonderful big puppy of a man.*

Sandrine took Jim's arm in her own arm and leaned her head into his shoulder and said, "Over there."

The couple walked along the sidewalk under the elm trees towards the tall Obelisk standing in the center of the magnificently broad Place de la Concorde, the Obelisk and fountains brightly floodlit against the dark sky. Sandrine said, "It's like walking across the stage of the Paris Opéra house and we're the dancers."

The couple continued across the square towards Pont de la Concorde, the bridge spanning the river. Looking across the river they could see the floodlit colonnade of the Palais Bourbon, home of the Chamber of Deputies. Reaching the bridge they started to walk across. Halfway over Sandrine tugged Jim to a stop and said, "Turn around. I want you to see the sight."

The couple looked across the blaze of light, the beautiful water sprays glowing white as they cascaded from the fountains, the floodlit façades of the ministry of marine on the right and the Hotel Crillon on the left, and up the brightly lit Rue Royale to the majestic Madeleine church sitting high on its pedestal, its brightly-lit Greek columns basking in front of the deeply shadowed portico.

Sandrine murmured softly to Jim, "I want to be French forever. I hope you understand."

"I do."

They continued across the bridge, past the Palais Bourbon, and up the crowd-packed Boulevard St.-Germain until they reached Place St.-Germain-de-Prés, the nearby cafés overflowing with festive revelers. They turned and walked over to Place St.-Sulpice and then up through the narrow streets of an old neighborhood until Sandrine said, "Ah, here is Rue Vaugirard, your street."

They crossed the street and walked along the sidewalk next to a high stone-wall, the Palais Luxembourg and the Luxembourg Gardens on the other side behind closed gates. Just past the gardens, Rue Vaugirard narrowed into a lane with high apartment buildings on each side. Halfway down the block they turned into the entranceway of the Hotel de Lisbonne and stopped in the small courtyard. Sandrine had been correct; the hotel was deserted, quiet as an empty church.

Jim said, "My room is up on the fourth floor."

Sandrine responded, "I've only been over here to see Sarah; she's on the third floor."

They walked up the stairs and went down to Jim's room and went in. They walked into the middle of the room, a pale light coming through the chintz curtains over the windows.

Sandrine came up to him in the soft darkness and undid the buttons of his shirt and pulled it off of him. Then she said, "This time you do the undressing," and she presented herself to him. He removed her blouse, then her skirt, pulled her slip up over her outstretched arms, and then knelt before her and slid her underdrawers down. She stepped out one foot at a time. She walked over and slid under the covers.

He stood next to the bed, took off his trousers and then his underpants and slid into the bed next to Sandrine, feeling the coolness of her smooth skin against his as he settled in.

"*Mon amour,*" she whispered as she kissed him. Then she slowly pushed his head and mouth down over her upturned breast and murmured, "Uhm." They entwined and drifted off together into raptures of their own creation.

In the dark gray before dawn, Sandrine nudged Jim awake and whispered, "They're back." They could hear the worn-out revelers saying their last goodbyes to one another as they came up the stairs and peeled off on the different floors for their respective rooms.

In the morning, Sandrine awoke and lightly shook a deeply sleeping Jim, one of her favorite things in a man, she thought, "I'm going to go out and get some coffee and a baguette. I'll be back in a few minutes."

"Whatever you say, dear."

She got up and put on her clothes while laughing to herself, *he domesticates easily.*

As she walked down the stairs she heard a door open along the third-floor landing and saw Sarah step out in a dressing gown. She walked up to Sandrine.

"So you were here. We didn't know where you had gone."

Sandrine smiled and laughed, "It was a night for love," then almost jokingly added, "He's not a hayseed anymore."

Sarah's eyes went wide with wonder, "You didn't," and she let out a little laugh, "You did." Once again Sarah was a little envious of young French women's ability to dip into affairs and then step out of them without losing sight of their eventual goal of husband, hearth, and children. This ability to sequence one's love life was so utterly foreign to the striving respectability of American middle class life, at least in the outwardly middle-class towns of middle America where she grew up, where grandmothers and mothers groomed daughters to believe sex began the night the wedding dress came off. *Yes, it was so different here.*

Sarah looked inquisitively at Sandrine, standing there expectantly, "Was there something else?"

Sandrine looked evenly at Sarah, reflective, then like a small girl she lightly said, "Yes, there was. There was something else. *Vraiment.* Really." Then she made a small curtsey to Sarah, turned, and continued down the stairs, smiling to herself as she went.

Sarah watched her cross the courtyard with her eyes and pondered: *yes, Sandrine had indeed taken another path. May be Toulouse is not as far away from Iowa as I thought.* She smiled and turned back to her room with a sense of almost maternal satisfaction.

Sitting at the small table in his room, Jim looked over at Sandrine sitting in the other chair, "Tonight is the going away dinner for Bob and Sarah Tompkins. At La Closerie des Lilas. Everyone will be there."

Sandrine simply answered, "I saw Sarah on my way out for the baguette. I am sad to see her go back to America, but I know that is what she really wants."

Jim nodded, "Speak to her?"

Sandrine answered, "A little." She continued, "This afternoon we'll go to the Luxembourg Gardens, afterwards lunch at a little café I know. Then we can go to my flat, *mon chéri.* I want you to see it."

She took a bite of bread and chewed and looked at him. Then she said, "I've never let any man come to my apartment before." She laughed, "You're the first."

He gave a half-amused smile, not quite knowing how to accept Sandrine's experience with bedroom pleasures.

She crinkled her nose and said, "I think may be you will be there a lot, if you like?"

He nodded his head in agreement, his only doubt that of a Mid-Westerner who could find no imperfection in this perfect goddess of a young woman. Then he smiled.

Sandrine quickly darted in, "What are you thinking?"

Jim expansively answered, smiling, "Some one in Chicago is paying a boy from Iowa to be in Paris. Who would believe?"

She laughed, "Let's get ready to go."

Later in the morning, Jim and Sandrine walked down Rue Vaugirard, crossed the street, and entered the Luxembourg Gardens through the large wrought-iron gate on the eastern side. They walked under the spreading plane trees to a parapet overlooking the Palais du Luxembourg, once the palace of Marie de Medici and now the home of the French Senate. They turned and walked along a semicircular line of statues.

Sandrine said, "These are queens of France. I like to walk along the terrace and look at them. They are my friends."

Jim laughed and said, "Do they speak to you?"

She turned and looked at him, "Of course they speak to me. They remind me of the duty and the opportunity to take my place in the great stream of French history, that I am part of the *patrie*—the homeland. I think women are more important in France than in the Protestant countries; we are not, how shall I say, viewed as 'fallen' here. Our sensuality is celebrated."

Jim let out his breath, "I'll say."

They walked across the gravel pathway and looked over the *grand bassin* and watched the children and old men set their small boats sailing across the wind-ruffled waters of the large circular pool.

Sandrine looked reflective and said, "May be when you are an old man you can set your boat to sail across this pond." She turned and looked up at him, "With our grandchildren."

Jim speculatively ventured, "In that case, may be in a few years you can push your baby pram along these walks."

She turned to him, pleased, and said, "*Peut-être.*" Perhaps.

She continued looking across the pond and watching the small children and old men. Then she said, "I know a nice little café up on Rue du Cherche-Midi."

Jim said, "Let's go." They walked out through the west side of the gardens and continued west several blocks to a street corner on Rue du Cherche-Midi where a little café overlooked the intersection. They took two seats behind a small round table on the shady side of the *terrasse.* A waiter came and they ordered a small bottle of wine and two *salades niçoises.*

Sandrine asked, "Where do you want your newspaper career to go? Be an editor like Monsieur Mac?"

As Sandrine watched, she saw that the bantering sunflower from Iowa had turned truly serious, even reflective. She smiled inwardly; she thought she would see that someday. He said, "International politics. Be a foreign correspondent. Write those big stories datelined the capitals of Europe. Wear a trench coat," and he laughed.

She replied, "Well, you're getting a start."

He turned to her, "Thanks to you, a great start. Writing anything from the Quai D'Orsay is a big thrill."

She said, a trace of hurt in her voice, "I'm not just a door opener for you, am I?"

He looked down at this glass and with upturned eyes looked directly across the table at her, dead serious, "Something more? Life companion? My queen of France? Something like that. You're going to have to kick me out, not the other way round."

She smiled warmly, "I like that. Yes, I like that."

They bantered on, sometimes serious, sometimes laughing, a sense of a future assured coming over the two of them.

Sandrine and Jim walked down Rue du Cherche-Midi, across a small square and into a narrow street with a stone gutter running down the center. At the far end Jim could see the little cobblestoned street intersect with the broad sunlit

Boulevard St.-Germain. The street was in a picturesque old-world quarter sitting right next to the big modern boulevard.

Sandrine said, "This is my street. Rue du Dragon. Some of the shops date back two hundred years."

They walked up to the front door of an apartment building on the west side of the street; Sandrine opened the door, and they walked into the foyer. An old woman dressed in black came out of her ground-floor flat and Sandrine said cheerfully, "Madame, this is *mon petit ami.*" Boyfriend. "He will be coming to visit me."

Jim smiled. He was pleased with the sound of *mon petit ami.* Pleased that he would be coming to visit.

The old woman smiled and said, "*Bonjour, Monsieur.*"

Sandrine turned to Jim and said, "Come on. I'm up on the third floor. We have an *ascenseur* here. Very modern. We can ride."

Reaching the third floor, they walked down the hall and she opened the door to a two-room flat with two large windows looking out over the street. Ornate wrought-iron balustrades fronted the windows.

Jim said, "This isn't a dormer?" referring to the ubiquitous rooftop garrets in the attic spaces of many apartment buildings.

"No, this building was built after the war. There are no garrets for starving artists here. They starve somewhere else. It is a wonderful when the sun comes through the windows in the morning; better than on the lower floors I think." She turned and looked at him, "You'll see."

Jim looked at the pleasant soft afternoon light reflecting from the building across the street that came through the open windows; the curtains were pulled back to the side.

Sandrine said, "It is modern. It has its own water closet. Not down the hall."

Jim said, "Very nice."

"My mother, my grandmother, and my aunts have provided for me. I am fortunate. They are like the queens in the garden."

She turned to him, "We will come back here after the dinner. For the night."

He smiled.

"But right now, I am sending you back to your room so you can get ready for tonight. I need to go see Irène about a lunch date, then I will meet you at La Closerie des Lilas."

He smiled again, stepped up to her, took her in his arms, and kissed her, "See you then." He let her go and walked over to the door, turned and looked at her, then went out and took the *ascenseur* down to the ground floor.

In the evening twilight, Jim walked up Boulevard St.-Michel towards Boulevard du Montparnasse, a little late for the Tompkins' going away bash. Entering from the sidewalk he saw tables pushed together on the gardened *terrasse* and a large group of boisterous Americans whopping it up. Spying an empty chair nearby, he walked over and started to push it into the group of celebrating journalists.

Mac stood up, lifted a glass high in his direction, and said, "Hear, hear. Farm boy is not a hayseed anymore. How will we keep them down on the farm after they've seen Parée?"

Jim's face went blank with astonishment, *huh?* Then red with embarrassment.

The other men jumped up and lifted glasses in his direction, "Hear, hear. The farm boy meets France. Tell us about last night!"

Jim blushed and stammered, "Whaddaya mean?" He looked over beseechingly at Sarah, still seated and calmly sipping a glass of white wine, "Sarah? How could you?"

She looked up, putting on her best air of sophistication, "Oh, Jim, are you talking about your ride in the horse-drawn carriage last night? Of course that's nothing but what us Ann Arbor girls were doing in those rumble seats while we were being debauched up at the big university. Remember how you told me that? My ex-little Hayseed. Remember? Should I hum a few bars of *Wolverine Rag* for you?" Her dark eyes danced in merriment and she said, "Boys will always be boys."

She took a sip of her wine, "I always liked the rumble seat wisecrack best. I really did. But you my boy, my little ex-Hayseed, in the back of a horse-drawn carriage with a French girl going down the Champs Élysées on Bastille Day," and she swept her hand past the joshing and drinking men standing around the tables and looking on attentively, "I guarantee you will be immortalized by our little Greek chorus in the drinking stories of Montparnasse for decades to come," and she laughed and said, "Come sit down and have a drink with me."

He sat down next to Sarah and she said, "What you did for Bob and me was wonderful. Sandrine knows that. She saw through you, too. I told her about the country boy slicking the slickers. She said, '*Voila*. That's him.' I'm going to tell you something else, too, she always told me, 'Never an American.' So you're something special."

Jim looked down, "This is all a dream. To be here in Paris. With people like you," and he swept his hand by the talking newspapermen, "and with her."

Then Mac jumped up, "Here she comes." Sandrine was walking along the sidewalk, smiling, coming up to the group.

Rewrite bolted up and called back over his shoulder towards a waiter, "Champagne for the show girl." The waiter waved and headed for the long zinc bar. The other men stood up as did Sarah.

Mac swung his arm and the journalists broke into a rousing rendition of *La Marseillaise*. Sandrine walked towards them.

Bewildered, Jim stayed seated, then with dawning realization he put his head in his hands, face blushing red, and peeked through his fingers as Sandrine came over to him.

She waved at the men, leaned down and kissed Jim on the cheek, and said to him, "Come on stand up. They're singing *La Marseillaise*. You're supposed to stand." She put her arm under his and pulled him up. With her left arm she made a swinging motion and started to sing along, nudging Jim in the ribs, "Come on. Sing."

Smiling broadly, Mac looked over at a group of Frenchmen staring at them from the other side of the restaurant and shouted to his friends, "Those are the Surrealists. They think we're crazy. Imagine that." Everyone laughed at the wise-crack and then they finished up with one last chorus of the French anthem.

The waiter came up with a big bottle of champagne, popped the cork to cheers, and poured Sandrine a glass, then offered it around to a half-dozen other upturned glasses from the thirsty journalists.

Mac looked at Sandrine, raised his glass, and toasted, "Madame Potter."

Sandrine beamed.

Everyone nodded in agreement. Sarah smiled warmly at Sandrine.

The revelry continued into the evening. Finally Sandrine leaned over to Jim, "*Chez moi.* Now?"

Jim stood up, offered her his hand, and the couple walked outside and across the small square. They started down the wide tree-lined sidewalk of Avenue de l'Observatoire, passing the large fountain, walking along arm-in-arm towards the Luxembourg Gardens. At the closed iron gates, they turned and walked through the dark summer stillness of empty streets to the little flat on Rue du Dragon.

July 16. Monday morning. Sandrine came up the stairway to the second floor of the Quai D'Orsay, said hello to the receptionist, and walked into the office of Madame Bardoux. Sandrine brightly inquired, "Is Monsieur de Davignon in?"

Madame Bardoux looked up, quite businesslike, and with not a trace of a smile, she responded, "Yes, I believe his office door is open." She looked back down at the papers on her desk.

Sandrine replied casually, "Thank you." She turned and walked down the hall and thought to herself: Yes, surprising how they always know. She smiled. Another small lesson.

Coming up to the door of Monsieur de Davignon's office, she rapped lightly with her knuckles and asked sweetly, "Can I come in?"

Davignon stood up, reached out his hand in a handshake, and said, "How nice to see you, Sandrine." He held his arm in invitation for her to take a seat.

Sandrine sat down, smoothed her skirt, and said brightly, "Philippe," she turned and looked over her shoulder to see if anyone could eavesdrop on this familiarity and then continued, "I wanted to explain to you a change in my personal circumstances."

Davignon looked concerned at what this development might be, obviously something affecting him. He nodded for her to continue.

Sandrine said, "I started something Saturday night with someone else, a beginning of another chapter. When a new chapter begins, then an old chapter must end, no matter how delightful."

Davignon looked momentarily hurt as the realization sunk in, then he replied, "It was always destined to be that way, Sandrine." He smiled warmly, "I, of course, understand," he added with well-practiced gallantry.

Sandrine, feeling slightly confessional, looked down at her lap, "I had always said 'never an American,' but the friendship ripened into something that I felt was truly my own little creation."

Davignon nodded sagely, "Of course."

Sandrine continued, "He, Jim, as you probably can guess, might not understand about us. He's from Iowa."

Davignon leaned back and, with a slightly amused look on his face, said, "Of course, Iowa's way out there to the west, beyond one, may be two, of those big rivers they have in America."

Sandrine added agreeably, "Yes, near what they call 'Injin Territory.'"

Davignon nodded wisely in his understanding, "Yes, primitive. Protestant, possibly Puritan, I believe."

Sandrine's shoulders relaxed and she said pleasantly, "You do understand."

Davignon dropped his chin in agreement, "Of course. We French are people of the world."

Sandrine asked hopefully, "I very much would like to stay friends, and I hope you continue to be helpful to Jim. He really appreciates your interviews."

Davignon turned slightly businesslike, "Of course. It is been very much in the ministry's interest to be able to explain our policies and thinking so successfully in the English-speaking press. Of course we will continue our professional relationships."

She smiled and said, "I am having lunch with your wife and Irène Friday. She is interested in Irène's dress shop. I look forward to speaking with her then."

Davignon beamed, "She will be delighted to continue your friendship."

Sandrine added, "Irène is like a sister to me. I know you will both like her."

Davignon caught the word 'both' and nodded in thoughtful agreement, a small delight of possible anticipation. He stood up and walked around the desk to escort Sandrine out into the hallway. In closing he said, "Sandrine, I look forward to following your career. You may not really believe it, but your relationship has been something special to me. There may be times in the future when we might again be closer."

She looked at him, looked into those dark eyes, and saw the sincerity, that distant "if" that might be way out there in the future—someday, somewhere.

She said to him softly, "Yes, may be it was all a little bit more than an adventure." She looked up and smiled warmly at him, turned, and walked down the hall.

Sandrine came up to Madame Bardoux's door. She rolled her fingers on the door in a little drum roll and asked, "Can I come in?"

Madame Bardoux looked up and said, "Of course."

Sandrine stepped just inside the door and said, "I wanted to explain about my relationship with my American colleague Jim Potter."

Madame Bardoux replied with a businesslike inquiry, "Yes?"

Sandrine replied in simple explanation, "Jim and I are, of course, colleagues on the American paper. We work together. But in our private lives, now," and she lingered on the word, "he has become *mon petit ami*—boyfriend. We are of course quite close."

Madame Bardoux's expression relaxed and she smiled, "Of course." In the French way she presumed.

Sandrine continued, "I did not want this close personal relationship between two people you deal with professionally to cause you any awkwardness. So I thought it would be best to explain."

Madame Bardoux's eyes lit up, "Awkwardness? To me? Why no." Madame Bardoux smiled inwardly and thought to herself, "What a nicely presented explanation. Cleverly diplomatic." She mused that one could see Monsieur de Davignon's interest, if not enchantment, with the young woman. Men. French men. If only foreign affairs would give way so easily to such charm!

Madame Bardoux stood up and came around the desk and escorted Sandrine to the door, "Thank you very much for sharing with me." She turned and looked Sandrine straight in the eye, "I believe your judgment is going to be richly rewarded, Sandrine. Please consider me among your closest friends."

Sandrine smiled and replied, "Thank you. Your opinion means so much to me." Sandrine turned and walked past the receptionist and started down the staircase.

Tuesday, July 17. Sandrine came up out of the Metro and hurried into the train station in the early morning brightness of what promised to be a hot summer day. She had left Jim sleeping in her apartment on Rue du Dragon. He had worked late the night before. It had been a rather exciting weekend for him, she thought to herself, highly bemused as she remembered the weekend's many events.

She quickly walked through the entrance hall, bright sunlight coming through the glass roof over the train tracks, and out onto the long concrete platform where the boat train to Cherbourg waited. In three hours time, the train would reach the *Gare Maritime Transatlantique* in Cherbourg and the passengers, and their baggage, would be efficiently transferred to an ocean liner heading for New York.

Sandrine could see at the far end of the platform, and at the head of a long line of railway cars, a big black locomotive wheezing out clouds of billowing white steam. Time for departure, she thought.

Sandrine walked along the platform, searching the windows of the railway cars. Up ahead, an arm waved at her from an open window. Sandrine raced over and looked up at Sarah, both hands on top of the lowered window, smiling out at her.

"So nice you could come and see us off," she said and she pointed at her husband Bob standing next to her.

"I wanted to thank you for everything you have done for me. I will never forget you," Sandrine shouted up to the open window.

"Sandrine, someday you will come to America. You will always have a welcome home with us. Remember that, if things go badly in Europe."

"I will."

A whistle sounded. Sandrine watched more steam billow from the locomotive at the open end of the station. The railway carriage started to move. Sandrine stepped back. She watched the railway car pull away. She waved until it was out of sight.

Friday, July 20. Sandrine looked out from under the awning of the café and across the brightly lit stone surface of Place St.-Germain-de-Prés to the church with its single stone bell tower reaching into the blue summer sky. She turned back and spoke to Irène sitting across from her at the little round marble-topped table, "I'm so glad you could come for lunch."

Irène smiled, "I appreciate very much the introduction to Madame de Davignon."

Sandrine nodded her head and continued, almost absentmindedly, "If it was just an affair with Philippe, may be…" Her voice trailed off. Then she looked at Irène, "You really feel the heat of his adoration for you when you're with him." Then she turned wistful, a trace of not-quite-understanding-something crossing her brow, "He is utterly devoted to her…" She looked down into her coffee cup, "She is very sweet, very polite, she looks at you like you are her daughter… or her younger sister…your friend."

Irène looked over the top of her coffee cup at Sandrine, "There are many different kinds of adventure in Paris."

Sandrine looked at her, "Yes, so you have told me." She made a small laugh, "Malka listens to you with wide-eyed fascination." Then Sandrine turned serious and said softly, a note of thankfulness lingering in her tone, "The Davignons have both been exceedingly nice to me."

Irène looked at Sandrine thoughtfully, "I like her. She fascinates me. And she is interested in my couture business. Genuinely. I want to like them both. This is an adventure I shall follow wherever it goes."

Sandrine saw the flash of excitement in Irène's pale blue eyes, the sense of longing in her face. Yes, Irène was a real adventurer. Sandrine felt comfortable with her introduction of Irène to the Davignons.

Again, Sandrine looked across the square and said, "Here she comes."

Irène turned and watched. An elegantly dressed woman, spare in figure, wearing a bright summer print dress and wearing a wide hat upturned to one side and sloping away casually on the other, was walking towards them. The woman saw them, smiled, and gaily waved. Sandrine waved back.

Anne de Davignon came up, both Sandrine and Irène rose, and then the three women sat down. Sandrine said, "You met my friend Irène at Longchamp."

Anne smiled brightly, "Yes, we were all going to visit your dress shop over on Rue du Cherche-Midi. I hope we still can?" She looked at both young women expectantly.

Sandrine said, "You can go with Irène. I have to go over to the newspaper this afternoon." Then Sandrine said light-heartedly, "I have a big new American boyfriend to keep an eye on."

Anne turned and said lightly, "Yes, Philippe told me. We wish you well with him."

Irène interposed, "We can go over to the shop and I can show you what we are doing. If you want, I can get some measurements of you there." Then she added, "Of course, usually I do fittings and take measurements in the privacy of the client's home."

Anne nodded her head in understanding, "Yes, of course, that would be best."

The waiter brought a coffee and set it down in front of Anne. She turned and smiled, "Thank you."

Anne looked over at Irène, "Yes, that would be very nice. You could come over tomorrow afternoon."

Irène said, "That would be excellent."

Anne looked at Irène and added inquiringly, "Yes. Then afterwards, if you like, you could join my husband and me at our country home for the weekend?"

Irène's eyes brightened and she nodded her head in polite agreement, "I would like that very much. I am sure we will have an enchanting time."

Anne smiled a pleasant smile of satisfaction and turned to Sandrine, "You are always everything Philippe says you are."

Sandrine said, "Thank you, Madame de Davignon."

"Please, Anne." She turned to Irène, "You, too, please call me Anne."

Irène nodded in pleasant agreement.

Sandrine said by way of conclusion, "Let me suggest that the three of us get together at the beginning of August. Let's say after the last of the shows exhibiting the winter lines. I will be writing stories every day."

Anne responded with approval, "A delightful idea."

Irène interposed, "May I suggest the little bistro across from our shop on Rue du Cherche-Midi?"

Anne said with a light touch of decision that came naturally to her, "Of course, we will meet there. Sounds so girl-like."

Sandrine quickly agreed, "That would be excellent. Shortly thereafter, I hope to go visit my family in Toulouse. Where I was a little girl."

Irène asked, "What about Jim?"

Sandrine laughed and replied, "I'm leaving him with Malka and Pascal. Continue his political education."

Sandrine stood up, "Please stay seated, *Mesdames.* Have a good time today. We'll lunch in August." Sandrine turned, made her way out through the tables to the sidewalk, and then started down Rue Bonaparte towards the river.

Country Weekend

July 21, 1934. Saturday afternoon. The large touring car drove down a wide and heavily tree shaded street in the wealthy suburb of Neuilly, stopped at the corner, and then turned right onto the even-wider Avenue de Neuilly and headed west. In the front seat was a driver with a chauffeur's cap on. Seated next to him was a prim woman dressed in the black dress and white collar of a well-appointed maid. Behind the pair was a glass partition separating the driver's compartment from the saloon in the rear.

Behind the glass partition, sitting on a jump seat, was Irène, smartly dressed and wearing a Peter Pan hat with a feather rakishly angled back. She looked with keen interest out of one window, and then the other. She faced rearwards towards Philippe and Anne de Davignon, who were sitting in a deeply upholstered rear seat looking idly out the windows. They had made the drive many times before.

Irène looked out the rear window of the touring car at Avenue de Neuilly receding into the distance until it merged into the even wider Avenue de la Grand Armeé, which stretched up a gentle slope into the far distance. At the top of the slope, almost floating on the horizon, was the imposing Arc de Triomphe, a reminder of the glories of victories long past.

Anne spoke to Irène, "We will be coming to the Pont de Neuilly in a minute. The bridge across the river was opened by Louis Fifteen with great ceremony over a century-and-a-half ago; he was the first to cross it in his carriage."

Irène said to Anne, "You have a great command of the history of the *ancien regime*, but you seem not to care so much for recent history."

Anne replied faintly, "Yes, of course, you are right. History has hardly been much good since." Then she added emphatically, " Guillotining the queen! My God! Where does it end?"

Irène agreed, "Yes, good manners and civility went with the grand manners then. It's all vanished now."

Anne nodded wistfully, "Yes." Then she sighed and said rather absently as an afterthought, "The Second Empire had its moments."

Irène smiled in agreement.

Philippe mirrored the smile; his eyes alight with merriment. He nodded his head towards Irène in approval, pleased with the understanding tone of her remark. Clearly, Irène understood his wife.

Irène turned and saw the river out the window.

Anne said, "You can see the Île du Pont on either side of the bridge as we cross."

Irène gazed at the long sliver of the island—Île du Pont—in the middle of the river with its tall trees.

Anne continued, "On the other side of the river is the town of Courbevoie, once a pleasant village but now a run-down industrial town of shuttered factories. We will go up the main street, Avenue de la Défense. Situated in the middle of the avenue is the Monument de la Défense de Paris, a bronze statue group by Barrias celebrating the defense of Paris. Why, I don't know since the Prussians got in anyway, I think, for a parade, I believe. Am I right, Philippe?"

Philippe answered casually, "Correct, my dear."

The big touring car crossed the bridge and proceeded slowly up the Avenue de la Défense and past the famous statues. Irène looked out the window at the decrepit buildings.

Anne continued, "To our left, over there," she nodded with her head towards the south, "is Puteaux, another run-down industrial suburb which in addition to shuttered factories has old munitions plants and chemical and dye works. Dreadful smells. The war never ends." She turned up her nose. "But we are not taking the river road today. We will go onto Chatou, then cross the river again, and out to the west. Our country house is about an hour away."

Irène looked at the passing ugliness of the industrial landscape, a rusting modernism situated in the bucolic forested lands of France.

Irène said, "It is sad. You see the Depression out here so much more clearly than you do in Paris."

"Yes, you do," Anne responded desultorily.

She thought for a moment. Then she nodded in the direction of the maid sitting primly up in the front seat, idly chatting with the chauffeur. Anne said, "We have all cut back. Now we get along with a maid-of-all-work. In the past, of course, there were different maids for different tasks. So much to do in a *grande maison*. But the parlor maids, of course, would not cook, and the personal maids would not, of course, clean." Then she sighed a deep sigh, "Of course, none of them would ever really clean."

Philippe smiled and listened to his wife's little tale of woe with bemused tolerance.

Anne came to her conclusion, "Of course, Josette has been nothing but a find for us. And now she has married Jean, the chauffeur. So we are blessed with domestic harmony."

Anne looked out the window and said absently, "Yes, the Depression. It has had its sacrifices."

Irène listened with amused interest and responded to Anne with seemingly great empathy, "Yes, of course. If it gets worse, what next? *Vin ordinaire?*"

The jest brought Anne quickly to a certain sharpness, she sat up, a lovely pout spreading across her face while she looked askance at Irène, her dark eyes flashing with humor. She took a quick glance at her husband, his face given to a wry smile, his satisfaction with Irène ripening. *She would be beyond expectation.* Anne's eyes met Philippe's, her laughing eyes dancing in front of his with hopeful allure. Philippe always liked to see that look in his wife, that special zest.

Irène watched Anne and Philippe and sensed that she was being brought into their little circle of private delights. She settled into warm contentment and relaxed expectation. She waited on Anne's response.

Anne looked back at Irène. She fixed her shining eyes directly onto Irène's eyes, seemingly grasping them to her own will, "My dear, I would hope not. That would simply be," and she searched for words, "a life without social distinctions, true poverty. *Vin ordinaire?*"

Irène smiled in warm acceptance of Anne's camaraderie, "Yes, wouldn't it."

The three sat quietly and watched the countryside pass by.

The touring car drove down a tree-shrouded gravel country lane, thick green woods on either side of the roadway. The car stopped in front of an iron gate and the chauffeur got out and swung the black gate open. He came back and got behind the driver's seat and drove the car forward onto a brick driveway that swept in a semicircle before a covered portico in front of a large stone country home. The car came to a halt.

Anne said to Irène, "We are here. Henri will help with the baggage," and she nodded at an older man in rough clothes who came off the portico to help the chauffeur with the baggage.

Anne, Irène, and Philippe got out of the car. Philippe stood and took a long circular look around the yard and house and pronounced, "Everything seems fine." He turned to Irène, "Henri does a great job keeping the property up."

Anne turned to the maid, "Josette, would you please show Irène to the little bedroom. Henri can follow with her luggage."

Josette smiled, "Yes, Madame."

Anne turned to Irène, "You can follow Josette and she will show you to your room. It is just next to the master bedroom. Both rooms share the *petit jardin*." The small garden.

Henri picked up the baggage that Irène pointed to. Irène turned and followed Josette through entranceway, into the vestibule, and followed her down a long hallway. At the second to last doorway, Josette opened the door and ushered Irène into the pleasant bedroom. Off to the far side was a door to a small bathroom. French doors opened up onto a stone verandah surrounded by plants and shrubs and enclosed by a tall brick wall creating a sense of utterly serene privacy. Another door was closed and Irène presumed it led to the master bedroom.

Henri walked in and put Irène's luggage on a small folding luggage stand next to the armoire. He tipped his hat and sort of backed out of the room.

Josette asked gently of Irène, "Let me put your things away."

Irène replied kindly, "Why, yes, that would be fine, Josette."

Josette opened Irène's luggage and took clothes out and hung them in the armoire while putting other things in a chest of drawers. She took out toiletries and carried them into the bathroom. Irène followed.

Josette said, "You have many nice things, Madame."

Irène asked, "Could I get you to call me Irène?"

Josette replied, "It would be better not to."

Irène smiled, "We will of course be friends."

Josette smiled warmly, "*Bien sûr*." Of course.

Josette turned and walked towards the door, turning and looking over her shoulder, "If you need anything, please call. I will either be in the kitchen or in our rooms, which are behind the kitchen."

Irène walked over to the dresser and looked at the little vases, the small dishes, and the family pictures in their little frames. In particular she looked at the pictures of the Davignons with a little girl, first as a toddler and then there was a picture for almost each year up until the girl was about six. Then the pictures shifted to simple portraits of the girl alone. The most recent one showed a pretty blond girl of about ten. A darling little girl, Irène thought. Possibly this was the niece. Yes, Anne would be most fond of her. And yes, she knew, just the mention of the girl brought a light to Philippe's eyes. She could see a resemblance.

Irène turned and started to dress for dinner.

Josette cleared the last of the dinner dishes away and then poured coffee. She turned to Anne, "Anything else, Madame?"

Anne replied thoughtfully, "No, that will be all for tonight, Josette. Oh, one thing, could you have Jean get the newspapers in the morning for breakfast."

Josette replied, "Of course," and then she did a small curtsey and retired.

Irène sipped at her coffee.

Philippe said rather matter-of-factly, "I will go to the study and work on my papers." He stood up, picked up the saucer with the coffee cup on it, smiled at Irène, and turned and walked towards his study.

Anne took a sip of coffee and said mildly, "He has so many papers. The foreign situation is a sea of worry."

Irène replied, "I only know that Berlin has turned wooden to fashion. Good for us in Paris, if you are couturier. I guess fashion can only thrive where there is freedom."

Anne looked at her, "I had never thought of that. It is probably true."

Irène changed the subject, "I have my measuring tapes with me. We could take your measurements, if you like, for the new outfits. I could draw a bath for you?"

Anne warmed and replied smilingly, "Yes, let's do. That would be nice."

The two women set their coffee cups in saucers, stood up, and walked out of the dining room.

In the last light of the twilight, Irène lay on her side in the middle of the spacious bed speaking softly to Anne lying next to her. Anne idly brushed strands of Irène's hair behind her ear and whispered, "I so enjoyed the bath, the warmth and the sudsy bubbles. It was like being a little girl again bathing with my sister."

Irène reached across and caressed Anne's hair off her cheek, "Me, too. You are milk-white and creamy." Irène heard Philippe come in the room.

He sat on the edge of the bed behind Irène and patted her on the shoulder with his palm and then he moved it down along her arm in a soft stroking motion. He reached over and brushed his wife's cheek. Then he said softly to both of them, "Turtledoves," then a little greeting, "*Bon soir.*" He leaned over both of their faces, "Ready to sing?" Anne looked up and smiled. Irène turned her head up, looked at Philippe, smiled weakly, and nodded in soft acquiescence.

He stood up and took off his kimono and draped it over a chair. He went back to the bed and pulled back the covers and slipped in behind Irène.

Irène felt the scent of his cologne mingle with the fragrance of Anne's Chanel. A sweet mixture of olfactory sensation overlay the slightly pungent odor from the bath soap that she and Anne had so thoroughly scrubbed into their skins in the bath. She let her head lay relaxed on the pillow. She felt his large hand caress her shoulder, he nuzzled her neck just under her ear, nibbled on the skin. She felt the sensual delight ripple across her skin like a soft breeze, the sensation was like little cats paws stepping down her belly, and then there was the tingling inside her deepest recesses. Now she understood: the presence of the man made everything feel so right. Yes, first the two women swirl lightly in a sea of fragrant femininity, and then the dusky male presence lights the first embers of passion. She smiled to herself: of course, they knew the power of this ritual.

Irène glided along in this mixed sea of sensual pleasure. She felt the flutter of small fingers across her body, the light pulling of long nails against the grain of her skin. Then she felt a large hand gently reach under her upper knee and slowly raise her leg. His belly pushed against her buttocks. Then she felt him, softly here and there, then poised, then…she gasped. She clenched Anne's upper arm with her left hand, turned her face into the pillow…and… with her last sentient thought let herself go into the moment…pleasurably… later wildly.

TRANSITIONS

July 26, 1934, Thursday afternoon. The secretary came into the office and handed the *chef* several dispatches. "News," she said.

The *chef* said, "Thank you. It is late. You can leave now."

"*Merci, Monsieur,*" she replied. She turned and went back to her desk, picked up her handbag, and departed, leaving the *chef* to his solitary labors.

The *chef* looked at the dispatches. "Ah," thought the *chef*, "François Coty died last night. Interesting. At the Chateau Louveciennes."

The *chef* leaned back and blew cigarette smoke up towards the ceiling. He watched the white clouds swirl. He recalled: yes, at the beautiful chateau where Monsieur had met with Colonel de La Rocque last February. Yes, the wily colonel had out maneuvered Monsieur, the would-be fascist strongman. Easily. The *chef* smiled.

What about Colonel de La Rocque? He pulled a file in front of him from the side of the desk. Reports from around France indicated that the *Croix-de-Feu* now had millions of solid middle class supporters.

He flipped some papers in the file: a typewritten report indicated that de La Rocque was on close personal terms with Premier Doumergue. The *chef* read on: the colonel was on friendly terms with a half dozen or more cabinet ministers, all very reliable old men from the conservative side. Of course, thought the *chef*. One could overhear the café gossips with their playful little question and answer: "Why is France ruled by seventy-five-year-olds?" And then the riposte, "Because all the men of eighty are dead." He smiled; Colonel de La Rocque was truly a supporter of the old order.

Continuing, the *chef* read the political summary: the colonel wants to strengthen the executive power of the premier while giving the President of the Republic the power to dissolve the National Assembly. Almost regal, thought the *chef*. Colonel de La Rocque was always a very interesting Royalist, he mused. Sometimes almost a republican, he thought. He laughed inwardly and set the file aside.

August 3, Friday. Jim walked down the marbled corridor of the second floor of the foreign ministry to the office of Monsieur de Davignon. He knocked lightly, looked in, and saw Davignon working on some papers. The diplomat looked up, smiled, and with a hand made a motion for Jim to come in and sit down.

Jim opened up, "Our paper would like to find out what a highly placed foreign ministry source thinks about Acting Prime Minister Stanley Baldwin's remarks to Parliament earlier this week?"

Davignon smiled warmly, "Yes, Mr. Baldwin very clearly said that today the Rhine is where Britain's frontier lies. That is of course the plain truth. These words will become historical."

Jim pondered Davignon's answer and thought to himself, "Baldwin had made an almost a complete turnaround in British policy; Davignon was discreetly polite in his comment." Jim decided to simply ask, "Were you surprised?"

Davignon quickly composed himself, "Surprised? No, it was a logical outcome from Foreign Minister Barthou's London meeting earlier in July. A fruit of diplomacy." Davignon beamed with satisfaction.

Jim continued, "What is the strategic significance of Baldwin's remarks?"

Davignon replied by way of explanation, "Taken literally, it indicates that France and Britain have the same eastern frontier, the Rhine River. From the French viewpoint, it expresses what may be termed a historic necessity."

Jim moved to the next question, "In practical terms, what does the British statement mean?"

Davignon said simply, "If the German Reichswehr should cross to the western bank of the Rhine, the French government believes that British would join with the French in confronting them and pushing them back to their side of the river."

Davignon leaned forward and said, "Just last week Italian Premier Mussolini rushed a hundred thousand troops to the Brenner Pass to keep the German Nazis out of Austria after the Nazis murdered Austrian Chancellor Dollfuss. The British statement is a similarly powerful deterrent."

Then Davignon leaned back in his chair and said reflectively, "On this twentieth anniversary of the World War, we observe that if such words had been pronounced in July 1914 in the House of Commons by the British government, it is probable that the civilized world would have been spared the cruel trial of the World War."

Jim added, "The proverbial ounce of prevention?"

Davignon firmly replied, "Exactly."

Davignon concluded, "The Italian response to the Austrian situation, and now Stanley Baldwin's declaration, are an important conjunction of events. The cause of peace is greatly strengthened, which is of course Foreign Minister Barthou's never-ending quest."

Davignon sat back and looked thoughtful for a minute, then he turned to Jim, "The British declaration will lead to a string of further successes for our foreign policy this year. Relations between Italy and France are improving. France is the architect for bringing the Soviet Union into the League of Nations in September." He looked at Jim, "That will be a major news event." Jim nodded in assent.

Then Davignon took on a distant gaze: "The state visit by Yugoslavian King Alexander to France in October will be another major diplomatic triumph for Foreign Minister Barthou."

August 6, Monday. Sandrine walked west on Rue du Cherche-Midi and, coming to Rue St.-Romain, turned into the doorway of the little dress shop on the corner. She saw Anne de Davignon and Irène standing together in the front showroom. Sandrine walked in and joined the two women.

Irène was showing Anne items from the fall and winter line. Irène held high a hanger displaying a black linen dress with a bright red belt to Anne's discerning gaze. Then Irène nodded with her head towards the wall, "And a hat to match." Both Sandrine's and Anne's eyes followed Irène's nod towards a hat sitting on a small wooden pedestal on a shelf by the wall. Sandrine and Anne made small nods of understanding: *yes, very stylish.*

Then, hanging the dress back on the rack, Irène continued, "Over here we have a sapphire-blue woolen dress, which goes with those red shoes over there." Both women looked over at the shoes and again nodded their understanding.

Then, by way of conclusion, Irène said, "These outfits are easy to pack and wear, an important feature for today's mobile woman."

Anne said with a touch of weariness, "Yes, there are so many out-of-town invitations these days."

Anne turned to Sandrine and said knowingly, "Wait to you start following your American fiancé to foreign capitals and diplomatic receptions."

Sandrine smiled at the expectation.

Irène then shifted subjects, "I want to show both of you our summer experiment." Then Irène said to Anne, "Sandrine introduced a fashion reporter from the London *Times* to our shop and specifically to this new line of summer apparel for us. The English lady wrote it up. We have been selling ever since. The story made our summer." Irène simply beamed and gave Sandrine the warmest of "thank you" smiles.

Irène walked over to a rack and said, "Right over here." Irène held up a fisherman's jersey fashionably adapted to slim figures. Then she pointed out some white duck shorts and skirts and said, "For the seashore." Moving over to another rack, "These tailored jackets go with the striped cotton pullovers, which are all the rage, while over here we have some rustic-looking colored prints."

Anne looked thoughtful and said, "Yes, I can see that holiday travel is an emerging new market. Your line fits beautifully with the new idea of vacation clothes."

She turned, stretched out both of her arms, and held Irène by both shoulders like a proud mother to a daughter, "I am so pleased for you, Irène. You are wonderfully talented." She looked over at Sandrine, beaming, and asked, "Don't you think so?"

Sandrine said, "Yes, I always admire Irène for striking out on the right path." Sandrine smiled.

Irène lightly addressed both women, saying, "I thought we could have lunch right across the street at the little bistro. They catch the overflow traffic from the Bon Marché."

Anne said pleasantly, "A new adventure. A touch of working class to go with the fisherman's jersey."

Both Irène and Anne clapped hands and looked at Sandrine with little-girl like pleasure. They were both such good friends, thought Sandrine. Yes, everything had worked.

Sandrine added happily, "Yes, and tonight this girl leaves to see her family in Toulouse."

Sandrine saw that the words 'girl' and 'family' seemed to strike a discordant chord with Anne, that she suddenly looked away and took on a distant and distracted air. Sandrine moved to say something, but Irène touched Sandrine lightly on the arm and looked at her with kindly eyes that said *let her be*. Sandrine relaxed; she knew without actually understanding.

August 9, Thursday. In the newsroom, the heat was stifling, a light air came in through open windows, a big circular ceiling fan made slow revolutions. Bill Wilshire sat sprawled at the far end of the horseshoe desk, his chin in the palm of his hand, his legs and feet angled out onto the seat of a nearby chair, his face a mask of resigned disgust and frustration.

Mac blew a ring of smoke out over the desk and said, "Bill, you've pestered every news bureau in Berlin for weeks. It's August. I hear even the Germans are on vacation."

Bill looked pointedly across the desk, "Mac, you know as well as I do that the story is in Berlin. How does a guttersnipe corporal replace Germany's greatest field marshal? Why does the most civilized society in Central Europe give way to the barbarism of hate? What happened after the last war to create this new monstrosity?"

Mac looked thoughtful, "Do you think reporting it will change what is happening?" He knew the answer. He looked inquisitively at Bill.

Bill took a deep breadth, "Probably not. But nothing better—and I mean nothing—will come about if there is not a huge and wide base of true facts upon which better opinions can be formed."

Mac nodded in understanding agreement.

The phone rang. Rewrite picked it up. "Yeah, he's here." Rewrite listened to the receiver for a while. Then he put his hand over the mouthpiece and said to Wilshire, "Bill, some guy in Berlin wants to talk to you." He handed the receiver to Wilshire and pushed the pedestal part of the phone with the mouthpiece in front of the reporter.

Wilshire dropped his feet in a flash, sat up straight, and grabbed at the receiver and the telephone pedestal in one smooth motion. "Hello, yes? Why Arnie, what have you got?"

Wilshire listened, "You bet."

"Hearst and the wire service? That's fine."

"When?"

Wilshire looked over at Mac. Mac nodded his head in slow-motion approval.

"I could leave Paris August 24 on the Berlin Express. Be there Saturday."

Wilshire listened some more, then spoke into the mouthpiece, "Fine. And thank you very much. See you in Berlin."

Wilshire hung the receiver back on its cradle. A look of thankful wonder crossed his face, satisfaction in his eyes.

Rewrite chirped, "Hey, you're going from worst to Hearst. Congratulations on the step down."

Wilshire laughed and leaned back, "But it's in Berlin."

Mac looked momentarily serious, "Bill, if you do the job I think you can do, Herr Goebbels will be in your face and the ministry of propaganda will make you think you have the creeping crud. Then there will be the other boys in the press, the old hands, the ones who don't want to give up the German girl friends, the life in nightclubs, the old decadence. They will 'understand' the new regime, ease back a bit, go along. Then you're going to have to write your own book on working under the nose of the secret police. When you contact a source, are you fingering him for a concentration camp? Lot of tough calls here."

Wilshire looked at Mac evenly, "I know. Shoe leather newspaperman against the modern state ministry of information."

Rewrite chimed in, tugging his arm up and down like pulling on a train whistle, "Whoo, whoo." He pumped his arm up and down again, "Whoo, whoo. Berlin night train. We'll have a going away party at the Gare du Nord. Whoo, whoo."

Friday, August 24, Paris. The taxicab swerved in front of other traffic and pulled up in front of the massive façade of the Gare du Nord. Jim put some coins in the driver's palm as Sandrine opened the door and stepped out. She reached back and grabbed Jim's hand and almost pulled him out onto the sidewalk in her enthusiasm.

She pointed up, "See. The central arch is over a hundred feet high. That statue on top symbolizes the City of Paris; she is of course the most beautiful statue on the cornice. Somewhere over there is the statue for the city of Berlin." She looked at Jim and asked, "Do you think they have a statue of Paris on the Berlin train station?"

Jim flippantly replied, "More likely a gold star on a military map."

Sandrine made a playful scowl, "That's why Bill Wilshire wants to go to Berlin. That's where the story is, he says."

The couple walked through the tall doors. Sandrine said, "This is the grand hall. Let's go over to the *salle de depart* where there's a little platform restaurant and we'll find the going-away party."

They walked under the impossibly high ceiling of the huge enclosure and came upon a small restaurant with a bunch of tables bunched together in front. A raucous group of Americans were quaffing beer and clinking red wine glasses in festive celebration.

Mac saw Sandrine and Jim walk up, "Look. Our girl in Paris is back from Toulouse."

Rewrite chimed in, "See Sandrine. Jim kept trying to go astray while you were away, but we kept him safe and sound."

Sandrine smirked at him, "Malka says something else. At least she saw to his political education."

Mac stood up and said to Jim and Sandrine, "Here, come along with us. We're going to walk Bill and his wife down to their railway carriage. First class with Hearst."

Mac nodded at Bill, who drained his wine glass and stood up. He held his wife's chair as she arose. He went over to a luggage cart and waved at a baggage porter. The whole crowd slowly and boisterously walked down the platform. Stopping at the rear door of a sleeper, Mac clapped Wilshire on the back and said, "Here's where we let you go. I'm sure personal representatives of Herr Goebbels, if not the Führer, will be at Friedrichstrasse Bahnhof to meet you."

Jim turned and said to Sandrine, "Boy, this is a big professional break for Bill. All the world will be watching those dispatches out of Berlin."

Sandrine held his arm and whispered up to him, "I can arrange an interview for you at the ministry of public works. Pascal is hugely interested in the subject of public projects."

Jim laughed, "The only one."

The crowd stood on the platform and waved at Bill Wilshire standing at the rear door of the carriage, holding his wife around the waist, as the train slowly left the station. The Americans watched as the train disappeared down the tracks into the Paris night. They started back down the platform.

Mac and Rewrite came over and walked along with Jim and Sandrine. Mac said gruffly, "There goes my foreign correspondent. Got to have someone who can cover Geneva and all those travels with Foreign Minister Barthou. Needs lots of experience."

Then he turned to Jim and said with disappointment, "But Chicago doesn't have any money."

Then Mac's face brightened and he said, "So we thought of you. Do you think you can fake it as a foreign correspondent?"

Jim just stopped and turned, a smile stretching across his face, "Hell, I can fake it with the best of 'em."

Mac beamed, "I knew you had it in you, kid."

Sandrine hugged Jim, "What about the interview at the ministry of public works?"

Jim laughed and then turned and walked along with Mac, "Wow, this is the big time."

Rewrite leered at Sandrine and said to Jim, "Don't worry about Sandrine while you're away at Geneva. We'll keep an eye on her."

Jim laughed, "That's all right. She says she's not interested in can-can dancers."

Tuesday, September 11, Paris. Jim walked up Rue Bonaparte just as the evening darkness was setting in. In the last light, he marveled again at the size of Eglise St.-Germain-de-Prés and the farm wealth that had gone into supporting the church's creation and operation over the centuries. He saw Sandrine sitting at an outside table near the sidewalk, wearing an overcoat to ward off the chill of the fall evening. He walked over to her and leaned down and kissed her sweetly on her upturned lips. He sat down close to her and gave her a short hug.

She could see the excitement in his face. She said expectantly, "You're leaving?"

He beamed triumphantly, "Yes, tomorrow morning. For Geneva. I'm going to cover the Assembly of the League of Nations. When it is over, I take the train to Marseilles and cover the arrival of King Alexander of Yugoslavia. Then I follow him up to Paris for the state visit. I will be back October 8 or 9."

Sandrine looked down and said softly, "You'll be gone for a long time."

Jim reached over and held her hand, "I know. But it's my big break. We'll live in Paris. You will have your work here. I'll be based here as a correspondent covering Europe."

Sandrine put her other hand on top of his, "We have unfinished business here."

"We do?"

"We do," she said evenly. "You were going to move in with me before you left."

Jim looked flustered. He stammered, "Yeah, I know. But can't we do it later?"

"Why?"

"Gee, I wrote my mother and family that I had met a swell girl in Paris. But I haven't told them about the rest of it," with a little bit of extra emphasis on "it."

Sandrine looked at him with disappointment, "I see."

He looked at her beseechingly, hoping for her understanding.

Instead, she sat back and looked at him with laughing eyes and said in a mocking tone, "Well, it seems to me you have been pretty enthusiastic about 'it' for the past two months. Most mornings and evenings, I might say."

Jim, agitated, looked at her with consternation, "That's not what I meant at all."

Sandrine then gently brought forth her skill as *une avocate*. Just a small insertion of the needle will do, she thought. "May be I'm just another Parisian girl, what you Americans call a 'student' in your light hearted way, to keep you company until you go home and marry the girl next door, like the ones in the pretty dresses and aprons in the refrigerator ads in the American magazines. That's what you mean?"

Jim, more than a little flustered, stammered, "That's not true at all, Sandrine. You know that. I want to marry you someday."

Sandrine sighed and looked at him lovingly, "You know, I really believe you."

Jim blushed and said, "I just haven't told my family. How do you tell your mother?"

Sandrine looked at him, eyes twinkling, and said helpfully, "In a letter?"

Jim sighed a sigh of relief, "That's it. I'll write her."

Sandrine coached him gently, "Tonight?"

Jim straightened up and said, overcome with a sense of determination, "You bet. Tonight."

Sandrine peered at him intently, "And?"

Jim replied, "I'll move as soon as I get back from Marseilles."

Sandrine now straightened up and looked forthrightly at him, the *avocate* now a judge. She grandly took up the pronouncement, "Malka and I will go over and get your things out of the Hotel de Lisbonne tomorrow afternoon when you leave." She let that sink in and then followed with, "Think of the money you will save." She smiled triumphantly at him.

Jim leaned back and brightly smiled at her, "Whatever you say, dear."

Tuesday, September 25, Paris. In the late afternoon, with darkness spreading across the street below, Sandrine sat at the big horseshoe-shaped desk of the newsroom by the telephone waiting. Mac blew a puff of smoke towards Rewrite and said, "We need to give Boy Reporter a new name. I hear some *femme fatale* wrecked 'Hayseed,'" and he smirked at Sandrine. Then he turned to Rewrite and said, "Let me suggest 'Dreamboat.'"

Sandrine looked at the two men and tilted her head to one side thoughtfully, "I like that, Monsieur Mac." Then she slowly repeated, "Dreamboat."

The telephone rang and Sandrine swept the receiver out of its cradle in one darting motion, "Jim?"

Her face relaxed and she looked up at the ceiling, eyes bright, smiling, "So nice to hear your voice. Mac has a new name for you: Dreamboat." Her face made a frown, "You don't like it? I do." She listened patiently for a few seconds, then said, "There, you see." Sandrine smiled and winked at Mac.

Mac smiled benignly. He watched Sandrine for a while, then blew out a puff of smoke and said, "Get the story, sweetheart."

She looked at him, nodded, and said into the mouthpiece, "Give me the story. I'll repeat it as I write it down."

Mac nodded his approval.

Sandrine started to write, saying the words as she went:

"Russia has entered Geneva today triumphant, furthering a major French foreign policy goal."

Sandrine wrote the words down and then repeated the following sentences as Jim read them to her:

"Foreign Minister Barthou in his comments at Geneva scarcely dares to make the argument that Russia's admission to the League makes for another ally against Germany. Rather, Barthou argues if admission were denied, then the Soviets might pursue other adventures."

Sandrine continued taking notes, "Barthou argues that admission of the Soviets is a real factor for peace and not just a part of a policy of encirclement of Germany, which always draws a sharp rejoinder from Berlin."

Sandrine looked over at Mac as she continued transcribing and repeating, "The official French view is that everything done against Germany is another link in the chain of peace, and it counts Russia's admission to Geneva in this category."

Mac nodded his head as he heard Sandrine repeat the story.

Sandrine stopped writing and lay her pencil down. She said softly into the mouthpiece, "I miss you. I can't wait for you to come home." She looked over at Mac to see if he had anything to add. He shook his head No.

She said into the mouthpiece, "*Au revoir*. Dreamboat." Until we meet again. She placed the receiver back in its cradle, ending the call.

Mac smiled and said, "Write it up and give it to Rewrite."

Sandrine smiled and said in her best American manner, "Sure."

GERMANY

Sunday morning, September 30, 1934. The early morning chill of fall had seeped into the hallway in the Davignon's country home during the night. Walking down the hallway towards the dining room, Irène stopped, opened her dressing robe and wrapped her white cotton nightgown around herself more tightly, then she overlapped the two folds of her dressing robe snuggly around her waist and cinched the sash tight and tied it off with a large bow. As she smoothed out her robe, she could hear sounds of conversation coming down the hallway.

Anne de Davignon was saying, rather earnestly, "Philippe, these articles on the Nazi rally at Nuremberg are dreadful. The news out of Germany is no longer dark, as you like to say; it is all black. Those blood-red Nazi flags are the symbols of a cult of hate."

Irène heard Philippe agree in a tone of worried anxiety that she couldn't quite place with the debonair diplomat, "I know. What should we do?"

Then Irène heard Anne reply with some decisiveness, "You must go to Germany. You have to get her out. Soon, otherwise it will be too late."

Irène listened now intently for what the answer would be. She heard Philippe say with some resolve, "I will go to Berlin. This week. I will arrange the visas and train tickets tomorrow."

Irène continued walking down the hall and into the dining room, "Good morning, hope I am not intruding?"

Anne said pleasantly, "Good morning, Irène. No, of course not, we were just speaking about the dreadful developments in Germany. Here, look at the illustrated magazines. They have pictures from the big Nazi rally at Nuremberg."

Philippe smiled and nodded at Irène, "Good morning. Germany is never too far away from our thoughts."

Irène said, "Yes, I know. You know so many people there."

Anne looked absently at the wall, "Yes." Then she turned and said softly to Irène, "For some of them, it is time to leave."

Philippe added, "We of course want to help."

Irène sat down at the dining table and answered, "Of course you would. I know that about you—both of you." She smiled warmly.

Tuesday morning, October 2. The *inspecteur* walked past the ministry of interior to the next street and then turned onto Rue de Miromesnil. He walked up the block, then turned into an apartment building. He checked in with the plainclothes guard on the ground floor and then took the elevator up to the fifth floor. He knocked on an office door and walked into the reception area, nodded at the secretary, and then walked past her into the office of the *chef*.

"What do we have today?" the *chef* asked as he looked up.

The *inspecteur* opened up his attaché case and took out some papers. He spread the papers on the *chef's* desk and then sat down.

"Davignon is going to Berlin."

"Nothing unusual in that."

"On the way back, Friday morning, he's stopping at a little town just outside Mainz. Then he gets back on the train later in the afternoon."

"Nothing really unusual about that, either. He's done that before, many times, but not so much since the Nazis came to power."

The *inspecteur* then said quite evenly, "He's purchased a second railway ticket from Mainz back to Paris. Someone is coming with him."

The *chef* leaned back in his chair, drew on his cigarette, then blew smoke up towards the ceiling, watching it ascend.

He softly said, "Who? Why?"

The *inspecteur* sat still. The *chef* left unanswered his own rhetorical questions.

The *chef* straightened up and said, "Very good work. Meet the train when it arrives Friday afternoon. Follow the second person."

The *inspecteur* stood up, nodded, and left the office.

The *chef* leaned back in his chair, took another draw on his cigarette, and again blew the smoke up towards the ceiling, his eyes following the gray swirl upwards.

All those little stops at Mainz over the years. Of course there was that little unexplained question from years ago. An answer now seemed near.

The *chef* straightened up and called in his secretary.

Wednesday morning, October 3. The train headed east across the rolling countryside of France. The *chef* looked out the window; the scars of the late Great War were still too evident outside the train window. Soon he would be in Strasbourg, the French city on the Rhine looking across the river at the ancestral enemy, Germany. He knew as he headed for Strasbourg that Philippe de Davignon was on another train going to Berlin. Why? Was it simply a routine diplomatic meeting to sound out the Wilhemstrasse about the upcoming meetings in Paris between Yugoslav King Alexander and the French government? May be that was the pretext? What was the real reason?

The *chef* leaned back into the comfortable seat of the first-class compartment and thought back. He had been younger then, in 1924. He had been in Mainz attached to the French occupation forces. He had worked undercover in the shadowy world of German separatists still hoping for French sponsorship of some sort of autonomous German republic along the Rhine River after the collapse of the Rhenish Republic in 1923. From a distance he had watched the smoothly assured young French diplomat Philippe de Davignon represent the foreign ministry at the French military headquarters. There had been the wife, elegant and pretty, presiding over beautiful dinners with local German leaders at the Davignon's rented villa situated on a beautiful estate just outside the city. A Frenchman who moved so effortlessly through the upper reaches of German society caught your attention.

Then, he remembered, suddenly the Davignons were gone. Some talk, very vague, about a possible mistress. Nothing unusual about that. The Davignons were back in Paris, his career at the Quai D'Orsay as a German expert on an ever-increasing arc. But what had happened?

In the early afternoon, the *chef* walked out of the Strasbourg train station and hailed a cab. He gave directions to an address outside of town. Arriving in front of the small house situated on a hill, the *chef* got out, paid the driver, and walked with his bags up to the front door. The door opened and an older man ushered him in with the greeting, "Nice to see you again."

The *chef* walked in, put his bags down in the entranceway, and turned to his host, "It is nice to see you again, *directeur.*"

"We'll go out on the verandah. You can see the river."

The two men walked outside and took chairs around a small table. The *chef* said, "Yes, the river."

The *directeur* warmed up, "Former President of the Republic Raymond Poincaré retired nearby. He, too, would look out from his home at the river. Then he would say, 'The Germans will come again.' And he would look across the river."

The *chef* said, "That is the great eternal truth that France's leaders must always remember."

The *directeur* said, "Yes, forty French kings kept them out for a thousand years, the sacred duty of the monarchy. Then the Presidents of the Republic," and his voice trailed off.

The *chef* said sadly, "Now the President of the Republic sits in the *Palais* and cries."

The *directeur* turned businesslike, "You said you needed to know something about what happened in Mainz ten years ago?"

The *chef* took out a pad and pen, "Yes, I remember that a young diplomat named Philippe de Davignon left hurriedly. There may have been a scandal."

The *directeur* searched his memory and said, "Yes, I remember. I, of course, would never have anything official, but may be there are some personal notes that might jog my memory. Let me go see."

The *directeur* stood up and went inside the house. The *chef* could hear a door open and then footfalls going down a stairwell to the basement. The *chef* sat and looked out across the river.

Ten minutes later the *directeur* returned. "Yes, I have the details clear in my mind now."

The *chef* reached for his pad and pencil.

The *directeur* started on his explanation of the long ago events, "Davignon had an affair with a young German girl, an *au pair* girl in the household. She confessed to her priest."

The *chef* looked inquisitively, "Not so unusual. These situations occur, as you know, rather regularly with our diplomats."

The *directeur* disregarded the comment, "The girl also confessed to the priest that she was in a relationship with both the husband and the wife. The relationship with the wife troubled her, felt some form of unknowable retribution might await her."

The *chef* nodded in understanding, "Yes, a country girl. Outside her experience."

The *directeur* continued, "The wife, Anne, just before this time had had a miscarriage, a dead baby girl. After the miscarriage, she could never have children of her own."

The *chef* looked at the *directeur*, "And?"

The *directeur* continued, "The wife, Anne, developed a deep attachment to the girl, and in particular to the baby she was carrying. She developed a belief that somehow God was delivering her another baby through the girl."

The *chef* replied, "I am starting to see."

The *directeur* said, "The German girl got upset at this attention, feared Anne would somehow steal her baby. Went to the priest. Confessed all—outside the box."

The *chef* mulled this over, "So this went to the French headquarters?"

The *directeur* nodded his affirmation, "Yes." After a pause, he continued, "It was hushed up. Davignon was posted back to Paris, almost immediately. Arrangements for a stipend to the girl were of course made. Davignon comes from a family of industrialists. His wife comes from one of the Two Hundred Families."

The *chef* looked momentarily startled at the words "Two Hundred Families." He made a very appreciative nod, "Of course, diplomats usually have family money. But the Davignons are top tier. I hadn't realized that."

The *directeur* said with a certain admiration, "Davignon was quite generous; the girl and her mother have not been in want. Madame de Davignon has ensured the little girl was exceptionally well provided for. Before the Nazis, the Davignons used to visit the little village outside of Mainz where the girl and the mother and grandmother lived."

The *chef* looked up with interest, "We knew he visited Mainz often, but we thought he was keeping up with German contacts. We never had the time to really follow him."

The *directeur* gave a judgment, "Davignon's work was always greatly admired. He seems to really understand Germans." The *directeur* cleared his throat; then he looked into the distance.

The *chef* looked at him and asked, with that small question that searched out the last little secret, the overlooked tidbit, "There's something else?"

The *directeur* shifted uncomfortably in his chair, "I mentioned the mother had spoken with a priest. During our investigation we noticed that the mother's mother was Jewish." The sentence fell like a lead weight in the room, an oppressive fact of momentous gravity and gloom.

The *chef* sighed and said, "That explains the last piece of the puzzle." He looked over at the *directeur* and by way of explanation said, "We in Paris learned that next week the German minister of interior, you remember Wilhelm Frick, will announce the new racial card, the so-called *sippenblatt*, that every German will have to carry. The registration officers must gather the most minute details of every German's race, tracing it through ancestry and kinship, supposedly for the purpose of keeping the race pure from foreign admixtures. The cards will certify ancestral origin."

The *directeur* sagged and said, "I understand. Under Nazi law, if the grandmother is Jewish, then the grandchildren are Jewish."

The *chef* looked evenly and said, "May be I shouldn't say this. But we have Davignon's itinerary. He is stopping at a small village just outside of Mainz early Friday afternoon. He has done this before. But this time he bought a second train ticket for the journey from Mainz back to Paris before leaving Paris. We were wondering why."

The *directeur* straightened up in his chair, "Very decent." A wave of concern crossed his face and he added, with a tinge of admiration, "Very risky."

Both men stood up. The *directeur* gazed down the slope towards the river, "*Les allemands. Oui, ils vienent.*" The Germans. Yes, they are coming.

The *chef* went outside. Soon a taxicab arrived. He got in and mulled over the surprising turn of events as he drove back into Strasbourg. In the far recesses of his mind he had thought Davignon would be up to something like this. He tried to think evenly about the options available. Always a chess game, yes, but now the adversary, his lifelong adversary, was totally ruthless—merciless men whose first instinct was to use death to clear chess pieces off the board in one fell swoop. *Dangerous to go over to their side of the chessboard.* Nevertheless, he knew one chess piece on the German side of the board. Could he be trusted? After all these years?

Thursday, October 4, Berlin. The taxicab driver pulled over to the curb and with somber correctness said, "Wilhemstrasse 73." The driver never turned his head around towards his passenger. Philippe de Davignon put some marks into the driver's upraised palm, got out of the taxicab, and walked across the sidewalk glancing upwards at the massive stone-block edifice of the German foreign office. He presented his credentials to two uniformed security guards at the entranceway. They carefully checked his credentials, gave him a look of scorn, then stepped back a step, clicked heels together, raised their right arms in the Nazi salute, and said, "Heil Hitler." They nodded that Davignon was free to enter the building.

Inside some of the warmth and charm of the old foreign ministry returned. He walked over to a receptionist and made a discreet inquiry. The young man made a telephone call, listened, "*Ja,*" he repeated. He put the telephone down, called over an orderly, whispered something, and then turned to Davignon, "He will escort you upstairs, Herr Davignon." The receptionist smiled blandly. It was the blandness of the heel clickers that got him, Davignon thought.

Davignon followed the orderly up a large staircase to the second floor, then down a long marble hallway. The orderly opened the door and ushered him into a secretary's reception room. Davignon entered, the orderly closed the door behind him. A woman secretary said warmly, "Welcome, Herr Davignon, nice to see you again."

Davignon smiled, nodded his head, and said, "Nice to see you again, Fräulein Schmidt."

"The director will be with you shortly."

The door opened and a distinguished looking man stood in the entrance and said, "Philippe, so nice to see you again. Please come in."

Davignon entered the office, looked around, and the German pointed over to one of the wing chairs and said pleasantly, "Have a seat." Davignon sat down.

Davignon said, "Nice to see you, Manfred."

The German sat down behind his desk and beamed, "What brings you to Berlin?"

"I just wanted to hear with my own ears what the German position is on various issues. Get a feel for the tone. Foreign Minister Barthou will be in Paris hosting King Alexander of Yugoslavia next week. We of course want to improve the situation for all concerned."

The German heartily agreed, "Of course. I see you have a copy of the *Berliner Tageblatt* under your arm. Something in particular you want to talk about?"

Davignon replied, "Why, of course. We read the paper's editorial with great interest. It suggests that Germany might have an interest in returning to the League of Nations at Geneva."

The German took on a serious, officious air, "Of course an issue of some gravity, Philippe, and there is a delicate matter of not appearing to do an about face. The Führer…"

Davignon interjected, "Of course."

The German nodded his head sagely, then continued, "The unofficial emissaries at Geneva, Dr. Schnee and Colonel Haselmayer, have contacts at the highest level here in Berlin," and the German cleared his throat, "both men can speak unofficially, of course, but also with the greatest authority…"

Davignon nodded and said, "Yes, of course."

The German looked straight at Davignon, "The central point is that Russia's entry to the League of Nations would make consideration of a German return a live issue."

Davignon responded, "Live?"

The German replied evenly, "Live."

Davignon nodded with his head, "Any conditions?"

The German shifted in his chair, "None. We presume that German equality in armament would have already been accepted by that point."

Davignon suppressed a smile and dryly replied, "Yes, of course."

The German searched Davignon's face for some sign of affirmation about the armament position. Military equality with the other European nations was the only thing Germany wanted. Getting rid of the shackles of the hated Versailles Peace Treaty was paramount, thought the German. The German looked at Davignon again for a sign: he saw nothing.

Davignon sat for a moment, letting his blankness settle in, a statement in and of itself as he knew from years of cross-table negotiations. Sidestepping the armament issue, Davignon started to speak, "A German return to Geneva would probably facilitate resolution of issues raised by the Saar plebiscite."

The German saw the counterstroke for what it simply was—a shift. "Yes, the German government wants to work with France and the League on a successful plebiscite." No talk about armaments today from Philippe.

The German summed up, "As you know, Philippe, Foreign Minister von Neurath has indicated to foreign diplomats that Russia's entrance into the League would make it desirable for Germany to return, his words now, 'as soon as it could be done decently.'"

Davignon replied with a smile, "Yes, by all means, 'decently.'"

The German shrugged his shoulders and looked at Davignon glumly. He said nothing. Davignon had scored one tiny point of honor on him. Some of the things that went on in Germany nagged at him. Philippe knew that. Oh, well.

The German sat up a bit and asked, "What about the Americans?"

Now it was Davignon's turn as he replied in a weary voice, "The Americans? The Americans support the League, strongly in private, but officially they are preoccupied with trying to find work for the unemployed, as we all are."

The German said, "Yes, and that is where the Führer is having great success in Germany. You need to fully understand that, Philippe."

Davignon looked at him, "You know I do, but I wish we would build all European employment through increased trade and cooperation, not autarky and arms races."

The German nodded, looked at the wall beyond Davignon's shoulder and said, "Results count in Germany."

Davignon stood up, "Let me not keep you from your work any longer."

The German stood up, "Please stay in touch, Philippe."

"Yes." Davignon turned, opened the door, and left the office.

Friday, October 5. Philippe de Davignon stood in the parlor of a small house in a village just outside of Mainz, Germany and near the railroad line leading to France. The woman, about thirty years old, stood in the middle of the room behind a ten-year old girl, her daughter. Behind her was a woman in her fifties, her mother, the child's grandmother.

The woman, distraught, tears in her eyes, said, "I know it is best, but..."

She turned and looked over her shoulder, "I can't leave my mother behind. I simply cannot. We have always been German. How can you be an enemy among your own people?"

She looked into Davignon's face, "I can't believe we will not be all right in the future." She said it as a hope, with the despair of having little personal conviction.

Davignon looked at her evenly, "I hope so."

She responded, "Herr Davignon..."

Davignon broke in, "Philippe, please, always and forever, Philippe. Giselle, for all time, we share something together, something we brought to this world together. You and I. We must protect the girl so that she will have the future we all want for her." Davignon looked at the grandmother for approval.

The grandmother sighed and gave a faint nod of acquiescence. To have to send away one's only grandchild. Who knows where? What will happen?

Davignon looked at the mother again. The woman looked at him from tear-drenched eyes, "Philippe, I know it is best. Ilse needs to go to France with you. Please ask your wife to look after her like she was her own."

Philippe looked at her. "You know Anne. She has a deep belief that she somehow shares in the motherhood of Ilse."

The woman pleaded, "I know. But I am the real mother, *muti*. I can't lose that. It's all I have."

Philippe said, "I promise you, you always will be her mother. You know you have my word on this. Besides, Anne would never think to try to take that away from you, or diminish it in any way. She has perfect integrity in this."

The woman looked at Philippe, beseechingly, then turned the little girl around, knelt down and hugged her and held her close. She said into the little girl's ear, "He is your father. He will take care of you. I love you."

The little girl started to cry. The grandmother came over, knelt down, hugged the little girl, and said to her, "It is best." Tears streamed down the grandmother's cheeks.

Philippe waited. After a while, he stepped forward and took the little girl's hand. "We have to go now." His eyes looked ever so kindly into the mother's worried eyes. Then he nodded, putting an everlasting finality to the leavetaking.

Philippe and the little girl Ilse walked out the front door and down the small walkway to the taxicab waiting in the street.

At the railway station, simply a long concrete slab with a covered roof running along the tracks, Davignon and the little girl Ilse got out of the taxicab. The driver got out their bags and handed them to a porter, who put them on a small pushcart. Davignon and the girl walked up a ramp followed by the porter. The train for Paris was stopped alongside the concrete slab. Davignon and the girl started to walk towards the middle of the train where the first-class cars were.

Davignon saw him up ahead. What was he doing here? This was Germany. Dangerous for a French secret service man to be in Germany. Why? Then he noticed the other man, a big lumbering bear of a man in a trench coat with a homburg hat pushed down on his head. He had seen so many like him over the years in Germany, a plainclothes policeman. State police.

Davignon was perplexed. His plan was going wrong. He looked at the French secret service man, the *chef*, with a questioning gaze.

The *chef* nodded ever so slightly to Davignon towards a first-class car, signaling him to get on. Davignon took the little girl's hand and said, "Over here, darling."

He walked over to the rear steps of the car, lifted the girl up onto the first step, and followed her. The porter followed with the baggage. Davignon walked with girl down the corridor, saw an empty compartment, slid open the door, and guided the little girl in before him. "Over there by the window, Ilse."

The porter brought the bags in and put them up in the racks. Davignon handed him some change as a tip. The porter left, sliding the door closed behind him.

A few seconds later the two men appeared. The *chef* slid the door open and the two men entered and sat down together opposite and towards the door, away from Davignon and the girl. The *chef* gave a slight glance of approval with his eyes to Davignon. Davignon leaned back in his seat. He turned to the girl,

"The train will take us to France, and then to Paris. My wife will be there, you remember Aunt Anne?"

The little girl replied softly, "Yes, she was so nice. She gave me things."

Then the little girl said, sharply, "I wish my mother could have been your wife. Then we would be a happy family."

Davignon looked down at her, lifted her chin up with his fingers, and looked into her eyes, "I truly wish that could have been true, too."

Davignon sat back up, looked blankly at the vacant seat across from him, and felt the ideas flood his consciousness. There will be so many unhappy families. So many.

Then he looked down at the little girl and said, "We will all have to try to do our best where we find ourselves. That is what your mother wants."

Ilse nodded her head in sad acceptance.

The train gave a small jerk and then started to pull out of the station.

Philippe de Davignon looked out the window. He had made this journey so many times. The French border was just ahead. He was sure Ilse's papers would be okay. They were genuine, from the Germany embassy in Paris.

The train came to a halt. Up ahead Davignon could see the candy stripe border pylons. There were footfalls in the hallway. A German immigration official came in, officious, military like.

Davignon stood up and gave the official his passport and Ilse's papers. The official looked at the French diplomatic passport. He looked at the photograph and then squinted at Davignon. He scowled with distaste at Davignon. He took up Ilse's papers. Ah, now here was something. These diplomats, always circumventing the Reich and trying to get "friends" out for money.

The immigration official brought his heels together, "Herr Davignon, these papers are not in order. I must get my superior."

Davignon took a slightly forceful manner, "The papers are completely correct. They are from the Reich's embassy in Paris. Approved by the ambassador."

The big burly German stood up and stepped forward, tapped the immigration official on the shoulder, and snapped open his identification and badge in front of the official.

The immigration official looked startled. Of course. They have paid off the police. They profit handsomely in this trafficking. He should have noticed. Then a thought crossed his mind, "May be my own supervisor is involved?"

The German policeman said softly, "The girl's papers are correct."

The immigration official stammered, "Of course."

The official looked at the other man. The *chef* opened his diplomatic passport. The immigration official nodded. He looked at the little girl. Of course. The granddaughter of a wealthy Jewish industrialist. They can still buy their way out, the swine.

He turned to the police officer. "All the papers are in order. My mistake."

The German policeman nodded and stepped back and let the official pass by on his way to the corridor.

The official stepped out, slid the door closed, and went onto the next compartment.

Several minutes later, the train moved forward very slowly. The border pylons went by the window. The train came to a second stop. Davignon could see French immigration and customs officials board the train. He relaxed back into his seat and turned to Ilse, "We're in France. You're safe."

The policeman and the *chef* stood up. The policeman slid open the door to the compartment and stepped into the corridor. The *chef* followed. The two men walked to the end of the car, down the steps, and onto the cement platform.

The German turned down the platform and started walking back towards the German end of the station. The *chef* stood and watched him go.

The German stopped, turned around, pushed his hands further down into the pockets of his trench coat, and said to the *chef*, "My last favor." He let the words seep in. "There are no old friends in the new Germany." He turned and kept walking slowly back towards the border.

The *chef* watched, then turned, and walked over to a second-class car, mounted the steps, and walked down the middle of the passenger car and took a seat for the trip back to Paris.

MARSEILLES

Tuesday, October 9, 1934. Marseilles. Jim Potter lugged the tripod to the newsreel camera down to the promenade overlooking the Quai des Belges in the *vieux port*—the Old Port—of the ancient city of Marseilles. He helped his newfound friend Ed set up the newsreel camera on the tripod. It had been a stroke of luck to meet Ed, an American newsreel cameraman in his early thirties with game-cock pride in this exciting new medium that was coming into its own with the advent of sound newsreels. In turn, Jim was promised a place as an "assistant" in the motorcade that would take the king and the foreign minister to the Prefecture for a reception and then onto the train station two miles away where the party would board a train for Paris.

Ed stood on the promenade and pointed his arm out over the large stone pier and said, "The king will be coming into the small dock in his launch. He will be at a distance so we will need a telephoto lens. Long-distance lenses require that the camera be held very steady otherwise the resulting movie will jump around on the movie screen, an unacceptable annoyance to the movie-going public. So we will use the tripod."

Then Ed turned and looked up towards the broad avenue where the motorcade waited and said, "When we get up to the motorcade, I've got us in the front seat of the second car back from the king. I will use a regular lens. I can anchor my elbow on the side of the door and my right arm becomes a post," and he demonstrated by plunking his elbow down on an imaginary car door and holding his forearm upright. "We will be able to shoot the picture straight up along the right side of the king's car. We can frame the rear of his head in the left side of the picture and the waving crowds behind the police line on the right side. It will be heartwarmingly triumphant."

Jim admired Ed's sense of scene and resolved to keep that skill in mind as he wrote his dispatches. He asked, "What do you want me to do?"

"You will feed me new film reels as I run through them, and store the exposed reels in the film bag as I use them up. We will really burn through the film today."

Looking over Ed's shoulder, Jim said, "Look."

Ed turned around and exclaimed, "Here they come."

Jim looked out over the blue expanse of Marseilles harbor, little wavelets sparkling in the fall afternoon sunshine, and watched as the massive gray battlecruiser the *Dubrovnik*, pride of the small Yugoslavian navy, rounded the massive seventeenth century fortress overlooking the harbor entrance. The ship slowly came forward into the middle of the inner harbor, tugboats standing off either bow. At the stern of the gray ship, Jim could see the sideways tricolor of the Yugoslavian national flag, a horizontal blue band at the top with white and red bands layered below, symbolic of the long relationship between France and Serbia, a relationship continued by the successor state Yugoslavia. Yugoslavia itself was the personal creation of the dynamic king riding on the battlecruiser, a rare European monarch who in this modern age not only reigned over but ruled the politics of his kingdom.

As the two men watched the ship slow, an anchor let loose. The majestic ship came to a stop. Several minutes later a launch was put over the side, a boarding ladder lowered, and an honor guard of sailors lined up along the rail of the ship. Soon an entourage surrounding a white-uniformed figure moved along the deck of the ship, there was a fanfare from a band assembled on an upper level, and the white figure descended the ladder and boarded the launch among a bevy of saluting officers. The ensign of Yugoslavia was run up a small staff at the stern of the launch; then a small flag, the king's personal ensign, broke from the bow. The white-uniformed figure of King Alexander waved at the sailors lining the rail, who in turn cheered as the launch pulled away. Several hundred meters away from the battlecruiser the launch stopped and bobbed in the water. Two French submarines slowly came up and took station off the port and starboard stern quarters of the launch. French sailors in dark blue uniforms lined the small afterdecks of each submarine. The little flotilla got underway and headed for the stone quay.

On the quay, a group of dignitaries led by Foreign Minister Louis Barthou, in top hat and frock coat, and General Alfonse Joseph Georges, resplendent in the uniform and decorations befitting a leading young French general, stood watching. As the launch tied up to the quay, the French army band struck up the Yugoslavian national anthem. The king ascended the stone steps and then walked across the stone quay, stopped, saluted the French and Yugoslavian flags, and then walked over to Foreign Minister Barthou and reached out and shook his hand and said a few words, then he turned towards General Georges, who promptly saluted. The king returned the salute and then stepped forward and clasped the general's hand in both of his and spoke a few words.

Up on the promenade, the newsreel cameras hummed and Jim watched both the ceremony on the quay and the smooth professionalism of the newsreel cameramen going about their work. He marveled at both.

The officer at the head of the honor guard gave a command, and the assembled French troops came to attention. The king walked along the file of soldiers and sailors with the escorting officer in the traditional rite of inspection. Foreign Minister Barthou and General Georges followed several steps behind. At the end of the inspection, the officer turned and gave another order. The troops snapped their bayoneted rifles to upright positions in front of their chests in the ancient salute of present arms. The army band broke out into a rousing rendition of *La Marseillaise*. The dignitaries stood and listened.

As the last sounds of the anthem drifted across the harbor, the dignitaries moved up the walkway to a broad avenue, the famous Canebière, where the motorcade was assembled for the drive to the Prefecture for a formal reception.

On the avenue and near the front of the waiting cars, Lieutenant Colonel Priollet sat on his horse and surveyed with practiced eye the two columns of mounted Republican Guards formed up on each side and in front of the motorcade, eight horsemen on a side. In front of the mounted columns were motorcycle-mounted Mobile Guards. Colonel Priollet shifted in his saddle and looked back and saw two mounted guards in station just behind the king's open limousine. Looking up the parade route, the colonel could see police at intervals of about twenty feet keeping back the thousands of bystanders lined up to watch the passing royal motorcade, a chance to see a crowned head visit the great republic. The police were facing in towards the motorcade route, not out towards the crowds as required by procedure. Ah well, thought the colonel, in two hours the reserve police will be back wrapping fish in newspapers, as they should be. All was about as could be expected.

As Colonel Priollet watched, the king, the foreign minister, and the general got into the third car in the motorcade. The king took the right-hand customary seat of honor in the rear seat, the foreign minister seated next to him. In the jump seat in front of the king sat the general.

Colonel Priollet looked back over the motorcade; in the first two cars were uniformed police and plainclothesmen of the Sûreté Nationale. He watched as the newsreel cameramen got into the cars in the fifth and sixth position. Farther back were more police and plainclothesmen in other cars. Behind the last car came two-dozen more mounted Republican Guards. All was ready. He shouted an order to the front. The mounted guards drew their sabers. The colonel drew his own saber, then turned in his saddle, stood in his stirrups, and looked back and held his saber high in the sky. The mounted guards at the rear of the motorcade drew their sabers, flashed them skywards in acknowledgement, and then brought the sabers down along their right legs to the ready position.

The colonel turned back and shouted another order to the front. The motorcycle outriders moved forward, the horse-mounted Republican Guards lightly spurred their horses forward at a walk, all eyes scanning the thronging crowds for signs of trouble. All knew the danger: an assassin bursting out of the crowd to murder a crowned head. This was exactly what happened at Sarajevo twenty years before. There, a Balkan assassin had killed the Austro-Hungarian archduke and set off the fuse to the biggest wartime conflagration in human history. Balkan hatreds burned with the fury of Hell, thought the colonel.

The motorcade slowly crawled forward, King Alexander smiling at the crowds, Foreign Minister Barthou beaming at the warm reception, the sidewalks and balconies of the ancient Mediterranean city crowded with enthusiastic onlookers. The motorcade passed the intersection of Queen Elizabeth Street and started past the Bourse, the city's stock exchange, overlooking a large plaza.

Colonel Priollet saw the heavy-set man shouting *"Vive la roi"* dart around a momentarily startled policeman, the policeman frozen for a brief second by the mistaken belief that the man was an over-enthusiastic supporter of the king. Colonel Priollet was under no such illusion; he moved his horse into the path of the charging man while watching the man pull an automatic pistol from his pocket. Skillfully, the man grabbed the horse's bridle and forced the colonel's horse around while dodging around the other side of the animal and jumping up on the running board of the king's limousine. With one arm the man grabbed a handhold on the door while simultaneously firing two or three shots into the king's chest and stomach from his Walther automatic pistol.

As the man darted around him, the colonel whirled his horse like a polo pony in a quick turn and brought his saber crashing down on the man's neck as he heard the third shot fire. A second slash of the saber sent the assassin sprawling onto the pavement where he continued to wildly fire at the limousine. Police and the crowd rushed forward. The man moved to put the pistol into his mouth and kill himself when bullets hit his body from the charging policemen rushing up to the scene.

Inside the limousine, a wounded but fully conscious Foreign Minister Barthou moved to try to help the mortally wounded king. General Georges slumped in his seat from gunshot wounds. The chauffeur moved the limousine forward surrounded by a screen of mounted Republican Guards.

Two cars back the American newsreel cameraman Ed exclaimed, "My God," as he watched the man charge towards the mounted colonel, then turn the colonel's horse, dodge around and jump up on the running board. He heard the crack of the pistol shots and saw the colonel's saber flash in the sunlight as it came down on the gunman's head and neck. The newsreel cameramen kept slowly cranking as the policemen rushed forward and then to his amazement he watched as the enraged crowd tried to tear the assassin away from the police. The police grabbed the wounded assassin and moved him to a newsstand where they could keep the maddened crowd at bay.

Jim had been looking out through the windscreen at the cheering crowds as the king's limousine passed in front of the Bourse. Out of the corner of his eye he saw the man dart around the policeman holding back the surging crowd. In horror, he watched the assassin turn the colonel's horse. "Something's going wrong, Ed," he shouted to his friend cranking away on the newsreel camera. Then he saw the man jump up on the limousine's running board. He saw the flash from the muzzle of the pistol and the king slump over to the side. Then his eye caught the flash of the saber and the man was gone, hacked down by the enraged colonel.

Jim could see that Foreign Minister Barthou was stricken but still moving. General Georges was slumped over. In two seconds, the backseat of the limousine had become a slaughterhouse. Jim watched the limousine accelerate forward, saw the horsemen of the Republican Guard form a phalanx around the car as it moved forward through the dense mass of people swarming onto the street trying to see what had so obviously gone wrong. The limousine moved up the Canebière and came to a stop behind the two cars that had been in the front of the motorcade. Ed cranked his newsreel camera as some policemen moved Foreign Minister Barthou to the rear seat of one of the cars. Then other policemen moved General Georges from the rear floor of the king's limousine to the other car. A police official came back and pointed to the two cars with the wounded French officials in them and indicated they would be going off in some other direction; the chauffeur was to drive the king's limousine towards the Prefecture.

Jim said to Ed, "I think that means the king is dead. They're not taking him to a hospital."

Ed, still cranking his camera, said, "Stay with the limousine."

Just then, the limousine inched forward into the crowd and continued heading for the Prefecture.

Jim turned to the driver and said, "Let's stay with the limousine."

The newsreel car moved forward and followed the limousine, two police-men standing in the rear keeping gawkers from reaching in and grabbing at the white-faced body of the deceased king.

Arriving at the Prefecture, the limousine pulled into the driveway while police with batons pushed the unruly crowds back from the front entrance. Other police came out with a stretcher and the king's body was gently moved from the rear seat onto the stretcher and carried inside the building.

The newsreel car came to a stop behind the limousine. Jim and Ed got out and moved towards the entranceway, but were stopped by the police cordon. Jim saw a press attaché from the foreign ministry and waved to him. He came over and Jim explained. The press attaché saw the newsreel camera in Ed's hands and the film bag over Jim's shoulder and spoke to one of the policemen, who escorted the two journalists into the building and over to a large office off the lobby. Another official came up and said to Ed, "I will take the camera and the film bag."

Ed stamped his foot and harshly yelled, "You can't do that. I'm part of the press. I'm an American citizen."

The French official waved two policemen over and gave them instructions. One policeman said to Ed with firm determination, "Monsieur?"

Ed and Jim handed over the camera and film bag.

The other policemen handed a receipt to Ed, "Your camera and film will be quite safe."

Ed grumbled, "Thanks."

Jim saw several officials in rapid-fire conversation on some phones across the room. He asked the press attaché, "Are you in touch with the Quai D'Orsay?"

The press attaché nodded yes.

"Could I speak with Madame Bardoux at the foreign ministry?"

The press attaché looked at Jim and considered the situation for a moment: the reporter knew Madame Bardoux? Yes. He might tell Madame Bardoux what he saw? Yes. That would be useful. He replied to Jim, "Yes."

Jim and the press attaché walked over to the telephones. The press attaché spoke with one of the callers, who handed the earpiece over to Jim, who then sat down in front of the mouthpiece.

"Madame Bardoux?"

"Why yes. Who is this?"

"This is Jim Potter. Is Sandrine there?"

"Why yes, let me put her on," came the reply.

Jim could hear her come on the line, "This is Sandrine."

Jim became formal and started, "Yes, Madame Bardoux, let me tell you what I saw so you can make an official report to Monsieur M."

The press attaché looked a little puzzled: he didn't recall a Monsieur M. Possibly a code word.

"But Jim, it is Sandrine."

"Thank you, Madame Bardoux. I will begin." He put on his most officious air.

In Paris, Sandrine quickly caught on. She looked at Madame Bardoux with twinkling eyes and smiled demurely: words from a boyfriend.

Jim began, "I was an eyewitness."

Ah, thought the press attaché: just as I thought.

Then Jim recounted the shooting that had occurred out on the crowd-filled plaza in Marseilles.

Finishing, Jim said, "Monsieur M will be most interested. Could I speak with Suzanne now?"

Sandrine said into the mouthpiece, puzzled, "Suzanne?"

Madame Bardoux, hearing her name, pointed her finger at her chest.

Sandrine said, "Oh yes, here she is."

Madame Bardoux spoke into the mouthpiece, "Jim could you tell me what you saw?"

Jim said, "I would be happy to summarize all the events I saw."

The press attaché nodded knowingly: yes, probably much confusion at the ministry. By all means go over the facts one more time. Get them transcribed. Official.

Jim recounted all that had happened in short, factual sentences.

Madame Bardoux said, "Thank you so much Jim. Your account is most helpful. Is my press attaché there? Good. Let me speak with him."

Jim handed the mouthpiece over to the press attaché and stood back.

The press attaché spoke, "We have seized all the newsreel film that we can find and we have embargoed all dispatches from the reporters pending instructions from the ministry. No news will get out. We have the situation under strictest control."

From where she was standing, Madame Bardoux looked across the room and watched Sandrine pick up the receiver and pedestal mouthpiece of one of the phones reserved for members of the press. She watched Sandrine give the operator a number, watched her wait, and then she saw Sandrine speak rapid-fire to the listener at the other end of the line. Like a human teletype, thought Madame Bardoux. She smiled and said into the phone to Marseilles, "That is very good of you. For now, in particular, keep the newsreel film. Undoubtedly the police and security inspectors will want to look closely at the newsreels before they are released to the public."

"Yes, Madame Bardoux." The press attaché nodded his head gravely.

Madame Bardoux looked up to see an assistant bringing a long printed-out sheet of paper from one of the ministry's teletype machines. She said into the mouthpiece, "Hold on. We have developments." She set the pedestal mouthpiece down and scanned the news report. She put the paper down and again picked up the telephone pedestal with its mouthpiece and began to speak:

"You can remove the embargo on the correspondents' dispatches. I have in front of me a teletype report from one of the wire services about the assassination. In these situations, it is best to let the news dispatches go forth so the public gets fresh and accurate information. But keep the newsreels. You are to be commended for your resourcefulness in following ministry policy."

The press attaché sounded mildly troubled with the compliment, "Yes, Madame."

Madame Bardoux said soothingly into the mouthpiece, "Your future as a *fonctionnaire* is assured, Monsieur."

He beamed and placed the receiver back in its cradle. He turned to the two journalists and briskly said to Jim, "You are free to make a dispatch."

Jim suppressed a smile.

Then he turned to Ed, "I am sorry. I have been instructed to keep the newsreel film for now."

Jim turned to Ed and said, "We're still a team. Let's go work the story."

Ed brightened and said, "Now I'm your assistant. Where do we go?"

"The hospital."

As the two men walked back into the lobby of the Prefecture, they saw that the large reception hall had become a funeral parlor, the welcoming table so recently stacked with long, elegant flutes and large magnums of champagne had now become a bier for a casket, and the flowers had been rearranged for mourning rather than celebration.

Jim said to Ed in a low voice, "The story is at the hospital."

Ed replied, "Right. But damn, the picture is here. Okay, I'm following."

The two men walked across the street and found a cab disgorging passengers. Jim quickly asked the driver, "Can you take us to the hospital?"

"*Bien sûr.*" Of course, the driver replied, grateful for a new fare.

Late Tuesday afternoon, October 9, Marseilles. Arriving at the hospital, Ed put some coins in the driver's hand while Jim opened the door and got out. Ed followed. The two quickly ran up the steps and into the lobby. An official hurriedly approached them and asked who they were. They both flashed their police press passes.

The official said, "You will have to wait here with the others," and he waved his hand at a couple of reporters sitting at the side of the lobby.

Another official came out through the double-swinging doors, whispered to the first official, who then turned around, nose up in the air, and said, "I have a bulletin."

The other reporters stood up and joined Jim and Ed, forming a circle around the official.

The official began crisply, "There has been a consultation among the doctors and it has been decided to operate on the foreign minister. We will keep you posted."

The reporters broke up and went back to the chairs, some of them writing in their tablets.

Several minutes later, the double doors swung open again and the official returned to the center of the lobby, visibly shaken, an ashen pallor to his face. The official said unevenly, "I have another announcement."

The reporters saw the official's pallid demeanor and were standing in front of him in an instant. The official said in a low, monotonous voice, "I have the sad duty to announce that Foreign Minister Barthou died of his wounds on the operating table several minutes ago at approximately six o'clock."

Jim turned to Ed and said, "I have to telephone the news to Paris."

Ed replied, "Go ahead. I'm going back to the Prefecture and start working on getting my film back."

Jim called to Ed as he turned to leave, "Good luck."

Late Tuesday afternoon, Paris. At the Quai D'Orsay, Philippe de Davignon walked down the silent corridor to the reception area where Madame Bardoux was working with the press. He sidled up next to her and whispered in her ear, "Any further news from Marseilles?"

She turned, tears glistening in her eyes, and said, "It is as we feared. Foreign Minister Barthou died in the hospital just now. The king was dead from the first shots into the limousine."

Davignon nodded absently to her and said, "Thank you."

He turned and walked back down the corridor to his office. He entered, closed the door, and walked over and sat down behind his desk. He swiveled his chair around so he could look out the window at the River Seine flowing slowly down its ancient channel.

He collected his thoughts. Probably not German. Some Balkan thing. The Italians? Davignon mentally shrugged his shoulders. French foreign policy? Undoubtedly a setback for bringing the Soviet Union into some larger European security alliance.

Davignon looked at the gray and leaden waters of the river flowing by. May be the eastern alliance is the wrong strategy? May be it's not too late to get Germany into some form of economic cooperation involving the coal and steel industries straddling the Rhine River? Should he even try? One voice crying out against a sea of nationalist chants and revanchist resentments now coming from all sides.

He swung his chair around, took on an air of determination, and started to write a paper recommending that a positive diplomatic démarche be made to Berlin. Possibly the assassinations will create a moment of thoughtfulness among the parties, a second chance for peace, he thought. Whatever, he concluded, such a proposal is the right path. We must always try. Someday, somewhere such a proposal will deliver the two historic adversaries to a state of peace. He would always believe that. He smiled in quiet satisfaction.

Wednesday evening, October 10, Marseilles. The taxicab pulled up in front of the Marseilles train station. Jim opened the door, reached back and lifted out his suitcase. He handed some coins to the driver through the front window. The driver tipped his fingers to the brim of his cap, "Thanks."

Inside the dark cavernous waiting room, Jim saw a minor uniformed railroad official and went up to him and asked, "Where's the party that's taking Monsieur Barthou's body back to Paris?"

The official shrugged and pointed over to the side of the waiting room and a dark long casket sitting on a wooden table. "There's the body. The officials are not here yet."

Jim looked over and saw the casket—unattended. He was thunderstruck. He had heard that cabinet ministers Herriot and Tardieu had come from Paris to Marseilles to escort the body back to the capital. Where were they? Jim looked again at the railway official for an explanation. The official turned his palms out empty handed and shrugged.

Jim got out his notebook and started writing some notes. He noticed a group of policemen come through a side door and walk over to the casket. They lifted it up onto their shoulders. Jim walked over to follow along; a police official turned and stood in his way.

Jim said, "I'm a reporter."

The policeman looked at him and simply shrugged. He didn't move out of the way. Jim showed his press pass and then said, "I am supposed to accompany the foreign minister's body back to Paris. I have a letter here from the press attaché at the Prefecture."

The word "Prefecture" brought a quick change in expression to the policeman. He looked at the paper Jim showed him. He said, "*Bon.*" Good. Then he indicated with his hand for Jim to follow the policemen carrying the casket across the darkened railway yard.

Jim fell in behind them. He watched as they carefully, and now and again clumsily, stepped over the many railroad tracks of the sprawling rail yard as they carried the casket towards the waiting train. Yardmen were hurriedly coupling up the last railway carriages to complete the train.

Over to the right, Jim saw two overcoated figures escorted by several policemen also stepping across the railroad tracks, trying to keep their feet on the railway ties where possible while heading towards the train. Jim presumed they were Ministers Herriot and Tardieu. The two men took station outside the door of a baggage car. The accompanying police formed a small honor guard next to the two ministers. The small party watched the casket being born towards them. They saluted. One of the ministers said to a police official, "Please arrange a Tricolor over the casket."

The police official handed the casket bearers a large Tricolor flag. The flag was neatly arranged over the casket, and then the casket was hoisted up to waiting hands in the baggage car. The two ministers nodded their approval. The door to the baggage car slid shut.

The casket bearers saluted and walked back across the yard.

The two ministers and the other policemen walked back towards a passenger carriage. Jim walked over towards them. Minister Tardieu stopped, turned, and looked at him, then in a flash of recognition, he said, "Ah, the young American. Come to join us for the return to Paris?"

Jim replied, "Yes, Monsieur. It is my sad assignment. I am truly sorry. Fate stopped the hands of a clock yesterday afternoon on the streets of Marseilles."

Minister Tardieu wearily said, "Yes, I am afraid so."

He turned and grabbed the handrails to hoist himself up onto the first step of the railway car. The others followed. A policeman stood aside and let Jim step up.

Early Thursday morning, October 11, Paris. The train from Marseilles slowly pulled into the cavernous glass-roofed arrival hall of the Gare de Lyon. Jim looked out the window of the carriage and saw the somber delegation waiting on the platform. He recognized Premier Doumergue standing in front of a rank of bareheaded cabinet ministers. Behind them were more officials, then Republican Guards and police.

Jim walked to the rear entrance of the railway carriage and stepped off onto the platform. A policeman eyed him. He showed his police press pass. He looked forward and saw Ministers Herriot and Tardieu step down from the front steps of the railway carriage. They walked over to Premier Doumergue and shook his hand. Then they walked over and joined the front rank of cabinet ministers.

The door to the baggage compartment slid open, soldiers walked up, and the casket, covered with the Tricolor and heaped high with wreaths of flowers, was handed out. The soldiers placed the casket on a motor-hearse. The assembled men and spectators came to attention as the motor-hearse slowly made its way down the platform and out to the gray, drizzly streets of Paris heading for the Quai D'Orsay, where the casket would lie in state.

Jim watched, wrote some notes in his notebook, put it in his pocket, and followed the crowd inside the large station to the waiting area. He decided to walk to a Metro station and ride to mid-Paris. Then he would walk up to the newspaper office composing his thoughts as he went. Follow-up stories on Barthou. Who were the assassins? What about the rumors about lapses in the French security arrangements for a state visit?

Then find Sandrine.

Late afternoon, Thursday, October 11, London. The American reporter walked up to the doorway of the small theater in a newspaper building with a group of British and American journalists. At the door he gave his name, "Ferdinand Kuhn, *New York Times*." The person at the door checked his name off the list. Kuhn thought: an invitation only showing.

Inside he took a seat in the darkened auditorium. A man stood in front of the white-lighted screen and said, "We have several of the newsreels from Marseilles. They have reached us apparently without the cooperation of the French authorities." The reporters laughed. The spokesman continued, "In addition to the filmed footage, these newsreels have very good sound tracks. The French foreign ministry had worked closely with the newsreel companies for first-class coverage of the state visit. The best of modern Hollywood-style technology."

Kuhn smiled inwardly at the dark irony.

The first newsreel came on. The film showed the Yugoslav battleship entering port, the party coming ashore in motor launches, the walk through the crowds up to the motorcade. There were filmed sequences of a squadron of cavalry in front of the motorcade.

Kuhn noticed the next scene: only two horsemen were near the king's limousine.

The newsreel then panned up the street the motorcade was to take: policemen standing idly about one every twenty feet, their backs to the crowd. Kuhn knew that this was the opposite of established French procedure for a state visit. The police were supposed to face the crowd and be vigilant for assassins.

Then the camera focused on the king, a whimsical smile on his face. Next to him Foreign Minister Barthou was beaming. As the car moved forward, the king began to intently stare at the crowds. Kuhn thought: very dramatic scene setting when you knew what was coming next.

Watching the movement on the screen, suddenly Kuhn heard shots ring out from speakers in the auditorium. Almost like you were there, he thought. He could see the limousine stop, then a mounted Republican Guard officer hack down the assassin with mighty blows of his saber. Surely these must have killed the assassin? Then coming through the speakers into the auditorium were the maddened shouts of the crowd. A pan of the horse-mounted soldiers' faces showed shock followed by consternation. Then another series of shots rang out. Where from?

The film broke to a picture of the king slumped in the seat of the car. A close-up showed him with wide-open, staring eyes and a puzzled smile still on his lips. Kuhn wrote down his impressions hurriedly in his notebook. Hands could be seen comforting the king. Barthou was nowhere to be seen.

Then the cameras panned back to the crowds who were attacking the assassin, who was apparently being trampled below them and out of sight of the camera. The camera swung around and the horse squadron could be seen galloping ahead to clear a path up the street through the surging crowds. The last scene showed the limousine slowly moving up the street through the lane cleared by the horsemen.

The lights came on. The spokesman came out again and addressed the journalists. "As you can see, all the action could be seen plainly except the actual figure of the assassin leaping onto the running board." Kuhn wrote this down. He had read the French procedure: limousines with running boards were not to be used for just this reason.

Kuhn's attention went back to the spokesman: "As a piece of history and as a human record these newsreels are among the most thrilling ever made." Kuhn quickly wrote these words down.

An emphatic statement, almost posed as a question, popped up from the audience, "These newsreels are glaring evidence of police negligence in Marseilles."

The spokesman coolly replied, "Gentlemen, you must form your own conclusions."

Kuhn stood up and walked outside into the lobby. He walked over to a small writing desk and sat down. He looked at his notebook. The vividness of the newsreels was striking; hearing the gunshots ring out was startling, to say the least. Yes, the other reporter was correct: the security arrangements had been completely negligent. All the reporters would lead with that conclusion.

But that wasn't the story, Kuhn thought, something else was? Then he understood. The newsreels, particularly with sound, were a new medium of journalism, a vivid visual moving picture of exciting history taking place before the viewers' own eyes and in their own ears. Millions of people would see history happen before their very own eyes in movie theaters around the world. That was the story.

Like almost everyone else in the room, he had thought: what would it have been like in 1914 if newsreels had captured the assassination of Archduke Ferdinand in Sarajevo, the event that set off the First World War? Kuhn then thought: we have just seen it. We will see it again and again. The newsreels will be there for every state visit, for every motorcade of a world leader. Darkly he wondered, will it bring forth every assassin for his moment in front of the newsreel cameras? Another first had been made.

He hurriedly finished his dispatch and put it on the wire to New York.

Thursday evening, October 11, Paris. The *inspecteur* stepped out of the elevator on the fifth floor and walked over to the closed office door. He knocked gently. A voice from inside said, "It's open. Come on in." He entered and walked through the vacant reception area and into the office of the *chef*.

The *chef* said, "Before we begin. Minister of the Interior Sarraut has accepted responsibility for the security arrangements in Marseilles and resigned. The ghost of Alexander Stavisky will of course be resurrected yet again for another public beating over police corruption."

The *inspecteur* nodded his head in understanding agreement.

The *chef* got to the point, "Any basis to the story that the Nazis that killed Chancellor Dollfuss in Austria last July had a hand in killing Foreign Minister Barthou?" Is there an international band of Nazi assassins about?"

The *inspecteur* shrugged, "No."

The *chef* said thoughtfully, "Yes, too disciplined." He blew cigarette smoke towards the ceiling.

Then he snorted, "As I thought. A Balkan thing then?"

"Yes," the *inspecteur* replied.

Then the *inspecteur* opened his valise and brought out some papers. He started to explain, "There was a band of six assassins from various parts of Yugoslavia. They drew lots on who was to shoot the king. Petrus Kaleman, the gunman killed in Marseilles, lost. All knew that a failure to carry through would result in their own brutal death. The group lived a shadowy existence in Hungary, whose government succored them because of their anti-Yugoslav activities. They drew financial support from the Croatian Ustashi, who feed Macedonian assassins into these groups. Italy provides some financing; once again, because of the anti-Yugoslavian activities."

The *chef* completed the explanation, "The assassins are in Hungary, never in Yugoslavia or Italy. No trail back. False passports. Travel through Austria to Switzerland and then across the French border. Correct?"

The *inspecteur* said simply, "Correct."

Then the *inspecteur* leaned forward, "Two of the conspirators were arrested today trying to cross into Switzerland at Thonon-les-Bains. That makes three. My sources in the police say they will get the other three shortly."

The *chef* replied, "Very good." Then he looked thoughtful, "Any international repercussions?"

The *inspecteur* leaned forward again, "Yes, my police sources say that they are closing in on two of the masterminds in Turin, Italy. They will ask the Italian police to make the arrests next week."

The *chef* scratched his chin, "What do you think will happen?"

"The police sources think the Italians will arrest them, but not let us question them. They will imprison them for awhile and then release them sometime in the future for some other intrigue."

The *chef* nodded his head, "Yes, that will at least confirm to our security services that the Italians had something to do with this, if they needed any convincing."

The *inspecteur* added, "The Italians will know we operate in Turin."

The *chef* sighed, "But what can they do about it? Nothing I think. A lot of Italians don't like other Italians." He smiled. So easy.

Then the *chef* turned to the *inspecteur*. "Berlin is not here. Yet. We must stay very low and wait. Very low. Let the other offices handle Italy."

The *inspecteur* nodded his head in slow agreement.

PARIS

Friday morning, October 12, 1934. Sandrine awoke in the gray light of early morning, a light drizzly rain falling outside the window. Across the narrow street, darkened clouds floated in the sky above the rooftops. Her arm was draped across Jim's chest. He was in a deep sleep after several hectic nights of interrupted sleep following the Barthou assassination. She smiled. His big weakness as a foreign correspondent, she reflected, was that he liked to sleep like a baby. She slid out of bed and put on a housedress and then a big over-coat, grabbed an umbrella, and silently crept out of the warm little apartment. She took the *ascenseur* down to ground floor and went outside heading for the *boulangerie*. Bakery.

Returning with a baguette, the concierge came out and spoke to her, "I have a letter for your *petit ami*. From America." She looked at Sandrine with hopeful eyes and asked, "Can I have the stamp?"

Sandrine smiled and said, "*Bien sûr, Madame.*" Of course. She tore the corner of the envelope off and handed it to the concierge.

Sandrine walked over to the *ascenseur* and stopped outside the little gated doors. She looked intently at the letter. From a Mrs. Potter. In Iowa. Had Jim given his mother his new address?

Walking into her apartment, Sandrine set the baguette down on the counter, set a pot of water to boil, and put the letter down on the table. She took off the overcoat and housedress and put on a simple bathrobe. Jim stirred. She sat down on the edge of the bed and ran her hand across his chest, caressed his cheek, brushed some hair away from his forehead. He awoke.

Not able to contain her curiosity, she said, "You have a letter from America."

"Really? Let me see it."

She stood up and went over to the table. He sat up in bed and put his legs over the side, his feet firmly planted on the floor. She handed him the letter. He opened it and began to read. Then he smiled.

"It's from my mother. I told her I had moved out of that hotel with all the drunken and carousing journalists to be with my girlfriend."

He looked up at her and smiled. Then he made a big, "Whew." He let the word float in the air.

Sandrine looked at him with a questioning gaze, "Well?"

"She understands." Then he looked down at the letter again, "Boy, does she understand."

Sandrine looked at him again, "Well?"

Jim looked at the letter, "Let me read some of it to you. First the brimstone."

"Okay."

"Jim, you say that this young woman Sandrine is the one for you. Well, if you are going to move in and live with her I should sure hope so. Our family has always believed that this commitment should be sanctified by wedding vows. That is to put the man and the woman into the same harness. No wandering off. So when you go and make this commitment to a young woman without wedding vows, then you yourself take on the even greater responsibility of being the steward of your own commitments. When you announce this to your family, you solidify your commitment before community. Undoubtedly God will be patient in waiting for your arrival at the altar."

Jim looked up at Sandrine, "Now comes the fire."

He looked back down at the letter and continued to read, "But He will be completely unforgiving of lack of commitment. Your family bears witness and watches in His stead. You have taken on a solemn obligation, all the more solemn because it is not presently sacred."

Jim looked at Sandrine and continued reading, "We trust the young lady will drag you before an altar soon. Someday we all hope to meet her. So, we put great confidence in you, and trust that will in turn bring you the happiness that attends lifelong commitment."

Then Jim said softly, "Your mother."

Sandrine hugged herself and enthused, "Oh, your mother is a great mother. Such a way with words."

She jumped around Jim and sprawled across the bed and reached out with her arm and open hand like a little girl, "Let me see the letter, Jim."

He handed her the letter.

She clutched it to her bosom like a doll and said, "Such a wonderful family. Let me read it again."

She held the letter out in front of her and read. Then she went back over the letter and whispered the words. She smiled. She spread her arms out across the bed and looked up at the ceiling, gently kicking her feet in joy, "I can't wait to go to Iowa."

Then she sat upright and looked at Jim and firmly pronounced, "We will get married in the cathedral at Toulouse. Irène will do the dress. Malka will be maid of honor."

Jim took a half step back and a look of wonder and astonishment spread across his face. He said abashedly, "In a Catholic church?"

Sandrine looked at him and pouted, "In a cathedral. In a language you don't understand."

She added solemnly, looking at the letter, "Two thousand years of sacred tradition behind the commitment."

Then she turned and impishly said, "Yes, a Catholic church. We'll put the Christian back in the Protestant."

Jim sighed and said, "Whatever you say, dear."

"Your mother raised such a good boy."

Saturday afternoon, October 13. Jim and Sandrine walked across the grass holding hands, mufflers around their necks to keep the chill away on this gray overcast fall day. They pushed their way past the long-barreled cannon on the raised ground overlooking the Place des Invalides until they were standing on a small escarpment gazing out across the broad square. Jim looked up over his shoulder at the dark stone edifice of the Hotel des Invalides. The gold dome was just visible above the highest ramparts. He turned to Sandrine and said, "Look, even the gold dome above Napoleon's tomb has a dull luster today. Sad and somber."

The Hôtel des Invalides with the golden dome over the tomb of Napoleon.
The Place des Invalides is the square in front of the building.

From the raised ground, they looked across the broad grassy Esplanade des Invalides towards the River Seine. Crowds in the thousands lined the street leading from the Quai D'Orsay, which was down on the river, up through the center of the Esplanade to the Place des Invalides. Along the route of the funeral procession, the street lamps, shrouded in black crepe, glowed weakly. A row of soldiers, elbow to elbow, lined the route. Behind the soldiers was a rank of Republican Guards. Between the two uniformed ranks plainclothes detectives, spaced at ten-foot intervals, formed a line keeping a careful watchfulness over the black-clothed crowds. No assassinations today, thought Jim.

Through gaps in the crowds, Jim and Sandrine glimpsed the approach of the funeral procession towards the Place des Invalides. First came a mounted squadron of Republican Guards in polished silver helmets with drawn sabers, followed by the mournful drummed cadence of a slow-marching regimental band. Then came the gun carriage carrying the Tricolor-draped coffin of Louis Barthou flanked by ten pallbearers. Just behind the gun carriage walked twelve khaki-clad junior officers holding cushions on which were pinned the many decorations awarded the foreign minister in his forty-five years of service to the Republic. Then came the President of the Republic, Monsieur Lebrun, followed by Premier Doumergue and the cabinet. Behind them came on foot the black-coated ranks of ambassadors and ministers from countries around the world. The procession stretched for almost two blocks.

Entering the Place des Invalides, the pallbearers placed the coffin on a flag-draped catafalque. Premier Doumergue stepped up onto a small wooden rostrum to address the thronging crowd spread across the vast Esplanade. Doumergue began by citing Barthou's great pre-war achievement when as premier he raised the length of army service from two to three years in 1913, a bold stroke that helped in 1914 to "hold back the invader and save France from mortal peril." Then he went onto say that in that war "his son was killed in action, a loss leaving a wound which never healed."

Sandrine winced and held Jim's arm closer to her, her mind reaching back to thoughts about uncles and cousins she had never met but were always missed. And as always in these ceremonies, she pondered that small little kernel of selfishness she always carefully kept hidden away, that little secret feeling of relief, that her own father had been spared to come home again. Just to her. For her. And her mother, of course. But through her girlhood, she could always remember when she would be standing dead square in the center of his affectionate gaze, a look of quiet thankfulness that she was in fact there, that she existed. She was something special, even in a land where children existed in a very special state of specialness.

Premier Doumergue continued, "Let us bar the route to the powers of evil that are loosened everywhere and doing the work of death…Disunited peoples are weak, and weak peoples are a prey and a danger. To be ready to be strong is for France an absolute necessity." Then his voice breaking, he summed up, the words almost lost in the vast open space, "To desire peace is not to obtain it…our will for peace…with an unbreakable resolution to hold force in check whenever it is not in the service of right."

As the premier concluded, orders reverberated, drums rolled, troops came to attention, and then a general and his staff, resplendent in their uniforms, stepped out leading a long column of troops past the catafalque, giving the last salute, as the crowd quietly watched.

Jim looked down at the tear-laden eyes of Sandrine. He got a strong sense of the assassination being another in a chain of heart-rending events weighing on France's immediate history, an accumulation of fears bending her people's optimism to despair. He just knew he wanted to be with her for whatever future was coming their way.

Sandrine looked up at him, "There's a memorial service in Church of Saint Louis inside. It will be very sad. May be we should just go file our story?"

Jim readily agreed, "Let's walk across the bridge."

"I would like that," and she held his hand just a little tighter.

Jim and Sandrine walked across the bridge, then along the Cours de la Reine, the grand boulevard bordering the river, underneath the bare-limbed trees while watching the gray water idly flow by. At the Place de la Concorde, Sandrine said, "Let's walk out to the Obelisk. I think we'll find Malka and Pascal." She smiled.

The couple walked across the great square and Sandrine saw Malka and waved. Malka waved back.

Jim said, "Your friend Irène is with them."

Sandrine said, "Oh, good. I haven't seen her lately."

They walked over and Jim reached out and shook Pascal's hand. The women hugged and kissed cheeks.

Irène smiled at Sandrine and said, "I was just telling Malka that I was going to meet the Davignons. The assassination is yet another shock to Philippe's hope that some rapprochement can be made with Germany."

Jim asked, "You are close to Monsieur de Davignon?"

Irène, taken slightly aback, said, "Why, yes I am. To both him and his wife Anne."

Malka quickly added helpfully, "Irène has been outfitting Madame de Davignon and some of her friends for the fall and winter seasons."

Irène hastily added, "Yes, I have." She smiled at Jim.

Sandrine said, "Here they come. They are walking over here. They have a little girl with them." Sandrine turned and said to Malka, "She looks like the little girl whose portrait I saw at their afternoon cocktail party last May. Their niece."

Irène said softly, "I don't think she is a niece."

Sandrine quickly gave her a questioning look, then turned to Malka to see if she knew anything. Malka's eyes answered No.

Philippe de Davignon, well turned out in a black suit and white shirt, walked along with the little blond girl. Anne de Davignon walked on the other side of the girl holding her hand, tenderly, and with concern.

Coming into the circle of friends, Davignon held out his hand to Jim, "Nice to see you again. Sad duty covering the foreign minister's funeral." Then he held his hand out to Pascal and engagingly said, "Ah, our engineer. The events are a call to both of us, a reminder of our duties to the future, Pascal."

Pascal replied, "Why, yes. But the parties of the Left are marshaling their collective strength even as we speak. The Communists have called for a broad

Front Populaire with the Socialists, but also to everyone's surprise, with the Radical Socialists. The call is to combat fascism while being for work, liberty, and peace."

Davignon nodded in agreement, "Noble goals. A new coalition of the parties of the Left might bring victory in the 1936 elections." Then he said to the entire group, almost as a benediction, "France has lost the last of its great statesmen from the War generation. Knowing war, he could speak ardently for peace. It was said of Monsieur Barthou that in his life he had many adversaries, but no enemies." Then, turning to Pascal, he concluded, "Pascal has told us about one avenue of hope."

Anne de Davignon stepped forward with the little girl, signaling a new direction for the conversation. She looked in turn at Sandrine, Malka, and Irène and then down at the little girl, "These are our friends, Ilse."

The little girl replied, in a German accent, "*Bonjour.*"

Anne said by way of explanation, "She is our daughter. She is my stepdaughter, actually, but she is Philippe's daughter. Her mother is still in Germany."

The little girl took on a faraway look and said softly, "*Muti.*"

Anne knelt down next to her, "Yes, *muti* is in Germany. Here in France I will be *maman.*"

The little girl said, "Yes, I know. *Maman.*"

Irène stepped forward and knelt down on one knee in front of the little girl and spoke softly to her in German. The little girl smiled and immediately warmed to her.

Irène said, "I am from near Germany. You and I will be friends."

The little girl said, "*Ja. Du?*"

Irène smiled and replied, "*Ja. Du.*" She hugged the little girl and then held her out at arm's length, "Here in France, we will be *tu. Tu?* Understand."

Ilse replied, "*Oui.*" And she looked at Anne, "Like *maman.*"

Irène answered, "Yes, and you and I and *maman* will always remember *muti.*"

Ilse seemed greatly relieved. Here was a big sister who understood her sadness, her loyalty to her only mother. She looked over at Philippe and faintly smiled and said, "Popa."

He smiled warmly back.

Sandrine watched this interplay with sharp interest. Jim noticed the keenness with which she followed each little sentence between Irène, Ilse, and Anne.

Each interchange was followed with a quick glance at Malka. This was a world of women; he could have been in another country.

Irène stood up. Then Anne de Davignon. Anne spoke to Irène, "Irène, I was so hoping you would be able to help us get some clothes for Ilse. She starts school soon."

Anne addressed Anne de Davignon with a touch of correctness, "Of course, Madame de Davignon."

"Oh, please, it is Anne."

Irène smiled and slowly repeated, "Madame," and she let the word hang for emphasis, "I will be pleased to meet you and Ilse," she looked down at Ilse and shaped her lips into the word, "*Tu*," then looked up, "at the Bon Marché tomorrow. And of course, we can follow up at my shop.

Then Irène stepped a half step back and made a hint of a curtsey, "Madame." Then she looked over at Philippe de Davignon, "Monsieur de Davignon, your daughter is a delightful. I will be of course at you and your wife's service."

Philippe de Davignon looked admiringly at Irène, so gifted at the little diplomacies, he thought. He broke into a warm and understanding smile, then nodded his head agreeably, and said, "Mademoiselle Fabré, it is always our pleasure."

Irène's eyes smiled brightly. She saw his approval. She looked at the little girl and then turned and looked at Sandrine and Malka, giving each a radiant smile of satisfaction for something having been done oh so well.

Sandrine smiled warmly at Irène. She looked at Philippe de Davignon and smiled, Jim sort of thought it was a very knowing kind of smile, and then she looked at Anne de Davignon and said pleasantly, "I am so happy for you. I have known of your longing for this moment."

Philippe turned to his wife and said, "We must be going." He turned back to the others and said, "*Au revoir*." Then Philippe turned to Sandrine and gave a small bow of his head, "Mademoiselle Durand." Next, he made a small turn towards Malka and dipped his head, "Mademoiselle Monterino." Then he guided Ilse and his wife in a turn and headed across the square towards the Hotel Crillon for dinner.

Sandrine turned to Malka and said, "Jim and I have to get up to the newspaper office and file our story." She turned to Jim, bringing him back into the world of conversation, and said, "Isn't that so, honey?"

Jim agreeably said, "That's right." Then he said to Pascal, "May be later we can meet for dinner. That place on Place St.-Germain-de-Prés?"

Pascal said, "The Deux-Magots?"

Jim said, "That's it. You get the table?"

Pascal said, "*Bien sûr.*" Of course.

Sandrine put her arm in Jim's and turned him away and started across the square towards Rue Royale whispering, "My favorite place."

The terrasse of Café des Deux-Magots today across from Place St.-Germaine-de-Prés and Eglise St.-Germaine-de-Prés and about a block away from Rue du Dragon. (Photo by the author.)

Irène walked over and put her arm in Malka's and leaned around and smiled at Pascal, "You don't mind?"

"Of course not."

Malka looked at Irène and said, "What is she like?"

"Madame de Davignon?" Irène stared off into the distance absently and then said, "She walks on two paths at the same time. When you look at her, it is like seeing the face and the silhouette in one portrait at the same time. You have to see the two sides of her as one."

Then Irène looked away, recalling her memories, "She is perfectly correct, always polite. They both are. When you are with them, you feel like you should be with them, even though something deep inside you says may be you should not. It is the perfection of the experience that is left in your mind."

Malka said, "I think I understand."

Irène said softly, "I am not sure I will ever completely understand. But I think her being reunited with the little girl, with Ilse, completes something in her."

Malka nodded her head, "I saw that. You put the new relationship together right before our eyes. All the relationships."

Pascal looked over at Irène with a slightly quizzical look. Yes. He had watched everything. But, apparently he thought, I had understood nothing. Engineer, he thought, and laughed to himself.

Irène continued, "I have never had such affection for two people. That is the interesting thing: it only works for me, at least, when you are with both of them."

Irène looked over at Pascal and decided to say nothing about Sandrine. Malka saw and understood. Sandrine had had a different experience. Adventure. Big shoulders.

Jim and Sandrine walked along Rue Lamartine towards the bistro, the sidewalk deeply shaded in the fall afternoon. Sitting outside at a small table in overcoats to ward off the autumn chill, the three journalists—Mac, Rewrite, and Phil Roberts—were deep in animated conversation about the week's events. Jim and Sandrine came up and stopped, standing in front of the three men without making a move to sit down.

Jim said, "We got the story, chief."

Mac blew smoke from his cigar and said, "I knew you would. Tell you what, kid," and he winked at Phil Roberts, "it's been your story from the start, why don't you and Sandrine go up to the newsroom and write it up. Night lead Chicago. Put it on the wire."

Mac looked over at Rewrite with a concerned look, "Do you think he can get the spelling right by himself?"

Rewrite chirped, "Of course." And he winked at Sandrine.

Mac turned back to Jim, "Double byline. Ladies go first." He smiled.

Sandrine grabbed Jim around the waist and gave him a big hug and looked up at him, "Dreamboat."

Jim, putting on his most abashed Iowa look, replied, "Gee, thanks, chief." He grabbed Sandrine's hand and the two turned and walked up the sidewalk towards the newspaper office.

Mac turned to the other two, "He's getting off to a great start. We're going to be needing young guys like him."

Phil Roberts said, with a touch of foreboding, "Yeah, history is coming at us like a freight train."

Rewrite said wistfully, "Farm boy walks off with Paris belle. Who'd think it?"

Mac added absently, "Even if it were true."

Mac watched the couple walk up the sidewalk. He focused his gaze on the slowly swaying hips undulating beneath Sandrine's thin summer dress. He shook his head and gave a short laugh, "Lucky bastard."

In the last light of the autumn twilight, the gendarmerie colonel walked across the deserted Place de la Concorde, past the soft rushing sound of the water from the fountains, past the Obelisk, and towards the bridge. He had just come from the funeral service for the foreign minister at Père-Lachaise Cemetery. The colonel's eyes were fixed on the Palais Bourbon across the river, with its great columns and Parthenon-like façade, cold gray symbols that France was a Republic. Across the facade in gold letters was written *CHAMBRE DES DÉPUTÉS*. Now almost a term of insult, the colonel thought bitterly.

Walking out on the bridge, the colonel stopped midway and turned around and looked back across the vast expanse of the square. He thought of the night the previous February when the battered forces of order were able to move that one last time against the anti-Republican rabble. And prevail. Yes, prevail. The Right had not been able to bring down the Republic.

He looked across to the far side of the square, at the stately edifice of the Hotel Crillon. Then he looked into the dark gray sky beyond, lifting his eyes towards the towering dark-edged cumulus clouds of a rain front moving east. With that gift given to those who have been marching soldiers, he could see written on the night sky the images of past and future events, some deeply remembered, others portentously imagined. He remembered another day like this, in November 1918 after the shooting had stopped, marching alongside a column of his great-coated soldiers, helmets strapped to their belts, rifles slung on their shoulders, the stink of the trenches lingering in their garments, as they marched into Germany towards the Rhine River on a cold and dank day.

He remembered: the last of the *grandes armies*, that great *poilu* army, almost anti-Napoleonic in its government drabness, nevertheless that great symbol of the enduring steadfastness of the Third Republic. Now he could see in his mind's eye that column of soldiers lift off the muddy road of Germany and climb into the gray sky, into the eternal glory of its achievement.

The future? He looked down at the vast vacant square and knew that the victory in the Great War had also gone to its *gloire*, a victory that would now live in exile from the perilous events that a dangerous future was bringing to a tired and weary France. A once great victory was now in retreat.

He turned and continued across the bridge and past the *Chambre des députés* without looking up.

SOME SOURCES

NOTE: This is a work of fiction interwoven with actual historical events. All the principal characters are fictional. The exception is fictional character Bill Wilshire who gives voice to the experiences described by correspondent William L. Shirer in his memoirs, particularly events of February 6, 1934 and Colonel Simon's dramatic actions on the Pont de la Concorde that night.

SOME SOURCES - BOOKS

Calmer, Ned. *All the Summer Days: A Novel of Paris in the '20s.* Boston, 1961.

Clunn, Harold. *The Face of Paris: The Record of a Century's Changes and Developments.* London, 1933.

Glassco, John. *Memoirs of Montparnasse.* New York, 1970.

Hemingway. Ernest. *The Sun Also Rises.* New York, 1970 (first printing 1926).

Horne, Alistair. *La Belle France: A Short History.* New York, 2005.

Hussey, Andrew. *Paris: The Secret History.* New York, 2006.

Paul, Elliot. *The Last Time I Saw Paris.* New York, 1943.

Shirer, William L. *20th Century Journey: The Start 1904-1930.* Boston, 1985.

_____. *The Nightmare Years: 1930-1940.* Boston, 1984.

_____. *The Collapse of the Third Republic.* New York, 1969.

Sherwood, Robert E. *Roosevelt and Hopkins, An Intimate History.* New York, 1948.

Weber, Eugen. *Action Française.* Stanford, 1962.

_____. *The Hollow Years: France in the 1930s.* New York, 1994.

SOME SOURCES – NEWSPAPERS AND PERIODICALS

Kuhn, Ferdinand, Jr. "Police Sparse in Marseilles, Film Shows; Shots and Crowd's Cries Ring in Newsreel," *New York Times* (Internet archives) (October 12, 1934). Note: This wireless news dispatch datelined London provides the factual substance to a scene in the chapter "Marseilles" describing how Kuhn might have viewed the newsreels in London. The excerpts from his dispatch are real. Reporters were quite aware of the power of the new visual media.

Birchall, Frederick T. "Hitler Justifies Killings as 'Reich's Supreme Judge'; Defies Boycott by World," *New York Times* (Internet archives) (July 14, 1934) (datelined Berlin, July 13, 1934). Discussed in chapter "Quatorze Juillet."

New York Times (Internet archives). Numerous news and fashion articles from 1934 generally datelined Paris, France, Berlin, or London.

Times of London (Internet archives). Numerous news and fashion articles from 1934 generally datelined Paris, France, or London.

Time (Internet archives). Articles from 1934 datelined Paris, France, or Germany.

LIST OF ILLUSTRATIONS

"Quai D'Orsay" by Simdaperce, August 2008, GFDL, Wikicommons.
"Place de la Concorde" photo by author, May 2009.
"Palais Justice 1933," scan of photo from *The Face of Paris*, 162 (see above source note).
"Fourrures André Brunswick: le grand couturier de la fourrure" by Louis Gaudin, c. 1930. ("The grand couturier of furs"), public domain, Wikicommons.
"Aerial view of Hôtel des Invalides and Esplanade des Invalides" by Eric Gaba, August 2002, GFDL, Wikicommons.
"Place de la République," photo by author, May 2009.
"Place de la Nation," photo by author, May 2009
"Hôtel des Invalides" by MarkGGN, May 1, 2005, GFDL, Wikicommons.
"Café des Deux-Magots" photo by author, May 2009.

Acclaim for Paul A. Myers and the maritime history *North to California: The Spanish Voyages of Discovery 1533-1603*

"Congratulations upon the publication of North to California. It is a book that only someone who is at once a trained historian and an experienced sea-going captain could have written. It will command the field for a century to come. As an historian, I have always admired these voyages. Having read your book, I now have even more reason to do so."

> —Kevin Starr, University Professor and Professor of History, University of Southern California

"We often think history is boring. Myers proves that it is not, with the exciting true story of the Spanish voyages of discovery to California. Describing colorful people, bold journeys, and a mystery, this volume is both education and entertainment."

> —Google Book Search (the entire book is readable at Google Book Search)

"Here is the story of how California was discovered by the Spanish explorers, starting with Hernan Cortes and covering the early years of exploration by sailing ship. This book brings the history of California to life, and makes a sailor feel like part of it."

> —*Latitudes & Attitudes*

" Juan Rodríguez Cabrillo, the discoverer of Alta California, was a tough Castilian kid off the streets of Seville who rose out of the conquest of Mexico City, a Stalingrad with swords, to become one of the top conquistador commanders in the conquest of Guatemala under the famed Pedro de Alvarado. Where did Cabrillo die? A gravestone marked JRC and discovered in 1901 on Santa Rosa Island becomes the touchstone for recasting the place of Cabrillo's death to Santa Rosa Island instead of San Miguel Island. The Cabrillo story finishes with the daring voyage led by his successor, Bartolomé

Ferrelo, as he leads his two ships far out into the Pacific on the Long Tack and then rides a winter storm north to Point Reyes. The two ships then battle winter seas north to the California-Oregon border before returning to Mexico."

—*Llumina Press*

Book Review from the Historical Novel Society

VIENNA 1934: Betrayal at the Ballplatz

by Paul A. Myers

It is Vienna, 1934. The Austrian government is starting to become a Fascist state as German-supported Nazis decide to overthrow Chancellor Dollfuss's government. Once Dollfuss's government is dismantled, then Austria will belong to Hitler. In Myers' story, Geoffrey Ashbrook is a British journalist who has come to Vienna to write news dispatches for the London papers and to write secret reports for the British cabinet. While in Austria he falls in love with Anna Marie Linden, daughter of an Austrian land owner. The plot thickens as Anna's stepbrother falls in with the Nazis and both Geoffrey and Anna's lives are in danger.

This book will appeal to readers who are interested in Austrian politics in the early 1930s. The story takes place in the early days of World War II— before Mussolini joined Hitler as a member of the Axis. In 1934, the Austrians were counting on Mussolini to keep them safe from Germany. Unfortunately, as Myers relates, there were many people within the higher ranks of police and government officialdom who were pro-Nazi.

Myers' characters feel true to the era. He loosely based several characters on real people of the era—such as writers and journalists, socialites and politicians. For example, Ashley's uncle is based on W. Somerset Maugham. These fabricated characters are woven into the storyline along with real people such as Empress Zita of Austria, Crown Prince Otto von Habsburg, G.E.R. Geyde, Edda Ciano (daughter of Mussolini), and many more. Myers did an excellent job of making the story real due to his good research and fine storytelling. The interweaving of fact, fiction, real, and fictional people makes this book exciting and romantic. -- *Naomi Theye*

from the May 2009 HNS Online Review

www.ingramcontent.com/pod-product-compliance
Lightning Source LLC
Chambersburg PA
CBHW060801120626
46557CB00001B/51